PRAISE FOR LISA EDMONDS

"An action-packed debut with a strong, compelling heroine. Heart of Malice is sure to cast a spell on urban fantasy readers and leave them clamoring for more adventures with Alice Worth."

— JENNIFER ESTEP, NEW YORK TIMES BESTSELLING
AUTHOR OF THE ELEMENTAL ASSASSIN URBAN
FANTASY SERIES

"The complex magic system throughout Heart of Malice is a genuine joy to read and there's danger and intrigue throughout. The characters leap off the page and the secrets which Alice Worth carries make her a wonderful character. I can't wait to read more of this thrilling series!"

— HELEN HARPER, AUTHOR OF THE BLOOD DESTINY
AND LAZY GIRL'S GUIDE TO MAGIC URBAN FANTASY
SERIES

"Heart of Malice hits the ground running with the perfect blend of magic action, compelling characters, and sizzling romance. Snarky and cynical Alice Worth is a complex and flawed woman who is not simply kickass but refreshingly intelligent. Lisa Edmonds conducts the twists and turns of the plot like a maestro conductor, spellbinding the reader with her original and innovative worldbuilding, solid magic system, and a compelling backstory that haunts the main story in surprising ways. It's an absolutely delightful, one-sitting, devour it now read."

— DEBORAH WILDE, AUTHOR OF THE UNLIKEABLE DEMON HUNTER AND MAGIC AFTER MIDLIFE URBAN FANTASY SERIES

"Fast-paced and action-packed, the story created by this author is both intriguing and addictive, as is the world she builds. Her prose is lively and entertaining and laced with just the right amount of humor. [...] This suspenseful urban fantasy pulls the reader into an imaginative world—one that seamlessly marries reality with the supernatural—through the author's outstanding storytelling skills."

— IND'TALE MAGAZINE

"Edmonds has an eye for both detail and entertaining characters, and her story is fun and energetic. Readers will enjoy this installment and look forward to more in the continuing saga of Alice Worth."

— PUBLISHER'S WEEKLY

"It's no secret that this is one of my favorite series and that Alice is my girl. The author shook me with this book. From the story to the action to the characters, it left me with a huge book hangover. [. . .] I. Loved. Every. Minute. Of. It."

—THE LITERARY VIXEN

Heart of Vengeance

ALICE WORTH SERIES

BOOK SIX

LISA EDMONDS

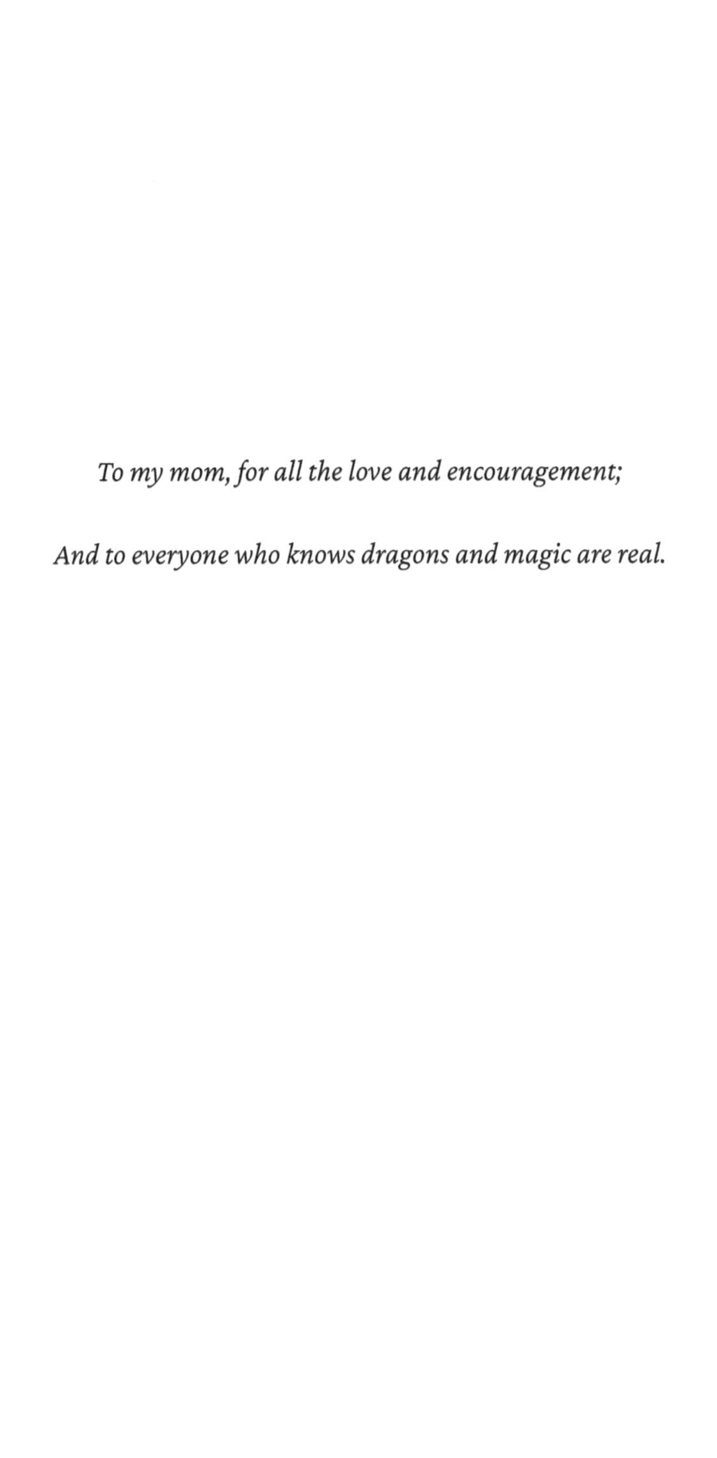

To my mom, for all the love and encouragement;

And to everyone who knows dragons and magic are real.

Also by Lisa Edmonds

The Alice Worth Series

Heart of Malice

Heart of Fire

Heart of Ice

Heart of Stone

Heart of Shadows

Heart of Vengeance

Heart of Lies

Heart of the Pack

Heart of the Damned

Short Stories and Novellas

From the Ashes

Just For One Night

Blood Money

Ghosting 101 (included with *Blood Money*)

Perfectly Magical

Alice Worth and the Elite Death Machine

The Alice Worth World Novels

Mortal Heart

CHAPTER I

"YOU SHOULD GO IN. THE OWNER DOESN'T BITE."

Startled, I turned. The speaker was a lanky college kid with long blond hair, wearing a Love and Rockets T-shirt and ripped jeans, sitting at the other end of the bench.

"Excuse me?" I asked.

He gestured with his half-eaten sandwich at the record store across the little outdoor pavilion from where we sat. "I'm just saying, go in and check it out. You've been staring at the place for like twenty minutes. Daniel doesn't bite."

"Thanks. Maybe I will." I crossed my arms and resumed watching the store.

My body language was lost on him. "We're the last real record store anywhere around," he said with obvious pride. "New and used, all genres. We'll order anything you want if we don't have it."

I didn't reply. My attention was on the figure of a tall, well-muscled older man inside the store. In the past half hour, he'd helped customers, sorted through bins of new inventory, and cleaned the glass door. At the moment, he was ringing up a couple of guys and talking with them, maybe about their purchases. I hadn't seen him smile...or sit down for one moment. Shifters tended to have a lot of energy, but he seemed more restless than most.

Mr. Love and Rockets was talking again. "What are you into? I bet classic rock." He finished off the last of his sandwich in one big bite and gulped water from a reusable bottle.

He seemed friendly, I supposed, and might be a good source of information about his boss. "I am, actually," I said, turning toward him. "How could you tell?"

He grinned. "I've been working in this store since I was sixteen. I get a vibe about people, you know? And I'm almost always right. So, who are your favorites?"

"Pink Floyd, The Eagles, Led Zeppelin, AC/DC, The Who, Queen, Fleetwood Mac."

"On vinyl?"

I feigned confusion. "Are there any other options?"

"Rock on. I'm Detroit." At my expression, he laughed. "It's really Henry, but Daniel's been calling me Detroit since forever."

"Are you from there?"

He shook his head. "Nah, I'm from here. I'm super into KISS, though, so I guess that's where it came from. Daniel claims he doesn't remember how he thought of it—just says Henry doesn't suit me."

I couldn't imagine a world in which this guy was named "Henry" either. "Daniel sounds interesting. He owns the store?"

Detroit nodded. "He's been running it for something like twenty years. It's his life."

That's what the file I'd received from my hacker contact Cyro had reported. Daniel had a simple life: the record store, a house on the outskirts of town, and a truck. No wife, no kids, no living family.

Except me.

"Daniel loves classic rock too," Detroit said, folding his insulated lunch bag. "He'd probably enjoy talking with you. Pink Floyd is his favorite band of all time. If you think *Dark Side of the Moon* is one of the best things ever made by a human, you and he will get along just fine."

My throat went dry. "The first vinyl album I ever bought was *Dark Side of the Moon.*"

"Then come inside and see what we've got. Bet we have albums you need. I'll even slide you a first-time customer discount." He stood and stretched. "You from around here?"

I shook my head. "A couple hours away."

"What brings you to town?"

I had an answer prepared for that question. "I planned to go on the ghost tour tonight."

"Mary Ann's tour? You'll like her. She knows all the local lore—and what she doesn't know, she makes up." He winked. "Coming in? I'll introduce you to Daniel."

I rose, but I made no move to follow him toward the store. I'd faced demons, ghosts, vampires, sorcerers, witches, poltergeists, angry werewolves, blood mages, panther shifters, an angel, a demon lord, and Vlad the Impaler, but the prospect of being introduced to Daniel Holiday made me want to run.

Running was not an option, however, because someone else might be coming after Daniel: my grandfather, crime lord Moses Murphy. For some reason he wanted Daniel dead for knocking up my mom with a half-mage, half-shifter baby. Why that would make Moses want to kill Daniel, I wasn't sure. I'd recently unearthed a forgotten memory from my childhood that indicated Moses would have killed all three of us back then if he'd known my real father wasn't John Briggs, the man who'd raised me as his own daughter.

Both my mom and my dad were long dead, murdered by Moses when I was eight. Now Moses knew I was part shifter, and he might be hunting for the man who'd fathered me. Luckily, ace hacker Cyro had found Daniel first. I had a chance to warn him that Moses or his goons might be headed this way.

As far as I knew, Daniel had no idea I existed, and I had absolutely no clue how to break the news. Since the day I learned about him, I'd rehearsed it a hundred times, saying it a hundred different ways, but none of them seemed right. My alpha werewolf partner, Sean Maclin, had kissed me goodbye this morning and assured me the right words would come to me when it was time. As I stared through the front windows at my probable biological father, however, my brain was totally blank.

"For Pete's sake, Alice, show some fortitude." Malcolm crossed his arms and glared at me from where he floated a few feet to my right. "You heard Detroit Rock City over there—Daniel doesn't bite and he's got a sense of humor and he likes Pink Floyd. What else do you want?"

"A less judgmental ghost sidekick," I muttered.

Detroit turned around. "What was that?"

"Nothing." I ignored Malcolm's exaggerated eye roll and took a deep breath. "Sure, I'd love to check out your store."

"Awesome." Detroit headed for the front door of Blue Moon Records, whistling. "Oh, hey, what's your name?"

"Alice," I told him. "Alice Worth."

He opened the door and held it for me. The familiar sound of Aerosmith drifted through the doorway. I smiled.

Was it possible to inherit a love of classic rock through genetics? I certainly hadn't gotten that from my parents, and I sure as hell didn't get it from Moses.

Detroit made a gallant sweeping gesture. "After you, Alice."

"Thanks, Detroit." I let Steven Tyler's vocals carry me inside.

THE MOMENT WE WALKED IN, Daniel sent Detroit to the post office to ship some online orders. As nice as the shop assistant was, I was relieved not to have to make conversation.

Daniel was still talking with his customers, who were regulars judging by the way they chatted. I busied myself bin-diving in the classic rock section of the shop's used records inventory and listened to their discussion about the highlights of Black Sabbath's lesser-known tracks. Unsurprisingly, Daniel was highly knowledgeable on the topic. Though he didn't laugh or smile and seemed generally very solemn, he was friendly. We were the only customers in the shop at the moment—not entirely unexpected for a weekday morning.

I hadn't necessarily planned to buy anything, but darned if they didn't have several albums I really wanted, all in excellent condition. I made a stack and continued browsing.

Malcolm prowled around the store, "checking the perimeter," as he called it, and reported nothing strange and no wards. He floated beside me, arms crossed again. "You're stalling."

"Hush," I muttered. "He's busy with customers."

"They're just yakking. I'm sure if you went up there, he'd send them on their way and talk to you."

"What part of this seems like it would be easy?" I asked testily, still in an undertone, as I flipped through records. "I'm working up the nerve to go up there, okay? And I've still got six more bins to go through. They've got a huge inventory."

Malcolm sighed. "I know this isn't easy, but I think you're getting *more* nervous the longer you think about it. Just go ask him about some random album and chat for a bit. Break the ice." He glanced behind me. "Scratch that. He's coming to you."

I spun and locked eyes with Daniel, who was striding down the aisle toward me. The other customers were on their way out the front door, purchases in hand.

Before the plastic surgery that turned me into Alice, the disgraced—and deceased—scion of the wealthy Worth family of Chicago, I'd looked a lot like my mother, Moira, except my eyes were dark coffee brown instead of blue-gray. When I saw the photos of Daniel in the file Cyro had sent me, however, I recognized my own dark brown eyes staring back at me. I also saw some of my own face —or at least the face I *used* to have—in Daniel's. In that moment, I knew with more certainty than if I'd had DNA test results in my hand that Daniel was my biological father. And days later, I stood in his record store, wondering how the hell to tell him who I was and why I was here.

He wore a plaid shirt, jeans, and boots, as if he planned to go for a hike after work, or maybe out into the countryside to shift and hunt. Besides his physique, the only indication he was a shifter was the way light reflected in his eyes. I was sure he'd already caught Sean's scent on me, but he didn't comment on it.

"Can I help you find something?" he asked.

I showed him what I'd chosen. "Just adding to my collection. Your store is amazing."

"Thank you. I'm very proud of it." He looked over my albums. "Some excellent choices. Are you new to collecting vinyl?"

"I only started buying albums about five years ago. I didn't really have the means before that." I'd had no way to buy records while a prisoner of my grandfather, but I'd started building my collection as soon as I had my own place.

He nodded gravely. "I understand." He probably assumed I meant I hadn't had the money. "What other albums are missing from your collection?"

I smiled. "So many, it would take all day to list them. I can tell you a couple that are at the top of the list, though."

He didn't return my smile. Given what I'd read in the file Cyro sent me, his solemnity wasn't unexpected. Even thirty years later, the memory of seeing most of his pack slaughtered would be raw. He'd lost everyone because of Moses.

Other than some DNA, we had that in common too.

Think of it like this, Sean had told me last night as we lay in bed. *You are a gift to him. He believes he's alone in this world. He has no pack and no family, as far as he's aware. Not all lone wolves are lonely, but my gut tells me this is a lonely man. I don't see a scenario where your news isn't welcome, once the shock wears off.*

Sean had offered to come with me, but the presence of an alpha would complicate things considerably. I'd decided to just bring Malcolm, who'd drifted over to a different area of the store to give us the illusion of privacy.

"What's on your list?" Daniel asked.

I named a few albums. We found two in the used section and one more in the back, in a crate of new inventory he hadn't had a chance to go through yet. I ended up with a healthy pile of seven albums, all in great condition.

Detroit wasn't back yet, so when another customer came in, Daniel went to help him while I looked over the flyers plastered on the front counter. Most advertised local bands, record swap meets, and other locally owned shops. A couple of bands were holding auditions. One specified they needed a drummer with a working vehicle capable of transporting the band to gigs. I chuckled.

Daniel's voice startled me. "Do you play an instrument?" He went around the counter to ring up my purchases. The other customer left empty-handed, apparently unable to find what he was looking for.

"No. I sing a little."

"Ever sing with a band?"

"Never got the chance to try. I think it would have been fun."

He gave me the total. "I assume Detroit offered you a first-time customer discount."

"He did, but I know a small business counts pennies, so I won't hold you to it."

"I count happy customers." He hit a few buttons on the register and told me the revised total. "Cash or credit?"

I handed over my card and he ran it. As the slip printed out, he studied me. "Did you find out what he sent you to find out?"

I blinked. "Who?"

"The alpha of whatever pack you're associated with." His expression hardened. "I assume he sent you to do a little snooping on the local loner. You didn't make much of an effort to clean off his scent, so he must have wanted me to know. Tell him I'm not interested in joining his pack and not to bother sending any more cute girls to entice me."

"It's not what you think." I signed my name on the receipt and handed it back. "That's my partner you smell, and he didn't send me."

His expression didn't change. "Your partner? Not your mate?"

"Not yet. Maybe someday. We just bought a house together." I wasn't sure why I told him that. It just came out.

"The Council's letting him have a human mate?" Daniel sounded skeptical.

"They don't exactly approve," I said, which might be the understatement of the century. "And I'm not exactly human."

For the first time, his dark brown eyes glowed golden. "What are you, then, besides a mage?"

I took a deep breath. "That's why I'm here, actually."

Before I could say more, three SUVs pulled up in front of the shop. Warning bells went off in my head. Daniel turned to see what had caught my attention and snarled.

Men and women emerged from the SUVs. I didn't know any of them, but I recognized a team of cabal soldiers when I saw one. Shit.

The passenger door of the middle SUV opened. Nora Keegan, my grandfather's newest lieutenant, stepped out.

Double shit.

Nora was a high-level blood and air mage. She'd been one of local boss Darius Bell's top lieutenants but had switched allegiances and killed Bell on Moses's order as part of his takeover of the city. She'd also been present when Malcolm was tortured to death on Bell's orders and kidnapped one of my clients right from under my nose. We had a *lot* of unfinished business.

Our eyes met through the window. She looked very surprised to see me, which told me they hadn't followed me here. Moses had tracked Daniel down and sent Nora to bring him in.

Nora smiled at me and raised her phone to her ear. I knew who she was calling: Moses.

Triple shit.

Daniel turned to me, his eyes bright gold.

"You've got to get out of here," we said at the same time.

"They're here for me," Daniel said. He must have recognized someone in Nora's goon squad, or he knew Nora worked for Moses now. He might have been keeping tabs on Moses's organization.

I shook my head and spooled magic. "They're here for *us* now. Go. I'll hold them off."

"The hell you will," he snarled. "That's Moses Murphy's top lieutenant out there." So he *did* know who Nora was.

"I know. The first time we met, I cut off her left hand and she blasted me through two walls." In the interim, I'd absorbed the magic and power of a sorcerer I'd killed and developed some new abilities. I looked forward to evening the score between us.

Malcolm floated over next to me, his magic prickling my arms. "I can take out the humans with sleep spells," he told me. "Then we unleash hell on Nora and the other mages."

Daniel looked right at where Malcolm was. He couldn't hear or see my ghost, but shifters were sensitive to the presence of spirits.

"I've got a mage ghost here backing me up too," I said to Daniel. "We can handle them. Do you have another way out of here besides the front and back doors?"

Outside, Nora finished her brief call and stuck her phone back in her pocket. She waggled her fingers at me. Air magic coiled around her arms and her eyes turned white.

With a snarl, Daniel vaulted over the counter, picked me up with one arm, and ran toward the back of the store, moving so fast I didn't have time to protest. Malcolm was right behind us. Thank goodness Detroit wasn't back from the post office yet.

The front windows exploded in a massive burst of air magic that swept through the store, destroying everything in its path. Shards of glass flew toward us in a blizzard of potentially lethal edges. Daniel swung me in front of him and grunted as glass embedded itself in his back.

He kicked the door to the office open and shoved me into the small room. Gunshots rang out. He staggered in after me, slammed the door, and locked it with several solid-looking deadbolts. Belatedly, I noticed the door and the frame were reinforced steel. The office was a panic room, apparently.

"If they've got a high-level earth mage with them, they'll be able to get in here," I told him. He probably knew that, but it didn't hurt to emphasize that concern.

Inside the room, I couldn't hear anything from the store. I assumed Nora and her crew were destroying everything and surrounding the panic room.

Daniel pulled a pocketknife from his jeans pocket. He tossed it to me and turned his back. "Cut them out," he ordered, his voice hoarse.

His shirt was soaked with blood. His back had large shards of glass embedded in it, but the two bullet holes were the immediate problem. I pulled out the glass so he could start healing and ripped his shirt open. The skin around the holes was black.

"Silver bullets," Malcolm said grimly. "Son of a bitch."

"I guess their orders were to bring you in dead or alive. Brace yourself." I sliced across one of the entrance wounds, stuck my fingers into the opening, and used my earth magic to sense the silver. How he'd known I'd be capable of rendering this kind of first aid I had no idea, but shifters usually had good instincts about people. Or maybe it was some kind of test.

Daniel snarled. "Hurry."

"I *am* hurrying." I pulled the first bullet to my fingers using my earth magic. Daniel grunted.

Thankfully, the bullet was intact and easy to remove. I tossed it on the desk. "One down."

I tried to repeat the process with the second bullet, which was also still in one piece, but it had shattered his right shoulder blade and gotten lodged in something—probably his collarbone. "It'll be easier from the front," I told him.

He turned to face me. "We need to go before they figure out how to get in here." He wiped his mouth, leaving a streak of blood on the back of his hand. One or both of the bullets had punctured something important.

"I know." I cut into his upper chest and stuck my fingers inside his flesh. One quick pull with my earth magic and the bullet came loose. I dropped it onto the table beside the first one. "Done."

Daniel balled up his bloody shirt and pressed it to the wound on his chest. "Thanks."

"You're welcome. Nora is a monster. You should've let me kill her."

"I want answers about why you're here. You can kill her some other time."

He grabbed a tall metal cabinet and swung it away from the wall, revealing a ladder. He climbed up a few rungs, pushed a ceiling tile aside, and punched in a code. A door swung up, revealing a tunnel leading up.

Daniel jumped down off the ladder. "You go first. I'll follow."

I turned to Malcolm. "Go up and make sure it's clear."

"You got it." The ghost zipped away up the tunnel. A few moments later, he returned. "The tunnel leads to a hatch on the roof. It's clear for now. I'll go back and keep watch."

"Okay. Be careful."

He zipped away again. I started up the ladder. When I got to the tunnel, I glanced back to see Daniel pour liquid from a small container onto the bloodstain on the floor. I smelled gasoline. He tossed the container aside, left his bloody shirt on the floor, and started up the ladder behind me.

I climbed up the tunnel. When Daniel got to the tunnel, he took a metal lighter from his pocket. He flicked it, dropped it into the room below, and slammed the trapdoor on the flames. The panic room's air vents would supply oxygen, ensuring the fire consumed the contents of the office, including Daniel's blood and whatever else was in there he didn't want Nora to get her hands on.

He looked up at me, his golden eyes bright in the near pitch-darkness of the tunnel. "What are you waiting for?"

We climbed the ladder quickly. The record store was on the ground floor of a four-story building, so we only had to climb three stories to get to the roof.

When we reached the top, I found a glowing number pad on the wall. "Code is one three nine five," Daniel told me.

I punched in the number and the hatch unlocked. I turned a handle and pushed it open. Daylight blinded me.

Malcolm was waiting. "All clear. Hurry."

Squinting, I clambered out to the roof. Daniel emerged right behind me and shut the hatch. Shouts drifted up from the street. Sirens blared in the distance.

"Follow me." Daniel headed for the far end of the roof. Clearly, he had an escape route already planned in case something like this ever happened.

I scurried after him with Malcolm at my side. "What's the plan?"

Daniel didn't look back. "Get off this roof and get the hell out of here."

"They'll be watching your vehicle," I reminded him.

"I know. I have a backup plan."

I glanced at Malcolm. "Go check and see if there's anyone lurking around my car. If there is, come back. If not, stay and keep an eye on it until we get there unless I summon you."

"Will do." He vanished.

We reached the edge of the roof. I didn't see any way of getting down to street level. There was another building across the alley, but it was a good twelve feet to that roof and a forty-foot drop.

Daniel turned to me, his expression cold. He'd lost everything again. His beloved record store was gone. Even if we evaded Nora, he couldn't go home—they'd be waiting for him there. For thirty years, he'd made the best life a man could after watching everyone he'd ever loved die, and in a matter of a few minutes, it was all gone.

"Why did you come here?" he asked. He didn't sound angry, just resigned, as if he'd known this day would eventually come.

None of the imaginary scenarios I'd rehearsed involved standing on the edge of a roof while Moses's goon squad destroyed Daniel's record store. Soon Nora would realize we weren't in the burned-out panic room and start looking for possible escape routes, if they hadn't already.

I reached into my back pocket and pulled out a four-by-six photograph of two adults and an eight-year-old girl. It was a duplicate of the original, which had been damaged in my escape from Moses's compound five years ago. I held it up so he could see it.

"My mother's name was Moira Murphy," I told Daniel. "That's her husband John Briggs with us in the photo. He raised me as his child, but I wasn't."

I reached for the golden shifter magic in my chest. My eyes grew warm, and I knew they'd developed telltale golden rings. "I'm your daughter," I said.

The hard mask vanished. A parade of emotions crossed his face: shock, disbelief, grief, anger. A flash of fear. Not for himself—for me.

"Where's your car?" he asked finally, his voice tight.

I pointed. "A couple of blocks that way. I wanted to walk."

"All right." He gestured at the other roof. "We have to get moving."

I spooled air magic. "You go first."

He growled. "No way in hell I'm leaving you behind." *Again*, his expression said.

"I'll be right behind you. I think I can jump it with my air magic. If you're there waiting, you can catch me if I put a little too much oomph into the jump." Which sometimes happened when adrenaline got into the mix. Unfortunately, I knew that from painful experience.

Daniel held out his hand. "If you trust me, I'll get us both across."

Though the injuries had begun to heal, he'd been shot twice with silver bullets and had his back sliced to ribbons by shards of glass.

When I looked into his eyes, however, I knew he wouldn't have suggested it if he didn't know he could get us across safely.

I'd known him thirty minutes and he was asking me to put my life in his hands. Then again, I'd hired a hacker to track down my biological father and then driven three hours to meet him. What was one more leap of faith?

I took his hand. "Okay."

He didn't give me time to think about it too much and swung me onto his back. I locked my arms around his shoulders and my legs around his waist. I'd done this with Sean a few times, but for fun and certainly never to jump between buildings. Like most shifters, Daniel's body was solid muscle, and though he was quite a bit older than Sean, he was powerful and strong.

Without giving me time to reconsider, he circled back to pick up momentum, adjusted his pace to account for my weight, and ran full speed toward the edge of the roof. He launched off the low parapet wall, flew over the gap between the buildings, and landed with plenty of room to spare on the other roof.

I let go of him and slid to the roof. His blood stained the front of my shirt, but that was low on my list of problems at the moment. "Thanks for the lift. What now?"

He gestured at a rooftop door. "Down those stairs and out to the alley. My buddy who owns the deli won't mind if we borrow his truck to get out of here."

Before we went to the door, we peered over the edge of the roof to check the alley. It was empty and silent.

"Hey, what happened to the sirens?" I asked.

Daniel growled. "Murphy probably made some phone calls. The cops aren't coming. Let's go before they figure out where we've gone."

He opened the door, revealing a dimly lit stairwell. I followed him down. We moved silently and quickly.

At the bottom of the stairs, Daniel paused with his hand on the doorknob, listening for any sounds in the alley. Hearing nothing, he unlocked the door and opened it.

Two of Moses's goons stood on the other side of the door. They looked as surprised to see us as we were to see them.

I unleashed a blast of air magic that sent them both flying back to smash into the wall on the other side of the alley. They hit the ground and lay still, either dead or out cold.

I heard slow clapping and turned. Nora stood in the mouth of the alley, flanked by four more goons with guns raised. "Alice, it's lovely to see you again. It feels like fate keeps bringing us together."

I rolled my eyes. "It's not fate; it's that your dick bosses keep sending you on little errands."

Her smile vanished. "My orders are to bring him in. You can come too, if you like." She pulled a pair of spell cuffs from her belt and twirled them around her finger. "Just slip these on like a good girl and I'll make sure you get there without so much as a scratch."

"I think we'll take door number two," I said, inching in front of Daniel. He growled.

"There is no door number two, sunshine." She dangled the cuffs. "It's my way...or the dead way."

"Moses needs me alive," I murmured to Daniel. "She can't kill me, but she can kill you. I'll buy you some time to get out of here. When you can, get to Sean Maclin, my partner. Our pack will protect you."

He snarled. "I'm not leaving, and I'm not bringing danger to any pack, especially not yours."

"Come on, Alice," Nora called. "Don't make me insist. I don't know why you're here, but it's time for you to either run along home or decide to come with Mr. Holiday and visit my boss. I know he'd love to see you."

She had no idea how badly Moses wanted me, or why. Moses had to make sure no one knew I was really his granddaughter, who'd supposedly died five years ago in an accident at his compound in

Baltimore. If that news got out, everyone would be after me, from the feds to every cabal in the country, and every Vampire Court too.

"Do you have somewhere safe to go?" I asked Daniel.

He growled and didn't answer, but I saw from his expression that he did have a place to go.

"Do this for me," I said. I knew it wasn't fair of me, and the last thing I wanted to do was to send him away when we'd only just found each other, but I wanted him far away from Nora. "Come find me soon. We have a lot to talk about."

He planted his feet shoulder width apart. "You can't fight them all by yourself."

I smiled. "I'm not by myself. Trust me, Daniel." I paused. "The first album I ever bought was *Dark Side of the Moon*. When you come find me again, we'll listen to it together."

He stilled, his face a mask of both pain and wonder.

"Go." I repeated. Out of the corner of my eye, I saw two mages and two goons at the opposite end of the alley. Malcolm floated behind them, unseen and waiting for my signal. He gave me a thumbs-up.

I turned back to Nora. "A while back, I told you we'd have to take a rain check and finish that conversation another day."

Magic spooled around my arms in every color of the rainbow. My cells buzzed with the magic I'd absorbed from the sorcerer I'd killed. The power was enormous and strange and I was only just beginning to learn how to use it.

It was also slowly killing me, but that was a problem I'd have to solve another day.

My wolf raised her head and growled. My eyes grew warm and my vision went gold around the edges. "How about we finish it today?" I asked Nora.

She stared. The goons with her exchanged glances.

Beside me, Daniel smiled at her. It was a purely predatory smile —one I used myself from time to time. I guessed I knew now where

I'd gotten it from. If he was weirded out by my magic or my wolf, he didn't let on.

"You want to play?" I asked Nora. "Then let's play."

Instead of leaving, Daniel dropped to his knees and shifted in a surge of golden shifter magic. His wolf was enormous: dark gray with a band of black fur across his shoulders. He flattened his ears back against his head and showed Nora all of his teeth.

It occurred to me Daniel had just as much reason to hate Nora and anyone else from Moses's cabal as I did. Fair enough—we could do this together.

My wolf prowled restlessly. My skin prickled like fur was pushing at it from the inside. She wanted out. I feared releasing her, because once she left my body I had no control over what she did. However, my desire to see Nora pay for everything she'd done outweighed my apprehension, at least for now.

Go play, I told her.

With a growl, my wolf leaped out of my chest in a brilliant surge of magic. She was the same size as Daniel's wolf, but made of pure golden magic. She landed on the pavement, raised her head, and howled. I might be biased, but I thought her howl was the most beautiful and terrifying howl I'd ever heard.

Two of the people with Nora turned to run. She formed a blood magic blade and cut them in half before they had a chance to take two steps. Apparently, just like Moses, Nora did not suffer cowards to live.

The humans at the other end of the alley dropped, thanks to Malcolm and his sleep spells. The two mages, who couldn't be spelled because of their natural shields, headed in our direction, spooling magic.

"Sic 'em," I told Daniel's wolf. "I'll deal with Nora and the others."

He snarled, turned, and headed for the mages.

Judging by Nora's expression, she was trying to think of a way to take out my golden wolf. My wolf, on the other hand, eyeballed Nora like she thought she looked tasty.

"What *are* you?" Nora asked me, her eyes on the golden wolf. "And what the hell is that thing?"

My wolf showed her teeth.

"I'm a mage with some special skills, and this is my wolf. And *that*—" I hooked my thumb over my shoulder toward where Daniel's wolf was snarling at the mages "—is someone you aren't taking back to Moses, so maybe *you* should just run along and tell him if he wants Daniel, he can come get him himself instead of sending his lackeys to do it."

Needling Nora about being an underling was one of the few ways I'd found to get a reaction from her. People like her didn't let others get under their skin very easily, but she had an ego. Poking it was one of my favorite pastimes.

Nora's eyes turned white. I didn't know how much power she'd expended earlier blowing out the front windows of Daniel's store, but she could pack quite a wallop. Then again, so could I. Thanks to the sorcerer magic I'd absorbed, I had some new tricks up my sleeve.

I spun my blood magic into round blades on my fingertips. Nora smiled. As far as she knew, from this distance and without a focus, the blades couldn't harm her or her companions.

Surprise, bitch.

Dark magic flared on my hands, igniting glyphs on the blades. With twin quick movements and a burst of air magic, I threw them at Nora, and two more right after.

She reacted fast, her reflexes enhanced—I suspected—by drinking vampire blood. Her air magic sent the first two blades into the walls on either side of the alley. The second set of blades ended up in the chests of the man and woman on either side of her. They went down, gurgling.

Behind me, Daniel's wolf tore into someone with a snarl that made my hair stand on end. I glanced over my shoulder. One mage lay on the pavement, unconscious, thanks to something Malcolm had done. The other stopped screaming abruptly when Daniel's wolf tore out his throat. The wolf raised his bloody muzzle and howled. Malcolm appeared at my side, looking quite pleased with himself.

"You are just *the most* stubborn person," Nora said, shaking her head. She was spooling air magic again. "Why do you insist on doing everything the hard way? Don't you know you'll only end up suffering more in the end?"

"Why? Are you planning to talk me to death?" I jerked my head in Nora's direction. "Kill her," I told my wolf.

She headed for Nora, growling low.

Nora unleashed a blast of air magic. I formed an air magic shield in front of me, but I wasn't her target.

Instead, the magic hit the corner of the building whose roof we'd jumped onto. The impact was like a bomb going off. The entire corner of the building crumbled. I had no time—and no*where*—to run.

I hit the ground, grabbed a ley line, channeled its power into my air magic shield, and curved it over my head. Falling bricks couldn't hurt Malcolm or my wolf, but they could hurt me.

Debris piled on top of my shield. It wavered, threatening to give way and drop a ton of rubble right on top of me. I curled into a ball and made the shield as small as I could to focus my magic.

I gritted my teeth and channeled more ley line power. The pain was intense, but it was better than being squashed flat. Had the building stopped falling, or was the pile on top of me getting heavier? I couldn't tell.

My wolf came back. She spiraled up my arm and disappeared into my chest. The sensation was of a puzzle piece finding its home. Her power combined with mine and the shield held steady.

I could use air magic to try to blast away the debris on top of me, but I worried I would lose the shield if I did that. I couldn't tell how deep I was buried. If I lost the shield without clearing an opening big enough to get out, the result would be an Alice pancake. On the other hand, I had to get myself out soon, before I ran out of air or my shield broke.

Just as I was about to try an air magic blast, Malcolm's head and shoulders appeared in the tiny space occupied by my body and the air I had to breathe. I could barely see him through the dust.

"I knew it! You're alive," he crowed.

I coughed. "For the moment."

"Daniel's digging you out. Hang on—let me tell him where you are." He disappeared.

I heard the faint sounds of pieces of debris moving. The sounds got louder and closer. The pile on top of me lightened, and chunks of rubble crashed as Daniel picked them up and threw them aside. Holding the shield became far easier as he cleared the wreckage.

Suddenly, sunlight and relatively fresh air streamed through an opening above my head. "Alice!" It was Daniel's voice, growly and worried.

I coughed again. "I'm here. I'm okay."

The opening got bigger until there was nothing left above me. I let go of the ley line and let my shield dissipate.

Daniel appeared, covered with sweat and dust, his eyes golden. "Can you get out?"

I got to my feet, woozy from channeling the ley line and holding the shield for so long. The entire corner of the building lay in a pile around me. Sirens wailed in the distance again, and I had a feeling they would be responding to this scene.

"Nora's gone?" I rasped, doubling over to cough out dust.

"Yeah, she gave up and hightailed it out of here," Malcolm said. "I think we should do the same before the cops and feds arrive."

Daniel helped me climb out of the rubble. Bystanders and employees of the businesses housed in the building picked their way through the debris, looking for anyone else trapped in the wreckage.

Thankfully, Daniel had found some basketball shorts to wear, sparing me the sight of my father naked. They weren't his size;

maybe he'd found them in his friend's truck. When he'd shifted, his wounds had healed, though the silver bullets had left scars.

I followed Daniel to his friend's truck, parked at the other end of the alley in a small lot. "Come back with me," I urged. "Moses won't stop hunting you. For some reason, he's angry I'm part shifter, and he wants to take it out on you."

Daniel leaned against the truck. "I can't believe I have a daughter. All these years...you're sure?"

"I'm sure. I have it on the highest authority." That highest authority happened to be an angel named Tura, but I didn't think now was the time to tell him that. He'd had enough revelations for one day.

"Why the hell didn't Moira tell me?" he demanded, his eyes blazing gold. He was angry now that the shock had worn off. I couldn't blame him. "I never would have left. I never would have abandoned her, or you. *Why?*" He snarled.

"She wanted you to live—to get away from Moses and have a life. I don't know why, but she believed Moses would have killed all three of us if he'd known you were my father. She and my dad kept it a secret until the day they died. I only found out recently because of a spelled mirror that showed me a forgotten memory of overhearing them talking."

"She had no right to keep this from me." He scrubbed his face with his hands. "You look nothing like the picture you showed me." It wasn't an accusation, just a question.

"When I escaped from Moses, I had to steal someone's identity to hide from him. I had plastic surgery and became Alice Worth, who died in Chicago five years ago. My real name is Ava." I swallowed hard. "Come home with me."

He shook his head, his expression grim. "I'm better off on my own. I don't want to bring more danger to your door."

"I used to think that way too, but I was wrong. Out there, you're alone. If you come home with me—"

"Alice, stop," he said quietly. "I will find you again soon, I promise. I have to sort some things out."

The sirens were loud now, and there were a lot of them. "We've got to go," Malcolm urged.

Apparently Malcolm had taken some energy from Daniel, because my father heard him. He turned toward Malcolm and pointed at him. "You keep her safe, and tell Sean Maclin he'd better do the same."

"Yes, sir," Malcolm said. "Come on, Alice."

Daniel cupped my cheek with his hand. "You may not look like her, but I recognize Moira in your voice, and the way you faced Murphy's soldiers without fear," he said, his voice rough. "Go home. I'll see you when I can."

There was no use arguing with him; I could see that in his eyes. I told myself he was leaving to protect me, but it hurt nonetheless. I'd never imagined he'd refuse to come home with me.

"Let me know you're okay, at least," I said finally. "Get me a message when you're somewhere safe."

"I will." He got in the truck. The engine started with a rumble. He gave me a nod and floored it in the direction of the lot's exit. In seconds, he'd turned the corner and disappeared.

I wanted to punch something. "Damn it."

"Yeah." Malcolm touched my shoulder. "You okay?"

"Not even remotely." I headed for my vehicle with Malcolm trailing along behind me.

CHAPTER 2

I WOKE FROM A VIVID NIGHTMARE TO FIND MYSELF BATHED IN A COLD SWEAT. My arms and legs seized painfully as my body tried to shift to wolf form.

Damn it, not again.

I gritted my teeth and clutched the bedding, trying to ride out the pain and spasms. A tiny sound escaped my clenched jaw—a cross between a whimper and a growl.

Sean had already pulled me close and wrapped warm, comforting alpha magic around me. He must have sensed the problem before I'd even woken up.

Though I wasn't a werewolf, he'd had to treat me much like a newly turned shifter since my wolf started trying to force me to shift in my sleep. I struggled to understand the changes to my magic, body, and mind caused by the sorcerer magic I'd absorbed. My wolf's restlessness wasn't helping matters.

Sean pried my fingers loose from the comforter and gripped my hand. "Hold on to me," he murmured, rubbing his chin on the top of my head.

I squeezed his hand gratefully. I still wasn't used to turning to others for comfort, though I knew it made Sean happy and deeply contented to take care of me.

Usually these episodes passed relatively quickly, but this time the discomfort seemed to be getting worse instead of better. A particularly severe spasm made my back arch. Pain lanced down both of my legs. I cried out.

Sean cursed. His eyes flared bright gold in the darkness of our bedroom.

My wolf responded by pushing me aside roughly to look out through my human eyes. The feeling of displacement caused a wave of intense dizziness and heat. My vision turned gold around the edges.

"*Be calm,*" Sean told her, his voice resonant with alpha magic.

Before, she'd obeyed immediately and stopped trying to force my body to shift. This time, however, she responded with a low growl. She prowled in my mind, her ears back and lip curled to show a few teeth. My skin prickled painfully.

Sean snarled. Alpha power rose, but not the comforting warmth I was used to. Instead, it seared me and pushed my wolf back with brute force. He'd never done that to her before. She whined in pain and unhappiness.

"Stop," I snapped, but he kept pushing until she hunkered down. He wasn't just dominating my wolf; he was dominating me too, and I was instantly furious. I wouldn't be mastered by anyone, for any reason—not after twenty years of captivity by my grandfather.

My wolf growled, but she retreated into the shadows in my head, her tail between her legs. Finally, my limbs stopped seizing. I went limp in Sean's arms, gasping for breath and shivering. My arms and legs ached down to the bones. He tried to pull me against his chest, but I was angry and resisted. "Why did you do that?" I asked, my voice rough.

"Because I had to. I should have done it before, but I knew how much it would bother you." He rubbed his chin on my head again in a very wolfy attempt to comfort me. "You're like a new shifter, though you don't actually shift. You and your wolf have to form a partnership, and you're the dominant partner. You haven't learned that role yet—or how to make it clear who's boss—so I have to do it."

I still shivered, though it wasn't cold in our room. He pulled the covers over us and wrapped himself around me, trying to warm and soothe me with his body heat. "The wolf is an intelligent animal, but she's still an animal," he said, his lips against my hair. "She can't be the one in control. Even if you don't shift, she's dangerous. She's hurting you because she doesn't know or understand what she can and can't do. She could hurt someone else unless you set boundaries. The next time this happens, you have to do what I just did. I'll teach you how, just like I would a new werewolf." He kissed my hair. "I love you with every fiber of my being, but I can't coddle you, not when it comes to your wolf. There's too much at stake."

"That's an understatement." I took a shaky breath. "The Council already wants me out of your pack and your life because I have a wolf made of pure magic. Imagine what they would do if they thought I couldn't control her."

He snuggled us deeper under the covers and rested his head on mine. "You *will* learn to control her. And the Council are not going to do a damn thing—not to you, or to any of us. You, Nan, and I will see to that."

Our pack's new beta, Nan Lowell, had taken over the role when longtime beta Jack Hastings died fighting the sorcerer Miraç. Nan's transition from pack member to beta had not gone smoothly—not because of trouble from within our pack, but because Nan was female, and that seemed to make a lot of people angry. Fortunately, nothing they said seemed to affect her or undermine her confidence in the least. From the day she became beta, she'd been as dominant as Jack had been, and still as nurturing as ever.

Sean nuzzled my neck. "Will you be able to get back to sleep?"

"I usually can't after these things, but I'll try. Maybe it will help knowing what I need to do if it happens again." I wiggled into a more comfortable position against him and tried to relax.

Unfortunately, something else was keeping me awake these days besides my wolf's new habit of trying to make me shift in my sleep. I was keeping something from Sean, something very serious and potentially explosive, and I had absolutely no idea how to break the news.

I'd recently figured out that Charles Vaughan, a longtime acquaintance and a member of the Vampire Court, had been messing with my head. His goal had been to undermine my resistance to his advances, get me under his control and, more recently, force me to sabotage my relationship with Sean. I would have noticed any overt influence, so he'd done it subtly, one tiny push at a time.

I'd liked Charles, even been fond of him—or so I'd thought. Now I didn't know what had been real and what was a result of his manipulations.

Two things I knew for certain, however: I would never trust Charles again, and I had to tell Sean the truth. Sean hated Charles for a long list of reasons, most especially his well-documented history of taking advantage of me in moments of vulnerability. I wanted to wait until I'd had a chance to confront Charles about it myself, so it would already be resolved, but that wasn't fair to Sean.

I owed him the truth and my trust, but after twenty years of captivity and abuse at my grandfather's hands, both were so damn hard for me to give, even to Sean, and even now. I made a frustrated sound.

Sean kissed my ear. "As much as I love your little growl, I know something's chewing you up. Talk to me. Let me help."

Damn it, why was I so hesitant to tell him the truth? Even if he was angry—which he most certainly *would* be—I knew he wouldn't do anything irrational.

I had a sudden thought: was my reluctance part of Charles's manipulation? I was starting to wonder if anything I thought or felt related to Charles was real or not, and that made me even angrier than I already was.

Sean squeezed me gently. "Alice." His tone had changed. He knew something was very wrong, and now there was no way he would let the subject drop.

I unclenched my jaw and forced the words out. "Charles has been messing with my head."

His body went rigid, like he was holding himself back from violence by sheer force of will. "In what way?" he asked. I almost didn't recognize his voice. It was hard, cold, and deadly.

"When I was in Miraç's prison, I was behind powerful wards that disrupted all my magic and metaphysical connections to everyone." My voice sounded strained with the effort it took to speak. "I couldn't feel our bond or my bond with Malcolm. As I lay in my cell and thought about you, though, I realized I suddenly had none of the second thoughts about moving in together I'd had just the day before when we talked about the new house. It reminded me of how I felt after Carly removed the hex Lily put on me when she tried to break us up—like I was suddenly able to think clearly. The only thing that makes sense is Charles has been subtly influencing me. For how long, I'm not sure, but months at least. Possibly years."

Fury rolled through his body in waves I sensed as his muscles tightened. He literally vibrated with anger. Magic and alpha power surged, and I thought for a moment he might shift.

Instead, he let out a long, low snarl. "I've wondered if that was possible," he said finally. "When you came back from being Miraç's prisoner, with no memories and the slate wiped clean, so to speak, you were instinctively suspicious of Vaughan. Not just because you didn't remember your past, but because whatever he's been doing to your head, Miraç's magic reset it. Vaughan was angry when he interacted with you and you didn't respond to him like you had before you disappeared. Now I understand why." His chest rumbled. "He realized he'd lost the ground he'd gained with you with all these months and years of messing with your thoughts and emotions."

Too angry to stay still, Sean got up and stalked back and forth across the bedroom, his eyes glowing like golden suns in the dark room.

"I'm sorry I waited so long to tell you," I said as he paced. The more I talked about it, the easier it got, as if I'd broken through Charles's influence and freed myself. "I don't know if what he did made me reluctant to tell you the truth, or if that was my own fears. It's hard for me to know what's real and what's not now when it comes to anything related to Charles or the Court. I have to assume my suspicions and anger are my own, and everything else was a result of his influence."

He stopped pacing, his back to me. He took a deep breath, exhaled, and returned to the bed. He sat on the edge and pulled me into his lap. "I am so damned sorry. After what you've been through, control over your own body and mind is more important to you than almost anything. That makes what Vaughan did that much worse." He nuzzled my neck. "You must want to kill him slowly for betraying you so cruelly. I know *I* do."

"Obviously, I was furious when I figured it out. If he'd been in front of me in that moment, I might have done exactly that," I admitted. "I'm much calmer now—more just done with him than vengeful."

Sean snarled, his muscles going rigid again. "He has to answer to our pack, and to *me*."

Startled, I moved so I could see his face. "Isn't it enough if he answers to me? That's always been enough before."

"Not this time."

I scowled. "I don't need anyone to fight my battles for me."

"This isn't just your battle." His expression was cold. "It's mine, and our pack's. An attack on anyone under my care is an attack on all of us."

Irritated, I started to get off his lap, but he held me. "Let go," I said.

After a moment, he released me. I walked over near the windows and turned around, my arms crossed. "Since when am I *under your care?* I want to deal with it myself. I don't want it to be a pack issue."

"It's already a pack issue." He rose from the bed. "The moment you accepted the role of pack associate, anything that happened to you became a pack issue. Just because I've let you talk me out of doing what needed to be done on multiple occasions doesn't mean it was the right decision. I'm done allowing Vaughan to blatantly disrespect you, me, our pack, and the Council. It's possible he keeps harming you because I *allow* him to keep doing it, and it ends now." He picked up his phone and scrolled through his contacts.

"Sean, wait."

He looked up, his thumb hovering over the CALL button. "Why?"

"Doesn't what I want you to do matter?"

"Of course it does." The words were clipped. "It always has, and it always will. But in this case, what matters more is that I do what has to be done—what I should have done months ago."

"Which is what?"

"Inform the Court one of its members has committed an unprovoked act of violence against a member of the Tomb Mountain Pack, in violation of both human law *and* the Council's treaty with the Court, and demand Vaughan go on trial before the Council."

"I don't want the Court *or* the Council to know what Charles did," I argued. "Admitting in open court that Charles messed with my head is admitting not only a failure on my part, but also a weakness. I don't like parading my weaknesses in front of people—especially people who would love to know how to get to me. If what I want isn't important enough to stop you from making that call, then maybe you don't want everybody and their uncle to know I let Charles play me like a violin."

Sean was silent for a long time. "Don't make it sound as if I'd be choosing what I want or what's best for our pack over what *you* want," he said finally, his expression hard. "That's not fair. You know damn well you are the most important person in my life."

"I do know that." I took a deep breath and let it out. "I'm sorry I phrased it that way. But don't you agree we'd be better off if no one knew what Charles did, as long as I confronted him about it and made damn sure it never happened again?"

"I will confront him," Sean stated. When I opened my mouth to object, he raised his hand. "Alice, I'm trying to meet you partway, because I accept your argument that letting others know what happened might cause you harm. You have to compromise too. Swallow your pride and let me do what I need to do as the alpha of our pack."

I'd asked Sean to swallow his pride a dozen times for me, and he'd done it. He'd probably done it a dozen more times without me knowing. Of all the things Sean had done for me, that was probably the most difficult—not just because it went against every instinct in his body, but also because it had the potential to undermine his authority with the rest of the pack, other packs, the Council, and the Court. I'd known that, but suddenly the reality of what he'd been willing to do for me really hit me hard. He asked so little of me, and I'd resisted giving even that much. The realization of how selfish I'd been was physically painful.

I turned away, but there was no hiding that level of emotion from him. He tossed his phone on the bed and wrapped his arms around me from behind. "Stop," he said, his head resting against mine. "Don't feel guilty. You're still getting used to this new life and being cared for."

I sniffled. "Don't make excuses for me when I'm a shitty person. That just makes it worse."

To my surprise, he chuckled. "So it would be better if I called you out for being a shitty person instead of giving you the benefit of the doubt?"

Inelegantly, I wiped my eyes with the back of my hand. "Yes."

"I'll remember that. If you're ever a shitty person, I'll tell you so." He kissed my hair. "And for the record, I don't believe for one minute Valas doesn't know what Vaughan was doing. I don't think he does anything that would have ramifications for the Court without her say-so. He may have even done it at her direction. Did he have his own motives, like getting you into bed? Probably." He growled. "Valas has her own reasons for wanting you under the Court's thumb. Now you're bound to her. Even if that binding doesn't give her as much control over you as she thought it would, you're still hers, by vampire law. Which pisses me off to no end, even if it was your decision and the only way to free you from Miraç's control."

"I'll figure out a way to undo the binding," I reminded him. "It won't happen overnight, because it's going to be tricky, but remember she can't control me like she could a human or even a less powerful mage. If she ever tries to force me to do something against my will, I'll burn out the binding and deal with the consequences."

"I'm glad to hear it." He nuzzled my hair. "Ready to try and sleep? We can catch a few more hours before it's time to get up."

We returned to the bed. Sean sent a text message, received an immediate reply, and put his phone on his nightstand.

As he curled up behind me and pulled the covers over us, I asked, "Did you set up a meeting with Charles?"

"Tomorrow night at his estate."

"Am I going with you?"

He kissed my jaw. "Of course you are."

"Okay." I hesitated, then asked, "Do you ever wish I wasn't...the way I am?"

"Not even a little bit, Miss Magic." He nestled his nose into the back of my neck, where my scent was strongest. "I love you."

I smiled and closed my eyes, willing myself to relax and take comfort in his love and strength. "I know."

"Hi ho, hi ho, it's off to work we go," Malcolm sang from the front passenger seat of my borrowed Maclin Security SUV. My car had been stolen and burned by people working for the sorcerer who'd kidnapped me. I hadn't had a chance to go car shopping, or even decide what I wanted to buy, so I was using one of Sean's company vehicles.

I sighed and tipped my travel cup up to get the last few drops of coffee at the bottom. "Are you going to be cheerful all day?"

He grinned. "Probably."

"Damn it." I grabbed my bag and another full cup of coffee and got out.

He floated around to the driver's side as I shut my door. "You know you love me."

"It's a good thing I do, especially at moments like this, when you're way too damn cheery this early in the morning." I put my bag on my shoulder and headed for the front door of Maclin Security.

Malcolm snorted and followed. "I'm sorry—I guess I forgot it was the crack of nine."

"Some of us didn't get much sleep last night, remember?"

He sobered. "You're right. I'm sorry. And Sean had to be here at seven thirty for a meeting."

"Which is why I brought him this, plus two fresh blueberry scones." I raised the full cup of coffee I'd bought at Brew a Cup, the fantastic coffee shop owned by my friend Carly Reese. "I figured I owed it to him for keeping him up half the night, and not in any fun way."

"You know that man doesn't hold it against you," Malcolm scolded as we reached the main door. "And I'm sure he'll be happy to let you make it up to him properly tonight." He waggled his eyebrows suggestively.

"Can we not talk about my sex life right now?"

"Hey, at least you *have* one," he griped. "I may be dead, but I still remember the good things about being alive."

I opened the door and went inside. Cass Reynolds, Maclin Security's office manager, was watering the plants in the lobby when I walked in. I adored the petite redhead, who was perpetually cheerful and made coffee better than most coffee shops.

"Morning, Alice," she chirped. "I was going to tell you I just made a fresh pot, but I see you brought some with you."

I waved the cup. "This is for Sean, so I *will* help myself to your delicious coffee, thank you. Is he still in a meeting?"

She checked the soil of a plant and gave it some water. "He's in his *second* meeting of the morning, but they should be out in a few minutes. I'll let him know to swing by your office when he gets a chance."

"Thanks, Cass. You're awesome."

"I know." She winked and headed for the break room to refill the water can.

I headed down the hall to the right with Malcolm trailing along behind me.

When we reached the third door on the right, I stopped in my tracks and stared. When we'd left yesterday, my office door had looked exactly like all the others in the building: plain and unre-markable except for the little placard beside the doorframe with the room number, A05.

That plain office door had been replaced overnight with an opaque glass door with a steel frame and handle. The upper part of the glass had my company logo, and beneath it the words LOOKING GLASS INVESTIGATIONS.

"Hey, looky there," Malcolm said, grinning. "You're officially official now."

"Did you know about this?" I demanded in a whisper, in case anyone was within earshot.

"Of course I did," he said with exaggerated patience. "I'm sure Sean wishes he was here to see your face when you saw it for the first time, but I'll tell him your reaction was exactly what he expected: disbelief and dismay."

I made a little growly sound and tried my key. It unlocked the door. "I wasn't dismayed," I protested.

"Uh-huh." He followed me inside the office.

I hung my bag on my chair and opened the curtains to let in some light.

"Don't get me wrong," he added. "I'm proud of you for making this leap and renting office space in Sean's building, but you're still having trouble committing to it. That's why you've still got stuff in boxes, and you tiptoe around like you're in someone else's space instead of your own. Now this is *your* office. You're paying rent and your name's on the door."

I sighed. "Is that why he did it? So I'd stop acting like I was borrowing an office from his company?"

"It was a gift from the heart, like everything he does." Malcolm floated over to me. The sunlight shone through his transparent body and made him glow. "But sometimes you need a little nudge to take that final step."

"This was a bit more than a nudge, but I can't say you're wrong." I sat back in my very comfortable fancy new chair and surveyed the office. It was a good size—not too small, not too big—and had its own bathroom. The windows let in morning and early afternoon light, and I didn't mind the view of Maclin Security's loading dock.

I'd been evicted from my old office a few months ago during a wave of violence against mages and vampires. I'd left my things in storage in the interim while I tried to find a new office. Many commercial landlords had balked at renting space to a mage private investigator, citing safety concerns.

I'd initially refused Sean's offer to lease an office in the Maclin Security building, but I'd come to understand my reluctance had come more from my irrational fear of commitment than not wanting to mix my personal and professional lives. My grandfather's torment had left some pretty significant scars, both physical and psychological. I'd gotten much better at trusting Sean and Malcolm, but it was hard to let go of the fear of betrayal and the instinct to avoid tying myself down.

I'm fairly well tied down at the moment, I thought, somewhat ruefully. Sean and I had just signed the paperwork on a house, I'd contacted a realtor about selling my home, and I was bound to Valas—albeit not without an exit strategy for the latter.

Rather than think about that, I sent a text to Ben Cooper, who was third in our pack and the head of Maclin Security's installation division.

Me: Can I borrow a hammer?

His reply was nearly instantaneous.

Drac Fanboy: Be right there.

Scissors in hand, I went to the stack of boxes in the corner and started opening them. In the second box, I found what I was looking for: my mage private investigator's license, in its battered frame. Sometimes my clients didn't get the answers they wanted, and they tended to get salty about it.

Ben knocked on the doorframe and stuck his head in. He grinned. "Hey, Alice." He glanced around. "Malcolm here?"

"I'm here," Malcolm said cheerfully from over by the window. "What's up, bro?"

Ben waved a hammer. "As requested." He gestured at my license. "Is that what you want to hang? You have some hooks?"

"Somewhere." I dug around in the box and came up with a package of picture hooks.

Ben took them. "Where do you want it?"

I showed him the spot on the wall to the right of my desk. He produced a tape measure and went to work.

In the meantime, I unpacked boxes and decided where to put things in my new office. I had my back to my office door and I was focused on what I was doing, so when a warm pair of hands gripped my hips, I jumped.

Sean nuzzled the back of my neck. "Mmm. Hello, beautiful. You smell good."

I smacked his hand where it rested on my hip, but I smiled. "Not professional," I reminded him.

He kissed my shoulder. "If I could make looking at you my full-time job, I'd do it."

Despite his teasing, when I turned, I could tell by his expression something was wrong. He let me know with his eyes that we'd talk about it in private later. "Cass told me you brought coffee," he said instead.

I gestured at the cup on my desk. "It's that new ultra-bold blend Carly's trying at her shop. It's a little too strong for me, but I thought you might want to try it."

"I do." He sniffed. "And do I smell scones?"

I went to my messenger bag and produced the scones in a little paper sack with the Brew a Cup logo. "Fresh baked this morning. I didn't even eat them on the way here."

"You are my favorite mage." Sean took a drink of the coffee and nodded appreciatively. "Excellent. I'm a fan of Carly's new blend." He smiled as Ben finished hanging my MPI license and raised his coffee cup in a toast. "Name on the door and credentials on the wall. Looking Glass Investigations officially has a new home."

"Thank you for the door." I touched his hand. "I love it."

"Do you?" Sean's tone was light, but his eyes searched my face.

"I do," I assured him. "It's a lovely and very thoughtful gift."

"I'm having your company name and logo put on the front window as well. They're doing that this weekend. That way your clients will know they're in the right place when they park out front."

I squashed the panicky fight-or-flight reaction in my tummy and smiled back. He wasn't trying to tie me down; he was making a home for me. "That's really sweet. Thank you."

"You're welcome." He glanced at Ben. "Can you give us a minute?"

"Sure." Ben spun the hammer in his hand. He enjoyed making things, even if it was just putting something on the wall. "Give me a call when you're done so we can go over next week's scheduling. See you later, Alice."

"Thanks again for your help. It looks great." The license was nice and level and centered. Much better than I probably would have done. If I'd hung it crooked or off-center, Ben would have probably taken it down and re-hung it anyway, so it was easier to just let him do it right to start with.

The moment he was gone, I turned to Sean. "What's going on?"

He gestured at my fancy chair. "Want to sit?"

"Sure." I went behind my desk and sat. He settled into one of my client chairs and Malcolm hovered to my right.

Sean rubbed the bridge of his nose. "Ron and I had a meeting to talk about some changes we've seen regarding our clients. There's always some turnover, but suddenly we've lost several large business accounts and haven't gotten some new ones we were fairly certain we'd get. I didn't think much of it, other than to be frustrated, but this morning we lost another account—one we've had almost since the day we opened. I called the CEO personally, and after some bull-shit, he implied he'd gotten pressure to switch security providers. I called one of the other companies who dropped us and was told the same thing."

"Pressure from who?" I asked, frowning.

Sean said nothing.

Realization dawned. "Son of a bitch." Magic sparked on my hands, and a cold breeze blew through my office. "That *bastard*."

"Moses?" Malcolm asked.

Sean nodded. "No one we talked to wanted to say very much, but someone made sure Ron heard it was because of you."

I got up and paced. "Because of me? That doesn't make any sense." No one but Sean and Malcolm were aware I was Moses's granddaughter, and the fact I was the powerful mage nicknamed "Storm Girl" was known only by a handful of people.

"It does if Ron thinks it's because the Were Ruling Council doesn't approve of our relationship, which is what he was told. I can't tell him differently, for obvious reasons." Sean flexed his hands.

"So, from Ron's perspective, the company you've spent the last fifteen years building is losing clients and money because of me." I wanted to smash something. "I knew Moses would find a way to drive a wedge between us. I didn't expect him to go after your business. I guess I should have."

"There's no wedge between us," Sean stated. "And Ron knows it's not your fault. He doesn't hold it against you."

"For how long, though? It's already cutting into your bottom line. What happens when you have to forgo raises or lay off employees?" Magic swirled around my clenched fists. "It's only going to get worse. What if Moses starts going after other members of our pack?"

Sean got up and touched my hand despite the magic that snapped at his fingers. "If Moses targets our people, they won't turn on you—they'll be angry at him."

"I have to kill him." Too angry to accept his comfort, I pulled away and leaned against the wall. "I have to kill him before he destroys everything. I had a chance the night he killed Darius Bell out at the bordello, but he had Ben. Somehow I have to get another shot at him when he doesn't have a hostage. I'll have to outsmart him."

He kissed my forehead. "And we will," he promised, putting subtle emphasis on the pronoun *we*. "In the meantime, we strengthen our pack, live our lives together, and revel in the knowledge of how pissed off he is that you're happy and free."

I took a deep breath. My magic faded and stopped sizzling on my skin. "That *does* feel good to think about," I admitted, smiling despite my anger. "A happily-ever-after, or even a happily-for-now, is maybe the best revenge I can think of, short of turning him to ash." I rubbed my right arm.

"What's wrong with your arm?" Malcolm asked, frowning.

"I must have tweaked it picking up those boxes." My back ached too. I flexed my elbow a few times. Was the pain from unpacking, or from Miraç's poisonous magic? I couldn't tell.

Rather than worry them, I added, "Welcome to my thirties, I guess. I know I've got a big bottle of ibuprofen around here somewhere."

"Second box on the right," Malcolm said helpfully.

I sighed and reached for the box, hoping my flippant excuse sounded more convincing than it felt.

CHAPTER 3

Until I met Joshua Hayes, I'd never encountered a true omega werewolf. And until I met his brother Jesse, I'd never known someone so full of both love and anger that he seemed perpetually on a knife's edge, waiting for the slightest provocation to unleash the full force of his fury.

Sean, Nan, and I met the brothers at the land the Tomb Mountain Pack owned north of town. It was the first time I'd been part of a decision about prospective new pack members.

"Thank you for meeting with us," Jesse told us as he shook Sean's hand. His tone bordered on confrontational, though he had no reason to be. I wondered if he assumed we'd be unwelcoming or unkind since so many other packs had turned them away.

Jesse met each of our gazes for a moment and then dropped his eyes. He was a little under six feet tall but powerfully built, even by shifter standards. He clearly spent a lot of time in the gym. I wondered if his primary motivation was protecting his brother, or if he was trying to compensate somehow for Joshua's relative weakness by making himself as physically intimidating as possible.

Though several inches taller than Jesse and as muscular as any shifter, Joshua stayed behind his brother, his eyes fixed on the ground. I felt instinctively protective of Joshua, and was sure Sean and Nan felt the same.

"We're glad to have you here." Sean's eyes glowed golden. A shadow moved behind them: Sean's wolf, evaluating the brothers through his human eyes. Sean had explained that in this initial meeting, we would meet the new prospective pack members first as humans. Then they would shift and interact as wolves to see if Jesse and Joshua's wolves would be a good fit for the pack.

Sean's golden eyes moved from Jesse to Joshua. His expression softened and his tone gentled. An alpha was a protector first and foremost. "Hello, Joshua. What do you think of our land?"

Joshua didn't look up. "It's very big," he said. His voice was surprisingly quiet for such a large man. "We drove all the way around. It took a long time."

"We like to have a lot of room to run," Nan said with a smile, though Joshua kept his eyes on the grass.

Nan's graying hair and kindly expression didn't disguise her dominance, now that she no longer pretended to be farther down in the pack hierarchy than she should be. She was still the caring and motherly woman I'd known since I'd first met her, but there was more steel visible in her now.

"Given what you told me in your e-mail, we know about your past interactions with other packs," Sean said, turning back to Jesse. Joshua relaxed minutely when no longer the focus of Sean's attention. "You and Joshua have chosen to be on your own since leaving the Clear Lake Pack. Tell us why you think our pack might be a good home for you and your brother."

Jesse's eyes glowed amber. "We're not here to beg to join your pack, Mr. Maclin. If that's what you want me to do, we'll leave right now."

He was as angry as Joshua was meek. We didn't deserve his anger, but I couldn't blame him for it, given the abuse they'd suffered. My heart ached for both of them. I didn't let Jesse see my sympathy. He wouldn't want it. He wanted our acceptance, though he was too angry and proud to ask for it.

Sean studied him. "Obviously, I'm aware Joshua is on the autism spectrum, and as an omega wolf he has been the target of abuse from your original pack, other packs, and even lone wolves. I'm also aware of your reputation as a fierce fighter and a protector. You have a well-documented history of starting—and finishing—a hell of a lot of fights, especially when someone mistreats Joshua, or when you think they're going to. I understand how hard your life has been."

"Do you?" Jesse asked, his voice bitter.

Sean moved like lightning. In a blink, Jesse was flat on his back, staring up in shock as Sean pinned him on the ground with a fist in his shirt. The sudden violent act startled me, but Nan didn't react.

"Yes, I do," Sean snapped. "Just because I haven't lived it doesn't mean I can't understand it. I've seen my share of suffering."

I wondered if he was thinking about my memories of my life with my grandfather, which he'd seen when I got them back from the sorcerer Miraç. I hadn't intended for Sean to see them, and really hadn't wanted him to—not because I wanted to hide them, but because Sean had enough bad memories without having mine too. But it was over and done, and there was no undoing it.

Sean kept Jesse pinned on the ground as Joshua watched, fear in his eyes. "Let me make something clear. If we invite you to join our pack and you decide to accept, no one in my pack, least of all me, wants you to beg—for a place among us, or anything else. No one in my pack will abuse you or your brother, because that's not the kind of people we are, and because I won't tolerate it. No one in my pack will treat Joshua or you as anything but a brother. We will protect you both, and you will protect your pack mates. Before that happens, however, you will get that chip off your shoulder. We've lost two pack members recently who wouldn't let go of their anger. If you know about our pack, you know that."

"I know about that." Jesse avoided Sean's eyes. "Please let me up, so my brother doesn't get scared."

Sean released Jesse's shirt. The younger man got to his feet and backed up several steps. "He didn't hurt me," he told Joshua, who'd shrunk back when Sean put his brother on the ground. "I was out of line, talking to an alpha like that." His expression indicated he didn't think he'd been entirely out of line, but he wanted to reassure Joshua, who looked ready to bolt.

"I'm not saying you shouldn't be angry about what you and Joshua have been through," Sean said as the brothers stood silently. "You have every right to be angry. I'm angry on your behalf. You've seen the worst of toxic pack culture, power dynamics, and abusive behavior. A lot of packs measure their worth based on brute strength and how they cull those they think are weak. Since the days of my predecessor, this pack has never been that way, and as long as I'm the alpha, it never will be." He glanced at me, his eyes warm. "As Alice has said, mercy and love are not weaknesses."

"At the end of the day, they are our greatest strengths," I told them. "As you know already, you will never fight harder than to protect those you love."

Jesse and Joshua exchanged a glance, having a conversation with their eyes as only siblings could. "That's why we came here," Jesse said finally. "Because we heard your pack was different. Joshua deserves a pack and a home."

"You both do," I said.

Sean squeezed my hand. "What do you think about Nan, our beta?" he asked Jesse.

"I think she could whup me," Jesse said without hesitation. "And I think she'll help me take care of my brother."

"And what do you think of Alice?" Sean asked. If the question about Nan had been a test, this second question was even more pointed.

"I've never met anyone like her." Jesse met my eyes and then lowered his gaze. "She's human, but she's got a wolf. And she's so powerful. I can feel her magic from over here."

"Are you afraid of her wolf?" Sean asked.

Jesse nodded.

"You should be." Sean's tone was full of warning. "Alice is my consort. She and her wolf are part of our pack. If you're in any way uncomfortable with that, or with a female beta, you can go."

Joshua flinched and Jesse looked a little taken aback. I wanted to say something to soften Sean's words, but I remembered what he'd told me last night: *Let me do what I need to do as the alpha of our pack.* Sean's ultimatum was harsh, but he had to make our position clear so the Hayes brothers—and any other new wolves who wanted to join our pack—knew how things stood.

Sean had been too lenient on both Caleb Jennings and Delia Hastings. I'd come to realize, even before last night, that his tolerance was mostly my fault, both directly and indirectly. He'd always been a good man and never more authoritarian than necessary to lead the pack, but since he'd fallen in love with me, his heart had softened a little more than he could probably afford. He was nothing like any pack alpha I'd ever known, which was a big reason why I loved him. I had no use for alphas—or anyone, for that matter—who mistreated others, or used their strength to subjugate or harm instead of protect, or preferred a partner who stood behind them instead of at their side.

At the same time, I was starting to understand that just as I wanted and needed him to accept me as I was, he needed the same from me. Delia's death in particular had hammered that point home. In the days since Sean had killed her, I'd realized granting Delia mercy after she'd had me hexed had not made the situation any better. I'd had only the best of intentions, but if I hadn't spoken up and wielded my authority as consort to spare Delia from Sean's rightful punishment, she might be alive now. That was a painful truth, and it would weigh on me for a long time.

All I could do now was try to learn from that mistake and let Sean do what he needed to do. *Personal growth*, Malcolm called it. He wasn't wrong, but I wished personal growth didn't hurt so much sometimes.

"We're fine with having a female beta," Jesse said. "Now that I've met her, I know she deserves that position in the pack. And as for Alice, if she's willing to fight for me and Joshua as if we're her brothers, then we're willing to do the same." He glanced at me.

"I fight for this pack," I told him. I started to add *for as long as I'm a part of it*, but I changed my mind. They didn't need to know I was worried about my future.

"Joshua?" Sean prompted when Jesse's younger brother said nothing. "What do you think?"

"I would like to stay," Joshua said, his voice barely audible. "I have no problem with Nan or Alice."

"I'm glad to hear it." Sean gestured at the woods behind them. "Go ahead and shift and go running. We'll join you in a few moments."

The brothers went to their truck and quickly stripped, leaving their clothes inside the cab. Though I knew nudity mattered little to shifters, and neither Jesse or Joshua seemed the least self-conscious, I kept my gaze averted. Sean's eyes twinkled, but he didn't tease me.

Joshua shifted first. His shift took longer than most werewolves I'd seen. His wolf was tawny brown and average sized. He hunkered on his belly with his tail between his legs. Even Karen Williams, the pack's current most submissive member and smallest wolf, had never cowered like that in front of Sean. My heart ached for him.

Jesse stepped between Joshua's wolf and Sean and then shifted. He'd wanted to make sure Joshua was safely recovered from the pain of shifting and protected. His love for his brother was fierce. For all his anger, he was loyal and noble, and I liked him.

Jesse's wolf was the same size as his brother's, with darker ears and a streak of dark brown on his tail. He kept his tail halfway down, in deference to us, but I sensed his anger still simmering. He could attack at any moment, given provocation. That was worrisome, since a werewolf with a hair trigger was a recipe for disaster—for everyone.

Together, they disappeared into the trees, with Jesse in the lead and Joshua right behind.

Sean turned to me. "What do you think?"

"You can probably guess what I think." I exhaled. "I hate that they were abused and driven from their own pack and haven't been able to find any pack that will welcome them. Jesse is volatile and Joshua needs protecting, but that's no excuse for how they've been ostracized. Jesse came to us because he thought they'd be protected and find a home here. I can't think of a higher compliment for our pack than that."

Silence. I looked at Sean, and then Nan. Had I said something wrong?

"What you just said flies in face of everything most packs stand for, and would give several members of the Council apoplexy." Nan smiled. "In order words, it was exactly the right thing to say."

"Are we comfortable being the pack with the reputation for taking in those who have a difficult time fitting in anywhere else?" Sean asked.

It was a serious question, with a lot of possible repercussions worth thinking about. He'd been considering this very issue since the moment he'd received Jesse's first e-mail, and probably before.

I knew what my heart said, especially given what we knew about Jesse and Joshua, but what about my head? We couldn't make decisions based solely on emotion.

Nan spoke. "Here's a better question: are we comfortable being the kind of pack that turns away people like Jesse and Joshua?"

Sean thought about it, but not for long. Nan's question went to the very heart of who Sean was, and what he wanted his pack to be.

"No, we are not comfortable turning them away," Sean stated. "I believe Jesse wants to change his ways and Joshua deserves a home. I want to give them a chance."

"They deserve a chance," I said. "But if Jesse doesn't show right away that he's improving—"

"He gets one warning, and then they'll have to leave," Sean

finished. He kissed my forehead. "It's harsh, but it's what we'll have to do." I could tell he was thinking about Caleb, who, despite being given a dozen chances, had never been able to let go of his anger.

"I understand," I told him, and I meant it. "Just don't ever stop believing in people." I'd told him that after Caleb's death, when he'd blamed himself for the attack that nearly killed me.

"I won't," he promised. "But there are higher stakes now, and harder limits."

I kissed him. His mouth was hard. He was in alpha mode. I understood it, even if I didn't necessarily like it. "Go run with the others," I said. "I'll wait here until you get back."

He pulled his shirt off over his head. Mmm, that perfect chest.

Nan chuckled and headed for her car to take off her clothes and give us a moment of privacy.

Sean folded his clothes and left them on the hood of the Maclin Security SUV. I tried not to leer, but I was already thinking about getting back home after our meeting with Charles.

Sean kissed me, this time with enough heat to make my legs wobbly. To my surprise, he picked me up with his hands under my butt, encouraging me to wrap my legs around his waist. It was something we did in private, but I'd never done something so blatantly sexual in front of someone else who wasn't part of the fun—and he was naked, for crying out loud.

When I resisted, Sean drew back, his eyes bright gold. "What's wrong?"

I pressed my lips to his ear. "Nan's right there," I murmured.

"Nan knows we have sex," he countered, without lowering me to the ground. "It won't bother her." He leaned me back against the car and slid his hand under my thigh.

I was as aroused as hell—good Lord, who wouldn't be?—but I clearly wanted him to put me down, and he didn't. What was going on with him?

Nan was out of my line of sight, but a tingle of magic on the back of my neck indicated she'd shifted. Sean kissed me again. "Go," I said when we came up for air. I was breathing heavily, unable to ignore either his arousal or my own. I needed a cold shower. "Run with the others. As soon as we get home from Charles's house, we'll have some time to ourselves."

With obvious reluctance, Sean let me slide down until my feet hit the ground. "We won't be long," he said. His voice had a little edge of growl that indicated his wolf was close to his skin. "And we won't go far."

"I'll be fine." As soon as I cooled down. "I'll holler if I need you."

He took a couple of steps back, went to his knees, and shifted in a powerful surge of golden shifter magic. Black magic threads twisted through the gold—the traces of Miraç's power Sean had absorbed when I'd killed the sorcerer.

Every time I saw Miraç's magic in Sean's aura, I hated it more. Sean said it gave him more power and strengthened his bonds with pack members and that was all, but I had no more idea what effects Miraç's black magic would have on Sean than on my own magic or body. I knew Miraç's magic was slowly killing me. What if it was damaging Sean too? Or changing him? Black magic was evil, and we'd gotten ours from an evil man.

As much as Miraç's power added to my own, I had to get rid of it somehow to save my life. I wanted it gone from Sean too, but I had no idea how to do either of those things.

Sean's wolf was enormous—black and gray, with beautiful golden eyes. He raised his head and howled. Nan's gray wolf answered from near the tree line. In the distance, Jesse and Joshua howled from the field beyond the trees.

Sean nudged my hand with his nose, then headed off into the trees with Nan to join the Hayes brothers to run and hunt. If there were no issues, Sean would invite the brothers to meet the rest of the pack, and then they'd do the formalities of registering the Hayes brothers as pack members with the Council.

The weather was beautiful. If we'd been in Sean's truck, I would have sat on the tailgate, but his truck had been totaled by heavily armed panther shifters on motorcycles, so we were in one of his company SUVs. I got into the SUV, shut the door, and leaned back in the passenger seat. My back still ached.

When my phone buzzed, I glanced at the screen. *Mr. Sunshine Calling.* I hit the green button. "Hello, Matthias. What's up?"

Matthias Albrecht was a longtime enforcer for the Vampire Court. In the wake of the death of her traitorous personal guard Hanson, Valas had promoted Matthias to take his place.

He and one of my best friends, Vamp Court investigator Arkady Woodall, were in a rather volatile on-again, off-again relationship. At the moment they were back on, but their philosophical differences about what it meant to be employed by the Court and how much loyalty the Court demanded were major points of disagreement. Matthias obeyed Valas and other members of the Court in all things. Arkady didn't believe in following their orders when it conflicted with her own sense of right and wrong.

At the moment, they enjoyed the resulting angry sex, but Arkady confided she'd all but decided their relationship had to end. Matthias was loyal foremost to the Court, and despite how much he liked her, he couldn't understand why Arkady was so resistant to their system of complete and total loyalty.

"Ms. Worth," Matthias rumbled. "Madame Valas requires your presence at Northbourne."

I glanced out the window. The sun was still an hour from setting. The older the vamp, the earlier they rose. Valas was more than a thousand years old. When, where, and for how long she slept each day were closely guarded secrets, but I'd started to wonder if she slept at all.

"Sean and I have a meeting with Charles Vaughan at ten," I said. "What does Valas want? Because if it's another case for the Court, I'm probably not interested."

I didn't have to see his face to know Matthias didn't approve of the way I referred to his boss so informally, or that I would turn down a job for the Court. "Madame Valas did not tell me specifically what she wishes to discuss, only that it pertains to your *prior agreement*." He put subtle emphasis on the last two words.

Well, crap. I owed Valas a big favor in return for how she'd helped me save Sean's life. I got the sense she was about ready for me to fulfill my end of the deal.

"I can come to Northbourne after our meeting with Charles," I said reluctantly. "I'll let you know when I'm on my way there."

"Thank you, Ms. Worth. I will see you soon." He ended the call.

I made a face and stuck my phone in the cup holder. So much for fun with Sean back home. When they returned from their wolf run, there would be just enough time to swing by my house so I could pick up my vehicle and then drive to Charles's estate.

Someone from the Court could drive me from Charles's house to Northbourne and then home after my meeting with Valas, but I didn't want a Court chauffeur. My binding with Valas chafed, though she had far less power over me than a mundane human. After months or years of manipulation by Charles, I was even more conscious of my freedom than before.

I might as well try to rest while I waited for Sean and the others to come back. This might be a long night. I locked the doors, leaned the seat back, and curled up.

CHAPTER 4

WHEN SEAN AND I ARRIVED AT CHARLES'S HOUSE, HIS HEAD OF SECURITY, Bryan Smith, escorted us directly to Charles's office.

The enormous two-story room featured a sitting area in front of a massive fireplace, a full bar, and the office area, with a large desk and guest chairs. Charles displayed his collection of fine art in the upper gallery. Floor-to-ceiling bookcases covered three walls of the ground floor. A two-story window in the exterior wall overlooked the estate's backyard. The curtains were closed tonight.

As usual, Charles was not there yet. He preferred to make an entrance. I was a little surprised at how annoyed I was about that tonight. Before, I'd never minded because it was just one of Charles's habits. Now I saw it more through Sean's eyes, as a power play and a sign of disrespect, as if our time was worth less than his.

Bryan interrupted my thoughts. "Would you like a drink?" He gestured at the bar as Sean and I settled into the two armchairs in front of Charles's desk. "Water? Scotch?"

On previous visits, I'd usually said yes—if not to whisky, at least to water, but I wanted nothing from Charles. If I was right about him messing with my head, it might be all I could do to let Sean say what he'd come to say and not take a pound of flesh for myself. I didn't want his booze.

"No, thank you," I said. Sean also declined. Either he took his cue from me, or he felt the same way I did about accepting Charles's hospitality.

If Bryan was surprised by our refusals, he didn't let on. He went to the bar to pour a drink for his employer.

Sean leaned over and pressed his lips to my ear. "Morgan Clark and Vaughan had sex earlier in this room," he said, his words barely audible.

Stunned, I sat back in my chair. Morgan was the daughter of Bridget Clark, the High Priestess of the Silver Thorn Coven, a local coven of black witches. The Court had enlisted Bridget and Morgan to investigate how Miraç had been able to steal my magic and memories, and to restore my magic. My good friend Carly had once belonged to the coven, but left almost twenty years ago when they began to practice black magic in earnest. She and Morgan had been like sisters before her defection. Morgan's teenage daughter, Katy, had recently left black magic behind. She now worked in Carly's coffee shop and had joined her coven.

Jealousy and anger lanced right through me like a blade. Magic sparked on my fingers and the bowl of flowers on the small table on my right nearly slid off onto the floor.

Sean's expression darkened. I wasn't sure who he was angry at: me, Charles, the Court in general, Morgan, or all of the above.

I gritted my teeth and squashed both the surge of magic and my anger. I didn't care who Charles slept with. My thoughts and my reactions didn't match. My brain said "Hmm...that's interesting" to the news, while my body's response was irrational fury and jealous rage. To me, the dissonance was more evidence of Charles's influence.

"That wasn't me," I murmured. I hoped Sean would understand what I meant, and what had caused my near-violent reaction to his news. His frown deepened, but he gave me a slight nod.

Bryan set a glass of Scotch on the desk pad. He waited behind and to the right of Charles's chair, his eyes on me.

I stared at the glass on the desk. Charles and I had shared many glasses of whisky over the years—in his office at Hawthorne's, on my back porch, here in his house. Was there any truth in any of the things he'd said over those Scotches, or had it all been lies?

From the moment I'd met Charles during my first case working for the Court, I knew he couldn't be trusted. Later that same night, he'd told me he would see my secrets laid bare, and his meaning was clear. He wanted me in his collection and in his bed.

I'd told him it would never happen—"Not in this lifetime" were my exact words. He'd simply smiled as if to say, *We'll see.* I knew then he was planning something, and made up my mind he wouldn't win.

And yet, somewhere along the way, he'd gotten under my skin and into my head.

Maybe Sean wasn't the only person in our relationship whose heart had gotten softer than it should.

Sean glanced at me, then over his shoulder in warning. Charles was approaching. I strengthened my shields and waited.

Familiar footsteps shuffled on the carpet behind us. Charles's gait was slower than usual, his steps uneven. He'd nearly died when a vampire object of power that once belonged to legendary vampire Vlad Tepes poisoned him with dark magic. Nearly two months had passed, but he still hadn't fully recovered.

Charles came around our chairs and stood beside his desk. He wore a gray suit with a purple tie and pocket square. I caught a glimpse of matching checkered socks, like those he'd worn the night he'd traded the cuff I needed to save Sean's life for a drink of my blood. I had no doubt he'd chosen his attire deliberately to remind me of that night. It was such a transparent ploy that I almost laughed.

Though I never would have admitted it to anyone, I'd once thought Sean's anger and distrust of Charles was excessive, a result of his protectiveness or even a touch of jealousy of a romantic rival.

Now, with the benefit of a clear head—or at least, a less-clouded one —it occurred to me that he'd just seen Charles for who he was. How frustrating it must have been for Sean to not be able to get me to see what he saw.

Charles's eyes glowed softly. "You seem angry this evening, Alice."

I opened my mouth, but Sean spoke first. "We're here on official pack business, Vaughan. Our appointment was for ten o'clock. It's nearly ten fifteen."

Charles studied Sean as he seated himself behind the desk. "My apologies for my late arrival, then," he said, his eyes moving from Sean's face to mine. "Mr. Smith offered you refreshments, I assume?"

"This isn't a social visit." Sean's voice was cold.

Charles's eyebrows raised slightly, his eyes still on me. "Can Alice not speak for herself?"

"She can, and will, once you and I have discussed the matter that's brought us here tonight." Sean's eyes turned bright gold. "That matter is your attacks on Alice, which are attacks on me and our pack."

Bryan's eyes narrowed. Charles's expression was thunderous. "I have never attacked you, Alice," the vampire stated. "What is the basis of this allegation?"

Charles persisted in trying to address me, despite how clearly Sean had stated he was taking the lead in this confrontation. I gritted my teeth. "This is a conversation between you and Sean, as the alpha of our pack. Talk to him."

Disbelief flashed in Charles's dark eyes. "Why does he speak for you? When did you abdicate your authority to speak for yourself?"

I knew he said it to bait me and drive a wedge between Sean and me, but the accusation still stung like a whip.

Unwilling to be distracted from the reason he'd asked for this meeting, Sean ignored both Charles's words and my reaction. "By your own admission, you bit Alice without her knowledge or consent while she lay in a coma. That was not only an attack by any definition of the word, but also against both human and vampire law. She may not have pursued prosecution for your crime, but that doesn't make it any less of a crime."

"Is that why you are here tonight?" Charles asked me. "To demand redress for that lapse in judgment?"

If it had truly been a lapse in judgment rather than a coldly calculated act, I'd eat my boots.

"No," Sean said, which seemed to surprise Charles. "Alice exacted her own punishment for that bite, as I'm sure you recall. It was her choice to do so, and if she considers that debt paid, I accept it. We asked for this meeting to inform you we are aware you've deliberately manipulated Alice's thoughts, emotions, and actions for a period of months, if not years."

Charles seemed stunned by the allegation. "I most certainly have not."

Sean continued as if Charles hadn't spoken. "This physical attack on my consort is an unprovoked act of violence against our pack. Like your earlier bite, it was a violation of both human and vampire law. After discussing the matter with Alice, we agree the best option for justice is for you to provide a full confession of your crime and pay restitution. Both will be considered confidential, and the matter need not go beyond the walls of this room, unless you wish to reveal on the record in a trial what you've done."

I'd argued against demanding restitution, but Sean was adamant. The Vampire Court had provisions for settling such matters through remuneration, and since we had no interest in dragging Charles in front of the Court for a trial, it was the most logical choice. I told him if Charles agreed to pay any money—and that was a mighty big *if*—it would go to the pack's account. I wanted nothing from him, least of all money.

Charles was on his feet before Sean finished speaking. "These accusations are completely baseless. What you propose is nothing more than extortion. I am aware your pack faces numerous difficulties, most of which you have caused yourself through poor leadership, but I did not think you would stoop to such a level." He turned to me, his expression bordering on incredulous. "Surely you are not a willing accomplice to this, Alice. Our relationship goes back almost six years. I have been more honest with you than any person I have ever known since I was turned."

Bile rose in my throat. My fingers tightened on the arms of my chair.

"If that is true, which I doubt, it says far more about you than about Alice," Sean told him. "You've done nothing but lie and manipulate since you met her. If there were grains of truth, it's only because you had to sprinkle some in every so often. If that's as honest as you've been in two hundred years, I have less respect for you now than when I walked in here tonight."

It was Charles's turn to ignore Sean. "You know I have spoken my heart," he said, his eyes boring into mine as if no one else existed on Earth. "Many times I bared my soul, though it made me vulnerable to do so. Whatever the wolf has told you and you may now believe, that does not change our past. We are kindred souls, Alice." His eyes pleaded with me to remember the physically and emotionally intimate moments we'd shared.

Despite my shields, my body—my flesh, my blood, even my bones—surged in response to his words. My certainty about his manipulations faded, buried under an avalanche of protectiveness and longing. Maybe it was remembered desire, or maybe he'd just unleashed the strongest blast of suggestion he'd ever used on me.

Whatever the cause of my reaction, and whatever Charles hoped to achieve, what he got was two hundred pounds of angry werewolf leaping over the desk. Sean threw Charles into a tall bookshelf. Books, several sculptures, and an antique globe crashed to the floor.

With a hiss, Charles flipped to his feet and swung at Sean, who blocked the punch and drove him back into the bookshelves with his shoulder.

The last time Charles and Sean fought, it was at my house, over Charles's accusation that Sean intended to bite me and turn me into a werewolf. That fight demolished almost every stick of furniture in my living room and ended with Sean in Vamp Court custody for assaulting Charles. If I'd thought that fight was brutal and destructive, it was nothing compared to this one. Unlike the earlier fight, I didn't try to intervene. Sean had every reason to be angry.

Bryan, however, *did* try to interfere—and ended up sprawled on the floor with a swelling jaw and a dazed expression. I wasn't sure who had punched him, truthfully, and I wasn't sure if he knew either.

Also unlike that earlier fight, Sean didn't shift. That made sense given the potential consequences of attacking Charles in wolf form. But even in human form, with the power of the pack bonds and the fuel of his rage, Sean wasn't much slower or less powerful than Charles, and he was a more skilled fighter. Their punches flew faster than I could see.

The fight moved from the office to the sitting area, smashing bookshelves, two tables, three chairs, and various antiques and sculptures. Whether on purpose or accident, it didn't stray into the bar, for which I was relieved—both because of how much potentially deadly glass was in the bar, and because if Charles's collection of expensive single-malt whisky was destroyed, I might cry, just on principle.

Bryan was back on his feet, but he didn't try to interfere again or summon backup. That had to have been on Charles's telepathic order, which meant Charles wanted this fight to continue.

It ended very abruptly, and very differently than the first one. Sean slammed Charles against the wall by the throat, breaking the painting hanging there. They were both bloody, clothes torn and knuckles busted. Charles's fangs were out, and Sean's eyes blazed gold.

"Tell her the truth," Sean snarled into Charles's face. "Tell her the truth, you lying bastard."

"I have," Charles said icily.

Sean's grip tightened. "She knows already. She's known since the sorcerer's lair, when his wards cut through your influence and freed her. Deep down, on some level, I think she's *always* known. That's why your manipulations never worked. Someone who's been abused will do everything in their power to keep from being victimized again, even if they don't realize they're doing it." He lowered Charles to the floor but kept his hand on the vampire's slim, pale throat. "Tell her."

"Or what?" Charles sounded genuinely curious. "What will you do if I refuse to say the words you wish to hear? Will you kill me, wolf? Drag me in front of the Court so my peers may hear your baseless allegations? Call me before the Council and inform the world you cannot protect your consort from anyone—shifter, witch, mage, sorcerer, or vampire?"

For a moment, I thought Charles was deliberately trying to provoke Sean into trying to kill him. But though his eyes blazed, Sean didn't take the bait. Instead, he released Charles's throat and took a step back. "None of those things," Sean said. "I will give Alice the chance to make a choice between your truth and mine."

Confused, I rose from my chair. "What do you mean, Sean?" He'd gone totally off-script, and I had no idea what he was talking about—though apparently Charles did.

"It's the only chance you'll have to come clean and make your case," Sean added, without looking at me.

Charles glanced at me. "See how your wolf tries to possess you? I knew it would only be a matter of time. I warned you it would come to this. An alpha must assert control."

How had I never seen how manipulative Charles was before this? Did he have that much influence over me, or had I just not wanted to see it? Was he to blame for my blindness, or was I?

"I want the truth, Charles," I said. "Or this is the last time you speak to me outside of Court business."

Charles studied me. "Because the wolf says so?"

His tactic of trying to make this about Sean, rather than his own betrayal, was getting old fast. "Because *I* say so." I slid onto a tall chair at the bar and turned to face him, my legs crossed. "So if you have something you want to tell me, now's the time."

"And once she's heard us out, Alice is free to make her choice," Sean said. "It's a better deal than you would have gotten otherwise."

"Why do this?" Charles demanded. "She may choose to stay with me."

"She might," Sean allowed. He met my eyes with his softly glowing ones. "But whether she stays with you or leaves with me, or just leaves, I want us *both* to know she did it of her own free will, and with a clear head. So no more games, no more manipulation, no more influence." His voice turned to steel. "Tell. The. Truth."

"Will *you* tell her your truth?" Charles countered. "If I must speak plainly, so must you."

I was ready to dismiss Charles's comment as just another attempt to get under Sean's skin, but Sean nodded grimly. "I'll tell her."

I wanted to demand, *Tell me what*, but that would just play more into Charles's little game. Instead, I waited.

I didn't have to wait long. Sean turned to face me. "When we first met, Vaughan told you a member of my pack, Mike Holleman, let it be known I intended to find a mage and turn her into a werewolf to be my mate."

I nodded. "I remember. He spread that lie to try and get you killed."

"It wasn't entirely a lie." A muscle moved his jaw. "I *did* say I wanted to turn a mage to be my mate."

I felt like someone had kicked me in the stomach.

His expression was unreadable. "About ten years ago, not long after I became alpha, I heard of another alpha who'd turned a mage to be his mate and thought it wasn't a bad idea. I would never have turned someone against their will, but I did want to explore the possibility of finding a mage to be my mate and turning her if she was willing. Jack and I discussed it numerous times—which is how Mike found out about it later. Jack or Delia let something slip in a conversation, and Mike decided to use it to his advantage."

For so long, I'd believed there was nothing to the rumor about Sean's intention to turn a mage. Charles must have uncovered the truth and held onto the information until he could use it.

"And when did you decide against turning a mage?" I asked finally. My voice didn't sound like my own.

Sean kept his gaze locked on my face. "Jack and Delia talked me out of it years ago. You know how dead-set they were on my mate being a born shifter. Before too long, they had me convinced choosing anyone other than a shifter would be a colossal mistake, for me *and* the pack." He flexed his bloodied hands. "After that, I didn't think about it again. And I never thought of you as a powerful mage I wanted so my pack would be stronger, or that I wanted to turn you, especially after I knew you had no desire to become a shifter. For me, from the night we met, you've simply been Alice, the woman I want and love." He exhaled. "And that is my truth."

"All right." My voice still sounded funny. I turned my chair toward Charles. "Now, you tell me the truth—all of it, or I walk out of here right now, and I won't look back."

As Sean revealed the grain of truth behind the rumor that had almost ended our relationship before it began, Charles had weighed his options. I recognized the expression he wore when he was calculating the best move to make. Vampires were fairly inscrutable, but there was a slight tightening of his eyes and a tiny crease between his eyebrows when he had to make a difficult decision. I supposed whether to tell the truth *was* a difficult and unfamiliar choice for someone like him. I figured it was a fifty-fifty chance the next words out of his mouth would be a lie.

"It is as the wolf says," Charles said finally. He drew himself up to his full height. His aura of fragility vanished, and though he was still thin, I saw no hint of infirmity. The lingering sickness from the Tepes stone and depression after using the spelled cup to walk in the sun had been an act. He'd pretended to be weakened and almost suicidal to play on my sympathy.

It took every ounce of willpower I had to not get up and walk out right then.

"Go on," I said. If my voice had sounded strained before, it was like a taut wire now.

"My campaign to ingratiate myself to you began very soon after we met." Charles folded his hands behind his back, his gaze locked on mine. "As you may have surmised, my intentions were primarily focused on making you my lover and ally so I might utilize your power and ingenuity for my own ends, and to advance the interests of the Court. Because you proved so thoroughly immune to my overtures, I influenced you very subtly so you would not detect my manipulations."

"At Valas's request? Or was it your idea, and she approved the plan?"

A pause. "She approved my plan."

Sean had been right about that too.

After a moment, Charles continued, "Our acquaintance soon turned to a business relationship, and then to the closest friendship I have enjoyed since I was human. My motivations grew more... personal. I came to realize that in your presence, I am human again. I laugh. I feel sorrow, and hope, and curiosity, and protectiveness."

He took a step closer, despite Sean's warning growl. "Alice, I love you. I did not think myself capable of love after the loss of my wife, but I have found it again with you. What I did, I did for your sake. I can protect you from your enemies, far better than the wolf. I can ensure you will have a long and happy life, free from your past. You will want for nothing. I promise only truth between us from this moment forward. I ask nothing of you in return, not even your power or your body, unless you choose to share them with me. Stay with me, so I continue to feel as though I am human. I wish to learn to be a better man, so I may be more worthy of you."

"Did you know Darius Bell and Moses Murphy had teamed up to

draw me out?" I asked. "Did you deliberately feed me fabricated intel about the weapons deal Murphy was in town for, so I'd go out to his house and walk into the trap?"

He didn't hesitate. "Yes."

I could have asked him about a dozen other incidents, but I wasn't sure any of the answers would matter, really. Would it change how I felt to know he'd allowed me to be almost killed by the bomb that destroyed Hawthorne's, or to be shot by Kent Stevens, or nearly seduced by Niara? No, it wouldn't.

I'd listened to his speech with my senses tuned to detect the slightest hint of influence and watched closely and listened for any indication of deception. Every word he'd said sounded and felt true. I didn't feel any push to believe him or that he'd tried to sway me in any way. And yet...

...And yet, I didn't believe him. Or maybe I did, but that didn't change anything.

Something died inside me in that moment. I didn't know what it was, exactly, but it was a physical sensation of intense, painful loss. Maybe it was the last of my hope that Charles wasn't the lying bastard Sean had always said he was.

When I finally accepted the true scope of Charles's campaign to influence me, it called into question nearly every action I'd taken, every word I'd spoken, every choice I'd made for almost the entire time I'd been in the city. How much of my life had been of my own free will, and how much was influenced by Charles?

It really didn't matter, I decided. What was past was past. I could choose to let this kick my feet out from under me, or I could find a way to let it go. If I didn't, Charles would still be influencing me—only this time, it would be by my own choice. He'd already taken up far too much real estate in my head.

There was no sense prolonging this conversation. I'd sat in silence for at least a full minute already, while Sean and Charles watched me and waited.

I slid off the barstool and stood. "It's not my responsibility to make you feel human, Charles, or teach you how to be a better man. Don't put the burden for either of those things on me. Those are choices you have to make. And clearly my presence hasn't made you feel all that human if you see nothing wrong with what you've done to me."

His face was impassive. "I did not say I was not wrong to do it."

"You knew it was wrong, but you did it anyway because you believed the ends justified the means."

"Have you not done the same on many occasions?" he countered. "What would you not do for love, Alice?"

"I've done a lot of things for love, but one thing I would never do—would never even *consider* doing—is make someone my slave or steal their free will. I told you that months ago, when you tried to blackmail me into working for the Court. I put on that cuff to free Sean from his, went into debt with Valas, and died to free us both rather than bind him to me without his consent. That's how deeply I believe love and partnership mean nothing if they aren't freely given, or if they're coerced in any way."

Sean's expression told me he wanted nothing more in the world right now than to touch my hand or put his arms around me. He stayed where he was because he didn't know whether his touch would be welcome in the wake of his admission. That was fine with me, because I didn't want comfort right now. I needed space, and to finish this thing with Charles, once and for all.

"Alice—" Charles began.

"No." My voice was quiet. "What you did was the worst and cruelest thing anyone has ever done to me, and there is a hell of a lot of competition in that category. My free will is the most important thing I have. It's the only reason I'm alive and not in chains, and you knew that."

His eyes blazed. "My honesty has meant nothing to you?"

He just didn't get it. He never would.

"You don't get a medal for doing the bare minimum, Charles—especially when you only did so because you had no other choice." I headed for the door of the office. "And no, it doesn't."

It didn't escape my notice that nowhere in all those pretty words had there been any facsimile of an apology. If he *had* apologized, it wouldn't have changed how I felt, but it might have made a difference. Then again, if I'd learned anything from years of working with vampires, it was that they seldom if ever felt the need to apologize for anything.

"Alice, a moment, please." Suddenly, Charles was in front of me, in one of those uncanny flashes of movement vampires could do when they didn't care about appearing human.

He grasped my hand. *You will regret choosing the wolf,* he said in my head, his voice grim. *The sorcerer's power has changed him. He is not the man you knew.*

Magic blazed from my other hand, forming a black-edged blade. I slashed at his throat, but he released me and moved like lightning to avoid the deadly edge.

"Don't ever touch me again," I warned him. "The next time, I won't miss."

Sean joined us by the office door. "The next time you touch her without her permission, she won't have to lift a finger," he said, his voice cold. "It will be me who kills you, and I won't make it as quick and painless as cutting off your head."

Charles's eyes met mine. In them, I read a message: *I warned you. He has changed.*

"You might be right, but I've changed too," I said aloud. I lifted my hand to show him the magic blade on my fingertips and the rainbow spiral of magic down my arm. I let my wolf raise her head and stare out through my eyes, turning my vision gold. She growled, and the sound rumbled in my chest. "You'll never play me for a fool ever again, Charles. Not ever again."

My wolf snapped her teeth at him. He recoiled.

I turned to Sean. "You two can work out the particulars for the restitution. I'm going to Northbourne. I'll talk to you when I get home."

I turned on my heel and walked out.

CHAPTER 5

On my way to Northbourne, I summoned Malcolm, who was spending his evening with Liam at Moses's haunted mansion. I wanted backup for my meeting with Valas.

I gave the ghost's trace in my mind two gentle tugs, a signal I needed him to jump to me but it wasn't an emergency. About a minute later, the blue crystal on my new bracelet buzzed. I touched it. "*Release.*"

Malcolm appeared in the passenger seat area. He took one look at my face and flitted in place. "What the hell happened at your meeting with Vaughan?" he demanded. "You look mad enough to knock a satellite out of orbit with your glare alone. Did he deny he's been messing with your head?"

I flexed my aching fingers, loosening my white-knuckled grip on the steering wheel. "At first he denied it, of course. Then he admitted that's exactly what he's been doing, and Valas knew and approved of it. *And* he knew there was no weapons deal at the mansion that night, but he lied to me so we'd walk into Moses's trap."

Malcolm let out a string of creative expletives. My ghost didn't swear much, but when he did, he could scandalize a sailor.

But when I told him what Sean had said about having once wanted to turn a mage to be his mate, Malcolm was silent for a long time.

"Are you okay?" he asked finally, then snorted. "That's a dumb question; of course you aren't okay. Are you *going to be* okay?"

"About what Sean told me, yes, eventually. I obviously wish he'd told me sooner so I didn't have to hear about it like this, but it's not like I've told him everything I've said and done—not even close. So who the hell am I to hold it against him that he didn't tell me every last thing about himself?"

"You can still be angry about it, even though you're still keeping secrets," he pointed out.

"I know. I'm not angry, though—just a bit blindsided, and annoyed that I had to hear it in front of Charles, who was probably hoping I'd dump Sean on the spot."

"No doubt he was," Malcolm said with a scowl. "I guess he doesn't know you quite as well as he thought he did."

"I guess not. Sean said he wouldn't have ever changed anyone who wasn't willing, and I believe him. We're going to talk about it when I get home, after you and I meet with Valas."

"And what about Vaughan's meddling? How are you dealing with that?" He read my expression. "Not well, I see."

"Not well at all, but at least I didn't do anything rash like lop off one of his appendages or burn down his house." I cleared my throat. "Not that I thought about it, of course."

"Of course," Malcolm said dryly. "You probably also didn't almost cut off his head."

I coughed.

"Or smash a couple bottles of his fancy whisky."

I sucked in a breath. "What kind of monster do you think I am?"

He chuckled. "Good to know there's a line you won't cross." His smile faded. "I'm sorry he's such a bastard, but I'm glad you know the truth."

"Me too." I turned the radio volume up. "Anyway, we're headed for Northbourne to meet with Valas about that errand she wants me to go on. Sorry to interrupt date night."

"No worries. Ghosts are laid back about that sort of thing."

"You and Liam are pretty smitten with each other, though, huh?"

He gave me a look. "I like the guy, yes. We have a lot in common, besides being dead."

"Such as?"

"We're both snappy dressers, and we're both funny as hell."

I laughed. My heart still felt bruised, but as usual, Malcolm dragged me back from the edge of gloom.

I glanced at him. "I love you, you know."

"Don't get sappy, Alice," he said, but he was smiling. He loved me too.

I looked ahead toward Northbourne's gate and sighed. "Lots of protestors here tonight. You'd think they'd get tired of waving signs and yelling."

"Some people always seem to find energy for hate," Malcolm said.

Protestors frequently gathered in front of Northbourne's gate these days. Anti-supe demonstrations were rare in the city when I'd moved here, but ever since the West-Addison Harnad murders, they were regular occurrences—and they were getting larger and more violent. People were angry at vampires and mages. Hate groups like Human Future and the Daylighters fanned the flames constantly. With the rise of several prominent anti-supe politicians and attacks by domestic terrorist groups against supes, things looked to get worse.

I turned into the drive. The protestors moved aside, since by law they couldn't block the driveway. Several yelled insults and one spat on my windshield. Lovely.

A group of black-clad Court enforcers converged on the gate to ensure none of the protestors attempted to enter the grounds of the estate. The metal barricades in front of my SUV retracted into the ground.

As the gate rolled aside, it occurred to me there was no way Charles had confessed to meddling with my thoughts without Valas's permission. That meant she'd either ordered him to tell the truth when we demanded it, or she'd planned on this happening and already told him to do so. She'd also allowed me to be taken by Miraç and tortured, and then manipulated me into killing him so I would absorb his power. Why she'd wanted me to do so, I wasn't exactly sure, but it had to have been for her benefit. It sure as hell wasn't for mine.

I was so tired of dancing on the end of Valas's strings.

"I'm done with the vampires after this," I told Malcolm as I drove past the gate and headed up the quarter-mile winding driveway that led to the estate. I used my wipers and washer fluid to clean the protestor's spit off my windshield. "Once I fulfill my obligation to Valas, I'm done. No more cases, no more favors."

"Easier said than done, especially when you're still bound to Valas by her bite. And you know they're not going to let you go without a hell of a fight." Malcolm looked grim. "If you want out, you know I've got your back, but it's going to be an uphill climb and they're going to be dicks about it the whole way."

I rounded a curve and the enormous mansion came into view in front of us. A half-dozen black Court SUVs were parked out front. Enforcers patrolled the grounds, alert for any signs of trouble. The recent uptick in violence against supes had everyone on edge.

"If they want to play rough, I can play rough," I said as I parked to the right of the wide front steps.

"They won't just target you," he reminded me. "Like Moses, they'll have no hesitation about going after those around you. I'm not trying to talk you out of it, but they'll go to war if they think it's necessary."

I glanced up at the mansion and turned off the ignition. "So will we, Malcolm. If it's war they want, it's war they'll get."

I was met at Northbourne's front door by an enforcer I knew. Carlos Rodriguez and I met during the first case I'd ever worked for the Court, when I was still an apprentice mage PI working for my mentor Mark Dunlap. We crossed the enormous lobby. Malcolm floated at my side, on high alert.

"How are you, Carlos?" I asked.

"I'm well, thank you," he told me. "We're going downstairs."

I'd expected to be escorted to Valas's audience chamber. "I thought I was meeting with Valas."

"You are." He led me down the hall to a wide stairwell. "She awaits you in one of the workshops."

I disliked venturing into the sub-levels beneath Northbourne. Being underground made me antsy. I was also surprised Valas was downstairs; I got the impression she rarely left her suite unless the Court was in session in one of the courtrooms. With my status as Sean's partner, Malcolm at my side, my wolf on high alert, and the amount of magic I had running through me, I felt quite certain I could protect myself if Valas's intentions weren't what they seemed, and get out of Northbourne if push came to shove. Still, there'd better be a damn good reason for meeting in the basement.

We followed Carlos down to sub-level one. He placed his palm on the scanner beside the double doors that led to the magic workshop area. The doors unlocked and Carlos held one open for me. "After you, Ms. Worth."

Our little group walked down a long concrete hallway, passing doors I knew led to workshops used by mages, witches, and practitioners of other kinds of magic. One was marked with an inverted pentagram beside the door. I hurried past it. I'd faced black witches twice in that room, and none of those memories were pleasant.

Carlos led us to a set of unmarked doors near the end of the hall. The wards on the room sizzled on my skin.

"Damn," Malcolm said, clearly impressed. "Heavy-duty containment wards *and* a bunch of Gandalf wards too." Gandalf wards were what Malcolm called wards designed not to let anything through—as in *You shall not pass.* "Whatever's in there, they don't want anyone getting near it, or anything getting out."

I had a pretty good idea what was in that room. It was priceless, and quite possibly the most dangerous object in the building. And it was meant for me. Hooray.

The doors opened, revealing Matthias. I could see almost nothing of the room beyond, which was large and dimly lit. "Ms. Worth, welcome," he said, sounding very formal. "Madame Valas awaits you." He used two fingers to draw a rune on the wall near the doors and the wards formed a doorway.

I stepped inside with Malcolm right behind me. Carlos stayed in the corridor. Matthias closed the doors and the wards flared again.

The room was almost as large as Valas's audience chamber, but without its high vaulted ceiling. My senses tingled, alerting me that a lot of magic had been used in this room, including unfamiliar forms of occult magic and blood magic too. We were in a dark magic multi-purpose room, apparently, with embedded containment and perimeter wards for containing and protecting people and things kept inside.

A dozen large candelabras illuminated the middle of the room, leaving the rest in darkness. In the center of a wide stone circle inlaid in the floor was a tall, thin object covered with a red silk sheet: the mirror Valas had obtained from Elizabeth, the head of the Chicago Vampire Court.

Glyphs and runes filled the stone circle. Some were mage spells; the other spellwork was more ancient and invoked dark power. They could be the work of a sorcerer. Maybe Valas's own handiwork? I'd never seen her do spellwork, but I had no doubt she could.

Something moved in the shadows to my right—something

almost human-shaped, but not quite. My nose twitched at the all-too-familiar odor of burned paper and a dozen other exotic scents, many of them unpleasant. Dark magic slithered around me. Malcolm flitted in consternation.

I glanced again at the glyphs in the circle. Not the work of a sorcerer, but a vampire warlock—one I'd met recently and had hoped not to meet again.

"You owe me for the damages to the deck on my new house," I told the creature in the shadows.

Vlad laughed. The sound made the hair stand up on the back of my neck. Malcolm shuddered as the laugh became a low hiss and then faded.

"Thank you for attending me this evening." Valas's voice came from behind me.

Keeping my eyes on Vlad's shadow, I said, "Why am I here?"

She appeared out of the darkness and glided soundlessly across the floor to a chair facing the stone circle. She wore a floor-length midnight-blue dress and a ruby pendant, the signature color of her Court. Her long, dark hair hung loose to her waist, like a cape.

A second person emerged from the shadows. Despite my unease about Vlad's presence and the purpose for the meeting, I smiled. "Adam!"

Adam March, a psychic and Seer who had worked for the Court most of his life, had helped me during my investigation into the West-Addison Harnad.

He returned my smile, but his was brief. "Hi, Alice. It's good to see you." He looked at Malcolm. "Hello."

Startled, Malcolm blinked. He wasn't used to anyone addressing him directly, or even knowing he was present. After a moment, he waved. "Uh, hi."

"You are here because your *errand*, as you call it, has become urgent," Valas said. She settled into the chair. Adam and Matthias stood on either side of her.

"How urgent?"

"You must prepare to travel immediately. From what Mr. March has seen, we have no time to waste."

I took a deep breath and let it out. For months I'd waited for this moment, and now that it was here, I was strangely relieved. "Tell me everything."

Matthias handed me a red file folder. Since he was going with me, Malcolm read over my shoulder.

The first few pages were from a Court employee dossier for a woman named Mariela Diakos. Mariela was forty-one and athletic. The file contained her official Court identification photographs: one from the front, one from the side, like mugshots. She had short dark hair, dark brown eyes, and an intense stare. The file also included photos of several tattoos. They were intricate, beautiful, and no doubt as magically enhanced as my own.

I read through the information that wasn't redacted. "High-level blood and earth mage," I mused. "An employee of the Court for ten years. Formerly employed by the Bell Cabal." I glanced up at Valas. "Sold to the Court?"

"In return for a debt," Valas said. "That has no bearing on the current situation."

The fact Mariela had been sold to settle a debt, and Valas thought that was a perfectly normal sort of transaction, told me a lot about both of them. Mariela likely had no loyalty to the Court, and I didn't blame her. People weren't for buying and selling, despite what Valas, Moses, and their ilk might believe. Someday, I hoped to prove it to them.

I read on. The dossier didn't contain many details about Mariela's duties as a mage working for the Court, but several reports assessed her powers and abilities. She had impressive skill with spellwork, including wards and blood magic.

I looked up. "So this is who stole your doohickey?"

Valas gave me an almost imperceptible nod. "She was a trusted employee. This betrayal is most infuriating." Her eyes glowed.

I flipped through the rest of the file. "There's nothing in here about what she took or why she took it."

"That information is highly confidential. I do not entrust it to many." Her fingers tightened on the arms of her chair. "What do you know of the Book of Thoth?"

I frowned. "The real one, or the legend?"

A tiny smile turned up the corners of her mouth. "As you know, nothing is ever as simple as 'real' or 'legendary.' In ancient Egypt, Thoth was god of knowledge and writing. The Book of Thoth has referred to many texts over the millennia—some thought to have been written by Thoth himself, and others written about him. One such work, which exists today in fragments held by various museums around the world, references the so-called Writings of the House of Darkness."

"I've heard of the Writings of the House of Darkness. The phrase *House of Darkness* was thought to refer to the realms of the dead, as I recall. No one is sure if the Writings ever truly existed, as far as I know."

Valas folded her hands in her lap, her elbows on the arms of the chair. "The Writings of the House of Darkness are thirteen scrolls. Each contains funerary rites, rituals, incantations and spells regarding death and the Underworld, and invocations for various old gods. Because together they contain enough knowledge to bring an end to all life on Earth, the scrolls were spelled by their creators so no more than two could ever be in the same place at the same time, or even within a hundred leagues of each other."

"Wait—the Writings are real?" Realization dawned. "You had one of the scrolls and Mariela stole it?"

"Indeed." Visibly angry, Valas started to rise. Instead, she settled back into her chair. I suddenly wondered why she was sitting down while the rest of us stood. As head of the Court, it was certainly her privilege to do so, but I suspected there was more to it.

"Two scrolls were in the possession of the Court of Constantinople," Valas said. "When Crusaders sacked the city in the thirteenth century, many who would have been captured for torture were forced to flee. Some chose to take priceless artifacts from the Court vaults, to preserve them from destruction or looting."

"So you took a scroll, along with a few other items," I guessed. "Why the scroll, though?"

"For its spells, naturally." Her voice was crisp. "It is one of my most valued personal possessions, a treasure that reminds me of my homeland."

"How did Mariela get hold of it?"

Her expression darkened. "Through a lapse in security, which has since been addressed."

Behind me, from the shadows, Vlad hissed.

That was obviously all I was going to get in answer to that question, so I moved on to more pressing issues. "Why did she take it? And why did she take it through a mirror?"

At Valas's nod, Adam spoke. "That we weren't sure of until very recently. At Madame Valas's request, I've been attempting to ascertain Mariela's location and intentions, but it's damn hard to See things that far away. She's been using spells to hide herself. Last night, however, I finally received a vision."

"What did you see?" I asked.

"He will show you," Valas said.

I recoiled. I remembered all too well what happened the last time I'd shared one of Adam's visions. "No, thanks. You can describe it."

"You will not be harmed," she snapped. "I have little patience for your timidity today."

"Hey, screw you, vampire," Malcolm said hotly before I could reply. "She almost died of a brain hemorrhage last time. She's entitled to be cautious."

Valas's eyes glowed silver. "You will keep a civil tongue, or you will find yourself elsewhere."

I stepped between them. "Don't threaten him, Valas. If you've got something you want to show me, then do it, but take it easy on my brain. I'm not psychic, and I've recently had all my memories ripped out and then stuffed back in. If you scramble my egg, I won't be going on any recovery mission for you."

Her eyes narrowed. "Very well. Stand before me."

Letting her touch me, let alone share a vision, was the last thing I wanted. I might learn something from it I could use against her, however, and we needed to know what we were going up against.

I joined Adam beside Valas's chair. She wrapped her cold fingers around my wrist. The room around us plunged into darkness, and I fell into the void.

I stood knee-deep in bloody corpses. The stench of death was nearly unbearable.

Thousands of bodies, young and old, male and female, lay piled around me. All had horrible gaping wounds in their chests where their hearts had once been.

As if the scene wasn't bad enough, from somewhere among the corpses, I heard the nauseating sound of something gorging itself, chewing with unmistakable gusto on what I assumed was the missing hearts.

In the distance, three shadows pursued a group of fleeing victims, leaving a wide path of bloody bodies in their wake. The screams of the dying split the air.

Scattered among the bodies around me were blood-splattered banners and signs, all bearing anti-supe and anti-magic slogans. I recognized the T-shirts worn by many of the dead as belonging to anti-supe hate groups like the Daylighters and Humans First. I also saw police in uniform, their chests torn open and hearts missing. The slaughter had been indiscriminate.

I was standing in the middle of a massacre.

A woman spoke. "Justice for Ellie."

I turned.

Mariela Diakos stood behind me. She extended her arms to indicate the bodies. "Justice for Ellie," she repeated, and smiled.

A black snake coiled around her right arm, its body marked with red glyphs. Small wings protruded from its back. In her left hand, she held a cup of what looked like honey.

Mariela raised her arm to look the snake in its red eyes. "Glen Grove," she said, as if invoking a curse. Her eyes glowed with blood magic and something else—some other, much older magic.

The snake raised its head and hissed. In the distance, the three shadows headed back toward us, their eyes silver and wings outstretched.

"Justice and vengeance," Mariela whispered. The words were a curse and a promise.

THE DARKNESS RECEDED, taking with it the stench of decaying bodies and the screams of the dying.

I found myself back in the magic workshop in sub-level one, more or less still standing beside Valas's chair. The "less" part was that Matthias was behind me, gripping my upper arms. Judging by the ache, he'd caught me before I fell and had been holding me up for a while.

"Thanks," I told him. My ears rang and it took effort to focus.

Malcolm floated in front of me. "You okay?"

My legs felt rubbery, but I nodded. "I think so."

Matthias released my arms. I stayed upright without leaning against him or Valas's chair. Yay, me.

"You saw the slaughter?" Valas asked, her tone impatient, as if annoyed by my disorientation. She'd rarely been so short with me. Was her mood a result of Mariela's theft, or something else?

"Yes, I saw it." I turned to Adam. "What's the deal with the snake and the three shadows? And what the hell was feasting on all those hearts?"

Malcolm's eyes were like saucers. "Feasting on *hearts?*"

"I'm not sure what was eating the hearts," Adam admitted. "But I believe the three shadows are the Erinyes."

"The Erinyes?" I knew that name from somewhere, but it took a minute for it to click. I stared at him. "As in the Furies? *The* Furies?"

"I'm afraid so." Adam folded his hands behind his back, a habit many touch clairvoyants developed to avoid accidental skin contact. "Infernal goddesses of vengeance, more ancient than almost any of the old gods. The black serpent is their symbol."

"And the fact she has the snake wrapped around her arm signifies she's bound them, or she's invoked them?"

"That's how I read it," he said. "The snake for the binding and the cup of honey as an offering."

Malcolm muttered a few choice curse words.

"So she wants to unleash the Furies on anti-supe hate groups?" I asked. "Other than on principle, why?"

Adam's expression darkened. "Glen Grove."

I recalled Mariela mentioning the incident. "She lost someone?"

"She lost her brother, sister-in-law, and their little girl Ellie."

I swore. No wonder Mariela was angry enough to invoke the Furies.

"What's Glen Grove?" Malcolm asked.

"About a year ago, a group of anti-supe domestic terrorists targeted a party in Glen Grove," I explained. "The party was hosted by a man named Colin Carr. Carr was a mage and active in organizations that work to protect the rights of supes and mages. He had a reception to celebrate a federal appeals court victory. Someone put two pipe bombs in the reception hall. The explosions killed fifteen people, including Carr and his wife, and wounded several dozen. All of the victims were mages. No one claimed responsibility for the bombing, but Carr had received numerous threats."

Malcolm flitted. "That's horrible. Was anyone arrested?"

"One guy," Adam told him. "A member of a fringe 'human rights' group. His lawyers say he's mentally ill. The feds claim he acted alone, but a lot of people suspect there were others involved and the guy they arrested is taking the fall for the lot of them."

"So this Mariela wants justice for her family, and she's bringing in the big guns." Malcolm shook his head. "I gotta say, I'm not unsympathetic."

"I'm sympathetic too, but there were piles of corpses," I said. "Men, women, even kids. Something ate their hearts. She wants to unleash three chthonic deities and the heart-eater and kill everyone who gets in the way."

"What are chthonic deities?" he asked.

"Gods of the Underworld. They tend to like human sacrifices and inspire cult-like devotion." I turned to Valas. "So, my mission is to stop Mariela from unleashing the Furies, drag her back here, and return your scroll?"

"You must bring me the scroll and stop her from invoking the Furies," Valas replied. "If you determine bringing Mariela back is too difficult or impractical, you may bring me proof of her death."

"I'm not one of your henchmen, Valas. I'll bring her back and she can get a fair trial before the Court." I rubbed my face. "Okay, now we know what she's trying to do and why. Why did she need your scroll, and why did she go through a mirror to use it?"

"The scroll contains dangerous arcane knowledge and hundreds of spells, incantations, and rituals. Among them are instructions for opening a door to the Underworld and traversing that realm in relative safety. Burial chambers can be used as doorways, acting as conduits between the mundane world and the Underworld."

Malcolm and I exchanged a glance. "Did Mariela use your first mirror to get to the Underworld?" I asked.

"No," Valas said. "In our world, the boundaries between realms are not easily traversed, even with the magic of the scroll. Someone wishing to venture into the Underworld, locate the Furies, and invoke them faces a nearly impossible task. The old gods and goddesses reside very deep within the darkest parts of the Under-world, where our voices no longer reach, and where they may more easily ignore the thrashing about of humans." She paused. "The same is not true of *all* worlds, however."

My throat went suddenly very dry. "Are you telling me you're sending me through that mirror not just to another realm, but to another *world?*"

"Sending *us,*" Malcolm interjected.

"I call it the Broken World," Adam told me. "But don't let the name fool you—it's actually pretty terrible."

Fantastic.

CHAPTER 6

 home, where Sean waited for me.

The confrontation at Charles's house felt like a lifetime ago. The news about my impending trip through the mirror had pushed my anger at Charles not just to the back burner, but deep into the back of a dusty cupboard.

In the passenger seat area, Malcolm flitted repeatedly. "Alice."

I gripped the steering wheel and stared straight ahead. "Yeah?"

"This is bonkers. I don't want to go through a mirror to the Broken World to stop a vengeance-crazed blood mage from unleashing the Furies on our world."

"Join the club, dude." I glanced at him. "You don't have to go with me, you know."

"You're sure as hell not going without me. You'll need all the backup you can get, so I'd better get used to the idea." He sighed. "Hey, did you notice how tired Valas looked?"

"Yes, I did. And since when does Vlad hang around his maker like that? It's like he's protecting her." I drummed my fingers on the steering wheel. "I think she needs that scroll back for more than just sentimental reasons."

"Based on what?"

"Vlad being there, and a feeling I got when she talked about the scroll. I picked up on something because of our binding. She doesn't just want it back—she *needs* it."

"If she does need it back and that's connected to her physical condition, maybe you can use that to your advantage."

"Maybe. I'll have to really think on that." I yawned. "I need to talk to Sean when I get home and then try to get a couple hours of sleep. Are you going to spend some time with Liam?"

"Yeah, I should, since I'll be gone for a while. I'll be back in the morning to help you figure out what to pack." He shook his head. "I've never packed for a trip through a mirror to another world before. It's not like we can check a tourism website for packing tips."

"At least we have a little bit of information from Adam about the Broken World. That's better than nothing."

"I guess," he said dubiously. "It sounds crazy there. And I thought *our* world was nuts."

"Our world *is* nuts. Theirs is just *more* nuts."

"Can you imagine a world where the boundaries between all the supernatural realms and ours are fractured?" Malcolm clearly had a difficult time wrapping his brain around the idea. "I mean, from what Adam says, all the critters and supernatural beings we don't have to worry about here are *everywhere* there, and it's basically martial law. The vamps jockey with the Light and Dark Fae for power. Creatures you and I have only read about in storybooks walk down the street, and humans have to figure out how to survive when we're not at the top of the food chain."

"When you put it like that, it sounds kind of bad," I said.

He snorted.

I turned onto my street. "I've got to have a serious talk with Sean. Have fun hanging out with Liam. Say hi for me. We'll have to all get together when we get back."

"Okay, Alice. Have a good night. I'll see you in the morning." He vanished.

Sean's Mercedes was parked in my driveway, off to the side so I could get past. The SUV was a tight squeeze in the carport, so I parked in front of it and got out.

The door opened as I trudged up the walk toward the front steps. Sean stood in the doorway, worried and grim. He'd probably caught hints of my emotions through our nascent bond while I was at Northbourne, and that was on top of the strain already caused by Charles.

When our eyes met, I paused halfway up the steps, my hand on the railing. "Hi."

Sean came out to meet me. To my surprise, he scooped me up and kissed me hard, then carried me inside. He set me on my feet in the foyer and closed the door with his foot. "Are you all right?"

"I'm okay. Really," I added when he frowned. "Not about what Charles did to me, obviously, but I know the truth now and that's the first step toward dealing with it."

"I should have told you sooner that I'd once considered turning a mage to be my mate. I'm sorry you found out this way."

"I'm sorry I didn't believe you when you tried to warn me a dozen times what a manipulative, lying bastard Charles is."

"He was in your head, keeping you from thinking clearly. Even I didn't know how bad it was." He cupped the back of my neck and pressed his forehead to mine. "He didn't just try to steal you from me —he tried to steal your mind. I want to kill him for that."

"I know." My fingers tightened on his. "My heart hurts, and I don't even know if the pain I'm feeling is real or a result of his meddling."

He kissed me again, much more gently this time. "Vaughan was your friend, and he betrayed you in the worst possible way. It doesn't matter if your feelings were based on his lies—this is a loss and a hurt you're going to feel. I wish I could take that hurt from you."

"Thanks. That means a lot."

"So, what happened at Northbourne?"

I yawned. "Can I tell you in bed?"

He smiled, and the corners of his eyes crinkled. How I loved that about him. "Of course."

Sean let our dog, Rogue, in from the backyard and we all went upstairs to my bedroom. Rogue curled up in his bed by the window while Sean and I got ready for bed.

By the time I crawled under the covers next to Sean, I could barely keep my eyes open. "I used to stay up for days at a time and be fine. Now I can barely make it to three o'clock." I burrowed my face into his T-shirt and let his forest scent wrap me in comfort.

He pressed a kiss into my hair. "You've had a long, emotionally tiring day." He rested his chin on my head. I nestled deeper into his arms, trying to commit the feeling of his body wrapped around me to memory. I would have no such comfort and safety in the Broken World.

"What did Vaughan say to you, right before you left?" he asked.

"He said you've changed because of Miraç's power."

After a long silence, he asked, "Do you think I've changed?"

"I don't know," I admitted. "Sometimes I do. We're both different, but I don't know if it's because of the sorcerer magic or because of what we've been through these past few months. Or maybe Charles planted suspicion in my head as yet another way of driving a wedge between us." Magic sizzled on my skin. "I hate him for doing this to me—for making me doubt my own thoughts."

He squeezed me. "I'm responsible for the safety and well-being of my pack, and you most of all. If you ever truly believe something is wrong, I need you to make sure I'm not a threat to you or anyone else. Nan and Ben will know what to do." He brushed hair back from my face and tucked it behind my ear. "Promise me you'll do that for me."

"I promise," I told him. "Promise you'll do the same for me if I start to go over to the Dark Side."

He kissed the tip of my nose. "I promise. Who should I contact to help you, if it comes to that?"

"Ask Carly and Malcolm for help." I nestled my head against his chest. "We can't keep this power, Sean. It's going to kill me, and it will change us both. Every instinct in my body tells me it's bad, even if we haven't really noticed any effects yet. Black magic is insidious."

"I like the way the new power helps me sense everyone in the pack more clearly, and how much it's strengthened the pack bonds," Sean said. "But that's how bad magic works, right? It seems harmless at first, but before you know it…"

"Before you know it, you've gone so far down the rabbit hole you can't find your way back," I finished. "Power is seductive that way."

"Do you think you could kill Moses with Miraç's power? Could you use it to get to him, even through the wards at his compound?"

I said nothing for a long time. Finally, I exhaled. "Maybe. I could do some research. Big-time black magic requires more than just raw power, rituals, and tons of intricate spellwork. Miraç had to have a human heart for the spell to tear out my magic. The kind of magic it would take to get to Moses in his compound would take…something worse."

"But if he was outside the compound?"

"That might be more doable, but I probably won't be able to keep the sorcerer power long enough to put a plan like that together."

"If any good can come of what Miraç did to you, I hope it's that his power enables you to kill Moses." He tucked my head under his chin again. "So, about Northbourne?"

"Valas called in her favor."

He stilled. "What does that mean for you?"

"I can't tell you any of the details, per my agreement with Valas," I reminded him. "But it means Malcolm and I are going to be gone for awhile, and you probably won't be able to sense me through our bond. It also means I won't be here to help you deal with the Council, support our new pack members, and grieve with the rest of the pack for Jack, Delia, and Caleb, and I regret that very much."

He raised my chin with his fingertips. His eyes glowed and his expression was hard. "Tell me where you're going."

"I can't," I repeated. "My agreement with Valas—"

He cut in. "—Was a verbal agreement made under duress."

"That doesn't make it any less binding, as far as Valas and I are concerned. She could prosecute me for violating the agreement if she found out I revealed anything to you."

"How can I come to you if you need me if I don't know where you are?" he demanded. "Alice, if it were me doing this job for the Court, I wouldn't leave you behind feeling helpless, verbal agreement or no verbal agreement."

"You won't be able to come to my rescue," I told him, my voice quiet. "Where Malcolm and I are going, you can't follow. Don't ask me for more information than that, because I can't give it." I ran my fingertips over his bristly cheek. "I've never regretted the bargain I made with Valas, not even for a minute. I know it's asking a lot, but I need you to accept my choice. Remember, you would have done the same for me if our situation were reversed, and you know it."

"I do know that. I wouldn't have thought twice about it." He rubbed his chin on my head. "It's real damn hard to be left behind, especially when I don't know what you'll be facing and I won't be able to reach you or even sense you through our bond to know you're alive. It'll be like when Miraç had you all over again, and that was hell for me." A shadow moved in Sean's eyes: his wolf, pacing in agitation. "I don't want to lose you, and I sure as hell don't want to have to depend on Valas to tell me what happened to you. I've never trusted her, but now I don't believe a word she says."

I'd thought about this during the drive from Northbourne, and made a decision I hoped would offer him some peace of mind. "I'll leave you a letter. If too much time passes and it looks like we won't be coming back, you'll at least know where we went." I ran my thumb over his cheek. "I will tell you this: we're not running off on some frivolous errand. There are a lot of lives at stake."

"And so you're off to save the world again." He kissed my forehead. "This is what happens when you fall in love with a superhero, I suppose." His tone was light, but his expression remained grim.

"Not a superhero—just a mage who wants to save lives whenever she can." I slid my hand through his hair and stared into his eyes so I could talk directly to his wolf too. "Malcolm and I will come back," I promised. "You don't have to believe in Valas or Charles or anything else, but you have to believe in me."

His eyes turned to golden suns. "I believe in you, Alice Worth, and I always will."

I gripped his hair and pulled his mouth to mine, my exhaustion and worries all but forgotten in my need for him.

He let go of me just long enough to pull his T-shirt off over his head and toss it on the floor. I moved his stone wolf amulet aside and ran my nails over the hard muscles of his chest, eliciting a deep growl that told me both Sean and his wolf enjoyed the sensation very much.

His hand slid under my tank top and over my ribs to my breast. Magic sizzled on my skin, but it wasn't mine—it came from Sean's fingertips, and it stung like crackles of electricity.

I gasped, my back arching in a combination of pleasure and pain. "What was that?" I asked, breathless.

He didn't reply. His mouth was suddenly electric too as he kissed me along my jaw and then down my throat, his teeth grazing my skin in just the way I liked. Though I knew Sean would never hurt me in any way I didn't want, that little edge of danger was exactly what I wanted—exactly what I needed.

I didn't want to think any more about our angry confrontation with Charles, the horror of the vision Valas had shared with me, or learning I had less than twenty-four hours before I had to take Malcolm with me through a mirror to a world full of wonders and nightmares. I wanted to be loved, so I could take that feeling with me to the Broken World.

Impatient as always, he tore my top in half and continued moving down my body, exploring my curves and most sensitive places with his fingertips, lips, and teeth. His mouth closed on my right breast at the same moment his fingers gripped my waist. A sizzle of magic and power arced from the delicate skin of my breast to his fingertips.

With a shudder and a moan, I dug my nails into his biceps. "Sean."

He raised his head slowly, drawing out the searing pleasure as his lips tugged gently at my nipple and then released me. "More? Or should I stop?"

He'd clearly done some research on how to use magic for pleasure. Far be it for me to be ungrateful for all his hard work. "More, please."

He smiled wickedly, and I shivered. "I was hoping you'd say that," he murmured. "Let me show you what I've learned."

My pajama pants disappeared while he distracted me with his mouth on my breasts. I used my own magic to trace patterns on his arms, shoulders, and back, making him growl and snarl quietly while he bit, nipped, and licked. Heaven.

Soon he moved farther down the bed and I could no longer focus on anything at all but the sensations of magic and pleasure, and just the right amount of pain. My back arched as I gasped out his name. Even the tip of his tongue sizzled with magic, and for a moment I thought I might black out from the sheer power of the pleasure he was giving me. My hands twisted in the bedding and I let out a desperate cry as the wave inside me began to crest.

Sean raised his head, his fingertips moving slowly and deliberately. "Release your magic," he told me.

"I don't know what the sorcerer magic will do if I release it," I gasped. "You...Rogue..."

"Rogue's gone downstairs." He did something with his fingers that made me cry out. "Release your magic," he repeated, and this time it was a command. "Come for me, beautiful girl." He'd said that to me on our first night together, when he'd shown me, as he'd done many times since, how much seeing my pleasure meant to him.

He bent his head. I felt something different and started to raise my head to see what he was doing—

—And my world went supernova in the most intense orgasm I had ever experienced.

I screamed, my head flung back. I writhed and clawed at the bedding, fighting to get away from a release that terrified me with its intensity. I couldn't move because Sean held me down, even as he continued to do whatever he was doing to cause this tidal wave of pleasure.

I was suddenly afraid to release my magic, not just because I worried it might destroy the room and harm Sean, but because it always caused a second wave of pleasure and I didn't think I could take any more.

Impossibly, the force of the climax increased, and I couldn't hold back anymore. My magic tore free and thundered around us. I screamed again as power coursed through me in waves. Through the haze of pleasure, I called Sean's name over and over, pleading for him to stop, and to never, *ever* stop.

When I opened my eyes, he was above me. His eyes and skin glowed with hot golden shifter magic as he pushed into me. He pinned my hands to the bed on either side of my head and watched me writhing beneath him as he moved.

"Alice." He lowered his head to graze my earlobe with his teeth. "*Beautiful mate*," he growled in my ear. It was his wolf's voice.

The sound of the wolf's voice, the sensation of our combined magic blazing around us, and Sean's movements sent me over the edge again. Our magic rolled through us, bringing pleasure and power. Sean shuddered and groaned. My nails left deep marks in his arms. He wrapped me tightly in his arms as he pulsed hot inside me.

Our magic sizzled on our skin, then faded as it settled back into our bodies. I trembled so hard my teeth chattered. We lay together, breathing hard and unwilling to let go.

Sean finally kissed my neck and raised his head, his eyes still golden. "Are you all right?"

"I think so." My voice was wispy. "What did you do? How did you *do* that?"

"Just a bit of magic, in your most magical spot," he said, nuzzling my throat. "I was hoping for good results, but that exceeded every expectation. I thought you were going to levitate off the bed."

At least I was getting my breath back. "You gotta warn a girl next time you want to try something crazy like that."

"You said *more please*," he reminded me. He kissed his way along my collarbone, then placed my wolf amulet between my breasts and covered it with his hand. "My beautiful Alice."

Without warning, shifter magic surged inside me. My arms and legs went rigid, the joints popping audibly as my wolf tried to force my body to shift. Caught off guard by my wolf's sudden agitation, I screamed.

Sean cursed. In a blink, he was kneeling beside me, gripping my hand. "Use your shifter magic," he ordered. "Push her back, Alice."

"I don't know how," I gasped.

"You have to learn." He leaned over me, his eyes bright gold. "Be the dominant partner."

The agony in my arms and legs made it difficult to think, but I resisted the idea of shoving her down with brute force. Instead, I closed my eyes and found my wolf's angry golden gaze in the shadows. *Stop trying to make me shift*, I told her. *I can't shift. I will never be able to shift. All you're doing is hurting me.*

Want to run, she snarled. She surged again and my limbs seized painfully.

I set my jaw to keep from crying out. I drew on my shifter magic and pushed her gently back. *You can't run in this body, and you can't run alone*, I told her. *It's too dangerous.*

She showed me her teeth. *No danger to me. Danger to others.*

That's what I mean, I said. *If you hurt someone, our whole pack will suffer. Many people are afraid of you. They may try to capture you and me. We have to be careful. Please stop hurting me.*

My wolf settled down. My limbs stopped seizing. *Want to run,* she said. It sounded more like a request or a plea now than a demand.

I'll figure something out, I promised her. *Please be patient. I have to figure out how to keep us safe.*

She showed me the memory of her twenty feet tall and sinking her teeth into the throat of the demon lord Orias. *We are safe*, she stated. She faded into the shadows.

I opened my eyes. Sean squeezed my hand. "What did you do?"

"I asked her to be patient and stop hurting me."

He rested his forehead on mine. "That won't work long term. You have to dominate her, or she won't learn her boundaries. I know you don't want to, but you have to."

He was right: I didn't want to dominate her the way he had, because it caused her pain—pain I understood all too well. I also knew boundaries were important. Somehow I would have to make her obey me, even if it hurt both of us to do so.

"I will," I promised him. "She wants to run."

"Of course she does. She's a wolf, albeit one made of magic. Wolves need to run. I'll take her running at the pack land. When do you and Malcolm have to leave?"

"As soon as I have a chance to talk to Carly and see if she can make me some goodies to take with us. Depending on how long she needs to make them, we might be leaving as early as tomorrow night. We don't have much time."

"Then I'll take her now."

"What? Now?"

"Yes. You can stay here and get some sleep. When we're done, I'll bring her back."

I shook my head. "This is a bad idea."

"Alice, made of magic or not, she's a wolf in our pack, and she needs to run." He kissed my forehead. "Trust us both."

I took a deep breath and let it out. "Okay." I closed my eyes and found my wolf's golden eyes in the shadows again. *Go run with Sean*, I told her.

My wolf didn't need any coaxing. With a growl, she leaped from my chest in a surge of power and landed on the floor next to the bed, radiant with golden magic.

I sat up, rubbing my chest, which ached from her abrupt departure. "You can't go around glowing," I told her. "You have to be stealthy."

She showed me her teeth again. She shook herself briskly, then turned into a black wolf with a band of gray across her shoulders and a streak of white in her tail.

Sean kissed my temple and climbed off the bed. "Get some sleep. We'll be back."

I didn't know how I was supposed to sleep after what we'd just done, or while he and my wolf were gone, but I'd have to try. "Be careful. And don't let her eat Rogue."

He chuckled. "She knows he's pack, but I'll make sure she doesn't."

He dressed quickly, gave me one last kiss, and headed downstairs with my wolf at his side. The house wards tingled as they left. I heard the sound of the Maclin Security SUV as it backed down the drive.

A few minutes later, as I dozed, Rogue appeared at the side of the bed. He put his chin on the mattress and stared at me.

"Sean's going to be annoyed at me if he comes back and you're on the bed," I told the dog sleepily. "But come on anyway, fur-face." I patted the bed.

Rogue jumped up and settled in with his back against my shins. I pulled the covers up to my chin and tried to imagine Sean, in wolf form, running through the pack land with my wolf.

"I wish I could run with him," I murmured to Rogue. "I don't want to be a werewolf, but I'd like to run with Sean, just once, to know what it's like. There's no way for me to do that, I suppose."

Rogue wriggled closer and let out a contented sigh. I snuggled under the covers and drifted off to sleep.

CHAPTER 7

SEAN AND MY WOLF RETURNED JUST BEFORE DAWN, FAR MORE CONTENTED and happy than when they'd left. Apparently the run had done them both some good.

My wolf returned to my body and settled so deeply into the shadows in my head that it felt as though she'd gone to sleep. Sean changed into pajamas and joined me in bed for a few hours before he had to go to the office for a meeting.

After he kissed me goodbye, I dragged myself out of bed and showered. Malcolm hadn't come back from hanging out with Liam, so I put Rogue out in the backyard and headed for Brew a Cup, in desperate need of caffeine and Carly's blueberry scones.

As usual, the coffee shop smelled like I imagined heaven might. When I walked in, Katy Clark was behind the counter. She'd helped someone hex me, so we'd gotten off on the wrong foot. To make up for it, she'd protected me during a black magic ritual, and Carly believed she was sincerely trying to put her past behind her. Plus we both had evil families we wanted nothing to do with, so I'd decided to let bygones be bygones, at least in regard to the hex.

She gave me a shy smile and tucked her pink hair behind her ears. "Good morning, Ms. Worth. Your usual?"

"Alice," I corrected her. "Yes, please. Carly around?"

Katy rang me up and I handed over my card. "She's in the back. She said she had to get something done before you got here." At my expression, she laughed. "She's spooky like that. It's always weird when she knows I'll have to call in sick before I do." She handed back my card and went to pour my coffee. "Anyway, she'll be out to talk to you in a few."

I took my coffee to the little counter to add some half-and-half and sugar, then headed to the corner booth with the RESERVED sign. Carly's familiar parchment-scented magic welcomed me as I slid into the booth, which was spelled to keep conversations private and gently encourage other patrons to ignore those in the booth.

The blue crystal on my bracelet buzzed just as I settled in. I touched the crystal. "*Release.*"

Malcolm appeared. "Hey, Alice. You weren't home, so I figured you were here." He frowned. "You look tired."

"That's why I have this." I raised my coffee cup and took a drink. "How's Liam?"

He floated back and forth. I sensed a little spike of sadness from my ghost sidekick. "Not happy, to be honest."

"Because you're going away with me?"

He nodded. "He's worried about me. I didn't tell him where we were going or why, obviously, but I can't tell him it won't be dangerous, and I can't tell him when we'll be back. He doesn't understand why I want to go with you, or why I don't just want to stay in one place. I made the mistake of pointing out that he feels secure in the bordello because he's used to being tethered to a place, but I'm more of a free spirit—so to speak." His mouth turned down. "I tried to explain I'm safer when I'm with you, just like he's safer there, but that didn't go over super well either. We had a big argument about it. I'll give him some time to cool off and try to talk to him later. I don't want the last words we say to each other to be angry ones."

"I'm sorry." I rubbed my face. "Sean's not happy either, obviously. He's trying to make the best of it, but you can imagine how much he hates the idea of me going somewhere he can't go, even if you're with me. And I hate that I'm abandoning Sean and the rest of our pack right when they need me."

Malcolm smiled a little. "Things suck, but it makes me happy to hear you talk about the pack like that." He looked up. "Hey, Carly."

"Hello, you two." Carly set my scone on the table and slid into the booth with a mug of tea. The petite brunette witch wore a purple long-sleeved blouse, black jeans, and her coffee shop apron with her name embroidered with silver thread that glimmered with magic. "You're off on a journey, Alice?"

I smiled ruefully and broke a chunk off the scone. "What tipped you off? Your cards, or your witchy sense?"

"Both." She sipped her tea, which smelled minty. "Plus my eyes. You have the look of a reluctant traveler. On the plus side, your wolf seems more content than I've seen her in quite a while, so you must have worked something out."

I took a drink from my coffee. "Sean took her running in wolf form."

Malcolm's mouth fell open. "He did? How?"

I shrugged. "She jumped out of me. They drove out to the pack land last night at around four, ran until almost dawn, and then came home. It was just what the doctor ordered for both of them. As Sean said, she may be made of magic, but she's still a wolf, and she needs to run from time to time, especially in the company of our alpha." I was getting used to the idea of being a part of the pack, but that still felt weird to say. "They came back happy and she went right to sleep. I should have let Sean take her for a run before. I was just scared to let her out of my sight, I guess."

"I can't blame you for that, but you did the right thing to trust them." Carly patted my hand. "So, how can I help with your journey? And don't worry—I know what you're doing is confidential. I won't tell a soul."

I sighed. "I'd love some party favors, but we have to leave almost immediately. I thought I'd check to see if you had anything on hand."

She smiled. "I have a few things. I saw this journey on your horizon a week or so ago, so I've made some goodies I thought you could use. I have *Return to Sender* amulets, a couple of *Reveal* spells, and some odds and ends. I've got them in my office. You can take them with you when you leave."

"Thank you. How should I pay for the spells? A gift for your coven? For you? A souvenir or two, if I can make that work?" Though from what Adam said about the Broken World, I'd be lucky to get back through the mirror with Malcolm and my hide mostly intact.

Carly surprised me by handing over two small silver vials with stoppers. Naturally, she'd somehow known to have them on hand. "Souvenirs would be lovely, actually. Some rainwater and moss, please—or spring water, if there's no rain."

I tucked the vials in my bag. "It's a deal. Any advice about the trip?"

From the pocket of her apron, she brought out a deck of tarot cards wrapped in purple silk. "I had a feeling you might want some guidance. It's difficult, but not impossible, for me to see into other places. I'm willing to try."

As she unwrapped the cards and spread the silk out on the table, I closed my eyes, took a deep breath, and exhaled slowly, clearing my mind of distractions and tuning out the noise in the coffee shop.

With my eyes closed, I picked up the stack of cards and shuffled them. I thought about the trip through the mirror, the world that awaited us on the other side, and my goals for the trip: find Mariela and the scroll, bring both back as soon as possible, make sure the Furies stayed where they belonged, and keep both Malcolm and myself safe. My fingers slid over the smooth texture and edges of the cards as I shuffled. I visualized the backs of the cards, which showed bright green vines with small white budding flowers. Like the two other tarot decks I'd seen that belonged to Carly, these seemed hand-drawn, and smelled of parchment-scented magic.

One of the cards fell out as I shuffled. "Oops," I said, and reached to pick it up.

"No—leave it," Carly said. She turned the card over and placed it face-up and horizontal just above the center of the silk. The card was the Hermit. I set the stack of cards on the silk between us.

She placed the second card, a six of swords, face up on top of the Hermit to form a cross. Below it, she placed the third card, a seven of swords, face up and vertical. She folded her hands on the table and studied the cards.

"You will have a guide and a protector," she told us finally. "You must listen to their advice and accept their help."

"She's not super good at that," Malcolm pointed out. I scowled. He raised his hands. "What, you're going to tell me I'm wrong?"

"A guide and a protector sound *useful,*" I said, glaring at him.

"So I can remind you of this conversation once we're there and you tell your protector to take a long walk off a short pier?"

"Shut up."

"*Children,*" Carly interjected. She tapped the six of swords. Her brow furrowed. "I'm not sure if this is directly related to your journey or not. Did the angel Tura give you a message to deliver to someone?"

"Yes," I admitted. "She asked me to take a message to someone I'm supposedly going to meet over there, because she can't travel through the mirror and deliver it herself. I'm supposed to find 'a knight with no court or kingdom,' whatever that means. And then I'll have to give that person a big ol' smooch to deliver the message, which is apparently in the language of angels and stored in my body somehow."

Her eyebrows went up. "Dare I ask how Tura gave you the message she wants you to deliver?"

Nonchalantly, I sipped my coffee. "She kissed me."

"Hmm." Carly smiled knowingly and inhaled the steam from her tea. "It must be a very special message."

"Soooooo...does Sean know you made out with a female angel?" Malcolm asked finally.

"We did *not* make out, Malcolm. Her lips touched mine. It was like kissing a mannequin. End of story." I pointed at the cards. "Anything else?"

Carly was quiet for a moment. "I think the final card has more to do with your return than what you may find while you're there. Did you receive a prophecy from Tura as well?"

When I didn't reply right away, she added, "I know you didn't want me to know your sorcerer magic is killing you, partly because you don't really believe her, and partly because you don't like to give your friends a reason to worry. I've meditated and prayed about this, and asked my spirit guides for answers. I believe I should tell you I've seen the same thing more than once when I read my cards. I've also seen the possibility of another path, one you find only through sacrifice, which is why I struggled with whether to tell you. This card—" She tapped the seven of swords "—tells me you will face violence on your return—violence you've already been warned about."

"Yeah, I got that warning from Tura." I finished the last of my coffee and set the cup on the table a little louder than was necessary. "She told me soon I would have to choose between Sean's life and my own, and when that happens, I should choose my own. If I did, she said I would save him—that I'd *save them all*, whatever that means. She didn't deign to explain further before she turned into a pillar of light and sent me back to your living room. I haven't told Sean about that because I have no intention of sacrificing him, no matter what Tura said. I'll find another way."

When she didn't say anything, I sighed. "You've never steered me wrong yet, Carly; I know that. I trust you and your cards. If you tell me this is what I'm supposed to do, I'll give it more thought than if it was only Tura's word, but there's always a third option, another door to choose."

"And if there isn't, you'll kick a hole in the wall." Carly smiled.

"Nothing's ever as simple as some people make it sound, even angels. What were her exact words?"

I closed my eyes and thought. "She told me when I had to choose between my life or Sean's to choose my own. By doing so I would save him—I would save them all."

"Interesting." She sipped her tea thoughtfully. "So she didn't say you had to sacrifice Sean, or even that he would die—just that you should choose your life over his. So maybe what I'm seeing is a totally different event, one that forces you to make a sacrifice to find a new path. What that sacrifice is, however, I'm not sure."

"A sacrifice, huh? Awesome. Something else to look forward to." I hesitated, then added, "Not to change the subject, but before I forget, Sean says Morgan Clark has been sleeping with Charles Vaughan."

For the first time since I'd met her, Carly looked totally nonplussed. I'd thought nothing could possibly render her speechless, but apparently finding out her onetime coven sister and current quasi-nemesis was shagging a member of the Vampire Court was a total shock.

"Well, that's certainly a match made in somewhere," she said finally. She gathered up her cards, wrapped them in the purple silk, and tucked them back into her apron pocket. "No doubt she's using him and he's using her. Vampires like witch blood, and black witches like power. I'm not sure which of them to pray for, so I will pray for both." She pinched the bridge of her nose. "Let me go get those party favors from my office. You want more coffee to go?"

"Yes, please."

We slid out of the booth. She took my cup to the counter and asked Katy to refill it, then disappeared into the back.

I added half-and-half and sugar to my coffee while I waited. Carly came out of the office with a tote bag. She gave me a hug and handed me the bag. "Be safe on your journey, both of you. I'll be thinking of you. And I'll keep an eye on Sean too, as best I can."

"Thank you. I'm sure he'll be fine, but..."

"But of course you worry. And he'll be worried about you too."

She squeezed my hand. "I put instructions in the bag for how to invoke the various spells. Let me know if you have questions."

"Thank you, Carly. You're the best."

She winked. "I know."

Malcolm and I said our goodbyes and left the shop. My phone buzzed as I unlocked my car.

Wolf: Taking the rest of the day off to spend with you. Where are you?

Me: Just leaving Brew a Cup and heading home to pack.

"Alice, trouble," Malcolm warned.

Three people emerged from an SUV parked two spots away from my borrowed Maclin Security SUV: two men and a woman, all shifters. I recognized brothers Matthew and Zachary Anderson, who were tall and muscular, with blond hair and blue eyes. The woman, whose name I didn't recall, had long, dark blonde hair and green eyes. All wore business casual and identical hard expressions. Matthew Anderson and the woman were on the Were Ruling Council.

They must have followed me here from home, waiting for a chance to confront me when I was away from both Sean and the safety of my house. I put Carly's bag of goodies and my shoulder bag in the SUV so my hands were free and turned to face them. Malcolm floated beside me.

The woman approached me first. "Alice Worth?"

"Who's asking?"

"My name is Sarah Webber." She didn't offer to shake my hand. "We're from the Were Ruling Council."

My phone buzzed with an incoming text. "Excuse me," I said, and read Sean's message.

Wolf: Should I meet you at your house?

Me: Sarah Webber and the Andersons just showed up in the parking lot at Brew a Cup.

The reply was instantaneous. *Wolf: I'm on my way. ETA 10 minutes.*

I stuck my phone in my back pocket. "Sorry about that."

Matthew Anderson, the older of the two, gave me a hard stare, his eyes glowing. Both he and his brother were alphas of their respective packs. Zachary's daughter Lily had pursued Sean for months and had hexed me in an attempt to end our relationship.

When I didn't look away or back down, Matthew snarled. "You're disrespectful."

Something told me this was not going to be a friendly chat. Still, I didn't have any reason to be deliberately antagonistic—at least, not yet. "No disrespect was intended. To what do I owe the pleasure?" *Of this ambush,* my tone implied. "I'm guessing this isn't an accidental meeting."

"Not in the least," Sarah said. "We're here out of concern for Sean and his pack."

"If you're concerned about Sean, why aren't you talking to him?"

"We've tried. He won't listen to a word we say." Matthew flexed his hands. "Despite everything you've put him through, he remains blindly devoted to you and determined to name Nan Lowell as his beta. It's sickening to see such a good man brought down like this."

"Oh, fuck off," Malcolm muttered.

All three werewolves glanced in Malcolm's direction. Though none of them could see or hear him, they could sense him, especially when he spoke.

"You've got your ghost servant with you today, I suppose," Zachary said. "And you were seen at Northbourne last night, showing your allegiance to the vampires. I never thought I'd see Sean mixed up with someone like you."

I wondered if that meant members of the Council or their packs had been among the protestors last night. I made a mental note to mention that troubling possibility to Sean.

A dozen insults burned on the tip of my tongue. For the good of everyone involved, I held them back.

I figured there was zero chance of changing their minds about Nan or me, but it was worth a shot. "Sean's a good man and an ideal alpha. Everyone who knows him believes that. He loves me, and I love him. Our pack has seen some hard days and undergone some changes, but we'll be stronger for it, and our people will be safe and happy. Sean, Nan, and I will make sure of that."

"Stop saying *our* pack," Matthew snapped. "You aren't part of Sean's pack—and won't ever be."

"I don't know if you really love him, or if this is some kind of game you're playing," Sarah added. "And I don't understand why Sean would jeopardize his pack this way. We're all at a loss to explain any of it. But if you do love him, you'll do what's best for him and his pack."

"I *am* doing what's best for Sean and *our* pack," I said, ignoring Matthew's growl. "The Council has no authority to interfere with internal pack matters just because you disagree with our relationship or that Nan is our new beta."

"Female shifters cannot be betas," Matthew stated.

"Where is that written?" I countered. "There are no laws against it. Even if there were, they'd be wrong and needing to be changed. This isn't the Stone Age. If you don't want a female beta in your pack, you have the right to make that choice, just as Sean has the right to make his. Every member of our pack stands behind him and Nan. And as you know, Nan's earned her place as beta. Five fights, five wins."

"Nan Lowell's former alpha should have killed her." His expression was colder than his words. "And you should have died when Caleb Jennings attacked you."

Sarah seemed taken aback, but Zachary didn't blink. "Matthew's right. Things have a certain order for a reason, Alice. Sooner or later, both you and Sean will understand that. I'm just sorry you're too selfish to spare him and the rest of his pack everything that's to come."

"Is that a threat?" I asked.

He shook his head. "Just facts. My daughter would have been an ideal mate for Sean. He couldn't have done better than Lily."

Malcolm snorted. "That's debatable."

"Alice, I know you think you'll live happily ever after with Sean, but it's not going to happen." Sarah's patronizing tone set my teeth on edge. "Regardless of whatever dark magic you're using to influence him and however you've tricked him into believing you have a wolf within you that's anything more than a demonic illusion, the truth will come out. We'll see to that."

Instead of telling her what she could do with her taunts, I called into the darkness in my mind. *Are you there?*

My wolf raised her head.

Would you care to introduce yourself to members of the Were Ruling Council? I asked. *Be calm and civil. No biting.*

She curled her lip, her eyes glinting.

"In the spirit of truth, allow me to introduce my wolf," I told the shifters.

My wolf leaped from my body in a surge of shifter magic and landed on the pavement beside me in her all-black form, her eyes glowing bright gold. She shook herself briskly. It hurt less than last time. Maybe we were getting better at this.

Sarah took a step back involuntarily. Matthew and Zachary growled.

"She's a real wolf," I told them. "Made of magic, it's true, but as real as you and me. You want the truth about me and my wolf? You can sense the truth for yourselves."

"I don't believe it," Sarah breathed. "I've never seen anything like this."

"It's some kind of illusion," Matthew snarled.

My wolf showed him all of her teeth.

"No illusion." I glanced behind them. "Oh, that is excellent timing."

Sean's Mercedes pulled into the parking spot beside the SUV belonging to Matthew Anderson. He must have broken every speed limit on the way here from the office. He got out, his eyes golden.

To my surprise, my wolf left my side and met Sean as he

approached. She sat beside him, watching the others. I might have been imagining it, but I thought her expression appeared smug.

He put his hand on her head. "I see you've met the newest addition to my pack."

"This is unacceptable," Matthew exploded. "Completely unacceptable. The Council—"

"The Council will mind their own business," Sean stated. "I don't know what you were hoping to accomplish by confronting Alice like this, but I'm glad you've had a chance to see for yourselves that she does, in fact, have a very real wolf."

"Matthew was just telling me that Nan's former alpha should have killed her, and I should have died when Caleb attacked me," I interjected. "Oh, and Zachary wanted me to know we're bringing a lot of trouble to our pack. Sarah's concerned I'm controlling you with dark magic." I glanced at the three Council members. "Does that about sum it up?"

"All of which I've heard from the Council already." Sean shook his head. "Don't threaten us, Matthew."

To my surprise, Matthew didn't meet Sean's golden gaze. Was Sean more dominant than Matthew? "You're going to destroy your pack, Sean," he said.

"No, I'm going to have the best and strongest pack I've ever had."

"Not with this mage as your mate, you won't," Sarah told him. "Mages are only good at destroying things and killing."

"Some say that about shifters." Sean took his hand off my wolf's head. "Are we done here? Alice and I have plans for the rest of the afternoon. She needs to redo the dark magic spellwork on me."

My lips twitched. Malcolm laughed.

Zachary scowled. "This is no laughing matter." He too avoided Sean's gaze. I started to wonder whether their antagonism was more due to Sean's rising dominance than Nan or me. "I hear you met with the Hayes brothers last night. At this rate, you'll have no reputation left."

"On the contrary, I think we'll have a reputation we can be proud of." Sean gestured at my wolf. "Return home," he commanded.

She bounded across the pavement to me, turned to golden magic, and spiraled up my arm and into my chest. Contented and self-satisfied, she retreated back into the shadows. I let my eyes continue to glow with shifter magic, however, just to make a point.

"Freak," Sarah muttered.

Sean's eyes blazed. "Never speak to Alice that way again, Sarah—not unless you're ready to fight. The same goes for the rest of the Council. I won't tolerate your abuse of any member of my pack, especially Alice."

"This isn't over," Matthew warned.

"It is," Sean countered. "Now, either name a time and place for us to fight, or get the hell out of here."

Matthew took a step toward Sean. Shifter magic rose. Sean braced himself, and I spooled magic, ready for an attack.

Zachary put his hand on his brother's shoulder to hold him back. "Not here. Another day."

Matthew snarled and shrugged Zachary's hand off his arm. "Another day," he said, his voice edged with a growl.

All three got into their vehicle. Sean joined me beside the Maclin Security SUV. We watched them back out of their parking spot and leave the lot, turning into traffic with a screech of tires.

When they were gone, Sean kissed my temple. "I'm sorry."

"For what? That the Council is four-sevenths troglodytes and assholes?" I smiled up at him. "Thanks for riding to the rescue."

"You don't need rescuing." He squeezed my hand. "Let's get to your house so you can pack and still have some time to ourselves." He waved at the windows of the coffee shop. Carly waved back. She must have been watching our scene in the parking lot.

I gave her a little wave, then climbed into my borrowed SUV. Sean went to his Mercedes.

In the passenger seat area, Malcolm crossed his arms. "What a couple of jerks. You okay?"

"Yeah, just concerned about what the Council's going to do next, since I won't be here to help Sean deal with it." I backed out of my spot and followed Sean toward my house.

"Between Sean and Nan and everyone else, I think they'll have it covered. We're going to have our hands full tracking down Mariela in the Broken World. This is not going to be easy, Alice."

"It wouldn't be any fun if it was."

"Our definitions of *fun* are vastly different, apparently."

"Not *that* different. Remember how much fun you had helping me with Irene Miller's poltergeist problem?"

He grinned. "Oh, yeah—that *was* fun. Point taken. I still don't think the Broken World sounds fun, though."

"Adam says there are trolls. Trolls sound fun."

"Have you never read a fairy tale, Alice? Trolls are *never* fun."

"Maybe these trolls are."

"We could never be that lucky," he muttered. "Whatever, Alice. Just drive."

Despite everything, I chuckled most of the way home.

LATER THAT EVENING, with my packing done and Malcolm at the bordello saying goodbye to Liam, I lay on top of Sean with my head on his chest as we both caught our breath.

"As going-away presents go, that was pretty good," I said when I could talk.

He kissed the top of my head. "Pretty good? You nearly screamed the house down. I'm surprised the neighbors didn't call the police. One wonders what I'd need to do to be rated higher than 'pretty good.'"

"Okay, that was better than pretty good," I admitted. "Bordering on great, really."

He chuckled and rubbed his chin on my head. "Glad to hear it. After all, I take pride in my work."

"Is that an alpha thing?"

"It's a Sean thing." He wrapped his arms around me. "I believe you'll come back to me. I believe you'll beat whatever you're going to face. It's still killing me to let you go."

I raised my head to meet his golden gaze. "I know. If the situation were reversed, I don't know how I'd handle it. At least I've got Malcolm and my wolf. That's a pretty good team, really."

"It is a good team." He tucked some hair behind my ear. "You wrote me a letter?"

"I did. It's in my nightstand."

"How long do you expect to be gone?"

"I don't know." I laid my head on his chest again to listen to the steady, reassuring beat of his heart. "Could be days, or weeks. I have no way of knowing until I get where I'm going."

"So when should I open the letter?"

"When you think it's time. I think you'll know."

He laced his fingers through mine. "There's no way for you to even get a message to me while you're gone?"

"No. I wish there was, but there isn't." I played with little wisps of magic, letting them dance over my fingertips and his hand. "When I get back, once my obligation to Valas is fulfilled, I'm done with the Court. I already told Malcolm that last night. No more cases, no more favors or work. No more being a favorite of the Court or Valas's little errand girl. No more." I glanced up at him. "I know that may bring trouble to our pack on several possible fronts, but I'm tired of vampires and their games."

"You know I'd love nothing more than for us to be as free from the Vampire Court as we can be. If that's what you want too, we'll figure out a way to make it work." He squeezed my hand. "Do you have anything you can use against Valas or the Court if they decide to play hardball?"

I thought about Valas's apparent need for the scroll and my suspicions regarding her physical condition. "I might."

"Good. I'll give it some thought in the meantime, and when you get back, we'll weigh our options." He nuzzled my hair. "Ever since you indebted yourself to Valas to save me, you've had a weight on your shoulders. Everyone who works for the Court has that weight on them, even your friend Arkady. There's something about being around vampires that leeches at the soul. Maybe it's knowing you're just a pawn to them, or the constant stress of trying to keep their fangs out of your neck." He growled, probably remembering the sight of Valas biting me during our fight with Miraç. "Whatever your obligation to Valas is, I'll be glad to see you free of it and back to doing what you do best: solving mysteries with Malcolm and having a *pretty good* time with me."

I laughed and kissed his chest. "I want that too."

"Good." He ran his lips along my jaw to my ear. "I have time for one more shot at greatness before you have to go." He kissed my neck and inhaled my scent. "I love you, Alice. Come back as soon as you can. I won't be whole until you're at my side again."

"I love you too," I told him. "More than good boots, whisky, or coffee."

He raised his eyebrows. "More than *coffee?*"

"Yep. Not more than Carly's blueberry scones, though. You'd have to be truly fantastic to rank higher than scones."

His eyes glinted. He flipped us over so quickly that I let out a squeak. "Challenge accepted," he said.

CHAPTER 8

I sat cross-legged outside the stone circle in Northbourne's sublevel one, staring at the covered mirror in front of me.

Under my leather jacket, my arms and chest were covered with runes and intricate spellwork, all drawn by me in my blood. Magic hummed on my skin, full of potential energy, waiting to be unleashed. My backpack sat beside me, stuffed with clothing, magic implements, Carly's party favors, money and a few other items provided by the Court, and a picture of Sean and me. Nothing electronic would survive the journey, so I'd left my phone at home.

"You okay?" Malcolm asked. He floated a few feet to my right. At the moment, we were the only people in the room. Valas was on her way from her apartment to see us off. If Vlad was lurking around, neither of us sensed him.

I took a deep breath and let it out. "All I have to do is step through," I said, more to myself than him. "The spellwork is complete. I have everything I'm taking with me. We'll have to figure out the rest once we get there."

"How many times have you mirror-traveled?"

"A couple." I didn't want to provide any details, since the room was no doubt under surveillance. "It's a bumpy ride, even if you're just going next door. This will be my farthest trip." I glanced up at him. "You still have a chance to change your mind and stay."

"Shut up, Alice." He floated back and forth. "We'll be fine. I have complete faith in you."

I smiled wryly. "Thanks."

Malcolm didn't return my smile. His good-bye with Liam hadn't gone much better than their earlier conversation. At least their final words to each other had been kind and not angry. I hated to see him hurting.

He guessed what I was thinking. "Stop blaming yourself," he said testily. "Liam and I will work it out when we get back, or it wasn't meant to be. I'm never going to be content to haunt the bordello, nice and safe from the dangers of the world. I'm an action-adventure ghost. Like you, I want to save lives and make the world a better place than I found it, one fight at a time. So let's go kick it in the ass."

"Wow, that's right up there with King Théoden rallying his soldiers for the big battle in *The Return of the King*," I said, getting to my feet. "Well done."

"You are such a smart-ass." But he was smiling.

I hadn't heard a door open or close, but suddenly Valas and Matthias emerged from the shadows on the far side of the room. He escorted her to the chair that faced the mirror and took up a position to her right.

Less than twenty-four hours had passed since I'd seen her, but Valas appeared markedly unwell. Though her dress covered her from chin to feet and the long sleeves hid her arms, I spotted a discoloration on the back of her right hand. I couldn't be certain because of the low light, but I thought I saw another near her jaw. Was she decaying? If so, why?

I decided it would be to my advantage to not let on that I'd noticed the marks. Always better to let the other person believe they'd fooled you.

"I'm about ready to leave," I told her. "All the spellwork is complete. I'm just waiting on midnight."

Valas clasped her hands in her lap, her elbows resting on the arms of the chair. The pose hid her discolored hand. "Have you all you need for the journey?"

"I have the basics, yes. I won't know what else I'll need until I get there. Other than what little Adam could tell us about conditions in the Broken World, everything's a big unknown. There'll be a lot of flying by the seat of my pants."

"It is fortunate then that you excel at that form of flight." Her dark gaze met mine. "Time is of the essence. You must retrieve the scroll and return as soon as possible."

"And stop Mariela from invoking the Furies. I get it. I'll hurry." I glanced at my watch—a non-digital, self-winding model I hoped would survive the trip. "Speaking of which, we're T-minus two minutes. Time to get ready."

I pulled the red silk cover from the mirror. I'd already drawn the necessary spellwork on its surface, but had been forced to cover it when the vertigo-inducing reflections made my stomach churn and my skin crawl. Though the glass seemed to show only a reflection of the room, the image was like a chasm: infinitely deep and dark. It pulled at me like a magnet. I gritted my teeth and forced myself to take two steps back.

I hadn't traveled by mirror since leaving my grandfather's compound, and his mirror had been far less powerful than this one. This mirror was very, very old. Judging by the power I sensed radiating from its glass, it had seen many journeys and a lot of blood. That meant I was almost guaranteed to end up at my destination. On the downside, I would probably encounter echoes of past travelers along the way, and those echoes were not likely to let me pass unnoticed or unscathed.

I checked the leather cuffs on my wrists to ensure they were buckled tightly. Each had a half-dozen crystals secured between the layers of leather. Most were healing spells. Two crystals were for

Malcolm—one in each cuff. Both were heavily warded to protect him from detection and a wide range of dangers, including the journey.

"Ready to go?" I asked Malcolm. "All aboard the Mirror Express. Next stop, the Broken World."

"Ready as I'll ever be." He grinned. "I'll see you on the other side."

"On the other side," I confirmed. "*Contain.*"

Malcolm vanished. One of the crystals in the cuff on my right wrist buzzed reassuringly with his presence.

I put on my backpack and fastened the straps across my upper chest and around my waist. I checked my watch. Thirty seconds to midnight.

"Ms. Worth." Valas rose, moving a little stiffly. "I wish you a safe journey and a swift return."

"Thanks." I tightened the strap around my waist and bounced to test that the backpack was cinched as tightly as it could be.

I took a deep breath and approached the mirror. The reflection in the glass seemed a mile deep. Vertigo made my stomach lurch.

Ten seconds to midnight.

Based on previous experience, I knew it was best not to bring anything with me in my head. I closed my eyes and took several deep breaths, clearing my mind and relaxing my shoulders. *Just fall,* I reminded myself. *Just fall, and the spell will do the rest.*

I opened my eyes. Midnight exactly. The glass shimmered like the surface of a lake.

With my fingertip, I traced the spellwork I'd drawn in blood on the glass. The humming of the magic on my skin surged until I vibrated with power. The mirror's power rose as well, building to a crescendo along with my own, but the vibrations were discordant. The discomfort made my teeth ache. My chest heaved as breathing became difficult.

Finally, the vibrations synced as the spellwork on my body and my blood magic aligned to match that of the mirror. The sudden lack of pain was almost euphoric.

On the other side of the glass, the chasm yawned. I'd never

looked into the mouth of Hell, but I imagined it might look something like this.

Voices whispered just on the edge of my awareness—so many, I couldn't distinguish any one sound. The mirror was full of echoes. This would be one hell of a rough trip.

"Bombs away," I muttered. I pressed my palms against the glass. "*Tollat me.*"

The glass gave way under my hands. I thought the mirror was falling over. By the time I realized it was *me* who was falling, the spell had me and there was no turning back.

As I slipped through the glass, Valas's voice hissed something in my ear—or maybe in my mind. When her words registered, I raised my hands to stop my fall into the mirror, but there was nothing for me to grab onto and nowhere to go but down, down, *down*.

A wall of wind that smelled of old earth blasted my face and carried my scream of rage away into the darkness as I fell out of the world.

I FELL AND FELL.

Formless faces and bodies that were little more than eyes, mouths, and hands clutched and clawed at me as I passed. They screamed in many languages I didn't recognize and a few I did: German, French, maybe Middle English. Every traveler who'd passed through had left an echo of themselves, and the blasted mirror had to be a thousand years old. It was an artifact of enormous power. I wasn't sure what kind of deal Valas had made with Elizabeth of the Chicago Vampire Court to get this mirror, but I had no doubt she'd paid a king's ransom for it. Clearly she'd wanted to make damn sure I made it to the Broken World and back.

The farther down the rabbit hole I went, the darker, angrier, and more solid the echoes became. Streaks of fire on my arms, legs, and back told me they were leaving wounds as I passed. The oldest echoes had become something else entirely—more like shades, and shades were angry and potentially deadly. Instead of passing through them, I hit each one and careened off, only to hit another.

The speed at which I fell was probably the only reason none of them had managed to injure me seriously. If I didn't get to the other side soon, one of the shades was likely to score a serious wound.

My right shoulder erupted in agony. If I screamed, I couldn't hear myself. Another blast of pain, this time in my left thigh. Something laughed.

At this rate, I wasn't going to make it to the other side; the shades would carve me up in transit and I'd come out looking like a broken doll.

Just as I thought that, there were no more shades—only darkness. I barely had a chance to feel relieved before the mirror spat me out on the other side.

CHAPTER 9

I LANDED FACE DOWN ON A COLD, DIRT-COVERED STONE FLOOR. THE PAIN OF the impact registered only in a distant way.

I was bloody, bruised, and too disoriented to process more than three basic facts: I was alive, I still had my backpack and arm cuffs, and I was terribly sick.

I hadn't eaten before the trip for just this reason, but my stomach decided to rid itself violently of every last bit of contents anyway. When that misery was over, I wiped my mouth with my sleeve and crawled away.

To get my bearings, I leaned against a stone wall and waited for the nausea and dizziness to subside. After my eyes adjusted to the near-darkness, it took several seconds for my surroundings to make sense.

"Oh, shit," I breathed.

When traveling by mirror to another world without a corresponding mirror on the other end, a traveler emerged at their destination in the same place as the mirror they used. That meant I'd come out in the Broken World in what should have been their version of sub-level one of the headquarters of the Vampire Court of the Western United States.

And maybe it *had* been, fifty or a hundred years ago. Instead of walls and a ceiling carved with spellwork, I saw collapsed stone, no ceiling at all, and far above, a starry night sky in place of the manor's famous soaring rotunda. I'd landed not in an elegant mansion, but in the basement of an abandoned building.

In this world, Northbourne was a crumbling ruin. If I hadn't been so sick and hurting, I would have smiled.

The building wasn't the only immediately noticeable difference between this world and my own. Waves of natural magic rose and fell around me like swells in the ocean. I recognized earth and air magic, but to my surprise, they felt distinctly unlike my own. The little amount of water magic I had because of my connection to Malcolm told me the water magic here was different too.

The magic here wasn't just different; it was far more powerful, as if I were standing right on top of or conducting power from a ley line. That matched what Adam had told me, but hearing magic was more potent and experiencing it were two very different things.

I suddenly worried whether I would be able to use my magic here. As an experiment, I raised my hand and tried to create cold fire on my fingers with earth magic. Instead of the small green flames I expected, cold fire shot out with tremendous force, as if my fingertips were flamethrowers. If anything had been within fifteen feet of me at that moment, I would have incinerated it.

"Shit!" I tried to extinguish the fire. "Shit, shit, shit," I chanted as I struggled to rein in my own magic—something I hadn't had trouble doing since the age of five.

When the fire finally vanished, I took off my backpack and got to my feet. I ached like I'd fallen down the side of a mountain and hit every rock on the way to the bottom. Most of my injuries were minor except for the slashes on my shoulder and left thigh.

Now that I had my feet under me—both literally and metaphorically—I reached for the magic in the buzzing crystal in my arm cuff. "*Release.*"

Malcolm appeared. "Hey, Alice. Told you we'd make it. Jeez, you look like ten miles of bad road."

When I didn't respond, he frowned. "Why are you staring at me? Do I have something in my teeth?" He looked down at himself. His eyes widened. "Holy crap!"

I swallowed. "Yeah—holy crap." I poked him with my index finger. Normally, my hand went through him, and he felt like thick fog. Instead, my fingertip hit something solid. "You feel almost real."

He rolled his eyes. "I *am* real, Alice."

"You know what I mean. How do you feel?"

He started to float toward me, then paused. Carefully, he took a step forward, and then another. "Like I'm real," he said in disbelief. "Alice, I'm *real* here!"

I didn't point out that he'd just mocked me for saying the same thing not ten seconds ago. "You're almost solid and the magic here is completely different. So far, this is more like the Weird World than the Broken World."

Malcolm looked up from marveling at his own hands and gestured at our surroundings. "I dunno—Northbourne looks pretty broken to me. What do you think happened?"

"I have no idea, but this place has been abandoned for a long time. You good?"

"Better than good. Better than *you*. Looks like something tried to shred you."

"As I predicted, it was a bumpy ride." I unzipped my backpack, rummaged around, and took out a black velvet bag and a rolled-up cloth. "Time for a tracking spell. Let's see where Mariela and that scroll are. Hopefully they're relatively close by and not somewhere in Europe. Keep an eye out, will you?"

"It's pretty quiet. What am I watching for?"

"I don't know. Anything weird, I guess."

I unrolled the cloth and spread it out on the stone floor. To save time, I'd drawn the spellwork for the tracking spell on the cloth before I left. The cloth smelled like my home—and like Sean, who'd helped me cut the fabric and rolled it up for me when the spellwork was complete.

He'd hung out with me in the basement all afternoon, sitting on my work table while I decided what to bring, what to leave behind, and what I needed to prep ahead of the journey. We'd talked about a lot of things, most of them inconsequential, like movies we wanted to watch when I got back and painting a few rooms in the new house before moving in. Making plans for the future helped us both avoid thinking about the possibility I wouldn't make it back.

I reached inside my jacket and wrapped my fist around my wolf amulet. I breathed in the parchment scent of Carly's magic and smiled at the warm golden magic of Sean's shifter trace. The sensations were bittersweet.

Sean would have sensed the moment I went through the mirror. I pictured him at home, sitting in the living room with a glass of whisky, or maybe lying in bed, when our connection vanished and he knew I was gone. It must have felt like a punch right in the gut, even though he'd known it was coming. My own stomach contracted thinking about the pain it would have caused him.

I should have told him where we were going, Valas and the entire Vampire Court be damned.

I tucked the amulet back under my shirt so it nestled reassuringly between my breasts and got back to work. From the velvet bag, I took a piece of obsidian and placed it in the center of the spellwork on the cloth.

"That's the darkest magic I've ever sensed that wasn't straight-up black magic," Malcolm said, eyeing the stone. "The trace is strong. The stone must have been soaking up the scroll's magic for a long time. Good thinking on Valas's part to keep a stone with the scroll so if it ever went missing, we had some of its magic for a tracking spell."

"Yeah, yay for Valas." My voice was bitter. "She thinks of everything, all right."

Malcolm crouched beside me. His new almost-human physical presence was going to take some getting used to. "Is there anything you need to tell me?"

Best to just say it and get it over with. "As I was stepping through the mirror, Valas told me if we don't bring the scroll back, we aren't coming back at all. The mirror will be locked to us without it."

He stared at me, aghast. "That wasn't the deal you made!"

"No, it wasn't, which was why she waited until I couldn't turn back to tell me." I took off my jacket, wincing at the sizzle of pain in my injured shoulder. "We're stuck here until we get that scroll from Mariela."

"What are you going to do about it?"

"I don't know yet."

He whistled low. "When Sean finds out, he'll kill her."

"He might not get a chance." I removed my shirt and used a couple of wet wipes to clean off the travel spellwork. I started to burn the wipes, then remembered the accidental flamethrower and thought better of it. Instead, I put them in a plastic bag and stuffed it into the backpack. "First things first: we have to find Mariela and the scroll."

"How are you so calm?" Malcolm demanded. "Valas tricked us. If we don't find the scroll, we're trapped here forever."

"I have to be calm, Malcolm." My vision went red around the edges. Dark magic swirled between us. "If I let my anger get the better of me, I think the results would be very bad."

He put his hand on my arm. I'd never felt his touch before, not like this. We'd been friends—siblings, almost—for months, and this was the first time we'd made real physical contact.

I was angry at Valas. So very, very angry. Burn-down-the-world angry. But when Malcolm touched my arm, my anger morphed into something that might be useful—something I could control.

Malcolm appeared shaken. "Wow, I didn't realize how much I'd missed human contact until this moment." He squeezed my arm. "Hi. You feel really warm." He gave me an almost-boyish grin that made my heart ache.

I pictured him as a young man, long before Darius Bell's cabal got its hooks in him, when he was a chemistry major looking forward to a career as a researcher. Before he'd been tortured to death by a blood mage and ended up as a ghost because Bell had wanted him bound to a powerful mage, and before angels had decided I needed a companion and protector. He hadn't had much control over any aspect of his life—or death—for a very long time. I knew from personal experience exactly how much that sucked. And he hadn't been able to touch anyone for comfort.

Before I knew what I was doing, I hugged him. He was cold, but I didn't care.

He hugged me back. When we let go, his smile was a little crooked. "I warned you last night not to get sappy on me," he reminded me. "All this lovey-dovey huggy stuff...I kinda miss the angry, rude Alice I used to know."

I surreptitiously wiped my eyes and sat cross-legged in the center of the tracking spell with the obsidian rock in front of me. "Really?"

"You're all soft and squishy now. Hard to believe you're the same person who threatened to have me exorcised."

"Yeah, well, call me *squishy* again and see what happens." I closed my eyes and took several deep breaths, inhaling through my nose and exhaling through my mouth.

When my mind was clear, I picked up the stone and drew on the trace of the scroll's magic it contained. The tracking spell on the cloth shimmered on the edge of my senses, waiting to be unleashed.

I inhaled, exhaled, and grabbed the tracking spell with my mind. "*Adinvenire.*"

Magic flared. The spell should have shown me a vision of where the scroll was. Instead, a blast of power sent me flying as the tracking spell splintered. One moment I was sitting in the middle of the cloth

I'd brought, and the next I was crumpled against the wall on the far side of the room, with my ears ringing and nose filled with the smell of smoke and dark magic. My chest hurt like I'd been kicked by a mule.

For a moment, I thought Valas had somehow booby-trapped the magic in the stone, though that didn't make a hell of a lot of sense if she needed that scroll found. What *did* make sense was my magic, or even the spellwork I knew, wasn't going to work here in the Broken World—at least, not like it did back home. The tracking spell had failed and released its energy the only way it could. I was lucky I hadn't been knocked out—or worse.

"Alice!" Malcolm shook my shoulder. I'd already forgotten he could do that now. "Wake up! Your wolf's out!"

My eyes snapped open.

My wolf stood about ten feet away, in what I was starting to think of as her furry, real-wolf form. She must have jumped out of me when the spellwork fractured. Like Malcolm, she looked pretty damn solid. No wonder my chest hurt.

She sniffed the ground and air, then bared her teeth and growled.

"I know it smells weird." I sat up with a groan. Everything that didn't already hurt from the journey now ached from hitting the wall. "You can't be running around on your own here. We're strangers in a strange land. You need to go back where you were."

She growled again and resumed sniffing her way around the room. Blast it—the last thing I needed right now was a stubborn wolf refusing to return to my body.

Malcolm watched both of us nervously as I staggered to my feet and leaned against the wall. Nothing was broken, I decided after checking my arms and legs, but I would be completely black-and-blue by morning. I missed Sean's soaker tub so much in that moment I almost cried.

The cloth with the tracking spell was gone, blown to smithereens by the blast, which had also scoured the stone floor clean of all dirt and debris. The obsidian stone had probably met the same fate, or was permanently lost in the ruins around us.

I rubbed my face. "Son of a bitch. Without the stone, and without a tracking spell, how are we supposed to find the scroll? Mariela's got a massive head start on us. She could be anywhere."

"We'll have to study the magic here and develop a new tracking spell, or find one we can use. You've still got the bag the stone was in. It'll have some trace—for a while, at least." Malcolm frowned. "Hey, what's she doing?"

My wolf disappeared into the shadows on the far side of the room.

"Hey! Come back!" I dug a small flashlight out of my backpack and hurried after her, muttering curses at the pain in my left knee. "Damn it, I'm going to have to put her on a leash."

Malcolm snorted. "Good luck with that."

From somewhere in the darkness, my wolf snarled, seemingly in agreement.

I pushed the button on the flashlight, but nothing happened. Apparently mirror travel drained batteries too. I tucked the dead flashlight in my back pocket.

Two golden eyes appeared in the darkness. "Seriously, you can't just run off like this," I told my wolf as she emerged. "This place is weird and dangerous."

My wolf eyed me, as if to say, *Yes, but I'm weird and dangerous too.* She opened her mouth and dropped a small obsidian rock at my feet.

Malcolm blinked. "Wow—she fetches? Um, good wolf," he added.

My wolf showed her teeth.

I picked up the stone. Enough of the magic trace from the scroll remained that we could try another spell, if we found one that would work here. "Thank you," I said.

My wolf turned and headed for a pile of collapsed stone. She climbed the rocks, picking her way carefully up toward ground level.

"Hey, wait," I protested.

She ignored me.

"Damn it." I stuck the obsidian in my front pocket and hurried to put on my shirt and jacket.

While Malcolm floated up ahead to make sure nothing waited for us topside, I took a moment to settle the backpack on my shoulders and check on the portal I'd emerged from into the Broken World.

Our return gate was a distinctly familiar sensation on my skin —an echo of my own magic and the magic of home. The portal was only visible in my Second Sight, and only from an angle. I thought it unlikely anyone would find it, even if they were looking. Judging by the state of the building, I doubted people came here. Maybe Vamp HQ was simply in a different location—or maybe there was no Vampire Court in this world. Adam had said there were vampires, but we knew nothing of how they were organized, if at all.

As an experiment, I tried to push against the shimmery magic, but it snapped at my fingers with an angry crackle. I yanked my hands away. "Son of a bitch," I hissed. "She locked it, all right." Not that I'd thought Valas was bluffing about not allowing us to return without the scroll, but the grim reality of our situation was sinking in. It was not a good feeling.

Nothing else to do but start our search for Mariela. I buckled the straps of my backpack across my chest and climbed up out of the basement, following the same path my wolf had used along the fallen stones that had once been part of the manor. Whether on purpose or accident, she seemed to have found the path that would be easiest for me to climb, even with a sore knee and wounds to my shoulder and leg.

At ground level, I stopped to take in the sight of the ruins of Northbourne from the center of what remained of the lobby. So much of it was familiar, from the marble floor to the sweeping grand staircase and the second-floor gallery, but all were crumbling and overgrown. Chunks of the rotunda had landed in the lobby and smashed through the floor, demolishing the rooms below.

Malcolm's voice startled me. "This is eerie. I don't even have skin, but I've got goosebumps."

I rubbed my own prickly flesh. "Yeah." I spotted my wolf heading into the woods through a wide opening where the massive double doors had once been. "Wait for us!"

I picked my way carefully across the ruined lobby, worried what was left of the floor would give way under my feet. We emerged from the building to find ourselves looking not at Northbourne's sweeping circular drive and beautiful grounds, but thick, dense forest. What remained of the driveway was barely visible in the undergrowth.

"Don't say we're not in Kansas anymore," I told Malcolm as we surveyed our surroundings.

"Okay, I won't, but we are totally *not* in Kansas anymore." Malcolm shook his head. "This is trippy."

My wolf had already made it down the crumbling front steps and headed into the forest. "Where are you going?" I asked her, hurrying to catch up.

She turned and growled impatiently, as if the answer should have been obvious.

When I reached her, she nudged my hip twice with her nose, then turned and faced the woods.

I touched my hip where she'd bumped me and found the obsidian stone in my pocket. "Holy moly," I breathed. "She's tracking the scroll using the magic in the stone."

I dug the obsidian from my pocket and held it out. My wolf nudged my hand hard and headed into the trees.

"What do we do?" Malcolm asked as we followed her. "I don't know much about this world, but I doubt we can just run around with a wolf like she's your pet. Things are crazy here, but surely they're not *that* crazy."

"I don't know what to do except follow her for now." I pushed a branch out of the way. "We'll just have to deal with whatever problems we run into when we run into them. One thing I *do* know is I have no idea if I can force her to return to my body if she refuses, or what she'll do if I try."

"So, to recap: our magic doesn't work right, our spells don't work at all, and your wolf can track the scroll but she's committed to doing her own thing," Malcolm said, his voice drier than the Sahara. "We're off to a great start in the Broken World."

"Pretty much."

Magic surged. Ahead of us, my wolf froze in her tracks, raised her head, and howled.

Malcolm jerked and turned toward me. "Oh, shit, Alice—"

Power erupted from the earth like a volcano, and everything around us disappeared in a blaze of magic.

CHAPTER 10

I'D EXPERIENCED MAGIC FLARES BEFORE, BUT ONLY ON A SMALL SCALE AND certainly never anything this intense.

The force of it ignited every cell in my body. All of my magic responded to the flare. Despite my efforts to rein it in, it erupted through my skin and formed a hurricane around me—one that grew larger and more powerful as the flare continued.

A blast of water and earth magic indicated Malcolm was similarly affected. I could see nothing beyond the vortex of my own magic, amplified many times by the flare.

Something appeared in the storm: my wolf, made of pure golden shifter magic so bright it hurt my eyes. I thought she intended to return to my body, but instead she pushed her head under my hand, lending her strength to my fight to rein in my magic.

Slowly, I gained control over the vortex as the flare began to subside. I drew my magic back into my body, letting it fill me with new and unfamiliar power derived from the energies of the Broken World. The sensation was similar to when I'd absorbed the sorcerer Miraç's power, but this magic was pure and natural, not dark and poisonous.

The flare finally ended. I sagged against the charred side of one of the trees I'd inadvertently damaged with my cold fire. "I'm sorry," I told the trees.

My wolf, back in her furry form, shook herself briskly and curled her lip. I had no idea what that meant—maybe that I didn't need to apologize to trees.

Malcolm glowed with the power he'd absorbed from the flare. "You okay?" I asked.

He squinted. "Your aura is like a radioactive rainbow."

"You are a poet." I sighed and pushed away from the tree. "So, add massive magic flares to the list of things that are weird about this place."

"Hopefully those aren't frequent."

We set off again, following my wolf through the overgrown grounds of the estate. Rather than stick to the remains of the winding driveway, the wolf made a beeline toward what I believed was the main road that ran past Northbourne's main gate. Once we emerged from the woods, I had no idea what we'd find, or how I'd deal with having a wolf as a guide. Maybe I could talk her into returning to my body and guiding us from there.

"Carly said we'd have a guide and protector," I said.

Malcolm chuckled. "I'll be damned. Do you think she meant your wolf?"

"I don't know. If she meant the wolf, wouldn't she have said so?" I sighed. "Or maybe she didn't get the details, just the idea. In any case, it sure looks like my wolf wants to fill that role."

"Looks that way," he agreed. "Like you said, I'm not sure we have much of a choice but to follow."

We walked the quarter mile from the manor to the edge of the property. In our world, Northbourne's grounds were surrounded by a high wall and protected by a massive rolling gate. Here, only hints remained of a wall, and no gate. The road was there, though—a wide, two-lane country road. No vehicles were in sight. Not surprising in the middle of the night.

Without hesitation, my wolf turned left and trotted in the grass along the road, heading south toward the city.

"How do you suppose she's tracking the magic in the scroll?" Malcom asked as we followed. I plodded on the shoulder while he walked on the grass beside me.

"No idea. Not even a theory right now." Damn it, my knee ached. I ignored it and increased my pace.

"Is she making a beeline for the scroll, or are we following the same path Mariela took when she arrived here?"

"I don't see how we're following Mariela's trail so long after the fact, but we're walking along a road and not cutting through that field." I rubbed the bridge of my nose, which was just about the only part of my body that *didn't* hurt. "That makes it seem like—"

I stopped in my tracks. Ahead, my wolf growled at something in the trees to our left.

A large, dark shape moved in the undergrowth. Twigs snapped. Something growled back at my wolf.

"Alice," Malcolm hissed. "What the hell is that? Is that a bear?"

The creature lumbered from the trees. I slowly unzipped a side pouch on my backpack, took out my Smith & Wesson, and chambered a round.

The thing turned toward the sound and stood upright, its long, striped tail curled around its legs. Its eyes were bright red.

"That is *not* a bear," Malcolm said.

"Thank you, Captain Obvious." I raised my gun.

"You sure we should shoot the giant demonic trash panda?" Malcolm asked. "That might just make it mad."

The raccoon-thing growled at us. "Don't call it a trash panda," I muttered. "I think you hurt its feelings."

The creature went back down on all fours and lumbered in our direction. I took aim between its red eyes.

Something else rustled in the undergrowth to our left—several somethings, judging by the sound. Multiple pairs of eyes glinted in the moonlight. More raccoon-things, or some other Broken World creatures?

My wolf tripled in size, her golden magic swirling around her body. She snarled and raced toward the raccoon-thing, her teeth bared. It hissed, turned, and disappeared into the trees, crashing through the undergrowth.

My wolf stopped at the tree line, raised her head, and howled. The sound was almost deafening and must have traveled for miles.

Dead silence. Not even a peep or a rustle from the forest.

Malcolm cleared his throat. "I think she just established this as her territory."

"So much for keeping a low profile." I stuck my gun in the side pocket of my backpack where I could get at it quickly, readjusted the pack, and started walking again.

My wolf trotted ahead of us, staying close to the tree line—presumably in case something decided to try its luck and attack us. Nothing else did, however. That howl had apparently sent the creatures of the forest scurrying away.

We'd walked for about ten minutes when I heard a large engine approaching. It sounded like a heavy truck. My wolf slipped into the trees to stay out of sight. Not a bad idea, since I didn't know who that truck might belong to. We joined her just inside the tree line and hid.

Headlights appeared over the top of a hill ahead of us. A military-style vehicle with dark paint and a large gun mounted on the back passed our hiding place moving fast. As it went by, I spotted an unfamiliar but unmistakably military seal on the side: a circle with a Latin motto, a vicious bird-of-prey figure, and a scale of justice. Two people in dark uniforms rode in front: a woman, who was driving, and a man in the passenger seat.

When the vehicle was gone, we emerged from the trees. "I wonder who they were," Malcolm said.

"Some branch of the military they have here that we don't have." I hooked my thumbs in the straps of my pack and started walking again.

Malcolm floated along beside me. "Wonder if they're the good guys or the bad guys."

"That's the million-dollar question. I suggest we stay away from them, regardless. Any contact with law enforcement, military, or even nosy civilians could bring a quick end to what we're here to do. We need to be invisible and not attract any attention."

Malcolm looked pointedly ahead at my enormous wolf. As if sensing his stare, she turned her head to show us her golden eyes and sharp teeth, then returned her attention to following the trail of the scroll.

"Invisible," Malcolm said dryly. "Yeah. Sure. No problem."

CHAPTER 11

We walked for the rest of the night.

My wolf eventually returned to her normal size, though she kept a wary eye on our surroundings. Few vehicles passed us. We hid in the trees or wherever else we could find cover to stay unseen. Daylight would make hiding far more difficult. There would be more traffic, and the closer we got to the city, the less cover we'd have. At that point, I'd have to have a serious talk with her and try to get her to return to my body—or force her to return, if that was even possible.

Not long after sunrise, my energy flagged after walking ten or twelve miles. My wolf trotted along at the same brisk pace. Malcolm strolled beside me with annoying ease. I trudged up a steep hill, breathing hard and cursing under my breath at the pain in my wounded shoulder and leg and sore knee. I'd already taken off my leather jacket and stuffed it in my backpack, but I was sweating.

Malcolm frowned. "Doesn't it seem like there's way less traffic than you'd expect?"

"I was thinking the same thing." I grimaced and adjusted my heavy pack. "All we've seen is a couple of big trucks and jeeps and that one military vehicle. Not that I remember this road ever being super busy, since there's not much out here but Northbourne and other big estates, but it's past dawn on a weekday morning and it's eerily quiet."

"I'm going to start calling this place the Eerie World. Seems less broken than just freaky. It's almost..." He paused, searching for the right word.

"Post-apocalyptic?" I suggested. "Since the boundaries between realms fractured, it kinda *is* post-apocalyptic, minus the marauders in metal spike-covered trucks and dune buggies fighting over water and gasoline."

"I don't like the quiet. Quiet makes me nervous."

"Well, what *would* you like? Because I *definitely* don't want—"

A huge winged creature the color of coal blasted into view from the other side of the hill. Stupefied, I stopped in my tracks and stared as it swooped over us. The downdraft of air from its wings nearly knocked me over.

"Holy shit, it's a dragon!" Malcolm yelled. "Alice, it's a—"

"I see it!" I ran for the trees, where my wolf had already disappeared.

A large military jeep with its windows down flew over the hill in pursuit of the dragon, moving so fast all four wheels left the ground. The dark-haired woman in the driver's seat whooped as the vehicle's tires hit the asphalt.

Just short of the tree line, I tripped and went sprawling, hitting my chin on a rock. Ow. I scrambled the last ten feet into the trees, dragging my pack behind me.

Meanwhile, the jeep screeched to a halt in the middle of the road. The dragon wheeled around and spewed a stream of fire directly at the vehicle. I ducked for cover behind the large trunk of a fallen tree.

As the fire swept over her vehicle, the soldier activated some kind of sonic weapon. The shockwave made my ears and jaw ache.

Stunned, the dragon hovered in mid-air, seemingly too disoriented to either attack or flee.

BOOM! The small cannon mounted on top of the jeep fired at the dragon and hit it dead-on. Dark blood and liquid fire poured from a large wound in its throat.

The dragon's high-pitched screech was so piercing I thought my eardrums might burst. I clapped my hands over my ears but that did little to muffle the cry. Desperate to escape the painful sound, I crammed myself as far under the tree trunk as I could and wrapped my arms around my head.

Finally, the dragon's scream faded as it flew away, its enormous wings flapping like boat sails.

Malcolm shook my shoulder. "You all right?"

I raised my head. "Is it gone?"

"Yeah, it's gone."

I sat up and leaned against the tree, wiping my face with my dirty sleeve. Now, on top of all my other aches and pains, my ears hurt too.

Malcolm flitted. "Holy crap, Alice—a real live dragon! Liam is never going to believe it."

Tires crunched in the gravel of the shoulder as the jeep pulled into the grass near the tree line. A heavy door slammed and footsteps approached.

"Hey, you okay in there?" a woman called. "It's safe to come out. Dragon's gone."

She'd obviously seen me, so there was no point trying to hide. That would just make her more curious.

"Damn it," I muttered and got to my feet. "Stay here," I told Malcolm in an undertone. "I'll show her I'm fine and hopefully she'll just leave."

"If she gives you trouble, I'll hit her with a sleep spell and we can skedaddle," Malcolm said.

"No you won't," the woman said, her voice amused. She put her hands on her hips. "Come out, both of you, and let's talk."

Malcolm's mouth fell open.

"We're coming out," I called. Backpack in hand, I made my way out of the trees. Malcolm followed. I didn't look around for my wolf, but she was probably nearby, hiding and watching.

The young female soldier wore a black T-shirt and BDU pants with boots, her long black hair in a ponytail. Her only visible weapon was a handgun in a thigh holster. I saw no insignias that might explain which branch of the military she represented or what her name was.

Her sharp green-eyed gaze raked me from head to foot as I emerged from the trees. "You look like hell." She unzipped one of the pockets in her pants and took out a little first-aid packet. She tossed it to me. "You busted your chin when you fell."

"Thanks." I set my pack on the ground and tore open the packet. As I wiped my bloody chin with an antiseptic wipe, I glanced up. Sure enough, no sign of the dragon.

She followed my gaze. "Yep, she's going to be out of commission for a while. Should be a lot safer around here for at least a month or two. I got her good." She grinned. "I'm two for two this year, both of them on my own. Personal record."

"That's impressive." I stuffed the soiled wipe in my pocket and pressed a folded-up piece of gauze to my chin. "That dragon was huge."

"Pretty average for the ones they get around here." She glanced behind me. "Hi, I'm Lucy, by the way."

"Um, I'm Malcolm," he said, floating back and forth in consternation. "You can hear me?"

"And see you," Lucy confirmed. "I like the glasses. Not really necessary for a ghost, but they suit you."

"Are you a medium?" he asked.

She shook her head. "My mother's side of the family has...gifts, you could say."

"You feel different." Malcolm floated closer. "Sorry to be nosy, but why do you feel a little like a ghost yourself?"

Her mouth twisted in a wry smile. "I'm a little bit dead, Malcolm —everyone in my mom's family is. And the ones who are dead are still a little bit alive. Our family has always been weird that way." She turned to me. "And you are?"

"Alice."

She waited, but I didn't supply a last name. "How's your chin, Alice?" she asked finally.

I checked the gauze, folded it a different way so I found a clean side, and put it back to my chin. "I'll live. So, is this something you do often? Go after dragons by yourself?"

Lucy smiled. "It's against regulations, technically, but doing things that are against regulations is pretty much my greatest pleasure in life." She paused. "Well, my *second* greatest pleasure, anyway. The League goes where we're needed, you know."

"Of course," I said, as if I knew who or what she was referring to.

"Those wounds on your shoulder and leg look serious. How'd you get them?"

"I fell down some stairs."

The corners of her mouth turned up. She didn't believe me, but she didn't call me on it. "Do you need a doctor or a healer?"

"No, I'll be fine. We need to get going. Thanks again for the first-aid kit." I stuck the gauze in my pocket.

"Where are you headed?"

I nodded at the hill in front of us. "To the city."

"I'm not really supposed to give rides to civilians, but like I said, I live for breaking the rules, and this is a dangerous stretch of road. I'm headed south myself on another job. Want a lift as far as a road-house? You can probably find another ride there to wherever you're headed."

I wondered if the term "roadhouse" had a different meaning here, or if roadside dives were like Broken World truck stops or trans-portation hubs.

"All right," I said, though part of me worried it would be a mistake to get in a vehicle with someone from the military, regard-less of how pleasant she seemed.

Malcolm shot me a startled look. I was a little surprised myself, but she seemed nonthreatening and truly concerned for our safety.

I had to get my wolf to return to my body, however, since I doubted Lucy would let her anywhere near us. "Um, I need to take care of something before we leave." I gave her a sheepish look and nodded at the woods. "Sorry. Can I just take a minute to pee?"

She glanced over my shoulder. "Do you need to pee, or do you need to talk to your friend?"

I turned. My wolf stood just inside the tree line, her golden eyes fixed on Lucy. Double shit.

"She's not a wolf," Malcolm said quickly. "She's, uh, only part wolf. She's Alice's pet dog. Her name is...Daisy."

"Daisy" showed Malcolm her teeth.

"Mm-hmm," Lucy said. Oddly, her right hand was behind her head, as if she was reaching for something on her back, but there was nothing there. Maybe it was an old habit. She moved her hand to her sidearm. "Is Daisy going to stay in wolf form, or does she want to obey the law and shift to her human form and talk to me?"

Triple shit.

"Daisy doesn't shift," I said. "She isn't a shifter at all—just a wolf with a little bit of magic. I don't know how we can prove that to you, but please don't shoot my wolf." I wasn't sure if Lucy *could* shoot my wolf, but I didn't know what kind of bullets she had in that gun. I couldn't be sure my wolf wouldn't try to kill her if she fired the weapon.

Lucy studied my wolf. "I've never met a magic wolf that wasn't a shifter." She tilted her head. "I have a League collar in the jeep. If your wolf will wear it, it will make me feel better. If we run into any other Guardians or local LEOs, it will keep them from asking too many questions."

"What does the collar do?"

"Its main purpose is to keep her from shifting. It also identifies her as a League asset, which is why no one will hassle us about her. Once you're on your own, you'll have to figure something else out."

"Sounds reasonable." I hoped my wolf would allow us to put the collar on. "Daisy," I called.

She trotted to me immediately, showing no fear of Lucy. And what did she have to fear? I reflected grimly. She could grow to twenty feet tall and damn near tear the head off a demon lord. A lone Guardian—whatever the hell that meant—probably wasn't anything she needed to worry about.

We went to the jeep. Lucy rummaged around in the back seat and came up with a leather collar emblazoned with the same seal that was on the sides of the vehicle, along with the words LEAGUE ASSET and a serial number. A small amulet hung from the collar.

"What does the amulet do?" I asked.

"That's what keeps her from shifting."

Lucy clearly didn't believe my wolf wasn't a shifter. I couldn't say I blamed her for her skepticism.

She handed me the collar. "I'll let you put it on her. If she won't wear it, you'll have to keep walking."

I held the collar out so my wolf could sniff it. "Can I put this on you?"

She investigated the collar and the amulet thoroughly with her nose, flashed a few teeth at us, and then stood still for me to fasten it around her neck. When I clicked the buckle, the amulet flared. Without hesitation, the wolf jumped into the back seat of the jeep and settled in.

"Huh," Lucy said, pausing with her hand on the back passenger door. "Wounded a dragon and met a magical wolf named Daisy who seems to be more intelligent than the average wolf. Hell of a day, and it's not even nine o'clock." She shut the door. "Want some coffee?"

I almost sagged against the vehicle. "I would kill for some. Not literally." I paused. "Maybe literally."

"Same. Get in." Lucy held open the passenger door while I climbed in and put my backpack on the floor at my feet. The interior of the jeep was very utilitarian, as I'd expected from a military vehicle—except for the cartoonish vampire bobble-head stuck to the dashboard.

Lucy shut my door and went around to the driver's side. Malcolm floated into the back seat with Lucy's gear and my wolf.

When Lucy climbed into the driver's seat, I gestured at the bobble-head. "That's cute."

"Thanks." She hit the gas, sending gravel spraying out behind us. She made a fast U-turn on two wheels and headed south toward the city. "It was a gift from my sister Callie. She thinks she's funny." She sighed. "You got any brothers or sisters?"

I didn't turn around to look at Malcolm. "Just a brother."

"Well, if he ever wants to become a vampire, try to talk him out of it."

I coughed. "I don't think he'll ever want to be a vampire, or could even become one."

"That's good. One less thing for you to have to worry about." She was flying down the road now, the speedometer well over eighty and creeping toward ninety. "Vampires are weird—even the unbound. Not as weird as the Euro-vamps or Court vamps, of course, but still. Callie joined some commune in Denver, says she's happy and she'll meet up with me next time I'm in the area. My mom's going to hit the roof when she finds out. The Colorado communes are notorious." She sighed again. "Still, as long as she's happy, I guess it's okay. Sisters...what are you gonna do?" She flicked the bobblehead and watched it jiggle merrily.

Malcolm touched my shoulder. *Vampires living in communes?* His voice in my head sounded incredulous. *And what the hell does she mean by unbound vamps?*

And what the hell is the League? I added. *And Guardians? And why are there friggin' dragons?*

This place is weird, he complained.

At least they have coffee.

He snorted and floated back.

Lucy glanced in the rearview mirror. "You okay, Malcolm?"

"Doing fine." His voice was dry. "It's just been a long day."

"I bet. Sounds like you guys have traveled a long way." She stuck her arm out the window and smiled at the sensation of the wind. "We'll grab some coffee in town and then head for the roadhouse that's west of the city. I have an informant meeting me there. You can see about finding a ride to wherever you're headed."

I turned to look at the wolf to see if the delay upset her. To my surprise, she was lying with her head on her paws, eyes half-closed. Apparently we were still on Mariela's trail heading in this direction. When I turned back, my shoulder twinged. I flinched.

"You want another first-aid kit to take care of your shoulder and leg?" Lucy asked. "I've got more in the box under your seat."

"Thanks. Might as well." I felt around under the seat until I found the plastic box.

As I sorted through its contents, the radio in the jeep beeped. "Station Ten to Guardian Four-Oh-One," a brisk male voice said. "Come in, Four-oh-one."

Lucy sighed and picked up the radio. "This is Four-oh-one."

"What the hell, Stone?" the man demanded. "I told you to wait for the backup team and you went in alone, against orders. *Again*."

"There was no time to wait for the other team," she countered. "Civilians were in immediate danger." She winked at me.

"Any injuries to civilians?" he barked.

"None to me *or* them, and thanks for asking about me. The only injury was to the fire-breather. She won't be back for a while. I scored a throat wound. She'll have to return to her nest to recover."

A long pause.

"Damn it, Stone," the man said, sounding suddenly weary. "One of these days, your luck is going to run out."

Lucy didn't reply. Something dark flashed in her eyes—pain and grief. His comment about luck had hit close to home.

When she didn't say anything, the man said, "Fine, file your report by tonight. You still tracking those attacks?"

"Yes, Captain. I'm meeting with some sources here locally, and then I'll let you know where I'm going from there once I get some leads." Her tone had changed: less flippant and more military. "Any word on how my partner's doing?"

"He reported in ten minutes ago. Unlike *some people*, he reports in regularly without having to be hounded."

Lucy snorted.

"They're going to be on that basilisk nest for at least a couple more days," the captain continued. "You want me to send someone out to ride shotgun with you?"

"Not right now, sir. I'll let you know if I need backup. You'll have my report on the dragon incident and the civilian involvement by midnight."

"Copy that. Stay safe, Lieutenant."

"You too, Captain. Four-oh-one out." She returned the radio to its hook on the dash and put both hands on the wheel, staring straight ahead.

I glanced up from taping some gauze to the wound on my shoulder. "So, other than chasing the dragon—so to speak—what brings you to town?"

"I was actually in the area chasing something else when I got the dispatch about the dragon."

"The attacks the captain referred to? What attacks?"

She glanced at me. "So, you're not from around here?"

I shook my head. "What should we be watching out for?"

"Not sure, exactly," she said, and she didn't sound very happy about it. "We've gotten some strange reports for the last month or so, all centered around an area south of the city. There have been some casualties and property destruction. No one's gotten a good look at who or what's responsible—no one who's survived, anyway. All I'm hearing is rumors, and the rumors don't make any sense."

"What are the rumors?"

She tapped her fingers on the wheel. "It's no secret, I suppose. You'll hear about it at the roadhouse if you ask. People claim to have spotted creatures no one has seen topside for a very long time. I'd think folks had just gotten some bad weed, but the descriptions are fairly consistent and coming in from all over. If they're right, we could be dealing with a very, very serious situation."

"What do you mean, 'topside'?"

Another long pause. "As opposed to the Underworld," she said. "Nothing's come up out of there anywhere near here in a very long time—that's usually a European or far East problem, as you know. If there are Underworld critters running around up here, and shades loose topside, either we've got a new fractured boundary somewhere or someone's left a door open."

My stomach sank. Mariela had come here intending to travel to the Underworld. I didn't believe in coincidences. What if she'd succeeded in opening a doorway, and then accidentally left it open?

"Jeez, that sounds terrible and really scary," Malcolm said from the back seat. "Fractured boundaries and open doors to the Underworld. Hopefully it's not that."

"Yeah, hopefully." She turned back to me. "Let's grab some coffee and a snack and head for the roadhouse. We have to take the long way around because one of the local covens has apparently closed their territory again. By the time we get there, it will be about lunchtime and we'll be starving if we don't grab something. My source won't be arriving until around sunset, so we'll have some time to rest if you want. The roadhouse has rooms where we can catch a few Z's. I don't know about you, but I didn't sleep last night and I can't afford not to be sharp."

On the one hand, I itched to go after Mariela, but it sounded like Lucy might have some useful information—like where these creatures were coming from and what they were. Even if my wolf could track the scroll, I didn't like going in blind, especially since my magic didn't work right here, and the spells and amulets I'd brought might not work at all. We needed to know what we were up against.

"Sure," I said. "Coffee, lunch, and a siesta it is."

"That's the spirit." She winked at Malcolm in the rearview mirror. "So to speak."

"Great, someone else who makes ghost jokes," Malcolm muttered. "Just what I needed."

CHAPTER 12

WE WERE INDEED STRANGERS IN A *VERY* STRANGE LAND, AND "NOT IN KANSAS anymore" didn't even *begin* to cover it. The Twilight Zone was a more accurate description.

As we got closer to the city, I propped my head on my hand and stared out the window. With Lucy sitting next to me I had to keep my poker face in place, but it was difficult. We'd gone through the looking glass, quite literally, and this was not our world.

Many things were similar, from the makes of vehicles to businesses, infrastructure, and clothing. Beyond these basic similarities, however, the Broken World was completely different in every way I could think of.

I saw few small cars, even in the city. Most vehicles were heavy trucks, vans, SUVs, or jeeps. I did see a lot of public transportation, all heavily armored and many with weapons like the one mounted on Lucy's vehicle. No skyscrapers downtown, or anywhere else. The tallest buildings were about ten or fifteen stories, and there were only a handful. Instead of a few very tall buildings, there were lots of medium-sized ones—none of which had glass sides or lots of windows. I wondered if that was because of dragons, or a result of other factors. Doorways were taller, probably to accommodate those who were extra tall, and most doors had two sets of hardware: one for very tall persons, the other for the very short.

Pedestrian traffic was heavy in the center of town, and about one in twenty people seemed not-quite human—some far from it. Giants walked alongside dwarves, and neither paid the other much heed. One tall woman scurried across the street in a crosswalk using her hands and feet like a four-legged spider.

When Lucy turned into Mermaid Coffee, I had to bite my tongue to keep from chuckling. Even the logo was similar, down to the familiar green color. The mermaid on the sign looked like a real model instead of a design. *Oh, right—they have real, live mermaids here.* I gulped.

"What do you want?" Lucy asked me, pulling into the drive-through line behind an enormous truck with tires bigger than a standard car.

"I'll have to look at the menu," I said, realizing I had no idea if coffee drinks had the same sizes and names, or what anything cost. Adam's visions had indicated money was the same here, but prices of everyday goods were unknown.

"Definitely get both food and coffee. And you'll need food for Daisy too, I assume?" At my surprised expression, she added, "Or do you want to wait until we get to the roadhouse? It'll be cheaper there, but I'm not sure I want to ride a couple more hours with a hungry wolf."

I turned around to look at Daisy—er, my wolf. She licked her chops and stared at me rather pointedly. "Yes, something for Daisy too," I said, wondering what the hell a coffee shop had to feed a wolf. Then again, a Happy Meal for a wolf or large predator might not be too strange of an order here. I wanted to thump my head against the side of the vehicle.

We inched forward in the drive-through. A large, hairy arm came out of the passenger-side window of the truck in front of us and draped itself over the door. The hand had only three thick fingers, each tipped with a long, pointed claw. Behind me, Malcolm saw it and let out a strangled cough.

"It's such a nice day," Lucy said, propping her elbow on her open window. "So, where are you from?"

"About ten hours north of here." That was vague enough without sounding too evasive, I decided. "I'm between jobs at the moment, so I decided I wanted to see more of California."

"So naturally you set off hitchhiking with a ghost and a magic wolf." Her tone was dry. "No vehicle of your own?"

I shook my head. "Can't afford one. I've been all right hitching rides. Daisy and I ride in the back of trucks just fine, and no one even knows Malcolm's with us."

"And I suppose no one's messed with you, not with Daisy along." The truck pulled forward and Lucy rolled up to the menu and speaker.

A cheerful female voice welcomed us and asked for our order. Lucy ordered our coffee and food, then requested a medium-sized carnivore dinner. In the back seat, my wolf licked her chops again, much more loudly.

The employee gave us our total and said she'd see us at the window.

I reached for my backpack, but Lucy waved her hand. "I've got it. I've barely stopped for food or sleep these last couple of days, so I've got some per diem to burn through today."

"Are you sure? Most of that order was for Daisy."

She grinned. "I've never gotten to feed a magical wolf before. My treat, as long as she doesn't make a mess back there."

My wolf made a chuffing noise that might have been an indignant huff.

At the window, Lucy handed over a card to pay for our order. The smiling young woman working the drive-through had small, pointed teeth and little tips on her ears.

She caught me staring. "I love your earrings," I said, so she didn't think I was rude.

She grinned, flashing that mouthful of pointy teeth. "Thank you," she said. Was she fae? I'd only met two fae before, and they had teeth like that. They didn't have pointy ears, though. Maybe an elf? I felt an almost maniacal giggle bubbling up and squashed it just in time.

Lucy passed me an enormous cup of coffee and a wrapped sandwich and put her own in the cupholders between us. She handed me a heavy parcel and pulled away from the window.

Even through the thick paper wrapping of the package in my lap, I smelled raw meat. The packaging seemed to be designed for an animal to eat from; the bottom was thick, leak-resistant coated cardboard. I figured out how to tear open the top, fold down the sides, and turn it into a food dish full of hunks of raw meat. I'd seen two similar packages handed over to the truck in front us. Were they for animals in the truck, or the truck's driver and three-fingered passenger?

I set the food dish on the floor behind me so it wouldn't fly off the seat if Lucy had to hit the brakes. Daisy stood, stretched, and got down onto the floor to eat.

I hadn't eaten anything but a protein bar since throwing up after the trip through the mirror, but the sound of my wolf eating the raw meat with undisguised gusto made my breakfast sandwich less than appetizing. Her noisy noshing didn't bother Lucy, however, who nearly inhaled her breakfast and guzzled her coffee with enthusiasm while weaving through traffic with one hand on the wheel.

Finally, my grumbly stomach won out. I unwrapped my sandwich and was relieved to find a familiar sight of egg, sausage, and cheese on an English muffin. Broken boundaries or no broken boundaries, apparently humans would develop the same fundamentally satisfying breakfast foods regardless of circumstances. The coffee was better than I'd expected. Judging by the way she licked her dish clean and then settled onto the back seat to wash her muzzle, my wolf had enjoyed her meal as well.

"How far to the roadhouse?" I asked as Lucy drained the last of her coffee.

She checked the GPS directions on a screen on her dashboard. "Well, since we have to go around coven territory, the troll settlement, and the Jupiter Sinkhole, about two hours, assuming we don't get called to any emergencies between here and there. We'll be able to get some good rest this afternoon before things get hopping at the roadhouse, if you don't immediately find a ride out of town when we get there."

I wanted to ask what species the girl at the drive-through was, why a witch coven had a closed territory, and what the hell the Jupiter Sinkhole was. Instead I put our trash in a bag and stuck it under the seat. "I'll have to see how I'm feeling when we get there and what options I find for rides. Can I ask about those attacks you mentioned?"

She raised her eyebrows. "Not sure what else I can tell you. Maybe it's gravelings; maybe it's something else that *wants* us to think this is all due to escaped Underworld creatures."

What the hell was a graveling? "What would want you to think that?" I asked instead.

"Any number of things. Earth spiders, maybe, or Dark Fae, or hey, pick your trickster." Her hands tightened on the wheel. "All I know is, I want to find out who's behind this and deal with them."

"And who are you meeting at the roadhouse?"

"An alleged survivor of an attack." She made a face. "I'm not sure I can believe a damn word he says, but I'll hear him out—as long as I've got my gun pointed at his gut the entire time."

"What's the story there? You know the guy?"

She shook her head. "Shifter." Her ominous tone puzzled me, as if a shifter was something both incredibly dangerous and almost repulsive. Adam had said nothing about the shifters here. Were they different and more dangerous from shifters in our world? That would explain why Lucy was so wary of my wolf.

"Oh," I said, as if her response answered my question. "What kind of shifter?"

"Werewolf. He says the rest of his pack is dead. I don't know how he's alive if they were all wiped out, or how he's going to make it to the roadhouse alone." Her voice hardened. "If my captain knew that's who I'm meeting, he'd be pissed I'm going in without a partner."

"How come your captain lets you get away with so much?" I asked. "Disobeying orders, meeting alone with dangerous people, going after dragons by yourself?"

Her mouth twisted. "I've always subscribed to the theory that it's better to ask forgiveness than permission. Sometimes it bites me in the ass. Most of the time, it works out in my favor."

"I was under the impression the military doesn't like insubordination," Malcolm said.

"I'm sure they don't, but I've never been military. I'm not your typical Guardian either."

So the Guardians weren't military, then. Interesting.

"How so?" I asked.

"I'm not a sanctimonious asshole, and I'm not blindly obedient. Well, I guess a lot of us aren't anymore," she amended. "The ones who are left, that is."

That sounded like there was a hell of a story there. I was about to ask what she meant when the radio beeped again. "Station Ten to Four-oh-one. Come in, Four-oh-one." It was a woman's voice this time, and her tone was urgent.

Lucy had the radio in her hand long before the woman finished speaking, moving faster than I'd expected. Was Lucy not human either? That was an unexpected development—and something I'd have to find out more about. With all the strange ambient magic crackling on my skin, sensing others' magic was much more difficult here.

"This is Four-oh-one," Lucy said. "Dispatch, what's going on?"

"We've got a situation developing and local LEOs are requesting assistance from the League. You're the closest operative in the area not already engaged. Sending location to your GPS now."

The screen on the dashboard lit up with a red dot to the southwest. "Got it," Lucy said briskly. "Rerouting now. What have we got? Another dragon?" She actually sounded hopeful.

"Thankfully not," the dispatcher said. Lucy made a face. "Reports indicate a troll is causing property damage and civilian injuries at a community market."

I turned in my seat to look at Malcolm. His eyes were like saucers. *A troll?* he mouthed. I gave him a surreptitious thumbs-up. He rolled his eyes.

"Mission is to assess and contain," the dispatcher continued. "Local law enforcement will take custody once the troll is neutralized."

"Typical," Lucy muttered. "Let the League do the dirty work and then the locals take the credit." She activated the radio. "Ten-four, on my way. I'll report in when I've got him collared. Four-oh-one out." Lucy hung up the radio and glanced at me. "It's not that far off our route to the roadhouse, but this might take some time to sort out."

"We should probably strike out on our own, then," I said regretfully.

My wolf growled. When I glanced back, she stared meaningfully at Lucy, then rested her chin on her paws and eyed me. The message was clear enough: stay in the jeep and stick with the Guardian. What did she know or sense that I didn't?

"On second thought, we'll just come along to the market with you," I amended.

Lucy watched my wolf in the rearview mirror. "I get the feeling Daisy's more than just a wolf with some magic. Now that we've bonded over coffee, how about you tell me what she really is and what the three of you are doing here in California?"

Partial truths had always served me well in situations like this, so I sipped my coffee and tried not to flinch as she wove in and out of traffic on the highway at nearly one hundred miles an hour. "I'm looking for a friend of mine. She's been missing for two months. Last I heard, she was here. Daisy is really good at tracking people. She's leading me to find my friend. Malcolm is my best friend, and he came with us to help keep us safe."

"Sounds reasonable—and about half true." She smiled. "I know a professional when I see one, Alice. I'm guessing private operative. Were you hired to track this woman down?"

"Yes," I admitted, since further fibs wouldn't do much but make her more suspicious. "Track her and get something back she stole from my client."

"And your wolf? What is she?"

"Not a shifter," I said to reiterate the point, because I had the feeling being a shifter meant something different here than it did back home. "She's my companion."

Another glance into the back seat. "Is she an amarok?"

I didn't know what that was, but her tone indicated it was something to be very wary of. I shook my head. "She's smart and she can be dangerous if someone poses a threat, but mostly she just tracks people and things and tries to boss me around."

Daisy chuffed in agreement.

Lucy let out a snort. "Okay, I feel like I've gotten about sixty or seventy percent of the truth, which is good enough for right now. Maybe later I'll ply you with drinks at the roadhouse and try to get the rest." She sobered. "I've got to deal with a rampaging troll first. When we get to the market, stay in the jeep. I may be a maverick, but I don't want to have to explain to my captain that I had a civilian with me on a call and she got eaten by a troll. He'll be pissed about how much paperwork he'll have to do, and so will I."

Malcolm coughed. "Paperwork *is* the literal worst," he said dryly.

"You said it," Lucy said with feeling.

"Fair enough. I'll stay in the jeep," I promised.

As it turned out, I didn't end up staying in the jeep—but in my defense, the troll threw it across the parking lot, so it was a good thing I wasn't in it.

When we arrived at the enormous open-air building that housed the community market, the parking lot was total chaos, full of people running to their vehicles and trying to leave. All four exits were blocked by traffic.

Lucy swore and swerved away from the traffic jam. I hung onto the dashboard as the jeep jolted hard over the concrete curb, bounced across uneven ground, and slid to an abrupt stop just outside the building.

She threw the vehicle in park, unfastened her seatbelt, and jumped out. "Stay here," she barked.

Inside the building, heavy objects crashed, people screamed, and something very large bellowed obscenities. Shoppers and vendors, carrying items they'd wanted to save from the troll's rampage, stood outside, helpless and shell-shocked.

Lucy ran into the building, shouting, "Guardian coming in! *Make a path! Move!*"

I might not have known what a Guardian was, but everyone else did. They scrambled to get out of her way. She vanished into the market.

"I know she said to stay here, but I feel bad that she's going in there without any kind of backup. Plus I actually do want to see a troll," Malcolm said, floating into the driver's seat area to get a closer look at the chaos inside the market. "Why do you suppose her partner's not with her? And why didn't she want the League to send anyone else out to work with her?"

"I think Lucy likes to do things her own way." I turned to my wolf. "Are we still on the trail of the scroll?"

My wolf put her right front paw on top of Lucy's black duffel bag, which was on the floor behind the driver's seat, and stared at me.

"So, you want us to stick with her until the roadhouse? Why?"

Malcolm snorted. When I frowned at him, he said, "Sorry, this is like watching *Lassie*, except instead of a gentle collie, we've got a giant magical demon-eating—"

The troll roared. Lucy came flying out of the market, hit the front of the jeep, and landed on the ground. Another crash came from inside, followed by a triumphant bellow.

I pointed at my wolf. "Stay inside," I commanded. "If I need you, I'll call."

She gave me a disdainful look and returned her head to her paws.

I got out and shut my door. By the time I made it around to the front of the jeep, Lucy was on her feet, seemingly uninjured except for a cut on her forehead. "Damn troll won't listen to reason," she muttered, rubbing her arm. "What the hell are you doing out here?"

"We can help," I said.

"I don't want paperwork," she reminded me.

"Malcolm's a ghost, remember? That could give you an advantage."

She pushed loose hair back from her face. "Don't know how, but maybe he could distract the troll long enough for me to try to calm him down. You need to stay clear, though, for your own—"

"No! Put him down!" a woman screamed from somewhere in the building.

We ran inside the market and into a fog of every kind of magic I'd ever encountered—and many more I hadn't.

As Lucy disappeared into the crowd, I staggered against a support post, fighting the onslaught of smells, spells, and power. The market had the kinds of stalls I'd expect to find at a flea market or farmer's market back home: antiques, collectibles, homemade foods, handmade and vintage clothing, and so forth. Almost a third of the booths appeared to be selling magic in the form of amulets, objects of power, ingredients for rituals and spells, potions, and light weaponry.

While the more mundane stalls remained relatively intact, the troll appeared to have targeted the magic-related vendors specifically for destruction. The result was a highly volatile jumble of broken spellwork and spilled potions.

"No magic in here," I wheezed as Malcolm gaped at the carnage. "We could blow this place sky-high with our weird power."

"There's more loose magic in here than in a mage strip club," Malcolm quipped. "I don't even know what all those potions do, but some of them are eating through the concrete and I think I just saw a ferret with two heads hide under a table." He looked around. "Where's Lucy?"

The troll bellowed again. I pushed away from the post and stumbled ahead on rubbery legs, elbowing bystanders out of the way. "I'm with the Guardian," I told them, which was technically true.

They made a path for me. I had a hard time walking straight—or even seeing straight. My vision swam repeatedly, causing me to bump into people, posts, and tables as we made our way toward the sound of the angry troll. Even in the wake of an explosion in a mage workshop that destroyed a wing of my grandfather's cabal compound, I'd never experienced anything like this.

I pushed past a few more people, staggered into a wide aisle between booths, and found myself staring up, up, *up* at an honest-to-goodness, full-sized, very angry troll—and at the much-smaller but equally furious Guardian who stood nearly toe-to-toe with him, her hands on her hips.

The troll towered over Lucy. Eight feet tall and half as wide, he had long hair, bushy eyebrows, a thick beard, enormous fists at the ends of tree trunk-sized arms, and huge, wide feet. He wore, of all things, a suit, though the jacket had numerous tears. Something—maybe spilled potions—had eaten away patches of his pants and turned them various colors.

At the moment, the troll had an unconscious man tucked under his arm like a rolled newspaper. An angry woman stood behind Lucy, her face flushed and stained blue, presumably from one of the many spilled potions.

The troll opened his mouth to bellow again.

"*Stop*," Lucy ordered him.

I sensed something: a little surge of magic, but not any kind I'd ever encountered. Beside me, Malcolm flitted in place. Something about what Lucy had just done had unsettled him.

The troll's mouth snapped shut. He looked startled.

"I'm Lieutenant Lucy Stone of the League of Guardians," she said, and she sounded damned intimidating when she said it. "Tell me what's going on here."

"You should be shooting him," the woman behind Lucy said. "Why are you talking to him? Look what he's done!"

"*Quiet*," Lucy told her.

Again, I sensed that little nudge of magic. The woman fell silent. *Uh-oh,* I thought.

"Oh, shit," Malcolm muttered. He'd figured it out too. Lucy had magic, all right—magic we needed to stay very far away from.

"Talk to me," Lucy told the troll. No nudge this time, just an offer to listen to what he had to say.

The people around us reacted angrily. I overheard a few epithets directed at Guardians in general and Lucy in particular, and one or two vulgar comments. The crowd wanted the troll arrested or taken out, and Lucy's questioning wasn't of interest to them.

The power of Lucy's suggestion wore off rapidly. The troll's expression darkened and his eyes narrowed. Instead of bellowing or smashing a booth, he squeezed the man under his arm until I heard something pop out of joint. Maybe the man's shoulder.

"This man is *kebek*," the troll told Lucy. I didn't know what that word meant, but it clearly wasn't a compliment. His voice was very deep, and heavily accented. "He kidnapped my sister. He comes to these markets to buy potions and magic and sell those he takes. I want my sister returned."

"Why smash everything in this market?" Lucy asked.

The troll glowered at the woman behind Lucy. "These people—they sell magic here, they sell people in secret. It is known in my clan. This market does not just trade in potions and wands." He gestured at the smashed booths around us. "They sell people like my sister."

"Why not contact the League for help to find your sister?"

"My father *did* ask," he snarled, and gave the unconscious man another bone-crushing squeeze. "I was told no one was available, too many other problems, that I must wait. I cannot wait. My sister cannot wait. I find him here. I will make him tell me where she has gone."

Lucy muttered a curse. She'd said there were fewer Guardians now than before, and they were stretched thin. The troll's sister's case had apparently fallen through the cracks.

"I'm sorry," she told the troll. "Come with me. I'll see both you and this man are taken safely into League custody instead of local jail. We'll find out where your sister is."

The troll drew himself up. "I am the eldest son of the chief of our clan. I will not be arrested. I will find my sister for my family." He looked past Lucy at the woman standing behind her. "Tell me where she is, or I will break his neck."

Lucy turned to look at the woman. "You heard him."

The blue-faced woman shook her head. "I don't know what you're talking about."

Calmly, the troll broke the man's arm. The woman screamed. "Stop him!"

"Tell me where his sister is, and I will," Lucy said.

The troll grabbed the man's left arm.

"We sold her to a dealer in Denver," the woman said quickly, shooting Lucy a venomous look. "A woman named Kelsey. Patricia Kelsey. I have no knowledge of what happened to her after that."

Lucy pulled a set of handcuffs from her belt. "You're under arrest on a whole bunch of federal charges."

The woman sniffed. "Not for long, I won't be, *Guardian*. I know people. I'll be released before you finish the paperwork."

With a roar, the troll broke the man's left arm and threw his limp body across the market. He bolted, tossing aside people, tables, and anything else that got in his way.

The woman who'd sold the troll's sister tried to run past me. I tripped her, rode her down to the floor, and pinned her face down on the concrete with my knee in the middle of her back, right where it would really hurt. "Oh no you don't," I told her.

She called me something very rude.

I held out my hand. Lucy tossed me her cuffs. I locked them on the woman's wrists and made sure to grind my knee into her ribs as I got up. Lucy took off running after the troll.

My head was still muddled by all the loose magic, but I heard the sound of something very heavy colliding with something else very heavy in the direction of the parking lot. I had a sudden terrible feeling about what the troll's latest target had been.

I left the handcuffed woman on the ground, told someone who looked like a security guard to keep an eye on her, and pushed my way through the crowd to the edge of the building.

The jeep was no longer where we'd left it. It was twenty feet away, upside down, on top of a truck. I saw no sign of the troll or Lucy.

Near where our vehicle had been parked, my wolf sat calmly on her haunches next to my backpack, her lip curled to show a few sharp teeth. No one ventured within twenty feet of her.

An angry bellow rolled across the parking lot from behind a row of vehicles. The sound cut off abruptly.

I headed in the direction of the troll's roar. Lucy appeared around the side of a truck, dusting off the knees of her pants. "He's going to take a nap for a while," she told me grimly. "I'm sorry about his sister, but he destroyed a lot of property today, and I can't have him running around playing vigilante."

"Why?" a woman asked snidely as she walked past. "Do you think Guardians have a monopoly on it?"

"We aren't vigilantes," Lucy said, her tone weary. "Not as a general rule, anyway."

The woman snorted and headed for her vehicle, an enormous truck that had escaped damage.

I'd started to get a clearer picture of not just what kind of person Lucy was, but also who the League of Guardians were. I was deeply wary of her, but it took a certain kind of person to do a thankless, dangerous job.

"Well, I got the troll and a couple of traffickers, but that could have gone better," Lucy said. She headed for the jeep. "Hopefully the radio still works and someone can bring me another ride."

While Lucy checked on her vehicle, I approached my wolf. One of the straps of my backpack showed marks left by her teeth. She'd apparently taken it out of the jeep before the troll tossed it. How she'd known to do that, I had no idea.

"Thanks," I told her.

She nudged her head under my hand. Her magic and strength filled me and cleared the last of the fog away.

Malcolm joined us. "See, I told you trolls would be fun," I said.

He shook his head and didn't answer.

Well, *I* thought it was funny, anyway.

CHAPTER 13

SOMEWHAT MIRACULOUSLY, THE RADIO IN THE JEEP STILL WORKED, SO LUCY called her captain to report in. After some swearing, he dispatched personnel to pick up all three of the detainees and bring her another vehicle.

I sat in the grass outside the market with Malcolm and my wolf, who I was beginning to think of as Daisy. It wasn't the name I would have chosen, but she didn't seem to mind it—in fact, whenever someone said it, her ears twitched. I wondered what Sean would think of her name.

In the meantime, vendors in the market focused on cleaning up the mess the troll had made of their inventory. Most of the shoppers left. Several gave my wolf hard stares. In answer, she either stared back or sat on her haunches with her tongue hanging out, like a large, friendly dog. How she decided who to stare down and who to charm, I didn't know. I'd tried talking to her telepathically, as we'd done before she leapt from my body. To my disappointment, it didn't work, even when we were in physical contact.

While Lucy was occupied getting her bags and gear and keeping an eye on the unconscious troll, Malcolm and I discussed whether to head out on our own or go to the roadhouse.

Daisy's opinion was clear. When I suggested we part ways with Lucy, she growled.

"I know you want us to stick around, but I'm concerned about Lucy's special talent," Malcolm told her. "She can make people do things. We saw her use it on both the troll and the woman she arrested. Who's to say she won't try to use it on one of us?"

That was exactly what I was concerned about too. "She might decide she wants the whole truth from us about who we are and what we're doing here," I told my wolf. "I'm not sure my shields can protect me from that kind of magic."

Daisy raised her head. She looked at Lucy, then at me, then mimicked biting the air.

Malcolm rolled his eyes. "Here we go again with wolf charades."

I raised my eyebrows. "Oh, come on, Malcolm. That one's obvious. She's saying Lucy can't use it on me because she won't allow it."

He sighed. "Well, as long as Daisy's with you, I guess you're safe then, but what if Lucy tries to mess with me?"

Daisy chomped the air again, but in Lucy's direction.

I laughed. "Well, there you go. She'll protect you too."

"I feel honored," Malcolm said. "I've got a wolf bodyguard. This must be like how you feel when Sean's with you."

My smile faded.

"I'm sorry," he said immediately. "I didn't mean to bring him up. Way to go, Malcolm," he muttered.

"It's okay. I'm not that fragile." I turned back to Daisy. "We need to find Mariela and that scroll. Why do you want us to stick with Lucy? Is there something we need from her?"

She stared at me.

"Something we need from someone at the roadhouse?"

She snuffled and laid her head back down on her paws.

"Is that a yes?"

No reaction. I had a feeling she understood me perfectly well, but chose not to answer.

"Fine, be that way," I said, exasperated.

"Did you just lose an argument with a wolf?" Lucy asked, dropping her gear on the ground next to us. "Sorry, didn't mean to eavesdrop. The wagon should be here any minute. Once we get these jokers loaded up and our gear stowed in the new ride, we'll be on our way."

"Can I ask a question?" Malcolm asked. "Is there a name for that special skill you've got?"

She tore open a first aid pack and cleaned the cut on her forehead without needing a mirror. "I've got a couple of special skills. Some I'll talk about, and some I won't, just like you and Alice. I assume you're referring to pushing."

"Pushing, yes." Malcolm's tone belied his unease. "That's a handy skill. Seems like there might be some ethical concerns there."

"It *is* handy. And yes, some definite ethical concerns, if you're good at it. Luckily, I'm not that good at it." She wrapped the soiled disinfectant wipe in its packaging and stuck it in her pocket.

"Why 'luckily'?" I asked.

"Because like with most special skills, being good at something means you might be useful to someone."

I knew that all too well, unfortunately. "Good point."

She glanced at the far side of the parking lot, where two jeeps and a large armored personnel carrier were pulling in. "Finally. Let me sort all this out. Any chance your wolf can look less like a wolf?"

Daisy rolled onto her back and showed us her belly, her tongue lolling. In that pose, she looked very dog-like if you didn't look at her too closely.

Lucy paused. "I know she's not a shifter, but she understands every word we say. I'm also aware she chose to let us put that collar on. I don't know why I'm this comfortable around her. I'm not even really a dog person."

"Stone!" A familiar voice bellowed across the parking lot.

Lucy winced. "Captain Ellis. I was afraid of that. I'll be back." She turned and headed for the lead jeep, where a man in an officer's uniform stood with his hands on his hips.

"What do you think?" Malcolm asked when she was out of earshot.

I watched Lucy talking to her captain. He spoke at length, pointing at the unconscious troll, the market, and her smashed vehicle, and then waving his hands to encompass the area. She let him finish, then replied. Whatever she said, it was brief, and it brought an abrupt end to the captain's tirade. He gave her a nod and started issuing commands to the half-dozen soldiers who'd come with him to the scene. They fanned out to follow his orders.

"I think Lucy's a good Guardian," I said finally. "I also think she's really, really good at pushing, and we need to be careful."

"You think she pretends she's not good at it for the same reason you pretend to be a mid-level mage?"

"Yup. It takes one to know one, maybe." I gingerly rubbed Daisy's head. She showed me her teeth, but didn't move away.

"Takes one what?"

"A liar," I said. "A liar, and someone who's pretending to be someone she's not."

"So who *is* Lucy, then?" he asked. "Besides a maverick Guardian?"

"I don't know, but I get the feeling whatever the answer is, it's why Daisy wants us to go with her to the roadhouse." I scratched Daisy's head. "Is that right, Daisy-dog?"

She growled, then wiggled her back in the grass. I had no idea what that meant, but it looked like I was going to a Broken World roadhouse in the company of a Guardian with mysterious abilities, a snarky ghost, and a magical wolf.

What could possibly go wrong?

CHAPTER 14

Under the command of Captain Ellis, the Guardians moved like a well-oiled machine. Within minutes of their arrival, they'd loaded the unconscious troll and the two alleged traffickers into the APC in chains and under heavy guard. They supervised the removal of Lucy's jeep and the truck it had landed on by a towing service.

After a brief conversation, Ellis handed Lucy a set of keys, got in his own vehicle with a driver, and departed with the APC.

As I loaded our stuff into our new ride, Lucy thanked the security guard who'd kept an eye on the alleged traffickers and took one last walk through the market to check on the magic vendors. Some were hostile and turned their backs on her. Others responded with respect or even camaraderie. I was impatient to get moving, but I figured she had good reason to invest a few minutes helping with cleanup.

I itched to find out more about the Guardians and why their interactions with civilians were so polarized. Asking too many of that sort of question was likely to make Lucy suspicious, so I'd have to find another way to satisfy my curiosity.

About fifteen minutes after Ellis and the other Guardians left, two armored police vehicles turned into the lot, lights flashing.

Lucy emerged from the market and joined me by the jeep. "Just in time," she said dryly. "They'll document the scene, fill out their reports, and be on their way." She waved at the officers in the lead vehicle. One raised his hand briefly, but they didn't stop to speak with her. "Might as well leave them to it," she added, circling around to the driver's side. "At this point, we're not going to get that rest we wanted at the roadhouse before things get crazy there, but we can at least get showers and some food. Sorry."

"It's fine," I told her as we piled into the vehicle. Daisy was already dozing in the back seat. "If there's time to get coffee on the way, that's all I'll need."

"Oh, there's *always* time to get coffee," Lucy assured me.

Malcolm snorted. "Nothing like bonding over shared chemical dependence."

"Hey," I protested. "It's not chemical dependence. I just need caffeine to function."

"That is the literal definition of dependence, Alice."

"He's got you there." Lucy stuck her sister's vampire bobble-head to the dash with a piece of chewed gum, turned the key in the ignition, and stomped the gas. "Let's get the hell out of here."

OUR DRIVE to the roadhouse was relatively uneventful. To pass the time, I asked Lucy to tell us about some of her more interesting cases.

The really good ones were classified, she said, but she described an encounter with a nest of basilisks much like the one her partner was currently involved in eradicating. Dealing with serpents whose bite, stare, smell, and spit were guaranteed to either drive you mad or kill you required strategy—and a substance Lucy called acira, which sounded a lot like magic-infused napalm.

To get to our destination, we drove south out of the city and then west in a long loop around areas shaded black on Lucy's dashboard GPS. One such area she identified as the territory of the coven she'd alluded to earlier.

The only visible signs of the territory's perimeter were pentagrams and runes carved into trees along the road. I saw no walls or gates, but I assumed *closed* meant anyone who tried to cross that perimeter wouldn't like what happened to them. I wondered what Carly would think about witches having territory that could be closed to outsiders.

My curiosity finally got the better of me. "Why did the coven close their territory?" I asked.

Lucy chuckled. "From what I hear, this time it was because their High Priestess wanted her eldest daughter to marry a witch from another coven. Her attempt at matchmaking didn't go so well, apparently. Several members of her family developed very unsightly and painful sores in the shape of male genitalia."

"Oh, man," Malcolm said in awe. "Alice, you have *got* to remember to tell Carly about that."

"We have a witch friend back home named Carly," I explained to Lucy. "She's always curious about what other covens are up to."

"Well, if she likes that story, she'll love the one about the enchanted chinchilla."

I was about to ask what she meant when we reached the top of a particularly steep hill overlooking a wide valley. My mouth fell open.

"Holy crap—what the hell is *that?*" Malcolm leaned over my shoulder to stare through the windshield.

"That," Lucy said ominously, "is the famous Jupiter Sinkhole. Pictures just don't do it justice, do they?"

When she'd said earlier that we had to drive around a sinkhole, I'd wondered why that was something that would add an hour to our journey.

Now I understood.

Something had come out of the ground here—something so big and fiery, it had left a hole several miles wide and maybe a quarter-mile deep in the center, like the caldera of an enormous volcano. The earth in the pit and for a mile around it was blackened and lifeless, dotted with the skeletal frames of vehicles and houses.

From here, we also had a good view of the city. I was struck by how much smaller it was than back home. Not just fewer skyscrapers —fewer *everything*. Fewer interstate highways, fewer sprawling suburbs, fewer shopping centers and schools. And no massive airport—just a small, regional-looking airport with a single terminal and a couple of runways.

What the hell was I doing here? And what if I couldn't get us back home?

Malcolm put his hand on my shoulder. *Don't freak out*, he said, his voice urgent. *If you freak out, I'll freak out, and Daisy sure as hell will freak out, and then we'll really be up shit creek. Just pretend it's the sarlacc pit and take deep breaths.*

Out loud, he said, "Dang, you're right. Pictures definitely do *not* do it justice." He poked me hard in the shoulder—which was a thing he could do now, because we were in another world.

I shook myself out of my paralysis. "Yep, way bigger in person," I managed to say.

"That's what *she* said," Lucy quipped, and laughed.

Malcolm and I exchanged a glance, nonplussed. There was just enough of our world in this one to keep me constantly off-balance.

"How far to the roadhouse?" I asked.

"About an hour. Makes you want a drink, right?" She navigated a series of sharp turns along the side of the hill. "The first time I saw the sinkhole in person, I needed one too. Here." She reached under her seat, pulled out a flask, and handed it to me. "Go easy. That's a special homemade recipe made by a vampire friend, and it's no bark and all bite."

I unscrewed the cap and took a whiff. "Holy smokes," I gasped. The smell of it seared the inside of my nose. I took a swig and coughed. "Thanks," I croaked.

"Don't mention it," she said. "Really, don't. Trev only gives it out to his very special friends, and I'll fall off that list if news gets out about it. Plus he'll kick my ass—or he'll try, anyway."

"Our secret." I took one more sip, then handed back the flask. She returned it to its hiding place under her seat.

From our vantage point, I saw the gray ribbon of the highway we were on as it bypassed the sinkhole and the no-man's-land around it and disappeared into the hills in the distance. Somewhere down this road was the roadhouse. I hoped it was just what it sounded like: a roadside dive bar full of restless souls, run by a sarcastic bartender with a seen-it-all attitude, a well-stocked selection of whisky, and a willingness to pour generously. That at least would be a welcome reminder of home.

WHEN WE WERE about a minute from the roadhouse, Daisy got up, stretched, yawned to show all her teeth, and sat expectantly on the back seat.

Lucy glanced in the rearview mirror. "Can she read the GPS?"

"Your guess is as good as mine," I said, rubbing my face. My eyes were gritty. I longed to be clean. I looked forward to a shower, a stiff drink, and finding out why Daisy wanted us to come here—not necessarily in that order.

When we reached the turnoff, Lucy barely slowed the jeep to make the turn into the nearly empty gravel parking lot. Our wheels kicked up a spray of rocks and dust as she fishtailed, cut through the lot, circled around back, and slid to an abrupt stop near a screen door I assumed led to the kitchen.

She put the vehicle in park and turned off the ignition. "The owner prefers I park around back. Some of his best customers won't stop in if there's a Guardian vehicle out front." When I didn't respond, she waved her hand in the front of my face. "Alice? You okay?"

"Fine." I cleared my throat. "You know the owner?"

"Yep. I've been through here a couple of times. He doesn't like Guardians much—hell, most vamps don't—but I helped him with a problem the first time I stopped in, so we're cool."

When I didn't reply, she paused with her hand on the door. "He's not a Court vampire, if that's what you're worried about. I wouldn't bring you here if he was." She grinned. "Oh, and fair warning: he'll probably invite you to his bed, since he has a thing for dangerous brunettes. If you feel like saying yes, I won't judge you. You could do worse."

"I think I'll pass." Robotically, I got out and put my backpack on my shoulders. I opened the back door and Daisy jumped out, landing in the gravel beside me. She gave herself a long shake. "This had better not be the reason you wanted us to come here," I told her under my breath.

She sneezed and stretched.

"Alice, what are we going to do?" Malcolm hissed. "It can't be *him*, right? It's a coincidence."

"I couldn't be that lucky," I muttered.

Lucy slung her bag over her shoulder. "Let's see about getting a room to clean up."

We walked around the building. On the outside, it looked like any number of older roadside dives I'd seen, except for the wards carved into the exterior walls. Most of them were dormant. Others tingled on my skin. The building was three stories. I imagined the ground floor was the bar and the upper floors were rooms available for travelers to rent. The parking lot was enormous, and tire tracks indicated the field next to the building was frequently used for overflow parking. The roadhouse was clearly popular.

We climbed the front steps with Lucy in the lead. The windows of the double doors were covered, preventing us from seeing inside, but rock music drifted out.

Lucy shoved the doors open and marched inside like a Western lawman entering a saloon full of drunken desperadoes. I followed her in with Daisy at my side and Malcolm behind us.

The doorway wards flared as we passed. They blazed blue for Lucy and Malcolm, gold with multicolored threads for Daisy, and a rainbow of colors with black threads for me. The tall, blond man behind the bar watched the wards as we entered, studied us, and finished pouring a drink. The wards alerted staff to the type of beings who crossed the threshold.

Only a half-dozen patrons were drinking in the middle of the afternoon: three at the bar and three others alone in booths. One of the solitary drinkers was a troll. Everyone else appeared to be human —but then again, that didn't mean they were. I saw no other employees besides the bartender.

The room was enormous, with a raised stage at one end, a wide staircase at the other, the main bar in the center, and a second smaller bar near the stage, not currently in use. Despite my uneasiness, I relaxed just a little. A mostly empty bar in the middle of the afternoon was familiar territory, even in the Broken World.

The bartender slid the drink across to the man in front of him and wiped his hands on a towel. "Welcome to Hawthorne's," he said, his eyes on Daisy. "If that wolf causes any trouble, I'll shoot her."

Daisy showed him all of her teeth, but didn't growl. If I didn't know better, I'd have thought she'd just grinned at him.

"Nice to see you again too, Joey." Lucy dropped her bag on an empty barstool. "We've been on the road and we need a room to get cleaned up." She slid a card across the bar. "And a bottle of Charles's finest later."

Charles. Unbelievable. I'd traveled through a mirror to a whole other world and still ended up drinking at Charles Vaughan's bar.

Joey took Lucy's card. "You just passing through, or meeting someone later?"

"Meeting an informant around sunset. We'll need a booth. You got a band playing here tonight?"

He nodded. "Yeah, a damn good one. I'll reserve you a booth far enough away from the stage that you can hear each other. You need any backup with your informant, give us the signal."

"You got it." She slung her bag over her shoulder.

"Will the owner be in today?" I asked.

Joey slid two old-fashioned door keys across the bar to Lucy. "Second floor, room 202. He might be in later," he told me. "Never can tell. You got a message for him?"

"No," I said, maybe a little too quickly. "No, just wondering. How'd he get the idea to name this place Hawthorne's?"

He shrugged. "Told me he used to drink with Nathaniel Hawthorne. Not sure if I believe him, but he's old enough. Not many roadhouses get named after famous authors."

Back home, Charles had named his bar Hawthorne's for the same reason. I needed a drink now more than ever.

The bartender gestured at my wolf. "You want to get her some dinner before things get busy?"

Daisy licked her chops.

My stomach grumbled. That breakfast sandwich had long since ceased to hold my hunger pangs at bay. "Dinner would be good," I said. "For us too."

"We ain't got room service, but I'll have someone bring you up something," Joey said. "The parking lot'll be full in about ninety minutes. You let me know if you're heading out after, or you want to stay the night."

"We'll be back down soon as we're cleaned up and eaten." Lucy headed for the stairs. "Come on, Alice. Let's wash off this road dust."

I adjusted my backpack and followed her.

CHAPTER 15

Ninety minutes later, scrubbed clean, wearing clean clothes, and having eaten—hamburgers and fries for Lucy and me, and a hunk of raw deer meat for Daisy—we stowed our bags in a locked storage closet and came back downstairs to find the bar nearly full.

I paused on the stairs to scan the room. About half the patrons appeared to be human. I spotted a couple of trolls, several men and women with pointy ears and teeth, and a couple of dwarves. Others were less familiar: several four-legged human spiders like the woman I'd seen in the city earlier today, fae-like beings with pointed ears, and a number of half-human, half-animal creatures at tables or standing. The bar was loud, full of human and non-human voices talking and laughing. My senses were overwhelmed by the chaos and unfamiliar magic. At the far end of the room, the band was setting up on the stage.

Beside me, Malcolm chuckled. "You will never find a more wretched hive of scum and villainy."

"Let's hope we don't run into any bounty hunters," I muttered.

"If we do, just be sure to shoot first," he advised. "Like Han did."

A large bat-like creature hanging from the ceiling near the foot of the stairs turned slowly and peered at me upside down. "Hello," it said.

"Hi," I said after a beat. "How are you?"

"Oh, getting by." It stretched its leathery wings languidly and folded them again. "Long bit of travel today. Headed south to Mexico, you know. Where are you headed?"

"Not sure yet," I said, imagining myself describing this conversation to Sean when I got back. "Just wandering through the area."

"Safe travels to ya, then," the bat said. It turned back toward the wall, humming quietly along with the unfamiliar song currently playing on the jukebox.

That song ended. After a pause, the jukebox played the next song.

"Bon Jovi?" I blinked. "Is that Bon Jovi?"

"Yes indeed," a spider-man leaning against the wall on the other side of the bat told me. He held a bottle of beer in one clawed hand. "Great damn song."

I rubbed my face. "I need a drink."

"Good idea," Lucy said. She wore jeans, boots, a tank top that showed off her toned arms, and something on a long chain around her neck that was hidden inside her top. "If you're done gawking at everything, let's go get one."

She led the way through the crowd to an empty booth with a RESERVED sign, located halfway between the stairs and the front door. We sat, with Lucy and Malcolm on one side and Daisy and I on the other.

Before we had a chance to flag down a server, one appeared carrying an unlabeled bottle and two glasses. She plunked them on the table and disappeared back into the crowd.

"So, what's this stuff?" I asked as Lucy unstoppered the bottle and poured some for each of us.

"A local specialty." She set the bottle back on the table. "Almost as smooth as what Trev makes. I don't know where Charles gets it; he won't tell me."

More moonshine, apparently. I would have preferred Scotch, but when in Rome…

I took a sniff and my eyes watered. Yup, definitely moonshine. I sipped cautiously. It tasted fine, though; much better than any homemade liquor I'd tried before, other than what Lucy had in her flask. I might develop a liking for it.

"So, what's your story?" Lucy asked after we'd both enjoyed some of our much-needed drinks. "How'd you end up tracking people down for a living?"

"Just fell into it, I guess," I told her. "I wanted to do something that helped people. With my skill set, the options were somewhat limited. I got the chance to apprentice with a pro who taught me the ropes. He showed me how important it was to get justice for people who have nowhere else to turn." I took a drink. "He was a good man."

"You lost him?" Lucy asked.

I nodded. "Earlier this year. He was murdered while investigating a case we were working on together. I got the person who did it."

"Good for you. What was your mentor's name?"

"Mark."

She raised her glass. "To Mark, then."

We clinked glasses and drank.

"It feels good to help people when they have nowhere else to turn." Lucy toyed with her glass. "That's the part of my job I like."

"The name *Guardian* does imply you take care of people when they need you," Malcolm said.

Her mouth twisted. "But you know the history of the Guardians —where we came from, or *supposedly* came from. We're different from the Spartoi because we've chosen to change our ways, but it's still in our blood. Some lose the battle against those instincts." She tapped her glass absently on the table. "Some like to kill."

The term *Spartoi* rang a distant bell, but I couldn't recall who they were. Greek mythology, maybe? Then again, she'd made it sound like the Spartoi were real—and still around.

"So, what about you?" Malcolm asked. "How did you end up becoming a Guardian?"

She frowned and didn't say anything for a long time. "Well, it's a long story," she said finally. "The short version is someone very close to me who was a Guardian was murdered. I wanted nothing to do with them because they'd made my life a living hell prior to that, but I needed to find out who did it and why. The Guardians made me an offer I couldn't refuse, I guess you could say. I joined up, found the killers, got my revenge, and damn near destroyed the League in the process." She smiled, but without humor. "It's not like the Guardians have recruitment posters, but if they did, I sure as hell wouldn't be on them."

"What were you before you became a Guardian?" Malcolm wanted to know.

She chuckled. "A florist."

He blinked.

"A florist with a vampire sister, ghoul cousin, clairvoyant aunt, and poltergeist grandparents. And a mom who's a ghost, but only part of the time." She drained the last of her drink and poured herself more. "Like I said, our family has always been weird about death."

She hadn't mentioned her father. I wondered if he was who had been murdered, and why getting revenge for his death had almost destroyed the Guardians. And if she'd only reluctantly joined them, why was she still among their ranks?

She checked her watch. "My source is due to arrive soon. Sunset, he said. You're welcome to stay and listen to his story."

"I'd like to hear about these creatures that killed his pack, in case we run into any. I prefer to know what I'm up against."

She saluted me with her glass. "Fair enough."

Up on stage, the band was almost finished setting up. A rock or metal band of some sort, I guessed, based on their instruments and attire. The band seemed to consist of a lead singer, two guitarists, a bass player, and a drummer, all young and male. The shirtless drummer in particular drew my attention, with his long, blond hair and broad shoulders. He caught my eye as he picked up a speaker and carried it to the side of the stage. He set it down, flexed a bit, and winked at me.

As I scanned the room, I spotted a large, very muscular man with shoulder-length dark hair held in a silver clasp at the nape of his neck and several days' worth of beard, sitting alone at a table against the opposite wall. He wore a black leather jacket, jeans, and steel-toed boots. A half-empty bottle of tequila and a glass sat on the table in front of him.

A young woman with small delicate wings, wearing a tiny skirt, tank top, and tall boots, sauntered up to him and struck up conversation. She handed him a key. He put it on the table next to the bottle of tequila and passed her some cash. Deal made, she sashayed away, brushing his shoulder with her wing as she passed.

Lucy turned to follow my gaze. "Well, hello there," she purred. "Don't be discouraged by the key. He's just using it to keep the others from bothering him. He's not going to use it."

That confirmed my suspicions about who the girl was—or her trade, anyway. "How can you tell?" I asked.

She shrugged. "A vibe. He just wants to drink in peace until someone interesting comes along. Someone like yourself, maybe."

I smiled. "I have a partner back home, so I won't be accepting any invitations tonight, or offering any."

"And I suppose I'll be heading out once I get what I need from my source. No time for play. Pity." She sighed. "The sacrifices I have to make for this job."

A shadow fell over our table. Daisy let out a low growl.

A young African American man stood beside our booth, wearing a T-shirt and jeans. His eyes had a telltale golden sheen. "Stone?" he asked, glancing first at me, then at Lucy.

"That's me," Lucy said. "You're Isaiah?"

"Yeah." He stared at Daisy, his brow furrowed. Probably trying to figure out what she was. She curled her lip to show him a couple of teeth.

"Pull up a chair," Lucy told him.

He grabbed an unused chair from another table, put a battered rucksack on the floor, and sat at the end of our booth. "What are you?" he asked me, a growly edge in his voice. "Human, but with shifter magic."

"Don't worry about her," Lucy told him. "I want to hear what happened to your pack."

Isaiah growled. His attitude and body language reminded me of Caleb, the young werewolf who'd tried to kill me out of a misguided sense of loyalty to Sean's pack.

"She asked you a question," I said. My tone sounded like Sean's when he was setting one of his wolves straight. Maybe I was picking up some of Sean's habits, or maybe I was instinctively acting like someone near the top of a pack hierarchy.

Isaiah's eyes dropped immediately, but his anger remained. "They're dead—all of them," he snarled. "Nothing left but scraps. I buried them, fifteen miles outside Oakdale. I can take you to the spot, or I can draw you a map."

"What killed them?" Lucy demanded.

"I didn't see it." His rage made his eyes glow. "I wasn't there when they were attacked. I was at a motel with a woman. When I felt them dying, I got there as fast as I could, but it was already over." He stared at his hands. "My alpha was torn to pieces. They all were, even the females. Torn to pieces and chewed on. Organs missing. Eaten." He looked at Lucy, eyes golden. "They smelled foul, Guardian. Whatever killed them, it came from somewhere dark and filthy—some deep pit full of death."

"And you've never smelled anything like that before?" I asked.

He shook his head. "Not in my life."

"If I go to this spot near Oakdale, I'll find evidence of the attack?" Lucy's voice was skeptical.

He reached into his bag.

Lucy tensed. "Slowly," she warned him.

He pulled a bloody scrap of a T-shirt from his bag and threw it on the table. "You want evidence? Here."

I recoiled. Daisy snarled. Malcolm flitted in place. Lucy stared.

Blood magic surged within me. Blood magic, and something else: Miraç's black magic. Like a tide under the moon, it responded to the bloody cloth, filling me with the sensation of rotting things—and a strong desire. Mesmerized by the sensation of dark magic pulsing under my skin, I reached for the cloth.

Malcolm smacked my hand. "Don't touch it!"

My temper flared, along with the dark magic. "Back off!" I snapped.

Isaiah snarled in Malcolm's direction. "What the hell is going on?"

Daisy growled and shoved her head under my hand. Her golden magic seared me, cutting through the dark power unleashed by the bloody cloth. The desire to pick it up faded.

I blinked and shook my head to clear it. Something about the blood called to the black magic I carried, and that was more disconcerting and worrisome than almost anything I'd encountered here.

Malcolm's agitation prickled on my skin. "I'm sorry," I said to him. "I don't know what just happened."

"You good?" Lucy asked, her gaze locked on mine. Her question was part concern for me and part Guardian unease that I might act violently or unleash bad magic.

"Yeah, I'm good." I rubbed Daisy's head and studied the cloth. "What is this?"

Isaiah growled, his anger sizzling on my skin. His shifter magic felt distinctly different from what I was used to. This magic was darker and tinged with something unsettling. It reminded me of a shifter who'd gone mad. I'd encountered a few over the years. Sometimes madness was the result of mental illness; more often, it happened because the wolf took over, even in human form. Isaiah might be going mad. Because his pack was slaughtered? Or was there some other reason?

"From my alpha's shirt," he said, his hands balling into fists. "He wounded the thing that killed him. I tried to track it, but it didn't leave the scene. The others must have eaten it."

"They ate one of their own because it was wounded?" I kept my hand on Daisy's head, drawing on her strength to keep the desire for the bloody cloth at bay. "Or so they couldn't be tracked?"

"Could be either." Lucy studied the cloth. "Nasty dead things."

Up on stage, the band started their first song. I was right: hard rock. Not a song I recognized, but the bar's patrons shouted and whistled their approval. The drummer was excellent.

Lucy produced a plastic bag from her pocket and held it open for Isaiah to drop the cloth inside. She sealed the bag and put it on the seat beside her, out of my sight. "What have you heard about these things?"

He shook his head. "The rumors are crazy. They never leave any survivors when they attack. They eat the heart and the liver. They drain the bodies of blood. Then they vanish into the night. No one has seen them—no one who lived. Some Seers have said they're gravelings. You've probably heard that rumor yourself."

"I have," Lucy said. "Anything else to add? Anything that might help me find these things?"

"All the attacks I know about have happened at night, near cemeteries," he said. "They seem to like death. The ones that killed my pack came from the south, but there are others."

Lucy took out a cell phone and pulled up a map of the area. "Show me where the attacks have taken place that you've heard about."

He pointed to several places, spread throughout a large area of several hundred miles. She noted those locations and frowned at the map.

"Thanks for your help," she said finally. "I'll do my damnedest to kill these things. I hope that's worth something."

Isaiah's chair scraped on the floor as he rose. "I survived the attack and the journey here to meet you. I figure I lived this long so I could tell you what happened to my pack and bring you that scrap of Nate's shirt. That's about all the favors I expect to get out of God." He glanced over his shoulder. I wasn't sure if he was looking at anyone in particular, or just at the crowd in general. "I'm probably not going to make it out of the parking lot."

Malcolm's look of puzzlement mirrored mine.

"That's mostly up to you," Lucy told him. "You could stay here tonight, leave after things clear out. You don't have to walk out there now."

"Or maybe I do." He bared his teeth at her. "Maybe I got something waiting for me—something I dodged back in Oakdale because of a tall girl with real nice legs. Maybe that's fate out there waiting for me."

"I don't believe in fate," Lucy said, her voice flat. "I believe you make choices, like whether you stay in here and have a drink and a raw steak and listen to the band, or you go outside looking for trouble. And if you choose to leave now, don't say it's fate if you die out there."

Avoiding my gaze, he asked, "What about you? Do you believe in fate?"

I shook my head. "Nope, I'm with Lucy. You've got survivor's guilt because you lived and the rest of your pack died. That doesn't mean your life is forfeit, unless you choose that path. You can make a new path."

His lip curled. "You make it sound simple."

"Of course it's not simple—but to me, the choice is." I knocked back the rest of my drink and enjoyed the burn of the moonshine. "I choose to live because I want to, and out of spite. A lot of people have tried to kill me, or told me I had no choice. Screw that. There is *always* a choice. There is always another way. When all the doors are closed, that's when you kick through the wall."

Carly had said something like that to me at Brew a Cup. Had it only been yesterday? That conversation felt like a hundred years ago.

"Whatever you are, I imagine you've kicked through plenty of walls." Isaiah picked up his rucksack and slung it over his shoulder. "The Guardians have never done shit for any shifter I knew except kill them. How do I know you'll even go after these things that slaughtered my pack?"

"Because I said I would." Lucy's voice was flat. "And because your pack deserves justice."

I caught a hint of a strange scent. My senses were overwhelmed by the noise and competing odors of bodies, magic, food, and beer, but I could have sworn I smelled incense and iron. Daisy's nostrils flared; she smelled it too. Then, as quickly as it had appeared, the scent was gone.

Isaiah gave Lucy a nod. "Send 'em back to hell, then."

He turned to go and bumped into a man who was walking past. Isaiah snarled at the man, his eyes bright gold.

The man stared at Isaiah. It was the guy I'd noticed earlier, sitting by himself with the bottle of tequila. Isaiah was big, but this guy was massive—several inches taller and with about twenty or thirty pounds more muscle. His eyes were the color of glacier ice. I recognized the way he studied Isaiah, assessing his threat potential and deciding whether to let him live. My earlier appreciation for his looks and physique gave way to wariness. My gut said professional killer. Judging by Lucy's expression, she'd come to the same conclusion.

"Shifter," the man said, his tone thoughtful. "A loner."

I had no idea how the man could tell Isaiah had no pack, or why his lone-wolf status mattered. Isaiah held his ground, but his uneasiness prickled on my skin.

When Lucy spoke, her voice had that hard military edge I'd heard at the market. "This man came here to speak with me." She lifted the item hanging around her neck and showed the man a Guardian seal. She tucked it back out of sight. "And there's no violence permitted within the roadhouse, as you know."

That explained a lot—including her recommendation that Isaiah stay inside until the crowd cleared out. I wondered if that was a house rule, or some kind of law. The no-violence rule apparently didn't apply to the parking lot, though. Good to know.

The man turned his cold assessment on the rest of us. "Guardian, you keep poor company."

Daisy showed him her teeth.

"Rude," Malcolm muttered. "I'm damn fine company."

The man glanced at my ghost. "Maybe you are, but you shouldn't associate with shifters and mages. Someone like me might assume the worst of you."

Malcolm's expression was priceless. If the tension hadn't been thick enough to cut, I might have chuckled. He wasn't used to anyone but me seeing and hearing him, and this place was apparently chock-full of people who could do both.

Meanwhile, the man had just identified me as a mage when I hadn't wanted anyone to have that information, which pissed me off. Not many people could sense my magic when it was hidden behind my shields, so he had to have powers of his own. I tried to identify what he was, but my spidey sense told me nothing. He was a null space to my senses. That meant he had extremely strong shields and probably big magic. Fantastic.

Lucy returned the man's cold stare. "I'm not particularly concerned about your opinions—just that you adhere to the house rules if you're here on business. And if you're not, I suggest you go back to enjoying the band and that bottle of cheap tequila."

I caught a hint of silver shimmering in his eyes. That could mean a lot of things, most of them dangerous. Lucy raised an eyebrow, daring him to make a move.

Isaiah had disappeared into the crowd. I hoped he would take Lucy's advice and stay inside Hawthorne's rather than go looking for trouble.

The man glanced at our bottle of moonshine. "I'll leave you all to your drinks, then. If you decide you want to keep better company, Guardian, come see me later." He turned and shouldered his way through the crowd toward his table.

"Damn," Lucy said, watching him leave. "I'm not sure if I want to bed him or kill him."

"Same," Malcolm said. "Doesn't have to be an either-or decision, though."

Daisy nudged my arm. "Not you too," I told her, exasperated. She stared pointedly in the direction the man had gone.

Lucy chuckled. "Your wolf would make a good wing-woman. If I didn't know better, I'd say she was trying to get one of us laid." She slid her phone over to me. "Tell me what you see."

I picked up the phone and studied the map she'd made of the attacks Isaiah knew about, and some she'd added. "It's almost a circle," I said. "The things are coming out of somewhere and spreading in all directions. The Oakdale attack is the farthest north so far. The open door—if there is one—must be somewhere in the middle of that circle."

"It's a lot of ground to cover, but I think you're right." She rested her chin on her hand. "How you feeling? Got a bit of a buzz going?"

I considered. "A little bit. Why?"

"Just wondering if I could get some more truth out of you, or if I need to pour you another drink." She poured more of Charles's finest into her glass and offered me the bottle.

I shook my head. "I shouldn't."

She poured me about an inch of moonshine and set the bottle down. "Which is a good reason to have more. I paid for the whole bottle, whether we drink it all or not. So, how about it?"

"I can't tell you anything more than what I've already said. I've got a confidentiality agreement with my client."

She smiled. "You know those don't apply if it's law enforcement asking, right?"

"Are you asking as law enforcement?"

"Not at the moment. More like...a concerned friend who wonders why you're so interested in finding these creatures and the open door they came out of." Her smile faded. "Do you suspect the person you're after has something to do with this?"

"I don't know, and that's the truth." I gestured at my wolf. "Like I told you this morning, Daisy's tracking this missing woman and I'm following her lead. She wanted us to come with you to this roadhouse, though I'm not sure why. I'm hoping she'll let me know soon so we can get back to tracking. My client is impatient for results."

I caught a glimpse of Leather Guy through the crowd. He'd returned to his table and his bottle of tequila. He watched the band with a deliberately casual air: low in his chair, legs straight out in front of him, nearly empty glass in his hand. To the untrained eye, he appeared to be a moderately intoxicated bar patron relaxing after a long day, but he wasn't. His gaze was sharply focused on the band—specifically, either the drummer or the bassist, if I wasn't mistaken. I recalled Lucy's reference to the man possibly being here on business. If he was, was someone in the band his target?

Lucy raised her glass and waggled it to draw my attention away from Leather Guy. "I'm going to sit here and drink a little longer, and then I'll be ready to head out. If you want to go south looking for gravelings, you and your crew can ride with me. If you prefer to stay and try to figure out why your wolf wanted you to come here and then find another ride later, that's up to you."

I was about to thank her for the offer when magic surged. The rush of power wasn't nearly as intense as this morning's colossal flare. With so many witnesses—and potential collateral damage—around, I couldn't afford to let any of my magic escape.

To my surprise, the other bar patrons barely reacted. A bird-like creature standing near our booth shook herself, settled her feathers, and resumed bobbing her head to the music.

I tried not to flinch or let on that the flare was affecting me, but the pain was too much. I doubled over with a groan, holding in the surge with sheer determination. Oh, God, it *hurt*—far more than the earlier flare had, though this one was much shorter and less intense.

My fingers tightened in Daisy's fur. She pushed her power into me, strengthening my shields and lessening the agony.

The flare lasted only about fifteen seconds, but it felt like an hour before the rush of power subsided. I took a shaky breath, let go of Daisy's fur, and raised my head.

"You okay?" Malcolm asked. For some reason, the flare hadn't affected him nearly as severely. He must be adjusting to the magic of this world faster than me.

I reached for my drink with a trembling hand. "I'm good."

Lucy watched me, her hands folded around her glass. "Does that happen every time there's a flare?"

I got the impression my reaction was abnormal, so I said, "No—that was strange. Something's different here and it's messing with me a little. I'll be fine."

Up on stage, the drummer launched into an extended solo that elicited appreciative shouts, applause, and a few squawks from fans in the crowd.

Lucy sighed and took a drink. "I appreciate his skill and enthusiasm, if nothing else," she said. "Drummers are a strange breed. I dated one once. It was fun, while it lasted. You know what you call a drummer without a girlfriend?"

"I've heard this one." I chuckled. "Homeless."

She clinked her glass against mine. "To the drummers."

"To the drummers," I echoed. We drank. "I dated a lead singer once," I confessed. I wasn't sure what made me volunteer the information. It might have been the moonshine.

Malcolm's eyebrows shot up. "No way. For how long?"

"A really, really good six weeks."

Lucy grinned. "If it was that good, why only six weeks?"

"He was leaving to go on tour and I couldn't go with him. It wasn't ever going to be a long-term thing anyway. I still have good memories, and some comfy old band T-shirts I'll wear until they fall apart."

"Is that where you got all those shirts for Death Kettle you wear around the house?" Malcolm asked. "I wondered about those."

Lucy almost spat out a mouthful of moonshine. "*Death Kettle?*"

I hadn't thought about Cam in a while—really, not since Sean and I had gotten serious. I had no idea how Lucy would react to the news, or how half-demons were regarded here, so I kept the fact that Cam was a half-demon to myself.

Before Sean, all my relationships were brief. Most of them had ended abruptly when the person I was seeing wanted more than just a physical relationship. Cam had asked me to come on the road with him, even offered to pay all my living expenses and promised we'd travel in relative luxury. Not because we were good in bed—or not *just* because we were good. He liked me, and just sex wasn't enough for him anymore. Back then, I feared letting anyone get too close. I was afraid they might suspect I wasn't who I claimed to be, or betray me to the feds or my grandfather. So I pulled the plug and sent Cam off on his tour.

That pattern of short physical relationships lasted until an alpha werewolf, whose eyes crinkled when he smiled, introduced himself to me late one night at Hawthorne's and found a way into not only my bed, but my heart. Tonight, I sat in this rowdy, smoke-filled, Mos Eisley cantina version of Hawthorne's, and missed Sean so much that it hurt. We'd only been separated a day, but the distance between us—and the hollow sensation where our nascent bond normally offered quiet reassurance—gnawed at me.

The song finished with a thunderous roll of drums and a screaming note from the lead guitar. When the applause and shouts died down, the singer announced the band would be taking a short break. One by one, the band members left the stage. The drummer headed to a back hallway I assumed led to bathrooms and the others to the bar, where Joey already had drinks poured and waiting.

I caught sight of Leather Guy rising from his chair and ambling toward the bathrooms. There could be many explanations for his casual stroll, but the little hairs on the back of my neck prickled. Daisy nudged me and stared in the direction of the back hallway.

"I need to use the ladies' room," I told Lucy. "Hold down the fort?"

"You got it." She raised her hand, attempting to get a server's attention. "I'll get us some water and road snacks. They'll pack us a travel bag. Let me know whether you're coming with me or not."

I rose from the booth. "Daisy? You coming?"

She settled into the seat and rested her head on her paws, her eyes half-lidded.

Lucy chuckled. "I guess she doesn't have to go."

So Daisy wanted me to follow Leather Guy by myself. "Okay, then. I'll be back." I headed for the hallway, weaving through a crush of bar patrons of various species and levels of inebriation. Several men tried to talk to me as I passed, but I kept my gaze locked on the hallway and ignored them. A few made rude comments—or squawks—when I didn't respond. Ah, the joys of being a woman in a bar full of drunken idiots.

I spotted Isaiah sitting at the main bar with a bottle of beer and a plate of meat, an empty seat on either side of him. All the other chairs at the bar were taken. Were shifters universally hated in this world, or lone wolves more so than pack wolves? As a member of a pack, who loved a shifter and my pack mates too, that made my heart ache.

At least Isaiah had taken our advice and decided to stay relatively safe inside the roadhouse instead of taking his chances outside. He couldn't stay here forever, though; he'd have to venture out eventually, either to find a new pack or try to survive on his own. I wanted to help him, but there was nothing I could do. Lucy had promised to get justice for his pack mates, and I believed she would keep her word.

When I reached the back hallway, it was deserted. I found four bathroom doors: two marked with silhouettes of a human man and human woman, and two others marked with symbols I didn't recognize.

One of the mystery doors opened and the spider-man who'd identified the Bon Jovi song to me earlier emerged. "Excuse me," he said as he scuttled past.

So maybe the other two bathrooms were for patrons with

different anatomy. Curiosity made me want to look inside, just to see what a non-human toilet might look like.

A heavy thud against the door at the end of the hallway drew my attention. It was an exit, presumably leading to the parking area in the back where Lucy had left her jeep. I went to the door and listened.

Through the door, I heard the distinctive sounds of fighting: heavy thumps of fists against solid flesh, gravel crunching underfoot, and muffled curses. Carefully, I eased the door open and slipped outside, into the shadows along the building.

Leather Guy was fighting the band's drummer hand-to-hand. Neither appeared to have a weapon, but the drummer was bleeding heavily from a stab wound in his upper chest. They moved far too fast to be human.

Snarling, the drummer spun in Leather Guy's grip, trying to take the larger man to the ground. His eyes shone gold—a shifter. I wondered why he hadn't shifted to fight. He caught sight of me in the shadows and snarled.

In the split second the drummer was distracted, Leather Guy moved like lightning. He drew a sword from a spine sheath and took off the drummer's head.

Blood sprayed through the air, narrowly missing me as the drummer's head and body landed in the gravel at his killer's feet.

CHAPTER 16

Leather Guy stood with his back to me, studying the dead man. Voices and the rumbles of engines drifted around the building from the parking lot. Here out back, the only sound was blood dripping from his sword.

Without turning, he finally spoke. "Do you like to watch?"

I cleared my throat. "Sometimes, but generally I prefer to participate."

He pulled a dark cloth from his pocket and cleaned the blood from his blade. "I suspected as much."

The fact he'd suspected anything of me at all was intriguing. I'd gotten the impression he didn't think much of mages.

"I hoped you'd follow me out here," he added when I didn't respond.

"Why?"

"So we could have a chat, away from your Guardian friend and bound ghost."

Somehow he knew Malcolm was bound to me, though that binding wasn't usually visible to anyone but us. My eyes narrowed.

He slid the sword into its sheath on his back with practiced ease and turned. His eyes still had that hint of silver I couldn't identify. "I'd hoped to take care of this business first, but you wasted no time tracking me down. I'm flattered."

"Don't be," I told him. "I just came out to get a breath of fresh air. Why lop off this guy's head? He was killing it on the drums."

"That wasn't all he killed." He nudged the drummer's head with his boot. It rolled into the flickering glow from an overhead light. He took a photo with his cell phone and sent it to someone. I was beginning to suspect what his profession was, even if I still had no idea what *he* was.

He pulled a large plastic bag from his inside jacket pocket, picked up the head by its hair, and dropped it into the bag with a nasty squelch. He tied the bag, took it to a Harley parked in the grass near a fenced area, and put the bag in one of the saddlebags.

I emerged from the shadows and studied the body as he locked the saddlebag. I sensed a puff of parchment-scented magic; the saddlebag had some kind of witchy wards, in addition to the lock.

The skin around the drummer's chest wound was black. "You stabbed him with silver so he couldn't shift," I said.

"He liked to bite people and infect them. He'd been doing it for almost a year, leaving a trail of ruined lives and messes for people like me to clean up." He joined me beside the body. Outside, without all the competing odors of the bar, he smelled like leather, tequila, and—strangely—the sea. What *was* he? "It's a good bounty. Would've done this one for free, but it would set a bad precedent."

I was right about him: a bounty hunter. I had no quarrel with bounty hunters per se; the good ones played an important role and filled a gap in law enforcement. Whether Leather Guy was one of the good ones remained to be seen.

His ice-blue gaze met mine as we stood over the drummer's body. "Of all the strange, dangerous, and fantastical things I have found here, you and your wolf companion are the most interesting I have encountered in a long time."

By *here*, did he mean the roadhouse? His intonation made me think he was referring to something else. In any case, I didn't want this man to find me interesting. "Well, this has been fun, but I should get back inside. My friends will wonder where I am."

"You don't need to worry about them." His smile chilled me like an Arctic wind. "I've arranged a diversion to keep them occupied for a few minutes so we can chat. No harm will come to them," he added when I started for the back door. "Nor to you, if you tell me who you are, and why you've come here."

"I came to hear the band and sample some of the local moonshine."

His eyes went from glacier blue to dark storm clouds.

"I guess the band's done for the night, unfortunately," I added, glancing at the drummer's body. "There's still some of the good stuff left in that bottle on our table, if my friend hasn't finished it off."

The back door swung open. The light from inside the bar framed the figure of a slim man in the doorway, wearing a T-shirt and jeans. A cigarette glowed in his hand.

"Thank you for not making a mess inside this time," the newcomer said. His voice was all too familiar. He gestured at the drummer's body. "You can throw that in the incinerator before you leave."

"Charles," I breathed.

Charles Vaughan stepped outside and let the door close behind him. "Hello, my dear," he said, his eyes glowing like soft moonlight. "Have we met? Surely not, or I would remember." He approached. "Ronan, introduce me to your lovely friend."

Of everything I had seen since arriving in the Broken World, Charles in a T-shirt and jeans, smoking a cigarette and smelling of beer, was the most thoroughly disconcerting sight of all.

Leather Guy—Ronan—said nothing.

"My apologies. He is an ill-bred man," Charles said to me, shaking his head. He flicked his cigarette into the gravel and extended his hand. "I am Charles Vaughan, owner of Hawthorne's. And you are...?"

"Alice," I managed to say.

He took my hand. I expected him to kiss it, as the Charles I knew had a habit of doing, but instead he shook it. "Lovely to meet you, Alice. You are here as Lieutenant Stone's guest, I understand. She is dealing with the little rumpus inside that Ronan cooked up." He raised an eyebrow at Ronan's glower. "Am I interrupting?"

"You know damn well you are," Ronan said icily. "Alice and I were discussing the reason for her presence."

"Actually, I was heading back inside to rejoin my friends. If you'll excuse me?" I said to Charles, who stood between me and the door.

He smiled, his eyes glowing softly. "I would consider it a great honor if you would join me later for a drink. Any friend of Ronan's is, of course, an even more cherished friend of mine."

Fresh on the heels of finding out the Charles I knew had influenced me for years, my instincts made me want to get far away from this man. My rational self reminded me this Charles was not the one who'd betrayed me, however, and I didn't want to insult our host when our things were still locked in one of his storage closets.

"I'll think about it," I hedged.

Charles glanced over his shoulder at the back door. "I will need to inform the other members of his band that their colleague has fallen to the hand of justice. A pity you could not have waited until the end of their second set."

Ronan scowled.

The back door banged open. Lucy emerged, her Guardian seal visible on its chain around her neck. Malcolm and Daisy were right behind her.

Malcolm flitted to my side. "You okay?"

"I'm fine," I assured him as Daisy trotted over to stand beside me. "I was just a bystander."

"What the hell is going on out here?" Lucy demanded.

"This was a bounty kill," Ronan said curtly.

"Show me your credentials and the posting," Lucy said, her hand half-raised as if reaching for a sword on her back, though there wasn't one there.

He took a black leather wallet from his jacket and handed it over. While she studied his license, he pulled up something on his phone with the dead man's picture. She read it over, had him show her the bagged head, and then returned his wallet and phone.

"Thank you for the kill," she told him. "Looks like it was quick. Better than he deserved."

"He never should have lived this long." Ronan's eyes were glacial blue again. "He should have been dead a year ago."

"I don't disagree," Lucy said. "I don't know how he eluded justice this long."

"I think the reason is obvious. The Guardians aren't doing their job."

Her expression went flat. "We're working around the clock, seven days a week. None of the Guardians I know have had a day off in months. There aren't enough of us to go around."

"And whose fault is that?" he asked.

"Not mine." She stepped toe-to-toe with him. "I've driven ten thousand miles in three months, bloodied my sword a dozen times this week. Don't blame me or the League for this, Bounty Hunter. Claim your bounty and move on to the next one. Look at it this way: the status of the League is job security for you."

She flicked the collar of his leather jacket. He tried to grab her hand, but she was faster and eluded his grip.

"And one more thing," she added as he glowered. "If you bring up my dead friends one more time, I will make damn sure you regret it."

Ronan pulled his sword.

For a moment, I thought he intended to attack Lucy. Instead, he turned toward the woods behind the roadhouse. "Incoming."

Daisy growled.

"Oh, shit," Malcolm breathed.

A pack of enormous snarling wolves erupted from the trees. Eyes bright gold, ears flattened, and teeth bared, they crossed the distance between us and the tree line in a matter of seconds.

Behind me, the back door to the roadhouse shut with a bang as Charles darted inside. Maybe he was going after a weapon—or maybe he wanted nothing to do with the impending attack. Either way, we were outnumbered three or four to one.

"Stay in this form," I told my wolf firmly. If she decided to get big, Lucy and Ronan might think she was a threat too. I couldn't be sure Ronan wasn't capable of killing Daisy.

In a blink, Lucy reached up behind her head and drew a sword out of thin air. I had no time to think about how the hell she did that because the wolves were on us.

"Go inside," Lucy snapped at me. Without waiting for an answer, she and Ronan ran ahead to intercept the wolves, swords raised. They fought, moving almost as quickly as dhampirs.

Running away had never been my style, and despite their super-speed and training, she and Ronan were grossly outnumbered. No way in hell I was joining Charles inside.

Malcolm and Daisy flanked me. Daisy tore into two wolves who got past Lucy and Ronan, while Malcolm used air magic to fling back any wolves that got near. Like me, he couldn't use his power with any kind of finesse, but finesse wasn't required—just blasts of air to send attacking wolves flying, where Lucy and Ronan waited to cut them in half.

I flicked my right hand to summon my cold-fire whip. Instead of a six-foot coil of concentrated and deadly earth magic, however, the whip was pulled apart by the ambient magic around us. It split into thin strands that flared like lightning bolts. I gritted my teeth and fought the wild magic around me for control of my whip, my best weapon against the attack.

Or was it?

Dark magic surged inside me. Unlike my earth magic, which didn't work like it should here, the sorcerer magic I'd absorbed from Miraç seemed unaffected by the ambient power of the Broken World.

I feared using this magic. My instincts told me once it started to take hold of me, I might not be able to control its effects.

A black and gray wolf came at me from the side while Malcolm was busy trying to keep another at bay and Daisy fought two other wolves. No time to debate; I'd have to deal with the consequences later. I stopped fighting the dark magic and let it rise.

My vision turned red. The noise of the fighting faded as my senses sharpened and focused. Void-black magic edged with red glyphs spiraled around my arms and from my fingertips, forming dual whips made not of earth magic, but sorcerer power. The force of the magic seared the air.

Malcolm said something, but I didn't hear him. I spun, lashing with my whips, and cut the approaching black-and-gray wolf in half in mid-leap. Shifter magic, tinged with the same madness I'd sensed in Isaiah, pulsed up my whip and into my body as the wolf's power transferred to me. The rush was like four espressos straight to my bloodstream. I sucked in a breath as the energy infused my own.

Flush with magic I could command even in this place, I waded into the battle with whips blazing. Ronan and Lucy fought back to back, their swords moving almost too fast to see. The air stank of shifter blood and death.

One by one, our attackers died. One got past my whips and came so close to biting me that one of his teeth sliced my sleeve.

Lucy brought her sword down and the wolf's head hit the ground next to my boot. She was scratched and bloody, but I didn't see any bite wounds.

The last wolf to die was the alpha. Half again bigger than the second-largest wolf in the pack, his power and size were unmistakable even from a distance. Daisy threw him to the ground and ripped out his throat. She raised her head and howled, drowning out the sound of his death throes. Finally, the alpha lay still. It was over.

I stood in the middle of the scattered bodies, breathless and covered in shifter blood. My whips snapped and sparked at my sides like broken power lines. Daisy stood to my right, Malcolm on my left.

Lucy and Ronan turned to me, swords in hand. Daisy licked blood off her muzzle and showed them her teeth. Malcolm's tension prickled on my skin.

"Are we going to have a problem?" I asked. My eyes were warm, indicating they were glowing.

"That depends." Lucy studied me. "That magic you've got…it's not from here. Neither are you. And don't tell me you're from *a couple hours north of here*. You three are from somewhere a lot farther away than that."

Though they were wary, neither she nor Ronan seemed all that surprised that Daisy, Malcolm, and I weren't natives of this world. Then again, their world's fractured boundaries meant people, beings, and creatures came and went all the time, so that revelation would be less strange than in my own world.

"What if we *were* from somewhere else?" I asked. "Does that make us enemies?"

Lucy tilted her head. "Some people I know would say yes, but I've always been of the opinion that where you come from matters less than what you do once you're here."

"We're in the same business, for what it's worth. I'm trying to stop someone from killing a lot of people." I drew my whips back into my body and let the dark magic settle back into my bones. "Since Daisy insisted we come with you, there may be a connection between the person I'm after and these attacks by what you call gravelings. Once we find the person we're tracking, we'll take her back with us. I'm not here to cause trouble."

"Maybe not, but you may cause it anyway." She took a cloth from her pocket and cleaned her blade. "It might not seem so to you, but this world has a balance, just like yours. When people and things cross boundaries between worlds and realms, that balance is thrown off. Things that weren't supposed to happen do, and what was supposed to happen doesn't."

She returned her sword to its invisible sheath on her back. The steel blade vanished as quickly as it had appeared. What the hell?

"The pain you felt during the flare means you aren't supposed to be here," she added. "Your magic and your body aren't of this place. You won't survive here long term. The more magic you have, the faster you'll die."

Damn Valas. I flexed my hands. She'd consigned me to a slow death here unless I brought back her triple-damned scroll. Though I'd never given her any reason to doubt me, she hadn't trusted me to keep my word and bring back the scroll without the added impetus of locking the mirror-door behind us.

I'd done a lot for the Court over the years: hunted down rogue vamps and their makers, custom-built intricate wards to their specifications, solved cases, saved Valas from Miraç and Charles from the Tepes stone, and a dozen more tasks of varying levels of danger. My repayment was betrayal at every turn.

Never again, I vowed. If I made it back home, this was the last time Valas or anyone else from the Court would stab me in the back.

"If that's the case, we should get back to tracking," I said finally. I glanced down. "Hear that, Daisy-dog? The clock is ticking. Now's the time to let me know why we're here."

Daisy walked around the bloody bodies of the wolves. She stood between Lucy and Ronan.

"What's this?" Ronan demanded, glowering at her.

"Wolf charades," Malcolm said with a sigh. "We've been playing it a lot lately. Alice?"

Daisy looked up at Lucy and Ronan, then stared at me.

I frowned. "Um, I think she wants us all to follow the trail. Together."

The wolf showed me her teeth. I was getting better at deciphering her expressions. "I think that means I guessed right," I said.

Ronan sheathed his sword with practiced ease. "I have no interest in joining your merry band. I have bounties to claim."

Daisy growled. He stared down at her, his eyes taking on that strange silvery hue again. "I don't know what you want from me, wolf, but you'll have to find someone else for your quest. I've received five job notifications just since I've been here. Whatever you're here to do, between the lot of you, I'm sure you'll have it covered."

The back door of Hawthorne's opened. Charles emerged, a bottle of beer in his hand. He surveyed the carnage with a raised eyebrow. "Congratulations to all on your hard-won victory."

"Coward," Ronan said, but without rancor.

"As the proprietor of this establishment, I must be neutral. I can hardly become involved in disputes between werewolf packs and the constabulary." Charles saluted us with his beer. "The drummer's pack, I take it?"

Ronan nodded. "Lurking nearby, waiting for him to finish playing so they could hunt together. They must have known what he was doing, and they protected and abetted him."

"Good riddance to the lot of them, then." Charles set his beer on the step so he could light a cigarette. "I would be obliged if you would dispose of the bodies once you document the scene." He took a drag from the cigarette, exhaled, and smiled at me. "Alice, you are quite a sight—resplendent in the blood of your enemies. Would you care to use the bathroom in my apartment to shower? Perhaps we would have time for a bite while your clothes are laundered."

"Am I not also resplendent in the blood of my enemies?" Ronan asked, his tone dry.

Charles flashed his fangs. "Indeed you are, but your beauty cannot compare to this warrior queen. And for all your charm, I am quite sure your blood would not be half as sweet."

Lucy rolled her eyes. Daisy chuffed in what might have been amusement.

This Charles lacked the smooth sophistication—not to mention the sartorial flair—of his counterpart, but there was something strangely charming about him. I could only imagine how the Charles back home would react to the news that another version of him existed and had invited me upstairs "for a bite" while my clothes were in the washer. I had no intention of speaking to my Charles again, but the possibility of seeing him die of sheer horror at such a lame vampire come-on was almost enough to make me change my mind.

I wished I had some way to take a picture of this Charles and Hawthorne's back to show Sean. He wasn't likely to believe me otherwise, even if Malcolm supported my story.

"Thank you for the offer," I said. "That's very generous, but I think Lucy and I will have to leave immediately before the trail we're following goes cold."

"How cold-hearted you are." Charles's smile revealed a hint of fang. "I will be doomed to be alone tonight."

"I rather doubt that." I had a hard time envisioning any version of Charles who slept alone unless it was by choice.

While we were talking, Ronan and Lucy documented the scene with their phones, recording video and taking photos. Daisy remained fixated on Ronan, watching him as he put his phone away and set to work bagging the wolves' heads. It was a gruesome chore. I found myself standing near the back door with Malcolm, trying to ignore the activity going on behind me. Meanwhile, Lucy was in her jeep, talking to someone on the radio. Probably reporting the deaths to her superiors.

Malcolm touched my arm. *I'm worried about you,* he said in my head. *That sorcerer magic is black magic, Alice.*

My choice was to either use it or get chewed on by a werewolf again, I countered. *And since my magic doesn't work right here, the odds that I'd be able to burn out the werewolf virus are slim to none. I didn't want to use it, but I didn't think I had much of a choice.*

I know. His cool fingers tightened on my arm. *Promise me you will listen to me if I tell you the magic is changing you.*

I promise, I told Malcolm. *And if I don't listen to you, you have my permission to do whatever you need to do to save me from the magic, and myself.*

He didn't reply for a long moment. Finally, he said, *That could mean something pretty serious.*

I know. That's why I'm telling you this now, while I know I'm thinking clearly. Sean and I made the same promise to each other before I left.

He squeezed my arm again, then let go.

With the wolves' heads stowed in his saddlebags, Ronan carried their bodies to a fenced-off area on the other end of the roadhouse. That had to be where the incinerator was. Daisy watched him work, her eyes bright. He ignored her pointed stare.

"Daisy," I said.

She walked around the bloody area to join us near the door. I got down on one knee to bring myself eye level with her, grimacing at the various aches and pains from a rough day. "I don't think he wants to come with us," I told her as Ronan disappeared into the fenced enclosure with the last body. "And I'm not sure we want him to. I don't know what he is."

Her stare was unblinking. Clearly, my argument had failed to convince her.

Ronan emerged again and shut the gate to the enclosure. Daisy nudged me hard. I sighed and got to my feet.

Charles met Ronan near his Harley. Ronan handed the vampire a roll of cash and said something in an undertone. Charles's eyebrows rose, but he tucked the money into his pocket. I wondered what the payoff was for: Ronan's bar tab, or something else?

Ronan swung his right leg over the bike and settled into the seat, raising the kickstand with his boot. With a wink in my direction, Charles went back inside the roadhouse.

Daisy gave me a push that nearly knocked me over. I headed in the bounty hunter's direction with her at my side.

Surprisingly, even standing next to the saddlebags, I couldn't tell what was in them. The witchy wards must hide their contents—even the smell.

As he took a pair of black leather gloves from his pockets, I said, "Look, I don't know how she knows what she knows." I gestured at Daisy, who stood in front of his bike. "I don't know how she's tracking the person we're after, how she knew where we were headed or that you'd be here, or why she thinks you should come with us."

He raised his eyebrows. "Sounds like you don't know much."

"Screw you, Ronan."

He rested his gloved hands on the bike's grips. "I've got a long list of people and creatures to track down. Lieutenant Stone isn't the only person working around the clock and putting in the miles. I'm not going to put all that aside because you *think* your wolf wants me along."

Daisy growled.

"I'm pretty sure that's what she wants," I told him. "You don't think it's the least bit strange and significant that a wolf wants you to do something?"

"I think it's plenty strange. Significant, no." He turned his icy stare on Daisy. "Move," he warned her.

She bared her teeth.

"If I don't find this person in time, a lot of people are going to die," I said.

He turned on the Harley's gas. "If I don't find the people on the list I just got, a lot of people are going to die."

"Is that why you're leaving? Or is it because of the money?"

"Both."

The Harley's deep rumble drowned out my short and rather profane response.

"Be seein' you, Alice," Ronan said over the roar of the engine.

He put on his helmet, flipped the visor down, and took off. Daisy jumped aside, but snapped her teeth at his leg as the motorcycle went by. He raised his hand as he passed Lucy. She gave him a one-finger reply.

The motorcycle and its rider rumbled to the end of the roadhouse and disappeared around the corner. I listened to the sound of the engine as it faded in the distance.

"What an asshole," Lucy said when she joined Malcolm, Daisy, and me. "With things in the League being what they are, the bounty hunters are a necessary evil. Some of them are like Ronan. The rest of them are worse. Still, better than the Spartoi." She rubbed her face. "We can't go on the road looking and smelling like this. Let's see if we can charm Charles into letting us clean up."

"Ronan said he arranged some kind of disturbance in the bar to distract you while we talked out here. What happened?"

She raised her eyebrows. "A fight broke out in the back room over a poker game. I had no idea that was Ronan's doing. Crafty bastard. Gotta respect his ingenuity, if nothing else. Well, and his ass."

"It was pretty fantastic," I admitted.

"Bordering on legendary," Malcolm agreed.

Lucy sighed. "Come on—let's go get washed up again and then we'll hit the road. Next stop: a mass grave near Oakdale."

CHAPTER 17

A FEMALE SERVER MET US JUST INSIDE THE BACK DOOR AND HUSTLED US UP some back stairs to the room we'd used earlier. Apparently, Charles didn't want us traipsing through the bar covered in shifter blood. As I'd noticed some shifters in the crowd downstairs, it seemed like a good decision.

I washed my bloody clothes by hand in the sink with detergent provided by Lucy, and showered while she got our bags from the locked storage closet. I scrubbed myself from head to toe and rinsed with cold water to help wake up.

As I washed, my thoughts about the Broken World versions of Charles and Hawthorne's forced me to contemplate something I'd deliberately avoided thinking or talking about since I'd found out I would travel to another world. The moment Adam explained this world was very like our own, other than the fractured boundaries between the mundane and supernatural realms, I'd immediately wondered if an Ava Selene Murphy, granddaughter of Moses Murphy, existed here—and just as quickly banished those thoughts. If she did, she was not me.

As we prepared the spellwork for the mirror travel, Malcolm had wondered aloud whether some version of himself lived in this world, and if so, whether that Malcolm's life had been better, worse, longer, or shorter than his own. Almost immediately, he'd come to the same conclusion I had: that it would be better not to know. We'd made a pact not to try to find out, and I still believed that decision was for the best. If anyone else we knew existed here, I didn't want to find them, and I didn't want to know. I saw no version of events where that knowledge would do anyone any good.

When I came out of the bathroom, wrapped in a towel with another around my hair, Lucy had stripped to her underwear. She was well-muscled, with no visible tattoos. She was battle-scarred from head to toe. One scar on her abdomen must have been very nearly a fatal wound.

I wondered, belatedly, if there were no healing spells here. I had a variety of healing spells with me, but I wasn't sure if they would work, given no other magic I had seemed to work right except the sorcerer power. Or maybe Lucy had kept her scars by choice. She seemed like the type who would.

Daisy was curled up on the sofa, her eyes half-lidded. "Where's Malcolm?" I asked.

Lucy grinned. "He skedaddled when I took off my pants, bless his heart. I told him I didn't care, but he muttered something about 'the rules' and flitted out of here like his ghost ass was on fire."

"He's really careful about not spying on people. He says he knows ghosts who do that and it really bothers him. Plus, when we were first together, he and I established some rules about not coming into my room unannounced after he scared me to death once when I got out of the shower."

"I like your ghost. He's got manners and a sense of humor. Most of the ghosts I know are jerks." She collected her bloody clothes to wash and clean ones to change into. "Let me get cleaned up and then we'll get the hell out of here. Joey will be up soon with our travel pack. It's already paid for." She went into the bathroom and shut the door.

I dressed quickly, opting to wear the same clothes I'd worn when I arrived in the Broken World rather than use my last clean shirt and pants. I'd only packed two sets of clothes, since that was all the room I had left in the backpack after packing the other items I needed. My toiletry bag was decidedly minimalist: travel-sized two-in-one shampoo/conditioner, moisturizer, soap, and deodorant. I also had a first-aid kit, my Smith & Wesson with silver bullets, assorted magic implements—which might or might not work here—and a photo of Sean and me.

I used my towels to wring as much water from my hand-washed clothes as I could and sniffed them. They smelled clean, thanks to the detergent. I put them in a plastic bag and reorganized and re-packed my backpack so I would be ready to leave when Lucy finished cleaning up.

With my packing done, I sat cross-legged on the floor in front of Daisy. She raised her head. "We have to learn to communicate," I told her. "We can talk to each other when you're inside me, so there has to be a way to share thoughts. Either that, or you need to return to my body so you can explain what we're doing and why you think Ronan should have come with us."

She curled her lip. Clearly, she enjoyed her newfound freedom and didn't want to give it up.

I reached for her. She growled.

"I'm not going to force you back in," I promised. "I want to try speaking to you again."

She remained still as I held her head in my hands, my fingers combing through her thick fur. I closed my eyes and reached for the golden thread I sensed between us. Unlike my strong connection to Malcolm, it was thin and insubstantial. Our bond was too new, too undeveloped to allow me to share thoughts with her. Damn it.

Maybe I could strengthen the bond. I lowered my shields and

focused on that thin golden thread of shifter magic. I reached for the earth magic around me, and instantly regretted it.

The pain was like falling into a dumpster full of cheese graters. Everything hurt. My skin, my bones, every nerve and cell sent out distress calls to my brain. My earth magic—my body, even—was on a different frequency than the magic here, so much so that even using it as ambient energy was agonizing.

My instinct was to slam my shields back in place and end the pain, but I refused to give up. Magic was magic. I sensed it pulsing all around me with potential and power, and that meant I could learn to use it.

Until then, I couldn't just funnel it into my tenuous bond with Daisy; it would do nothing to help, and might hurt her. Instead, I drew on the magic within me I knew I could use and tried to strengthen our bond.

Daisy snarled and moved out of my reach.

I raised my shields, blinked until I could focus, and frowned. "What's wrong?"

She chomped the air between us, her eyes glowing.

"Alice? You okay?" Malcolm asked from near the door. He'd apparently returned while I was focused on Daisy.

I got to my feet with a grimace, using the couch to stand. "I'm trying to strengthen our bond, but I haven't learned to use the magic here yet. And when I tried to use my own magic, she wouldn't let me."

"Could be a couple of reasons for that." He walked over to the sofa. "Maybe she wants you to conserve the magic and power you *do* have." He glanced at the closed bathroom door and lowered his voice. "Or she's worried about that dark magic you've got and doesn't want it transferring to her."

"She has physical form because of that magic," I pointed out, also in an undertone. Lucy was singing quietly to herself in the bathroom as she got dressed, but I didn't want to risk being overheard. "She was born of it."

He shook his head. "She has none of that black magic in her aura like you do. The power you absorbed from Miraç gave her a physical form, but she's unaffected by the dark magic. I think that little chomp means she doesn't want it. You'd best learn how to use the ambient power here if you want to strengthen your bond. Your magic is tainted."

At my expression, his eyes widened. "I didn't mean that. Wait—"

The bathroom door swung open. Lucy came out in a clean black T-shirt, BDU pants, and boots, her Guardian seal around her neck and damp hair in a ponytail. Her wet clothes were in a plastic bag. She eyed us. "Am I interrupting something?"

"Actually—" Malcolm began.

"No, we were done," I cut in. "I'm ready to go if you are." I picked up my backpack. Malcolm hovered near the sofa, looking stricken.

Lucy went to her duffel bag. "Okay, then. They come by with our food and drinks yet?"

"Not yet. I guess I'll go downstairs and check on that. Meet you out back." I headed for the door with Daisy on my heels.

I opened the door and came face-to-face with Charles. He stood in the hallway holding three drawstring cloth bags in one hand, his fist raised to knock. He'd traded in his T-shirt for a clean button-up shirt with rolled-up sleeves and combed his hair. Music, shouts, and laughter drifted upstairs from the bar.

"Were you listening outside the door?" I demanded.

"Not at all. I only just arrived." He smiled. "Forgive the delay in delivering your supplies. Our kitchen is short-staffed tonight."

"It's fine." I reached for the bags.

He held them out of reach. "May I escort you to your vehicle?"

I had no desire to be alone with him, but I was stung by Malcolm's comment and wanted to take a walk. I shrugged. "It's your roadhouse, Charles. Lead the way."

He tilted his head. "You look at me as though we know one another and speak with such familiarity. I would swear I have never set eyes upon you before tonight."

I pinched the bridge of my nose. "I apologize, Mr. Vaughan. It's been a long day and I'm tired."

"I am not offended, only intrigued." He offered me his arm. "Allow me to have a word in private."

This wasn't the Charles Vaughan I knew, but he was a vampire and I'd be foolish to let my guard down around him. I figured my new bodyguard would like the taste of vampire just fine if he got any funny ideas.

After a hesitation, I tucked my hand into the crook of his elbow. "Sure. Come on, Daisy."

As my wolf joined us in the hall, Lucy looked up from packing her duffel. "We'll be along in a few minutes." Her voice held a note of warning, presumably directed at Charles.

Malcolm was clearly unhappy to be left behind. I shut the door of the room.

Charles led me down the hall toward the back stairs. Daisy followed. "Any trouble with the rest of the band when you told them their drummer was deceased?" I asked.

He chuckled. "Initially, they were very angry. I showed them their comrade's wanted poster, and their anger turned to shock and horror. They had no idea he was a predator. They believed he was, and I quote, 'a very laid-back dude, for a shifter.' His only failing, as far as they knew, was a penchant for leaving a trail of broken hearts."

"It was a trail of ruined lives, not just broken hearts. The bastard."

"Indeed."

We descended the back stairs and went out the back door. Someone had soaked the gravel area where the werewolves had died with water mixed with some kind of chemical to remove all traces of the carnage. Daisy sniffed the wet gravel and curled her lip.

When we reached the jeep, Charles put the bags on the hood, turned his back to the building, and lowered his voice. "You must be cautious. There are those, even among the unbound, who would send you back to your mistress, hoping for a reward."

I frowned. "I have no mistress."

"I sense your binding. She who bound you has great power and dark magic, and must have enormous influence. You cannot outrun her for long. She will send people to bring you back. They may well kill your companions and anyone they believe gave you shelter."

"Then why give us rooms?"

"I am a gambler." He flashed a hint of fang. "And I am curious about you and your beautiful wolf."

Daisy showed him her own sharp teeth, but didn't put her ears back.

"Not much to tell you about us, other than we're traveling with Lieutenant Stone for a while. And no one will be coming after me," I added. "The binding you sense...it's not what you think. I'm not running from her; I'm investigating on her behalf."

"Interesting." His lips brushed my ear. "How have we met before, Alice? You *must* tell me." His words were accompanied by a nudge of vampire suggestion. Through my shields, it was nothing more than a tickle.

He smelled of cigarettes and beer. Under that odor I recognized the familiar scent of wine I knew so well. This Charles had never betrayed, bitten, or hurt me, but anger and grief for what the other Charles had done left a bitter taste in my mouth.

"I've never met you before tonight," I said. If he could sense deception like Charles back home, he'd sense the truth in my words. "I was much too familiar with you earlier, and I apologize. All I can say is that I've had a long day and I forgot my manners."

"I have enjoyed your familiarity and hope for more." His eyes silvered. *There* was the Charles I knew, or thought I'd known: wealthy bar owner and seducer of dangerous brunettes. "I caught the scent of a shifter on your things. You must have encountered one on your travels. Surely you do not have a brute as a lover."

Though I knew shifters here were much different than back home, I still didn't like hearing Sean called a brute when he was anything but.

I stepped back. "Who I choose to sleep with is hardly your business, Mr. Vaughan."

Several emotions flashed in his eyes: surprise, dismay, even a hint of revulsion. Resentful of his judgment, I opened my mouth, then closed it. I didn't owe this Charles—or *any* version of him—an explanation for anything, least of all for who I loved.

The back door opened. "You two look cozy," Lucy said. She headed in our direction with Malcolm at her side, her duffel over her shoulder and several small cloth bags in her hand. "I ordered two travel bags of food and water. What's in the third bag?"

"Food for Alice's magnificent wolf companion, compliments of the house." He gave her a smile, again flashing his fangs. "In hopes you may find your way back here again and indulge in another full night's stay under my roof."

"Much appreciated. I never know where work might take me, and your rooms are much better than a lot of other places I've stayed." She tossed her duffel and the smaller bags into the back seat. "Let's roll, Alice. We have a long drive ahead of us, and the road is dangerous at night."

"If you are heading south toward Oakdale, travelers tell me Donestre are hunting along the highway," Charles warned. "Have care."

"Always. See you next time, Charles." She climbed into the driver's seat and turned the key in the ignition. The jeep started with a rumble.

Charles opened the passenger door for me. "I wish you safe travels." His voice was decidedly chilly. Apparently, knowing I had slept —or was sleeping—with a shifter unnerved him a great deal. It shouldn't have bothered me, but it did, though I wasn't exactly sure why.

"Thanks for the hospitality," I told him. "Hawthorne's is quite a place."

"Indeed it is. Farewell."

I got into the jeep, put the bags of food and my backpack on the floor at my feet, and shut my door. He stepped back and lit a cigarette, his expression thoughtful.

Daisy sat in the back seat behind Lucy. Malcolm floated behind me, his uneasiness and unhappiness buzzing on the edge of my senses. I knew we needed to talk, but not in front of Lucy—and not until I was less angry and hurt.

Lucy shifted into gear and headed in the direction of the front parking lot. She gave Charles a wave. He raised his hand and watched as we drove away into the night.

THE BRIGHT LIGHTS, loud voices, and full parking lot of Hawthorne's were an oasis of relative safety. As Lucy turned onto the highway and accelerated away from the roadhouse, the pitch black of night closed in on our jeep. All kinds of potential dangers, most of which were entirely unknown to me, filled the darkness around us. Lucy remained on high alert, as did Daisy.

Once the roadhouse disappeared from view in the rearview mirror, Lucy switched from standard headlights to a different set. They were brighter than the standard lights, with a bluish tint, and they illuminated not just the road in front of us, but the sides of the road as well.

"What are those lights?" I asked.

She kept her eyes on the road and our surroundings. Her caution upped my anxiety level considerably. "We call them supe lights. You'll see a lot of them around buildings and in towns, but they're not common on civilian vehicles."

"What do they do?"

"You'll see for yourself soon," she told me. "Just watch."

I didn't have to wait long to get my answer. Ahead, on our right, the silhouette of a man appeared alongside the road. He glowed in the supe lights. "A ghost," Malcolm said in wonder. We passed the ghost so closely he could reach out and touch the jeep as we went by.

Something large and dark moved in the trees on the other side of the road. I didn't get a good look at it, but I thought it might have been one of the raccoon-bears that had tried to attack us the previous night.

"The supe lights make it easier to spot supernatural creatures," I said.

She nodded. "During the day, too. Some things can change shape or use glamour to look like something else. The supe lights let you see beyond the glamour in most cases and reflect different wavelengths and colors if something is supernatural."

"Ghosts glow white?" Malcolm asked.

"It's more of an opalescent glow," Lucy told him. "With the supe lights on, we'll see all kinds of spirits. I kind of tune them out, since I'm keeping an eye out for bigger, nastier things."

"Like the Donestre?" I asked. "What are those?"

"Definitely something you want to avoid. They prey on travelers, especially people traveling alone. Their natural form looks like a human male with long hair, green eyes, and furry ears, though they've been known to cut their hair short and hide their ears with hats."

"You said they prey on travelers," Malcolm said. "What do they do?"

"Eat them," Lucy said matter-of-factly. "Everything but the head. They leave that behind. That's how you know it was a Donestre kill."

"Yikes," Malcolm said.

"Yup." She glanced at me. "So, obviously I have some questions. I'm sure you do too."

"So many, it's difficult to pick which ones to ask. I'll start with maybe an easy one: can I have a magical invisible sword?"

"Do you know how to fight with a sword?"

"Sure. The pointy end goes in the bad guy."

Lucy chuckled. "You're not wrong, though sometimes it's harder than you might think to know who the bad guys are." She sobered. "Then again, if you're a mage, you probably knew that. Actually, the sword itself isn't magical. My ability to hide my sword is part of my Guardian heritage."

"I wondered if there was more to being a Guardian than just joining up," Malcolm said. "Can you tell us more about the League?"

"The origin of the Guardians is rooted in myth. The legend says that Cadmus, founder of the city of Thebes, slayed a water dragon that killed many of his soldiers. On the goddess Athena's advice, he planted the dragon's teeth. From the earth rose a legion of fierce and bloodthirsty warriors, the Spartoi. They were vicious—so much so that Cadmus supposedly attempted to wipe them out by setting them against each other. Those who could better control their blood-lust survived. They were faster and stronger than humans, able to go long periods without food or water, and train for days without tiring."

"Sounds like a scary bunch," Malcolm said. "If all that's true."

She shrugged. "No one has ever come up with an alternate explanation for the Spartoi's existence—and by extension, the existence of the Guardians. Their children, both male and female, inherited the Spartoi's physical strength and abilities. Their most sacred law forbade them to marry or have children with anyone who did not have Spartoi blood. They wanted to prevent their abilities from disappearing through intermarriage with humans. The penalty for breaking that law was death—for the Spartoi, their lover, and their lover's entire family. It was ruthlessly enforced. That, as much as their reputation for slaughtering not only their enemies but anyone who got in the way, led to their well-deserved reputation for cruelty."

"So where do the Guardians come into play?" I asked.

"After Cadmus's death, the Spartoi and their descendants split into different groups. Some became mercenaries, protecting kingdoms and wealthy families. Others joined the Knights Templar. One group dedicated itself to protecting humans from various supernatural threats and became the League of Guardians."

"A-ha," I said. "Now it makes sense."

"The modern League operates like a branch of the military and serves as law enforcement for nonhumans. Our jurisdiction is the entire United States. We go when and where we're needed, usually either in pairs or teams, to deal with supernatural beings and creatures who cause problems."

"And the Spartoi?" Malcolm wanted to know. "Are they still around?"

"Unfortunately, yes. They work as individual operatives or mercenaries, generally. Some of them belong to a guild called the Brotherhood of Cadmus. When they're hired to deal with a supernatural problem, they tend to kill first and not bother to ask questions later. Collateral damage doesn't bother them. The end always justifies the means. Sometimes we're forced to work together, but the League and the Spartoi despise each other."

"I can see why," I said. "They sound just as nasty as the creatures you have to deal with."

"You're not wrong. With any luck, you won't cross paths with any while you're here."

"So that's why you looked at me funny when I asked how you became a Guardian," Malcolm said suddenly. "No one joins the Guardians—you either have Spartoi blood, or you don't."

"*Guardian* blood," she corrected. "Not Spartoi."

"Sorry. No offense."

She blew out a breath. "I wanted nothing to do with the Guardians, and I sure as hell don't want to be lumped in with the Spartoi. I'm only half Guardian. My father was a Guardian. My mother isn't."

"Do the Guardians not have the same policy as the Spartoi about children?" I asked.

"They had the exact same policy, up until the last few years, when the League underwent some major changes. Before that, it didn't matter what a Guardian wanted, or who they loved. They wanted to protect the Guardian abilities at all costs, and they were a bunch of elitist assholes to boot. I was never supposed to be born. The Guardians made my life a living hell because of it. But my father loved my mother, and they wanted a baby, and here I am." She smiled—a real, genuine smile. "I got my Guardian abilities from my dad, my connection to the afterlife from my mom, and my stubbornness from both of them."

"You said you joined up after someone you knew was murdered," I said. "Was it your father?"

Her hands flexed on the wheel. "I'd rather not talk about that, if it's all the same to you. Those wounds are still pretty raw."

"No problem." I knew all about those kinds of wounds. I spotted several more ghosts along the road in front of us, glowing in the jeep's supe lights. "I'm used to sensing ghosts, but not to seeing them everywhere."

"Welcome to my world," Lucy said with a chuckle. "I mean, literally, *welcome* to my world. We're got a three-hour drive to Oakdale. It's easier for me to drive and listen than talk. What are things like where you're from?"

"A lot less crazy," I admitted. "For starters, we don't have dragons."

"Weeeeeeird," she breathed. "I can't imagine...really? No dragons at all?"

"Oh, it gets weirder than that," Malcolm said. "No Donestre, no spider-people, no trolls, no talking bats, and no witch territories. And Alice is shacked up with an alpha werewolf."

"He's cute, though," I added. "He owns a security company and he almost never kills anyone."

Lucy drove for a few beats in silence.

"Your world sounds kind of broken, to be honest," she said finally.

Malcolm snorted. "Funny you should say that."

For two hours Lucy drove, on high alert for roadside dangers, while Malcolm and I told her what life was like back home.

We encountered numerous ghosts, more of the raccoon-things, which Lucy said were called lotoru, and a number of shadowy creatures that eluded the vehicle's bright supe lights. We saw no men with long hair and furry ears—and no other vehicles except a convoy of trucks guarded by armed soldiers in jeeps, heading back the way we'd come. Lucy identified the trucks as belonging to a shipping company.

Of all the differences between her world and ours, she marveled most at the ease of travel, especially air travel, and how little the existence of supernatural beings impacted the daily life of most humans. Clearly, she had as much difficulty picturing such a world as I'd had visualizing hers when Adam first described it to me.

"Imagine not being able to travel by airplane because of *dragons*," Malcolm said, shaking his head.

"They tend to go after planes during takeoff and landing," Lucy explained, her eyes scanning our surroundings. "Once a plane reaches a certain height, it's safe because most dragons can't fly above eight thousand feet. Below that they'll take the planes down, either trying to get at the people inside, or just for fun. All outgoing and incoming flights have to have gunship escorts, and airport command towers have to monitor radar and spotter reports about dragon activity in the area. Flights are very expensive, so most civilians drive if they need to travel—usually in convoys and during the day."

I would never take the ability to run to a convenience store at two in the morning for ice cream for granted ever again. In fact, there were a lot of things I wouldn't take for granted anymore after being here, like being able to take a near-spontaneous vacation to the

Bahamas with Sean. Not that I *remembered* that vacation, of course, thanks to Miraç stealing my memories. Sean had promised to take me back to the Caribbean to make new ones. I wasn't sure which of us hurt more over those lost memories.

Thinking about Sean and my missing memories would do nothing but make me sad, so I focused on spotting creatures in the woods and answering Lucy's questions about our world.

Given the dangers that lurked along the road, I expected an attack on our vehicle at any moment. Lucy noticed my anxiety. "Most critters are smart enough to stay clear of League vehicles," she told us. "They wait for easier pickings to come along. We're not safe out here, but we're less likely to be attacked than civilians."

As it turned out, our route to Oakdale took us through another coven's territory. These were white witches, Lucy explained, and wouldn't mind our passage—especially since she had planned ahead and brought gifts.

Even if I hadn't seen the runes carved into the trees and painted on the road, I would have known when we crossed the coven's border because their wards flared and scraped across my skin. I winced and rubbed my arms.

About a mile past the wards, Lucy slowed. Ahead, a tiny figure in a dark hooded cloak waited near the side of the road, sitting on a tall chair inside a small shelter, with a basket on their lap. I saw no car or other structures nearby, but lights glowed deeper into the forest. Houses were hidden back in the trees.

"It's like a spooky little toll booth," Malcolm said over my shoulder. "You sure these are white witches?"

"Pretty sure," Lucy said as she pulled to the side of the road and stopped. "I've never been through here myself, but the Guardian intel says they are." She reached behind her seat for one of the small cloth bags she'd brought from the roadhouse.

The little sentinel slid down from the chair and headed for us, basket in hand, their face and body entirely hidden by the cloak and hood. I wondered who or what had come out to meet us.

My window whirred down. "Merry meet," Lucy called.

"Merry meet," a child's voice responded. She set the basket on a tree stump next to our jeep. Small hands reached up and flipped back the hood, revealing a small girl of about ten, with braided dark hair and amethyst jewelry.

Given the dangers that lurked in this world, some might be surprised to find a child—or even an adult—by herself at night. Age and size had little to do with power when it came to magic, however, as I knew very well. Multiply that by the fact her coven thought her capable of defending herself, and it was crystal clear underestimating this girl would be a very bad idea.

She climbed up on the stump so she could look in my window. "I'm Torryn. Welcome, Guardian," she said to Lucy. She inclined her head toward Daisy, sitting on the back seat. "Welcome, caretaker wolf. Welcome, earthbound spirit," she added to Malcolm.

"Merry meet," Malcolm said, very respectfully.

Torryn turned to me, her expression solemn. "You bring black magic here, Alice. While you are welcome, the darkness you carry isn't."

First Malcolm, now a witch I didn't even know. "Hey, I didn't ask to have this magic dumped on me," I said.

Her brow furrowed. "You haven't cast it out."

I started to protest that I had no idea how to do that, but she glanced back at Lucy, ignoring me. "You have something to share with my coven?"

"I do." Lucy handed me the little bag. I passed it to Torryn.

She opened the drawstring and peeked into the bag. To my surprise, she giggled and bounced up and down with glee. Then she caught herself, stilled, and assumed a more dignified expression. "Thank you, Guardian," she said formally. "This is very thoughtful." She slipped the bag into a hidden pocket in her cloak.

"How did you know to expect us?" I asked.

"I saw you in my bowl," Torryn said simply. She must have the gift of scrying.

"And how did you know my name?"

She smiled in the same way Carly did when I asked her questions. "I have gifts, same as you...and curses, same as you." Her smile faded. "My coven sisters advised me not to speak to you because of the black magic, but I don't always listen. Our High Priestess trusts my judgment. They should too." I caught the odor of burned paper— the telltale scent of angry witch.

"Why do you want to talk to me?" I asked.

"Because when I know something about someone, I don't like to keep it to myself." She frowned. "It itches if I do."

"You're clairvoyant," Lucy said. "My cousin and aunt say the same thing—usually right before they tell someone something they don't want to hear."

Torryn shrugged. "I can't control what I see. If you want to know what I saw in my cards and my bowl, I'll tell you." She held out her hand.

At first, I thought she wanted me to touch her palm. When I hesitated, she made a face. "Seeing things is *hard work*," she said pointedly.

Understanding dawned. I reached into my backpack and took some cash from the wallet provided by the Court. I put it in her hand carefully. Many clairvoyants received visions from skin contact, and I had no desire to let Torryn get a glimpse into my past.

The cash disappeared into a pocket. "I saw three things. Always *three things*," she added under her breath. "You need two others to reach your destination. The first is a man you met tonight who is not a man, who carries two swords and serves no one."

Lucy muttered a curse. "Ronan."

I turned to look at Daisy. She stared at me, as if to say, *Told you so*.

Damn it, and he'd ridden off on his Harley, probably never to be seen again. I turned back around. "Who's the other person we'll need?"

Torryn picked up the basket and handed it to me. "Leave the cover on. She's sleeping."

I blinked. The basket weighed only about four pounds, and its contents were hidden by a purple blanket that shimmered with silver threads and magic. From under the blanket, I heard a tiny snore. "What on earth is this?" I asked.

Torryn smiled, suddenly mischievous. "A pūķis. Don't wake her up."

I didn't know what that was, but Lucy's mouth fell open. For the first time since I'd met her, she seemed flabbergasted. "That's a treasure," she croaked.

The young witch's expression grew solemn. "Some of my coven sisters will be mad I gave her to you, but I know what I saw in my bowl."

"I can't take a treasure from you," I protested, still unsure of what I'd been given. "And I'm in no position to care for a pet."

Torryn stared at me. I smelled that burned-paper scent again. The thing in the basket moved around, settled back down, and resumed snoring.

Lucy coughed. "Just say thank you, Alice."

Malcolm poked me in the shoulder.

"Thank you," I said helplessly. "Does she have a name?"

"Not yet—that's for you to choose." Torryn folded her hands. "Give her a strand of your hair when she wakes up."

"A strand of hair. Okay. So, I'll need Ronan and this pūķis. What's the third thing?" I asked.

"You have come here with three goals. You will succeed at none of them." After a moment, Torryn added, "Sorry."

I did have three goals: stop Mariela from unleashing the Furies, return the scroll to Valas, and bring back Mariela to answer for her theft.

Malcolm's fear and fury at the prospect of being trapped here prickled on my skin. My own response was anger and denial. "I'm not going to fail," I told Torryn.

"I didn't say you would *fail*," she countered. "You just won't get done what you came here to do. Nothing is ever as simple as winning or losing, Alice. You should know that."

Damned if Torryn didn't sound just like Carly when she said that. She was right—I *should* know better.

Chastised, I pondered the basket on my lap. "Thank you," I said finally. "For the gift, the information you've shared, and meeting us here."

"You're welcome." She raised a dagger with a beautiful jeweled handle and blade etched with runes and pointed it at me. "No black magic within the borders of our territory, under any circumstances."

I didn't ask *or what*, because the answer was obvious. "I understand."

The blade disappeared under her cloak. "Since you've used the black magic, you'll have to cut it out to get rid of it. The longer you wait, the more you'll have to cut."

"Metaphorically speaking?" I asked.

She looked at me.

I swallowed. "I guess not."

She pulled up her hood. "Safe travels to you all, and blessed be."

"Blessed be," Lucy said. Malcolm and I repeated her words.

Torryn hopped off the stump and walked away without looking back. In seconds, she'd disappeared in the trees. The little shelter and chair vanished like mist.

"That was the witchiest thing I've ever seen," Malcolm said. "As theatrical exits go, hers was a solid ten. And I thought *I* was dramatic at that age."

I wrapped my arms around the basket to hold it steady as Lucy rolled up my window and shifted into gear. "So what's a pūķis?" I asked.

She pulled back onto the road, flipped on the supe lights, and accelerated. "House dragon."

"*House dragon?*" Malcolm squeaked.

The purple blanket rustled. A gray kitten poked her nose out and peered up at me with two emerald eyes. "Rrrrrr?" she inquired.

"That looks like a cat," Malcolm said, nonplussed.

"*Now* she does." Lucy chuckled. "Just wait."

Remembering Torryn's instructions, I pulled a strand of hair out and offered it to the kitten. A little paw emerged from the blanket and swiped the hair from my fingers. Magic I'd never felt before tingled on my skin. It was light violet, with threads of purple. Fae magic. The pūķis must have originated in the fae realm. I had a fae kitten-dragon in my lap. Sean was never going to believe any of this.

The kitten disappeared back under her covers. A loud purr, edged with a growl, drifted out of the basket.

"I have a house cat-dragon," I said, just so I could hear the words out loud.

"It might be more accurate to say *she* has *you*," Lucy said.

Oh, goody. The basket vibrated with the pūķis's growly purr.

"What do you think about what Torryn said, about you not succeeding?" Lucy asked me.

"I think we're still going to do our damnedest to do what we came here to do," I told her. "We've beaten the odds before. And if I've learned anything about seeing into the future, it's that nothing is set in stone. Always in motion is the future."

Malcolm snorted. "Did you just quote Yoda?"

I shrugged. "You quoted Obi-Wan Kenobi earlier, so I thought it was only fair."

Lucy frowned. "Who's Yoda?"

Malcolm flitted. "You mean you don't have Star Wars here?"

She laughed. "Relax, I was only kidding. Of course we do. This is the Broken World, not the Sad, Empty World."

I sighed. "Don't scare us like that, Lucy."

"I had you going there for a minute though, right?" She grinned.

"Not cool, dude," Malcolm said, shaking his head. "So, have you come up with a name for your new cat-dragon, Alice?"

"Not yet. I figure something will present itself. She's so *tiny*."

"Don't judge her by her size," Lucy advised.

"I'm not about to. What can you tell me about her?"

"Just the basics. They emerged originally in northeastern Europe, but have obviously spread, just like all the other dragons." At my expression, she waved her hand. "Yes, there are many kinds of dragons. Anyway, pūķis are fierce guardians of people, property, and treasure. They're also little tricksters, though that tends to develop more when they reach adolescence."

"So when does she turn into a dragon, then?" Malcolm asked. "When she's angry?"

Lucy smiled. "Generally, from what I understand, they are in cat form when on the ground and dragon form when they fly. Your little guardian will be quite a handful."

I blinked. "My little guardian?"

"Fierce guardian for life. She's bonded to you now."

"What? I can't—Lucy, I'm going back home when all this is done. I can't take her back with me. She'd never survive the journey."

"She's a fae creature," she reminded me. "Never underestimate a fae, or anything from that realm. Boundaries aren't the same kind of obstacle to them as they are to us."

"Even if she did survive, I can't take a cat-dragon back to my world," I argued. "We don't have cat-dragons there."

Lucy kept her eyes on the road. I hadn't seen any ominous shadows in the trees since we entered coven territory, but hyper-vigilance seemed like a necessity for nighttime driving here. "Maybe you do, maybe you don't. Just because you aren't personally aware of one existing doesn't mean they don't. Smart little creatures like pūķis are very good at hiding."

"She's got a point," Malcolm said. "Just think of all the so-called mythological and legendary creatures we've got back home. What if even a percentage of those are real?" He grinned. "What if some of those people flying high on whatever they're on aren't just halluci-nating when they say they saw dragons?"

A furry creature that looked like a large, muscular beaver with two small wings on its back ran across the road in front of us. It shone greenish-black in the supe lights and had bright green eyes and big teeth. It disappeared into the trees.

I rubbed my forehead. "What on earth am I going to do with a cat-dragon?"

"Same thing you're going to do with a magic wolf: make it work," Malcolm told me. "Let's worry about one thing at a time. We've got more immediate problems, like getting out of witch territory, avoiding creatures that eat travelers, and finding a mass grave."

And proving Torryn's predictions wrong, I thought wryly. "Piece of cake."

CHAPTER 18

Thanks to Lucy's GPS and Isaiah's directions, we had no trouble finding the field outside Oakdale where he'd buried his pack's remains.

Even if we hadn't known the exact location, though, I could have guided us there once we were close. My dark magic roiled, making my stomach churn and my skin crawl, even as it pulled me toward the wolves' grave. I squashed the sensation with my own magic, though the queasiness remained.

The streets of Oakdale were silent and deserted at three in the morning. Now that I knew to look for them, I noticed supe lights among the streetlights, their bluish tint giving the empty streets an eerie, otherworldly glow.

The field was adjacent to an abandoned salvage yard. Lucy parked her jeep near a couple of motorcycles and cars. I wondered if they'd belonged to members of the pack.

I reached for my door. "Stay in the jeep," Lucy said. "This is a League investigation."

"I know how not to contaminate a crime scene."

"I'm not asking you." She unbuckled her seatbelt. "Stay put."

"If this is because of what happened at the roadhouse with that bloody T-shirt, I've got that under control."

She opened her door. "Whatever magic you've got that likes these things has been prickling since we rolled into town. I have no idea what you're capable of. If you lose control again like you did back at Hawthorne's, I'll have to do whatever needs doing to protect myself and others. That includes the use of deadly force, which I don't want to use since I kinda like you, and because I *really* do not like paperwork. *So please stay in the damn jeep.*" She got out.

"Can Malcolm go with you to look around and watch your back?" I asked as she reached to close her door.

She thought about it, then nodded. "Okay. Come on, Malcolm."

"Go on ahead," he told her. "I'll catch up."

Lucy shut her door, took a heavy rucksack from the back of our vehicle, and headed out across the field, picking her way through the grass by our headlights. To my surprise, her skin was pearlescent in the jeep's supe lights, similar to the ghosts we'd seen along the road on the way to Oakdale. She'd said she was part dead, whatever that meant, so I supposed that shimmery glow confirmed it.

"I'm sorry for what I said about your magic," Malcolm said to me when she was out of earshot. "I know you're mad about it and you probably don't want to talk right now, but I wanted to tell you that, at least."

"Apology accepted. We'll have time to talk about it later. Go spy for me and see what you can find out about what killed the werewolves."

"Roger that. Honk if you need us." He zipped away to join Lucy.

My new cat-dragon seemed to have gone back to sleep. I set her basket on the driver's seat and dug into one of the travel bags we'd brought from Hawthorne's. It contained a large refillable bottle of water emblazoned with the roadhouse's logo, several sandwiches wrapped in paper, an apple, an orange, and various snacks—some of which I recognized, and some I didn't.

I ate a sandwich and an apple as Daisy and I watched Lucy and

Malcolm investigate the wolves' grave. Lucy's gear bag included a camp shovel, which she used to unearth some of the remains. She and Malcolm studied what they'd uncovered, and she took pictures of the grave with her phone.

I unwrapped the other sandwich and ate it too while I waited. Despite the nausea caused by proximity to the grave, I was famished. When the sandwich was gone, I tore open a bag of chips.

Daisy nudged my shoulder. I patted her head. The growly snoring continued from the basket.

"I think I'll have to name her Sleepy," I told Daisy. "I wonder if she sleeps as much as a regular cat. Or maybe she sleeps as much as a regular dragon. I really have no idea what to expect from a cat-dragon. What do they eat? Will she need a litter box?"

Daisy snuffled.

"Hey, it's a real question," I protested. "Speaking of which, do you need to do your business? I'm not allowed in the crime scene, but I could at least stretch my legs."

She walked to my side of the back seat and waited by the door. I took that as a yes.

I got out and opened Daisy's door. She jumped out, gave herself a brisk shake, walked about ten feet away, and relieved herself in the grass near a large truck.

I ached all over, and my eyes burned with tiredness. Blast it, when had I gotten to the point where I couldn't stay up for a measly thirty-six hours without feeling like death? I'd hoped the food would give me energy, but instead I just felt *more* hungry, and no less tired.

Maybe it was all the sitting I'd done today, stiffening up my muscles after the beating I took falling through the mirror and getting tossed around by the failed tracking spell. I walked around the jeep several times, then did some stretching even though it hurt. Daisy stayed next to me, alternating between scanning the darkness for potential threats and watching me as I tried to wake up without the benefit of coffee.

The back of my neck prickled. Since Caleb's attack infected me with the shifter virus, my spidey senses had gotten sharper. My instincts told me someone was watching us. It might just be the people in the houses across the street, but if it wasn't, we could be in trouble.

I rubbed the back of my neck and crouched next to Daisy. "Do you see anyone out there watching us?" I murmured.

Daisy studied our surroundings, her eyes golden and ears forward, but she seemed calm. If something *was* lurking around, she wasn't aware of it. That should have made me feel better, but it didn't.

I got up and leaned against the jeep. My thoughts went to Torryn's pronouncement that I would have to cut the dark magic from my body. What blade or magic could do that? Magic wasn't a tangible thing, like a tumor or bullet—even dark magic. The sorcerer Miraç had stolen my magic in a black magic ritual, but I couldn't duplicate that feat even if I wanted to. Well, perhaps I *could*, if I studied the ritual, but I *wouldn't,* because it required a human sacrifice. I would die a hundred horrible deaths and never consider committing that kind of atrocity.

Beyond the apparent impossibility of cutting the magic out, Sean's suggestion the sorcerer power might be useful in killing Moses had stuck in my head. I knew better than anyone how difficult but necessary it was to kill my grandfather. If there was a way to use this blasted dark magic to get at Moses, I owed it to everyone to find out for sure before I tried to cut myself open, especially on the word of one little witch.

Finally, Lucy covered up what she and Malcolm had been looking at and re-packed her little spade. She stuck a flag in the ground to mark the spot for her colleagues, shouldered her gear bag, and headed back to the jeep, talking with Malcolm. I tried not to feel a little jealous at their closeness, but failed. It wasn't like me to be possessive of Malcolm. Damn it, I was tired, hungry, and perilously close to irritable.

I ate the last of my crackers as they approached and stuffed the empty package into my jeans pocket. Lucy went around to stow her gear bag in the back of the jeep, her face expressionless. I recognized the look of a law enforcement officer with her emotions on lockdown.

"What did you find?" I asked Malcolm as he floated back and forth at my side.

"A big mess, just like Isaiah described," he said heavily. "Be glad you didn't see it. It looked like someone dropped them in a food processor. Hard to tell what's missing now, with the remains all jumbled up, but we didn't see any hearts or livers."

"What else?" I prodded.

Lucy slammed the jeep's back door, startling me. I rubbed my arms. I wasn't usually a jumpy person, but this place was getting to me.

Malcolm looked even more grim. "Lucy thinks one of the women might have been pregnant, but the fetus was torn out and eaten too."

"Jeez." My stomach lurched. "What are these things?"

"We call them gravelings." Lucy came around to my side of the jeep, cleaning her hands with a wet wipe. "It's really a catch-all term for creatures from the Underworld. They come in all shapes and sizes. They're nasty, merciless, and bloodthirsty. They're incredibly difficult to kill because they're fast, armed with more teeth and claws than you'd think possible, and formed from some kind of primordial ooze and dark magic."

"So what's the bad news?" Malcolm asked dryly.

Lucy's laugh was short, almost like a bark. "They're most active at night, hide during the day, and are single-minded about slaughtering. The more violent their prey, the better they like it. You can't reason with them—you kill them."

"So we follow the trail to wherever they're coming from, kill the ones we find along the way, and shut the door," I said. After we got our hands on Mariela, anyway.

"*We* are doing no such thing," Lucy informed me. "This is a League problem, not a civilian problem."

I shrugged. "Deputize me or something."

Lucy crossed her arms. "*Deputize* you? What do you think this is, the Wild West?"

I spread my hands to indicate our surroundings. "This is more like the Wild West than the Wild West was. This place isn't broken—it's crazy."

"Hey," she protested, then paused. "Okay, fine, I'll give you that one. But I can't protect you *and* fight gravelings *and* shut that door."

"You won't have to protect us. I know you might not think so, but I'm kind of a bad-ass back home, and as soon as I figure out how to make my magic work, I'll be one here too. Malcolm can hold his own in a fight. Daisy is...whatever she is. I'm not sure what that cat-dragon can do, but Torryn seemed to think she'll come in handy too." I took a deep breath and let it out. "I know you prefer to work alone, and I'm sure there's a good reason for that, but sometimes you need a team."

"Wow...if the old Alice could have heard you say that," Malcolm said. "And it's true—she is a bad-ass," he added. "Her magic is kinda wonky here, and so is mine, but we're not liabilities. You don't have to protect us. Alice is right; you need a team. There are a lot of those critters running around, and there will be more and more getting up here until we get that door closed. We can save lives if we work together."

Lucy pinched the bridge of her nose. "As you've probably guessed, I have some trust issues with partners and teams."

I waved my hand. "I am literally the poster girl for trust issues. But you know what you can usually trust? Your gut. What does your gut tell you about us?"

She studied us. I brushed cracker crumbs off my shirt. Daisy showed Lucy her teeth, her eyes glowing. Malcolm gave her a ridiculously charming grin and floated back and forth.

Lucy sighed. "Get in the jeep." She headed around to the driver's side.

I opened the back door for Daisy to jump inside, then shut it and opened my own. "Hey, can I have one of those Guardian badges, since I'm your deputy?"

She gingerly moved the cat-dragon's basket from her seat to the floor on the passenger side. "Don't push it, Alice."

And that was when the gravelings attacked.

* * *

Monsters.

I'd fought a number of supernatural creatures in my life and held my own, but at the sight of the swarm of pitch-black, toothy, snarling creatures emerging from the darkness to converge on us, my brain locked up in terror. They were the worst nightmares given form, ranging from the size of a house cat to eight feet tall, and there were dozens of them, gnashing their teeth and howling for blood.

Monsters! my conscious mind screamed.

Fortunately, my subconscious knew what to do and my instincts kicked in, so I didn't just stand frozen in place half inside the jeep like some kind of dunce. Which was fortunate, because otherwise my new alliance with Lucy might have been the shortest partnership of all time.

If anyone living nearby heard the gravelings' howls, they stayed inside their homes—much as they'd probably stayed inside while Isaiah's pack died.

I guess I knew now what had been watching us from the darkness, hidden from all of us, even Daisy.

My own magic was still unusable. I reached for the sorcerer power thrumming in my bones. Dark magic erupted through my skin and from my hands to form my whips. The rush of power was pure pleasure, and twice as potent as the magic I'd used fighting the werewolves at the roadhouse. I'd been reluctant to use the magic then, but this time, I didn't fight to rein it back because I figured I needed the boost of energy to have a chance against the gravelings, and because it felt *so good*.

I had a fraction of second to worry about what that meant before the gravelings were on top of us and survival was the only thing that mattered.

They didn't fight like wolves; they fought like mindless things driven by a desire to slaughter and eat. In a way, that made fighting them easier, because there was no plan to their attack, unlike the wolves.

Lucy was right: they were very, very hard to kill, as I discovered when I lopped two legs off one and severed a third of its body from the rest, and still it half-crawled, half-jumped at me, trailing innards and thick, stomach-turning black gloop. A larger one chomped down on its injured buddy, tossed it into the air, and gulped it down before eating the parts I'd cut off earlier.

Malcolm slashed at the creatures with razor-thin blades of air magic, flitting so quickly I couldn't track him with my eyes. Why he could use his natural magic and I couldn't, I didn't know. On the other side of the jeep, Lucy was swearing a blue streak and slicing through the gravelings' leathery flesh. We cut and hacked and slashed as fast as any of us were capable of, but within moments it was painfully clear there were too many of them, and too few of us.

Something big knocked me aside. Daisy leaped from the jeep, having scrambled over the front seat. Golden magic swirled as she tripled in size. The collar Lucy had put on her when we'd first met— had it really only been this morning?—disintegrated.

She raised her head and howled, as she'd done when the lotoru tried to attack us. Her howl was deafening. I wondered what local residents thought about the sound.

The gravelings paused for a split second, as if some part of their primal brains recognized a bigger predator, but their drive to kill and eat us won out—much to our dismay, and Daisy's delight.

She'd fought like a wolf against the wolves that ambushed us at

Hawthorne's. Even twenty feet tall, she'd attacked the demon Lord Orias as a wolf.

Against the gravelings, my wolf became a glorious nightmare.

Enormous teeth bared, she launched herself into the midst of the horde and tore through them, leaving nothing but twitching body parts and black gloppy mess in her wake.

"Please don't eat them!" I shouted at her, slicing a four-foot ball of teeth and claws into four pieces with my whips. I had no idea what graveling flesh and blood might do to her. Maybe nothing—or maybe something very bad.

Daisy snarled back at me before shredding a very large creature that bellowed and spurted oily black gloop as it died. Whether that snarl was an acknowledgement or defiance, I couldn't tell.

I realized I didn't hear Lucy's sword cutting its way through graveling flesh anymore. "Lucy, you okay?" I yelled, taking the head off another creature. It was gobbled up quickly by a larger one, just before that one died in Daisy's jaws.

Lucy staggered around the side of the jeep, splattered with black gloop and sword in hand. She had a couple of small bite or claw wounds, but seemed otherwise unhurt. She took in the sight of Daisy, blinked, and then waded into the fray as if there wasn't an enormous wolf with bright golden eyes and magic swirling around her ripping gravelings to shreds ten feet away.

A small creature landed on my back and tore into the shoulder already injured during my trip through the mirror. I screamed and lashed at it, but missed. Its teeth and claws shredded my back, shoulder, and arm as it growled and hissed.

Suddenly my attacker was gone—ripped away from me by some unseen force. I staggered against the jeep and turned just in time to see the thing struggling and screeching in midair, held in the talons of a gray-and-scarlet dragon about the size of a house cat, with emerald green eyes and surprisingly powerful little wings.

"Holy cat-dragon," Malcolm said in awe.

My cat-dragon promptly ripped its prey in half, tossed the parts aside, and landed on my non-injured shoulder. Tiny claws dug into my skin as her wings folded in. She perched on my shoulder, perfectly balanced, and let out a growly, throaty purr.

Daisy and Lucy dispatched the last of the gravelings, who were in the process of trying to eat their fallen comrades. To my surprise—and disgust—the gravelings' bodies dissolved, their flesh turning to puddles of black goo even as we watched. The smell defied description. Soon there would be nothing left but the gloop and the stench, or maybe even just the stench.

Breathing hard, Lucy locked gazes with Daisy, who was large enough at the moment to look the Guardian in the eye.

"I know you can understand me," Lucy said to Daisy. I edged closer, my dark magic crackling on my skin. "You fought to help protect us, and I'm grateful."

Daisy inclined her head slightly.

"Behave yourself, though," Lucy added. "Don't assume that collar was my only way of reining you in."

Daisy showed her teeth, but in the friendly grin she'd shown Joey at the roadhouse, rather than in a threatening way. Interesting that certain kinds of threats she took as friendly chatter, while others were deadly serious. I had yet to figure out how she decided which were which.

I let my whips spiral back into my arms and let go of the dark magic. My shoulder screamed and hot blood ran down my arm. I was suddenly aware of a half-dozen other small wounds I hadn't noticed in the heat of battle. And I was famished again.

The cat-dragon lifted off from my shoulder and returned to her basket in the jeep. As she landed, her wings folded in, violet magic swirled, and a gray kitten stared up at me with emerald eyes. She lifted a goop-splattered paw and licked it primly.

"My life is weird," I said.

Lucy snorted. "Welcome to the club, Deputy."

CHAPTER 19

We cleaned up as best we could with Lucy's wet wipes, performed triage on each other's wounds, and then ate like starving werewolves —washing down our food with much-needed swigs from Lucy's flask.

The roadhouse had packed deer meat for Daisy. She returned to her normal size and ate it outside the jeep. Lucy divided the contents of her travel bag between us. If she wondered where all my food had gone, she didn't ask.

Between bites of her sandwich, Lucy used the jeep's radio to report the location of the werewolf pack's grave and the graveling attack. Luckily, the dissolving bodies meant she could under-report the number of gravelings that had attacked and avoid mentioning she'd had the assistance of a ghost, a mage, a pūķis, and a giant magical wolf.

She sent in the pictures she'd taken via her cell phone and promised to file a full report when she had a chance. The dispatcher took her brief account of what happened and asked where Lucy was headed next.

"South," Lucy told her. "Toward where I think the gravelings are coming from. When I find the source, I'll call in my coordinates."

"Ten-four," the dispatcher said briskly. "Keep us posted, Four-oh-one."

Lucy signed off, hung up the radio, and started plotting a route on her dashboard GPS.

"Where are we headed?" I asked, tearing into a package of cookies.

"South, like I told dispatch." She frowned and tapped on the GPS screen. "By way of a healer and a motel."

"A healer? Is that like a doctor?"

"A mage." She studied the screen, scrolling through information. "A healer uses magic to heal."

"What kind of magic?"

She glanced at me, then returned to searching for a healer on the GPS. "It depends on the healer. For our wounds, we're going to need something strong and fast." She tilted her head. "I see a mage healer on the way, endorsed by several Guardians I know and trust."

"Sounds good." As a general rule, I didn't like anyone but Malcolm to use healing magic on me because it reminded me of being a prisoner of my grandfather's cabal, subjected to both torture and healing by his blood mages without my consent.

My shoulder hurt like someone had driven a pike through it, though, and every bone in my body ached. Besides, I might be able to learn something from the mage that could help me figure out how to use my own natural magic instead of the dark magic I'd absorbed from Miraç. I'd liked the feeling of the dark magic a little too much for comfort.

Daisy had finished her food all too quickly; I was sure she was still hungry, and so was I. Apparently traveling to another world and battling werewolves and gravelings could cause one to work up an appetite. She waited outside the jeep on high alert, watching for any other threats that might try to sneak up on us.

Meanwhile, my cat-dragon had finished washing graveling goop off her fur and curled up in her basket at my feet, but she wasn't asleep. She watched me, her emerald eyes glittering and occasionally flashing with violet magic. She was a pretty little thing—and completely and utterly deadly. And I still had no idea what to name her.

Finally, Lucy had our route planned from Oakdale toward the center of the attacks by way of the mage healer, avoiding areas shaded black, except one.

"A colony of earth spiders," she said. "Shapeshifters. A form of yōkai. They generally keep to themselves and don't bother anyone, but this colony's leader is an isolationist. We should be fine to just drive through the edge of their territory."

"Shape-shifting spiders sound fun," Malcolm said. He'd been forcing cheerfulness since we got back in the jeep. Seeing the dead wolves had really rattled him.

I got out to open the back door, stifling a groan at all my aches and pains. "Let's load up," I told Daisy.

She looked meaningfully at the empty spot where her dinner had been, and then up at me.

"I know; I'm still hungry too," I told her. "We'll try to find some food on the way." Where we'd find some, I had no idea. I hadn't seen any businesses open, but there had to be somewhere to get food.

Clearly disgruntled, she jumped into the jeep. She sat down on the back seat with a snuffly chuff. I shut the door and got in.

When we were all settled, Lucy turned on the ignition and backed out onto the street. No one had stirred from their homes, even in the wake of the very noisy fight. A few curtains moved as we drove away, but that was the extent of movement I saw from people living near what I was starting to think of as the killing field.

Lucy noticed me looking around. "Unless they have special training or a death wish, most civilians stay inside with their doors barred and windows shuttered. It's just how things are here. It helps us because there's less collateral damage usually when something happens, and reduces the number of call-outs we get."

"I guess that's one way to look at it." Malcolm's voice was grim. "This is a tough world to live in."

"I suppose it would seem that way to you. To us, it's just Thursday." She glanced at me. "There's a waystation not too far ahead. We can get food for everyone and fuel so we don't have to stop again before we get to the healer. I'll pay for use of the facilities so we can clean up, but let's not stay long. I'd like us to get as far as we can by dawn."

"Got it." I winced and settled back into my seat. A waystation sounded like the Broken World equivalent of a convenience store or truck stop.

I was ready to go home to a world that made sense, with all-night fast food and no giant shape-shifting spiders. A world with Sean in my bed and threats I understood how to fight.

We couldn't go home, though—not until we found Mariela and the scroll and made our way back to our return gate.

The cat-dragon hopped into my lap. She turned around a few times, curled up, and lay her head on my leg, purring quietly.

We drove out of Oakdale and into the night.

THE WAYSTATION WAS INDEED A HEAVILY fortified version of a truck stop. We were in and out in less than fifteen minutes—a little cleaner, moderately refreshed, and carrying several bags of road-friendly food and drinks. Our blood and black goo-splattered clothes barely got second glances from other customers.

In addition to food for myself, I bought Daisy another good-sized hunk of deer meat, which she ate in the parking lot. The cat-dragon happily consumed a full-sized can of cat food and drank about a pint of water. She settled back into my lap, purring. I wondered if she sensed my dark mood, or if she just wanted a warm place to nap.

Either way, I appreciated her comforting warmth, even if I had no idea what to do with her when it was time for Malcolm, Daisy, and me to return home.

A waystation employee—a troll in blue coveralls, whose name tag identified him as Ureg—fueled up our jeep. He and Daisy growled at each other until the tank was full and Ureg ambled off to assist a different customer.

We headed south on a major highway that actually had some traffic—mainly semis and large vehicles traveling in caravans. The vehicles were equipped with supe lights and oversized metal bars on their fronts, presumably to protect from collisions with large objects or creatures.

Despite my best efforts, I fell asleep not long after we got back on the road and dreamed about witches with enormous blades etched with pictures of male genitalia.

I woke with a start some time later when Lucy turned the jeep down a rough country road. I rubbed my bleary eyes and wiped some drool from my chin. I suspected I'd been snoring. "Where are we?"

"Approaching the mage healer's house." Lucy drove slowly, trying to avoid the largest bumps and dips, but the vehicle didn't have much of a suspension and the rough road rattled my teeth.

Peering out my window, I spotted an enormous castle on top of a hill in the distance. Bluish-white floodlight supe lights illuminated the building, its roofs and towers, and lawns brighter than the midday sun. Nothing would be able to get close without being seen.

"What the hell is that?" I asked, pointing.

Lucy winced as the jeep hit a particularly deep pothole. "The local Keep."

"Which is...?" I prompted.

"Sorry, I keep forgetting this is all new to you. Fae citadel. A prince of the Dark Fae lives there."

"Gulp," Malcolm said. "I vote we stay the hell away from the citadel of the Dark Fae prince."

Daisy chuffed. "Sounds like we're all in agreement," I said.

Lucy slowed to a crawl as a small house built into the side of a hill came into view in our headlights. Despite the late hour—or early hour, depending on how one looked at it—several lights were on inside.

Powerful magic sizzled on the edge of my senses. I braced myself as we crossed the mage's wards. Like the wards on the roadhouse, they lit up in distinct colors, signaling the healer who was approaching and what kind of magic we had. Unlike the coven wards, they didn't hurt me, just prickled on my skin. I let out a breath.

Lucy parked the jeep and we got out. Malcolm had gone invisible to avoid detection by the mage healer. I sensed him on my right.

"Will you stay and guard the vehicle and our things?" I asked Daisy.

She studied the house intently, then sat on the back seat so she could see anything that approached. I wondered what she'd sensed or seen from the house that made her willing to let us go in without her.

My cat-dragon jumped onto my shoulder. "Stay in the jeep," I told her, trying to disengage her claws from my shirt. She growled.

"She's your guardian," Lucy reminded me, coming around to my side of the vehicle. "Bring some cash, or something to barter."

I had nothing to barter, so I took cash from my wallet and followed Lucy up the walk with my cat-dragon on my shoulder.

A hinged gunport in the middle of the door opened. The barrel of a shotgun appeared. We stopped in our tracks.

"These are loaded with spelled pellets and silver flechettes," a brisk, young male voice said. "State your business."

"We're looking for the mage healer," Lucy said. "We have cash."

"Let's see it."

Slowly, Lucy withdrew a roll of cash from her pocket and raised it. I showed my own cash.

"Not enough," the young man said. The barrel raised slightly. "Show me more, or get going."

"It's more than enough," Lucy countered. "Going rate plus twenty percent for us showing up in the middle of the night, and a little extra to get us back on the road in less than an hour."

"What's all that black goop?" he asked.

Lucy heaved a sigh. "You want to play twenty questions or let us inside?"

"I want to play twenty questions." His voice hardened. "What's the goop?"

"Graveling innards," I said. "We've had a long damn night."

"Graveling innards, huh? That's a new one." The shotgun barrel disappeared. "Fine. I'm intrigued. You can come in. Tell your ghost friend to stop lurking around my blood garden."

A muttered curse from over by the garden. If I hadn't been so tired, I might have laughed. Poor Malcolm. He'd gone from not being able to be seen to not being able to hide, even when he *wanted* to.

A lock clicked and the front door swung inward. No point having a bunch of deadbolts with deadly wards on the house.

A young blond man of about twenty stood in the doorway, his shotgun cradled in the crook of his arm. He wore a gray T-shirt, pajama pants, and slippers. "Take your shoes off, please. Don't want that gunk in my house." He ran his fingers along the doorway, opening a passage in the wards for us to cross.

Lucy and I took off our boots and left them on the front step. Malcolm turned visible and followed us into the house. The mage shut the door behind us, and the wards flared again. I rubbed my arms as the house's ambient energy tingled on my skin.

"What's with the cat?" the mage asked, eyeing my companion.

"She's scared to let me out of her sight," I told him. "You're not allergic, are you?"

He clearly thought there was more to the story, but he didn't push. "I'm Tom," he told us.

We introduced ourselves and looked around. The house was spartan by any standards, but with comfortable spots for reading and a nice kitchen. He must like to cook.

I sensed no magic other than the house wards. No doubt his work area was hidden behind masking spells like my own back home. "Where do you want us?"

Tom gestured at a straight-backed chair near the door. "Bring that chair."

Lucy picked up the chair. We followed him into the kitchen. He leaned his shotgun against the wall and rolled up a carpet to reveal a circle inlaid in the stone floor. Lucy placed the chair in the middle of the circle, its feet in four tiny indentations. A lot of magic had been performed in this circle—enough to wear away the stone.

Expressionless, Tom got a bucket from under the sink and set it next to the chair. He ran his fingertips over some runes on a cupboard. Wards shimmered. He opened the cupboard, took out a wooden box, and set it on the counter. "Who wants to go first?"

"I'll go first." Lucy sat in the chair. "Hit me with your best shot."

He held out his hand. She put the cash in it, returned her arms to the armrests, and waited.

Tom set Lucy's cash on the counter next to the wooden box. He raised the lid and took out a beautiful dagger with an obsidian blade and carved wooden handle. The blade was etched with runes I recognized.

"You're a blood mage," I said.

He glanced at me. "That a problem?"

"Not at all."

"Good, because you know where the door's at if it is." He stood in front of Lucy, dagger in hand. "Some of these wounds damaged muscle." In other words, this was going to hurt.

She draped her hands over the ends of the armrests and crossed her legs, casual as could be. "Whenever you're ready, let's get this show on the road."

He cut the pads of his fingers without flinching. Magic rose and Tom's eyes glowed. His blood magic danced on his fingers, filling the air with the scent of pepper and copper.

He brushed his bloody fingertips on Lucy's arm, painting a rune in crimson on her skin. When I used blood magic for healing, I didn't have to touch the person, but Tom wrapped his fingers around her arm. "*Heal*," he said.

Lucy inhaled sharply as blood magic swelled and rolled through her, making her shudder. A tiny sound escaped her clenched jaw.

"Scream if you want to," I told her. "You have nothing to prove to anyone."

She glared at me and stayed stubbornly silent. The healing spell pulsed. She jerked and shook as the various wounds healed.

Finally, Tom released her arm and stepped back. Red magic swirled in the air between them, then dissipated. Panting, Lucy hunched over in the chair, face pale and lips bloodless. She shuddered hard.

"The bucket's on your right," Tom said, crossing his arms. "If you miss it, you clean up your own mess."

"Screw...you," Lucy said raggedly. She straightened with difficulty and glared up at him. "Ass...asshole."

"*Guardian*," he said, mimicking her tone.

She lurched to her feet and staggered to the other side of the kitchen. She leaned against the counter and breathed deeply. "You're up," she told me.

I gingerly placed the cat-dragon on the counter. "Stay here, please," I told her. "I'll be fine."

Violet magic flared in her emerald eyes.

Tom stared. "What is she?"

"Just a very smart cat. I wouldn't mess with her, though." I sat in the chair and rested my arms on the armrests as Lucy had done.

Tom studied me. "Your aura is strange, and your magic is even stranger. What have you been messing with to make your own magic unusable?"

"I tried to learn Latin and mispronounced something. Damn near killed me and screwed my magic all up."

"I hate it when that happens." He contemplated his bloody

fingertips, then glanced at me. "You keep that dark magic to yourself and we'll be fine."

"It's a deal." I gripped the chair.

He painted two runes on my forearm with his own blood. One was the same rune he'd painted on Lucy; the other, a spell I didn't recognize. "What's that?" I asked.

"I'm going to try to heal your magic, just to see if I can. If it works, you can tip me."

"I have no idea if that will work," I said, startled that he'd offered.

He shrugged. "It's a challenge. I get bored healing bites and sword wounds and so forth. Might as well try something new once in a while."

"I can understand that." I considered his offer. I very much wanted to use my own magic here and not the sorcerer power. I was relatively certain I could re-tune my magic using the spell crystals in my cuffs. If not, I could definitely do it once I was back home. "Okay, see what you can do," I told him finally.

I caught Malcolm's eye. He read my expression and joined Lucy by the sink, ready to intervene if Tom got any funny ideas.

Tom's hand closed on my forearm. "Lock that dark magic down," he warned me.

I couldn't blame him for being concerned. If he'd known it was a sorcerer's black magic, not just dark magic I might have gotten mixed with my own, he probably would have told me to get the hell out of his house and burned the chair for good measure. But then again, who knew if sorcerers were the same in this world.

I took a deep breath and nodded. "Ready."

His blood magic rose again. I'd been on the receiving end of many healing spells in my lifetime. Every one of them had hurt—some so badly I'd vomited, passed out, or even wished for death, albeit briefly. But they'd all been familiar magic, and familiar magic was something I understood and could withstand.

Tom's magic, like this world, was not like my own. When the healing spell rolled through me, it was like a tidal wave of broken glass and white-hot needles, and it caused the dreaded healing-spell effect trifecta: I screamed, threw up, and passed out.

I woke up on the kitchen floor, hurting all over and full of someone else's magic.

Not someone else's magic, I realized. My own magic, partially tuned to the Broken World. The sensation was incredibly unsettling, like my body was out of tune with itself, but more in sync with the world around me. I groaned.

"You awake?" Lucy asked from somewhere to my left. "Get up, then. We gotta hit the road."

"Give her a freaking minute," Malcolm snapped. "Healing spells suck, and he messed with her magic too. That's like a whole-body root canal."

I opened my eyes and found myself staring into the bright green eyes of my cat-dragon, who was standing on my chest, her nose an inch from mine.

Tom crouched next to me. "You good? Or are you going to throw up again?"

"Good thing I don't feel like shit, or your comments would really be annoying." I carefully picked up the cat and sat up. The room tilted hazily, then settled itself. The area beside the chair was wet and smelled of cleaning products. They'd had time to clean up before I woke.

I checked my injuries and found them all healed. Someone had cleaned Tom's blood off my arm. "Sorry for the mess," I said.

He held out his hand. "Thank you for aiming for the bucket as you went down. I take it this is not the first time you've gone through a strong healing spell."

"Correct." I gripped his hand and he pulled me to my feet. He was stronger than he looked. I put the cat-dragon on my shoulder, where she perched and eyed him. "I don't usually lose my dinner or pass out, but like I said—"

"Like you said, you've had a rough day," he finished. "How does your magic feel?"

"Out of tune with what I'm used to, but like I might be able to use it, at least in a limited way. Thanks. I'll get you some cash when I get back to the jeep."

Lucy waited by the door. She'd washed Tom's blood off her arm and cleaned off as much blood and goop as she could while I was unconscious. "We've got lots more driving ahead of us," she reminded me.

"I'm coming." I paused. "I didn't get you with any of the dark magic, did I?" I asked Tom.

He shook his head. "You locked it down well. You have good training. Where did you learn that kind of control?"

"A long way from here, in a place that doesn't exist anymore." I headed for the door on rubbery legs, with Malcolm at my side. "You've got some impressive skills yourself."

"Thanks." Tom opened the front door. Lucy and I put on our boots. My magic thrummed under my skin, ready to be unleashed. The uneasy sensation faded as I adjusted to the feeling of my tuned magic.

I got money from my wallet in the jeep and brought it back to Tom as Lucy climbed into the driver's seat.

He tucked the cash in his pocket. "Thanks. Safe travels to you."

"Thank you. Fixing my magic was risky for you."

"What isn't a risk when you're a mage? Comes with the territory." He started to close the door, then paused. "Get rid of that dark magic, before it digs in any deeper."

"I don't know how." Why I admitted that to him, I wasn't sure. "I do know I don't want to turn into someone who likes that kind of magic." I hesitated, then asked, "Do you know of a way for me to get rid of it?"

"Get rid of it how?"

"I was advised that I might have to cut it out."

He studied me, his head tilted. "I don't know of any way to do that, with any kind of blade or magic. I'm sorry."

"It's okay," I said, since it wasn't Tom's fault I was in this mess.

"It's *not* okay," he said, surprising me. "However you got that black magic, I'm sure it wasn't your choice. One thing I do know is it requires dark power to take dark power."

"That's what I'm afraid of." And I was fresh out of sorcerers—not that I'd allow another one to get anywhere near me. "Before I leave, do you sell healing spells? If so, I'd like to make a deal."

"I usually don't sell blood magic healing spells. Too many ways they can be used against me."

"I know—believe me, I do. And I wouldn't ask, except I don't think my own will work, and I have nothing else."

He considered. "I've only got one made, and it's expensive."

"How expensive?"

We negotiated a price. I went back to the jeep again for cash and traded it for a red crystal that pulsed with Tom's healing magic. I slipped it into one of the little pockets in my right arm cuff.

"Anyone asks where you got that, you found it on the side of the road, far from here," he told me.

"Thanks again." I backed away. "Be safe."

"You too." He closed the door and locked it. The wards flared.

Lucy was drumming her fingers on the steering wheel when I climbed into the jeep. "What did he give you?"

"I bought a healing spell, just in case we need it later." The cat-dragon jumped from my shoulder into my lap and then into her basket at my feet, where she curled up. "I think I might be able to use some of my natural magic now, with practice."

"Good." She made a three-point turn and headed back toward the main road.

As we bounced along, I asked, "Why were you so harsh to him and in such a hurry to leave?"

She didn't reply for a long time. Finally, she said, "Because he reminded me of someone I knew. The longer I stayed, the more I saw that other person in him. I don't want to think about that. What's past is past. What's gone...is gone."

"I'm sorry."

"Me too." She consulted the dashboard GPS. "We'll be able to make about fifty or sixty miles before dawn, then we'll find a motel. We can't hunt gravelings during the day, and we won't be worth much unless we rest."

I couldn't argue with that. Fifty or sixty miles sounded like a thousand. Lucy had to be tired too. I'd force myself to stay awake until we got to the motel to keep her company. And then I planned to sleep, and sleep well.

CHAPTER 20

We checked into a roadside motel on the outskirts of a town called Lawrence, just before dawn.

After some arguing with the manager and handing over cash, Lucy got us two rooms next to each other on the ground floor and a promise we would not be disturbed. I dragged my pack, the cat-dragon's basket, and my sorry carcass inside, took Daisy for a bathroom break around back of the motel, and returned to my room.

"I'm going to go explore a bit," Malcolm told me. "I don't want to just hang out here and watch you sleep. I'll check back every so often. If you need me, summon me."

"I plan to be unconscious until further notice." I pulled my filthy shirt off and tossed it in the trash. "Be careful, okay?"

He rolled his eyes with characteristic exasperation. "Yes, *Mom*."

"Hey," I said, my voice sharp because I was tired, and because I worried about him.

He sobered. "I will be careful, I promise. Get some sleep. The big wolf and the teensy dragon will watch over you."

"Okay. See you in a while."

He gave me a little salute and left.

I was almost too tired to see straight, but I forced myself to shower so I didn't go to bed smelling like graveling goop. I damn near fell asleep leaning against the tiled wall in the shower.

I had no sleepwear, so once I was out of the shower and dried off, I put on underwear and my last clean shirt. With the window shuttered, the room was pitch-black. I left the bathroom light on with the door cracked because a pitch-black room was not comforting to me at the moment.

I put wards on the doorway and window, barred the door, and crawled into bed. My cat-dragon was already curled up on the other pillow, purring, her head on her paws. Her eyes glittered in the dim light.

My eyelids weighed a hundred pounds each. I checked on Daisy, to see where she'd decided to lay down. Instead, she stood by the door, staring at it expectantly. "Don't tell me you have to go again," I groaned.

Someone knocked. Daisy didn't growl, so it had to be Lucy.

"Damn it, you said we'd get some sleep." I flung the covers back, marched to the door, lifted the bar, and yanked the door open.

Ronan stood on my doorstep, bottles of tequila and what looked like local hooch in one hand, and nothing in his sword hand. His Harley was parked in front of my room. Either he'd wheeled it up or he'd shown up while I was in the shower, because I sure as hell hadn't heard him arrive.

He raised an eyebrow. "Very nice. I like the Wonder Woman underwear."

I slammed the door.

Daisy growled.

"Don't you start with me," I warned her. "I'm so tired, I can't even think. I don't want to talk to him. He's an asshole."

She stared at me pointedly, then at the door.

"Rrrrr?" the cat-dragon asked, standing on the edge of the bed, her eyes flashing with fae magic.

Torryn's prophecy. I ground my teeth.

Tap tap tap. Three measured knocks.

With a growl, I pulled on my clean jeans, decided I didn't care if I wasn't wearing a bra, and yanked the door open again.

Ronan held up the bottles. "Peace offering?"

"I don't want anything to drink. I want to be asleep." I crossed my arms before I realized that pose emphasized my lack of undergarments. Son of a bitch.

To his credit, Ronan kept his eyes on my face. "Then *I'll* drink."

"Why can't you go drink by yourself?" My sluggish, sleep-deprived brain finally kicked up the thing I should have demanded the moment I opened the door the first time. "How the hell did you know where we are?"

"Can I come in and not have this discussion on the sidewalk?"

I wanted to thump my head on the doorframe. "Ronan, I have been awake for three straight days, fought a werewolf pack and a horde of gravelings, and had my magic retooled. I am *so* not in the mood to ask again, but I will. How the hell did you find us?"

"I paid Charles Vaughan to put tracking devices in the bags of food you bought at the roadhouse."

My mind conjured up the memory of seeing Ronan slip Charles a roll of cash. I stifled a growl. Unbelievable. Charles Vaughan: not trustworthy in *any* world.

"Please bite him," I told Daisy.

She showed me her teeth.

Ronan held up the bottles again, indicating the unlabeled one with a nod. "This is from Charles's personal stash. I'm told it's worth dying for. It certainly cost me a lot of money." He looked down at the ward I'd placed on the threshold. "May I come in?"

His politeness and apparent honesty had me on guard. Then again, Daisy had insisted we go to the roadhouse so we could cross paths with him. Torryn had told me we would need him. The universe had clearly conspired to bring him to my door. My natural contrariness—not to mention my exhaustion—urged me to slam the door again, crawl into bed, and pull the covers over my head.

Instead, I flicked on the light and traced a rune on the doorframe with my finger. My ward shimmered. "Fine. Come in."

He brushed past me, smelling of leather, tequila, the sea, and the open road. I shut the door, raised my ward again, and turned around.

He set the bottles on the little table and studied the cat-dragon, who stared back at him with emerald eyes. "You have a pūķis."

"No wonder you're such a good bounty hunter, with observational skills like that." I knew I was being petty, but I was bone tired.

To my annoyance, he ignored my taunt. "Got any glasses?"

I spread my hands to indicate our surroundings. "Does this look like the kind of place that provides glasses?"

"Cups, then." Without waiting for permission, he went to the bathroom and returned with two paper cups. His ice-blue eyes sparkled with some secret joke.

I sighed. "Yes, my bra is hanging in the bathroom. What are you, twelve? You've seen bras before."

"I was actually amused by your travel bag, which is rather minimal in its contents, for a woman." He released the stopper of the moonshine bottle, poured a generous amount into a cup, and offered it to me. "I didn't see your bra, but I will go back and look if you'd like."

Scowling, I took the cup. "Stay out of my bathroom."

He poured himself a cup of tequila and raised it. "To long journeys and wondrous travels to faraway lands."

I tapped my cup to his and sipped my drink. Ronan hadn't lied. This moonshine was far and away better than what Lucy and I had drunk at the roadhouse. Something else this Charles had in common with his counterpart back home: a taste for the good stuff.

In one gulp, Ronan drained his tequila. He reached for the bottle to refill his cup. Daisy settled in beside him. My cat-dragon returned to her pillow and curled up with her eyes half-lidded.

"Why did you track us?" I asked as he refilled his cup. "I thought you wanted nothing to do with us."

"I wanted to collect my hard-earned bounties first." He set the bottle down. "Then I wanted to see you in action, so I knew who you were, how you fought."

"You didn't see enough when the werewolves attacked?"

"They weren't much of a challenge for us, were they?" He knocked back his drink and poured another. "I learned a little about you, like the fact you aren't from this world, but you were on your guard with me there."

"So you tracked us." My eyes narrowed. "How long have you been following us?"

"I caught up with you in Oakdale."

My hand closed on the paper cup, crumpling it. Liquor ran down my fingers and dripped to the carpet. "Were you watching when the gravelings attacked?"

He took a drink. "Yes."

I manifested my whip of earth magic and lashed at him before my brain even formed the thought that I wanted to attack. My anger gave me speed. It was *my* magic, and I'd formed the whip with ease. Yay for Tom's magical tuning.

He raised his arm, moving with the lightning swiftness I'd seen when he fought the drummer and the wolves. My whip wrapped around his arm, crackling with power that seared the air. It should have cut him to the bone, or lopped his arm clean off.

Instead, he grabbed it and held on. His eyes flared bluish-silver. Some kind of magic I didn't know blazed up my whip and stung my hand.

"Look," he said, holding my earth magic whip inches from my nose. "You see those black threads? That's black magic. Sorcery. You think I don't know how you got that?" He released my whip, almost throwing it back in my face. His face was cold, his eyes like a thunderstorm. "Blood magic. Sorcery. Travel not just between realms, but between *worlds*." He set his cup on the table. He hadn't spilled a drop during our scuffle. "I hunt things like you for a living."

That did it. "*Things* like me?" I raged. "What about *you?* You're far from human. You watched us fight for our lives against the gravelings and didn't lift a finger. We nearly *died*. You think I want to die in this nightmare world? You think I *wanted* this black magic that's killing me, and is probably eating away at the soul of the man I love while I'm trapped here chasing the only thing that can get us back home? You don't know a damn thing about me, you self-righteous killer for hire. What gives you the right to judge me, or anyone else, for that matter?"

My chest heaved—not with exertion, but with the force of my anger. The dark magic surged in response. I shoved it down and let my own magic crackle on my skin. "What gives you the right?" I repeated, more quietly.

We stared at each other.

"You didn't nearly die." His voice was even.

I blinked. That was not a response I'd expected. "What?"

"When the gravelings attacked. You didn't nearly die." He took my crumpled cup from my hand and tossed it in a trash can. He went back to the bathroom and returned with another cup. He poured moonshine into it and held it out to me. "You fought with courage and resourcefulness, and like someone who's fought for her life against the odds many times. Your wolf revealed she has other forms and fought with you, as did your little pūķis." He nodded at the cat-dragon, who'd watched our dust-up with bright green eyes but hadn't moved from her pillow. "You had no need of me. If you had, I would have joined you."

"Sure you would have." I belted down the cup of moonshine. On a nearly empty stomach and after three days with close to no sleep, it hit me like a wrecking ball. I steadied myself against the table. "What do you want?"

"I want to find out why your wolf and the little witch Torryn think I should join your merry band."

"You talked to Torryn?"

"She was waiting for me when I came through her territory. We talked." He poured more moonshine into my cup. "Now I want to know how you got here, *why* you're here, and what it will take to get you home where you belong."

"My dark magic had nothing to do with how I got here. Back in my world, I'm one of the rare kind of blood mages who have enough earth and air magic to use mirror travel."

He refilled his cup with tequila. "That's the how. What about the why?"

"I bartered my gift of mirror travel to a vampire in return for her help saving someone's life. She sent me here to chase someone who stole something from her and bring it back."

"And how will you get back, once you've found your prize?"

"The same way we got here. But why do you care? What happened to me being a *thing* you hunt for a living?"

"Just now, you had every reason to strike out at me with that black magic, but you didn't. You used your own magic instead, and you did so without thinking." He tapped his cup to mine once again. "That means the evil hasn't taken hold of you yet. Once it does, you'll have to force yourself not to use it. You won't be satisfied with the magic you were born with. You won't mind if it eats the soul of the man you love. None of that will matter. You won't even care if you die from it."

I drank the moonshine in my cup, trying not to let on how much I feared the very outcome he described. "The witch Torryn said I'll have to cut it out," I said. "I'm afraid of what that means. And if I have to cut it out of myself, what will I have to do to save Sean?"

His eyes darkened again, but this time, it wasn't with anger. "All good questions, Alice, but not questions you must answer now." He took my cup and set it next to his on the table. "Rest. Regain your strength." He gestured at the bags of food I'd bought at the waysta-tion. "Eat. The magic consumes energy. You're hungry all the time now, aren't you?"

I nodded.

He put the cap on his bottle of tequila. "Eat when you're hungry, rest when you're tired, as best you can. That will buy you some time."

"Time for what?"

"To figure out how to get the black magic out. To find what you've come here looking for. To get you home." He headed for the door, bottle of tequila in hand. "Sleep."

I followed him. "Where you are going?"

He turned. For the first time since I'd met him, the corners of his mouth turned up in a ghost of a smile. "Missing me already?"

"Asshole." I touched the doorframe to lower the ward. "Get out."

He opened the door. The early light of dawn spilled across the horizon behind him. "I'll be nearby. Sleep tight."

I wanted to slam the door. Instead, I closed it quietly and raised the ward.

Daisy chuffed.

"Quiet, you." I flicked off the light. The bottle of moonshine, half empty, remained on the table, next to our cups.

Outside, the Harley rumbled to life. After a moment, it departed, and the motel fell silent.

I didn't remember taking off my jeans, but they were draped over the back of a chair. Warm from the moonshine, I returned to the bed. Daisy curled up in front of the door, on guard. The pūķis purred on her pillow.

I pulled the covers up my chin and fell asleep.

I woke from a sound sleep to someone pounding on my door and my stomach cramping from hunger.

"Rrrrr," my cat-dragon said with a yawn, blinking sleepily on the pillow beside my head.

"Alice!" Lucy shouted through the door. "Wake up! We've gotta hit the road!"

I stumbled out of bed. Disoriented, groggy, and lightheaded with hunger, I nearly fell. Daisy was suddenly at my side to steady me.

I thought maybe only an hour or two had passed since I'd fallen asleep, and was prepared to yell at Lucy for waking me up so soon. To my surprise, the clock on the nightstand said it was a little after two in the afternoon. I'd gotten about seven hours of sleep, which should have been enough to get me back on my feet, but I felt almost as tired as when I went to bed.

The half-empty bottle of moonshine on the table confirmed Ronan had been in my room this morning and I hadn't in fact dreamed his visit. I dug a protein bar from one of the shopping bags from the waystation and unwrapped it on my way to the door.

When I opened the door, I found Lucy outside, already dressed, her bag at her feet. "You look like hell," she told me.

I took a bite of the protein bar. "Thank you," I said around my mouthful of food. I dropped my ward so she could come inside and stepped back to let her walk past.

She brought her bag inside and shut the door. I got my jeans off the chair where I'd left them and put them on as I ate the rest of the bar.

Lucy eyed the bottle on the table. "Where'd that come from?"

I went to the bathroom to put on my bra. "Ronan," I said.

"*What?* How—?"

Between bites of a second protein bar, I explained how Ronan had found us. As she cursed Charles, Ronan, his motorcycle, and all of their ancestors, I brushed my teeth, washed my face, and combed and braided my hair. My eyes were deeply shadowed and looked almost feverish. At least the hunger pains had eased.

When I emerged from the bathroom, Lucy was still livid. "*Tracking* us," she fumed. "Spying on us while we fought the gravelings. Rat bastard." She glanced at my rumpled bed. "You didn't sleep with him, did you?"

I gave her a look. "No, I did not. I have a partner back home who I love very much, and Ronan is an ass."

"You wouldn't be the first person to sleep with someone you thought was an ass, especially if he showed up with a bottle of what looks like Charles's very special reserve." She rubbed her face. "Where is he now?"

I packed quickly, stuffing my clothes and toiletries into my backpack. "No idea. He said he'd be nearby, whatever that means."

"Judging by how much he drank at the roadhouse, probably the closest dive bar." She picked up my shopping bags and opened the door of my room. "He's good with a sword, even after a bottle of tequila. He killed more of the werewolves than I did."

I got the cat-dragon into her basket and covered her with the blanket. "I didn't know it was a contest."

"Of course it was a contest." She carried my shopping bags and her own duffel to the vehicle. "Where's Malcolm?"

"Out exploring. I'll summon him." I put my backpack and the basket in the jeep, then returned to the room to remove my wards on the door and window and make sure I hadn't left anything behind. Lucy went to check us out of our rooms.

With my room emptied and the wards gone, I leaned against the side of the vehicle, closed my eyes, and tugged twice on the blue-green trace that connected me to Malcolm.

Almost instantly, he appeared beside me. "Hey, Alice. What's going on?"

I let out a breath, relieved to see he was unharmed. "We're hitting the road."

He frowned. "Did you not get any sleep? You look awful."

"If one more person tells me that, I'm going to start throwing punches." I yanked open the back door for Daisy. She jumped into the back seat and settled in. Malcolm floated into the jeep beside her.

I shut the door, turned around, and found myself nose-to-chest with Ronan, in a black T-shirt, black jeans, and his leather jacket.

I jumped and magic flared on my fingers. "Son of a bitch!" I yelled.

His brow furrowed. "You do not look rested."

I punched him.

He didn't expect an attack, and I didn't really expect my blow to make contact, so we were both caught off guard when my fist connected with his jaw. It felt like punching a tree. I shook my injured hand and swore. Belatedly, I noticed his Harley backed into a parking space several spots down from ours.

Ronan barely flinched. I figured his reaction was more from surprise than anything else. He raised an eyebrow. "Did that make you feel better?"

I scowled. Damn it, it wasn't like me to be so jumpy, or to take swings at someone—especially when I didn't know what they were capable of doing in retaliation. I reached for another protein bar, hoping food would help me feel more like myself.

"We're leaving," I informed him, as if loading up our bags hadn't probably tipped him off.

"Did something happen?"

I shook my head. "We're heading south, toward where we think the gravelings are coming through from the Underworld."

Lucy's voice cut in. "Don't you ever track me again, Ronan. Not for any reason." She approached the jeep from the direction of the motel office, her fingers twitching like she wanted to reach for her sword.

"My apologies, Lieutenant." He inclined his head. It didn't escape my notice that he didn't say he wouldn't do it again. "Shall we continue south, then?"

"You follow my orders if we run into trouble," she warned. "This is a League operation."

He studied her. "And if I refuse?"

"Then you can go back to swilling tequila and collecting boun-ties." She opened her door. "People are dying. I don't have time to measure dicks with you, and I don't give a shit about your ego. Either join the team or don't. Let's roll, Alice." She slammed her door.

I eyed Ronan. "So what's it going to be?"

"I don't play well with others, which is why I'm in the business I'm in." He put his hand on my door. "But if a wolf made of magic and a ten-year-old clairvoyant witch tell me I'm supposed to go with you, I should go, just to find out why. Maybe I'll get to bag a few more bounties along the way."

Gotta pay for that tequila somehow, I thought, perhaps uncharitably. Out loud, I said, "I'm interested to find out what use you might be."

He smiled slightly. "I look forward to proving my worth."

I got in the jeep and buckled in. He shut my door and watched as Lucy put the vehicle in gear and pulled away without looking at him. Ronan turned on his heel and headed for his Harley.

By the time he'd reached his motorcycle, Lucy had already turned onto the street headed south, following the directions provided by the GPS.

"He smells like tequila and no sleep," Lucy said. "Pass me one of those protein bars, will you?"

I handed over one of the bars. "It's five o'clock somewhere, right?"

She sighed. "How do you feel about having him at your back?"

I gulped water from my refillable Hawthorne's bottle and eyed the box of protein bars. Thirsty, hungry, and achy seemed to be my new normal. "Better than I should," I admitted. "Though I'll be damned if I know why."

Her mouth became a grim line. "Same here. Goodness knows he's given us little reason to trust him."

Daisy growled quietly.

"You may trust him, wolf, but I don't," Lucy said.

"Do you know what he is?" I asked.

"No, I do not, which is more worrisome than how much tequila he consumes. He sure as hell is *something*." She glanced over her shoulder. "Malcolm, you have any thoughts about what Ronan is?"

"I wish I did," Malcolm said, floating close to the gap between the front seats. "He looks plain-Jane human to me, but he obviously isn't, so he's capable of hiding what he is."

"There could be a lot of reasons for that," I pointed out. "Not all of them are bad."

Lucy snorted. "Yeah, not all of them—only most."

"Some people with special skills just don't want to be noticed."

"Touché."

In my side mirror, I spotted Ronan's Harley behind us. The rumble of its engine grew as he gained ground on us.

Lucy's eyes flicked to the rearview mirror. She scowled and put her foot down. The jeep accelerated sharply. The Harley closed the distance again. I expected him to pass us, but instead he fell in behind, content—for the moment—to follow her lead. How long that would last, I had no idea. There wasn't much about Ronan I *did* know, other than he was leaning hard into the lone-wolf bounty hunter vibe and he knew when to bring a girl a bottle of damn good hooch.

Weaving through traffic at well over one hundred miles an hour, we raced south, hopefully toward Mariela, the scroll, and a door to the Underworld.

CHAPTER 21

THE APPARENT CENTER OF THE GRAVELING ATTACKS WAS ONLY ABOUT A TWO-hour drive from our motel in Lawrence. Lucy kept the accelerator nearly to the floor the entire way, except for a brief stop for coffee and food.

About an hour into the journey, we passed through earth-spider territory. To Malcolm's and my disappointment, we didn't spot any giant spiders. Lucy assured us we should be grateful, but Malcolm pouted.

Something had been bothering me since I woke up—something worrisome I hadn't thought of until a strange dream last night about Lucy and Charles made me wonder if my subconscious was trying to get me to put something together. The more I thought about it, the more sure I was that I would have figured it out sooner if I hadn't been so distracted by the weirdness of the Broken World and muddled by sleep deprivation.

Once we were safely past spider territory and on a well-traveled highway, I cleared my throat. "Lucy, did you push me to accept a ride from you when we met?"

Her silence was an answer in itself. She was expressionless. Behind me, Malcolm flitted, his anger prickling on my skin.

"I ask because before we met you, Malcolm and I discussed at length, *several times*, that we needed to stay clear of military, police, and anyone like that, for obvious reasons. And then minutes later you rolled up in a military jeep and offered us a ride, and I immediately thought it sounded like a good idea." I turned in my seat to face her. "I need the truth."

Her hands flexed on the steering wheel. "I was suspicious of you. I wanted to know why you would be walking along a stretch of road infamous for fatal attacks by lotoru and other creatures, in the company of a ghost bound to you by magic I didn't recognize. You felt out of place, though I had no idea just how *out of place* you are. Once I saw your wolf, I had to know who you are and what *she* is, because that's my job, and because I didn't want you to get eaten. So yes, I gave you a nudge to ride with me." She glanced at me. "But after that, I never nudged you again. Everything you've done since has been one hundred percent of your own volition."

Dark magic and nausea rose along with my anger. Just like Charles back home, she'd forced me to act against my will. My shields, tuned to the magic of my world, had done nothing to prevent her from forcing me to get into her jeep and put all of us— Malcolm, Daisy, and myself—at her mercy. I hadn't even noticed or suspected she'd done it, which was worse because it proved just how dangerous her ability was. She could have nudged me to do or tell her anything, and I might have done so without thinking twice.

"Alice, I'm sorry," Malcolm said, shooting Lucy a venomous look. "I had no idea. I wondered why you accepted the offer, but I figured you had a good reason. I should have said something, I guess."

"You weren't the only one who watched it happen." I turned to look at Daisy. "So much for not letting her use her magic on me."

Daisy put her paw on one of the bags from the roadhouse and stared back at me with golden eyes. Her motive for letting Lucy push me was clear enough: she'd wanted us to go with Lucy to the road-house to meet Ronan.

Malcolm could be forgiven for not understanding what had happened, especially because we'd had no idea at the time Lucy was capable of pushing, but Daisy's choice to let Lucy nudge me into accepting a ride cut like a knife. I would never have expected that kind of betrayal from my own wolf.

Lucy was a Guardian, tasked with tracking down potential threats and solving mysteries, much like myself. I could understand her motives, though I firmly believed stealing someone's free will was wrong, regardless of the reason.

Sick to my stomach and almost too angry to feel anything at all, I turned toward the window.

"Alice—" Lucy began.

"Just drive," I told her, my voice toneless. "Don't talk. Just... drive."

Malcolm's fingers touched my shoulder. I shrugged him off. He floated back away from me.

Lucy drained the last of her coffee and set her thermos in the cup holder. Daisy let out a little whine. I ignored them both.

Ronan's Harley rumbled behind us. I wished I was riding on the back of his bike, so I could focus on the wind and sun on my skin, and not on the pain of having my will stolen yet again and the knowledge Daisy had permitted it.

My stomach growled. Damn it. I tore open another protein bar. If Lucy wondered why I was eating so much, she didn't comment—which was good, because I was in no mood to answer questions or make polite conversation.

No one in the jeep said a word for at least an hour, when we reached the edge of a town called Walliston and found ourselves in the middle of a nightmare.

LIKE MOST LITTLE towns we'd passed through on our journey south, Walliston was small, picturesque, and home to several hundred inhabitants who lived in modest homes and worked in the same kind of short, squat office buildings we'd seen since our arrival.

Unlike those other towns, however, Walliston was now a ghost town—quite literally.

Our two-vehicle caravan rolled slowly down Main Street, past empty shops with broken windows, silent houses still shuttered and locked down for the night, and office buildings still dark in the afternoon because their employees had never come to work—at least, not in a form in which they could do their jobs.

Ghosts of men, women, and children wandered the streets, visible in our supe lights. Some wept, some screamed, and some flitted frantically, calling out for family members or friends. Most moved out of the way of our jeep, but others stood rooted in place and didn't react even when Lucy drove slowly around them. Daisy whined when a ghost's outstretched arm passed through her.

I checked my side mirror and saw Ronan still behind us, riding slowly in our wake. I might have been imagining it, but I thought the ghosts seemed to be giving him a wide berth.

"Oh, this is bad," Malcolm breathed. "This is *so bad.*"

My dark magic rose and swelled like ocean waves in response to the lingering traces of power around us. The sensation was less like how my blood magic reacted to spilled blood, and more like the way proximity to a ley line energized my earth magic. I inhaled deeply. The scattered traces of dark energy promised power, if I just reached out and took it. I stifled the impulse, but the hunger remained.

Whatever had happened here, it wasn't gravelings that did it. Something else had slaughtered the people of Walliston, and it called to my dark magic as like called to like.

I was still furious about Lucy's push and Daisy's betrayal, but all that had to go to the back burner for now. "What can we do?" I asked. My question wasn't really directed at anyone in particular, and I was referring to more than the dozens—or maybe hundreds—of ghosts haunting the streets.

Lucy had a white-knuckled grip on the steering wheel. "How's your magic? Sensing any gravelings or their handiwork, like you did back in Oakdale?"

I shook my head. "Not like Oakdale, but something similar. What else can come up out of the Underworld?"

"What can't?" Lucy pulled to the curb in front of a home with two vehicles still parked in the driveway. "There are creatures and people and gods down there—things you wouldn't believe even if you saw them with your own eyes. Not that we have much to go on in terms of intel; it's mostly reports cobbled together from records of things that have made it topside and legends that are probably part truth and part complete fiction. But like I said, stuff getting out is rare here."

A ghost ran in front of our jeep, calling for someone—her daughter, maybe. Lucy took a ragged breath. When the ghost was past, she went on. "Cultures that worship certain Underworld deities open gateways with some regularity, but traffic through them is tightly regulated on both sides. A lot of inhabitants of the Underworld don't want anyone from here going down there. Most magic practitioners here don't want to open any kind of portal, because there are things down there capable of unleashing death and destruction on a massive scale. And once opened, portals are sometimes damn near impossible to close."

"Well, that sucks," Malcolm said, his tone curt. He was still angry about Lucy's push, but like me, he'd apparently decided to put that aside to deal with more immediate problems.

"Yeah." She turned off the jeep's engine. Behind us, the Harley rumbled, then went silent.

"What are we doing?" I asked.

"We have to know what happened to these people." She got out and shut her door. I got out and opened the back door as my little cat-dragon hopped onto my shoulder.

Malcolm floated out. Daisy got up, stretched, and jumped down beside me. She gave herself a long shake and stared at the house in front of us, her lip curled to show some teeth.

I listened. Other than ghostly keening, an eerie silence reigned in Walliston. No vehicles, no music, no dogs barking, no...nothing. Somewhere down the street, a flagpole rattled in the wind. I rubbed my arms.

Ronan joined us on the sidewalk, his helmet and gloves stacked neatly on the seat of his bike. "A house of death," he said.

I didn't know how he knew what was inside, but my spidey senses told me nothing was left alive in this house, or in any house on this block.

My blood magic tingled as we crossed the lawn. "It's a mess in there," I told my companions.

"I'll take point," Lucy told us. "Ronan, watch our backs."

Daisy growled.

"With the wolf's help," Lucy amended. Ronan snorted.

When we reached the front step, I raised my hand and held it near the door. "House is warded." I closed my eyes and studied the spellwork. "The wards target nonhumans."

"Most wards around here do," Lucy said. "Human invaders are less of a worry than all the things that go bump in the night."

"Allow me to earn my keep." Ronan placed his palm flat against the door. I flinched as the house wards broke. The flash of pain faded as the magic dissipated.

"I could have done that," Malcolm muttered.

Ronan raised his boot and kicked in the door. The door, the bar behind it, and the doorframe exploded into the entryway of the house.

"I could have done that," Lucy said.

I caught a flash of a shadow heading for us. Its dark magic was unmistakable. I knew—though I didn't know *how* I knew—that it was death incarnate. A blood magic blade emerged from my fingers.

Ronan drew his sword and sliced the shadow in half. It let out a bone-chilling scream as it disintegrated.

"A shade," Lucy said grimly. "Shit."

"I could have done that," I said.

Ronan sighed. "You are all very difficult to impress."

"Stop trying to impress us," Lucy snapped.

He raised his hand. A ball of silver-blue light formed on his palm, illuminating the interior of the house. "No."

Lucy rolled her eyes. "Come on." She handed me a small flashlight. "Supe light. If you use it, keep it low, out of our eyes."

"Got it."

She reached behind her head and drew her sword soundlessly from its invisible sheath. Blade raised, she entered the house. I followed her in, with Malcolm and Daisy behind me, and Ronan at our backs. The cat-dragon's little claws dug into my shoulder as she balanced herself.

The thick, coppery scent of blood and eviscerated bodies made my stomach rebel. I set my jaw, swallowed hard, and forced myself to ignore the stench. The house wards, while sufficient against most threats, had apparently done nothing to protect against shades.

The first two bodies we found were large dogs—or what I thought had been two dogs—in the blood and flesh-splattered nightmare of the living room. Two adults had been slaughtered in their bedroom, one on the bed and one near the door, as if she'd tried to run to the children's rooms before she died. I went into investigator mode, shutting down my emotions as best I could so my brain could process this house of horrors.

The three children—toddler twins and an older child—had died in their beds, their blood and bits of flesh strewn throughout their rooms and into the hallway. After I looked more closely, I realized the killings were done out of instinct, but the scattered remains were the result of play. The shades had *played* with the bloody remains before moving on.

It was, by a significant margin, the most horrific scene I'd ever had the misfortune of seeing...

...and it was repeated, with variations in the number of victims found, in the next four houses we entered.

An hour later, I sat on the front steps of the last house on the block, my hands dangling between my knees. My mouth tasted sour from throwing up, though I'd rinsed it repeatedly and taken a swig from Lucy's flask. I might never get the smell of death out of my nose. I'd sure as hell never get the memory of the slaughter out of my head, or the keening of the ghosts out of my ears.

The others were in the house, searching for shades. So far, the only one we'd encountered was the one from the first house. They didn't need me to search, so I'd come outside to be alone with my anger. Some of it was directed at the shades, though I knew they were little more than mindless echoes, killing because it was all they knew how to do. Most of my fury was directed at Mariela.

According to Lucy, shades and gravelings almost never made it out of the Underworld. I'd had a sinking feeling from the moment I heard about these attacks that Mariela was indirectly responsible. Lucy's comment last night that visitors from other worlds and realms upset the balance of her world and caused things to happen that shouldn't had resonated deeply with me—not because of myself or Malcolm, but because Mariela had set all this in motion. The people of Walliston weren't supposed to be dead. The kids in this house should be in school today, not in pieces. Their parents should be at work. Their dogs should be playing or sleeping in the backyard. Mariela should have stayed in our world, where she belonged.

I understood her desire for justice for those she'd lost—I under-stood it all too well. I also understood how that desire became a need for revenge when the perpetrators of the Glen Grove massacre escaped prosecution. Somewhere along the way, however, her need for vengeance had blinded her to the collateral damage she might cause, and all the suffering and death.

I had no idea if some residents had holed up somewhere with better wards, or escaped. The fact no one else seemed to have responded indicated no one had made it out to warn about the shades or alert law enforcement from neighboring towns, the army, or the League. There was a good chance everyone in Walliston was dead. Unless there was some other explanation for the shades' presence here, their blood was on Mariela's hands.

That thought, and the memory of the torn bodies, propelled me to my feet. My anger turned cold, became resolve. I would find these shades, and I would destroy them. And then I would locate that door, go through it, find Mariela, and bring her to justice for what she'd done.

I caught a familiar scent on the breeze: iron and incense. It wafted over me like a puff of air exhaled by a newly opened tomb. I'd smelled it at Hawthorne's, when Lucy told Isaiah his pack deserved justice. The breeze shifted and the scent disappeared. What the hell was it? Some kind of strange Broken World magic, or a figment of my imagination?

The traces left by the shades didn't feel all that different from the dark magic I'd absorbed from Miraç. That made sense, because black magic included death magic, and the shades were death. Natural magic like mine, even blood magic, was life.

I had a sudden thought. Since the night of Miraç's death, when Sean and I had absorbed the sorcerer's power, I'd thought of the dark magic as Miraç's and treated it like some invading, alien force. Why couldn't I shape that power and make it mine? Magic was shaped by intent. Miraç's intentions had been entirely evil, or nearly so. Mine weren't. So, as Tom had tuned my natural magic to the frequency of this world, could I not tune Miraç's power to my own and command it?

No time like the present to find out. I took a deep breath, held it, and exhaled, clearing my mind of distractions.

"Rrrrr?" the cat-dragon asked.

"Hold on," I told her. "I'm going to try something."

I closed my eyes and reached out to the traces left by the shades. This time, I let my own dark magic connect with the remains of their energy. Power pulsed through me, heavy with death. My natural magic tried to rise, but I pushed it down and focused on the traces of the shades, seeking the ebbs and flows that would indicate where the shades had come from and where they'd gone.

The patterns were erratic and tangled, but the threads all originated from the same direction—and led to the same place now. Dark power thrummed at the end of those traces. The shades were nearby. All I had to do was follow those threads and I would find them.

I thought of Malcolm and the others. Should I let them know where I was going? No, I wanted this for myself. I was angry—angry at Valas for trapping me here, angry at Miraç for tormenting me and stealing my memories, angry at Moses for hurting Sean's company, angry at Daniel for refusing to come home with me, angry at Mariela, angry at Daisy and Lucy...angry, angry, *angry*. I needed to do something with all this anger, or I'd explode.

Malcolm would ream me for going off by myself. So would Lucy. I didn't care.

I started walking.

Using my Second Sight, with all my focus on following the traces of the shades, I walked across yards, over curbs, around cars, and through the ghosts of the dead. My cat-dragon stayed on my shoulder, her claws in my skin only a distant pain.

Following the trace took me to the locked gates of a cemetery. I manifested my earth magic whip and cut the chain in two. I pushed open the gate and entered the cemetery.

The moment I stepped through the gate, I knew where the shades were: a large above-ground mausoleum about a hundred yards away. In my Second Sight, it was black and so full of dark magic and death that I was surprised it hadn't crumbled. The shades had taken refuge from the daylight in the mausoleum.

I used earth magic to melt the metal of the gate and hold it closed. It wouldn't keep anyone out for very long, but I didn't intend to take long.

As I approached the stone building, my dark magic sensed the dead in the graves beneath my feet. Their decay felt like potential sources of power—which was unsettling, to say the least. I was used to earth, air, ley lines, and blood feeling like power, and even water now that I'd shared water magic with Malcolm, but never death itself. I hated the sensation, but I liked it too, just a little. Some part of my brain told me that was bad, but all I cared about for now was those shades. I'd worry about the rest later.

When I reached the doors of the mausoleum, they were closed and locked. Behind them were thousands of shades. Maybe I should have feared them, but I didn't. My dark magic surged along with my blood magic. I let both rise and spooled power around my arms. The cat-dragon arched her back and hissed. Not in warning—in anticipation.

In the distance, Lucy shouted my name. The cemetery gate clanged.

I reached for earth magic and placed my palms against the doors of the vault. "*Discindo*," I commanded. *Divide.*

My earth magic, only partially tuned to this world and therefore wild, blew the building apart. The shades erupted from the ruin. Thousands of them flew screaming toward me, full of rage and hunger that could never be sated.

With my blood magic and dark magic, I gripped them as if with talons and tore them apart. Their screams nearly deafened me.

When I'd used my dark magic whip to kill the werewolves at Hawthorne's, each death had transferred power and life energy from the shifter to me. The shades had no life energy, but they were full of power. As they discorporated, that power became mine.

I sensed other shades throughout the town, stranded in homes and other buildings like the one we'd encountered in the first house we entered. I tore them apart as well. Finally, no more shades remained anywhere within the radius I could sense.

I pulled my magic back. My skin and bones hummed with new power. I felt better than I had in days, because I'd let off steam and done what I could to keep the shades from harming anyone else.

Something warm bumped against my hand: Daisy's head, nudging its way under my palm.

"Alice?" Malcolm asked from somewhere behind me. He sounded worried.

With my back to them, I sensed rather than saw that Ronan and Lucy had their blades raised.

I turned, switching hands on Daisy's head. Lucy and Ronan stood about ten feet away. Malcolm floated between us, watching me.

"I found where the shades were holed up," I said, scratching Daisy's head. "Decided to just take care of that for you."

Lucy's blade didn't move. "You just killed thousands of shades by yourself."

"They were already dead," I pointed out.

"You know what I mean."

I lifted one shoulder—the one that didn't have a cat-dragon sitting on it—in a half shrug. "I told you I'm kind of a badass. What, you didn't believe me?"

"No, I believed you." She studied me, then lowered her sword. "Are there any shades left in Walliston?"

I shook my head. "All gone."

"Good. So now all that's left is to find that open door and close it."

"Yes," I said. And I would, but not until I found Mariela and dragged her back here to answer for what she'd done.

Ronan had watched me while Lucy and I talked, his face expressionless. When I said I intended to close the door, the shape of his glacier-blue eyes changed. He knew I wasn't telling Lucy the truth about what I planned to do.

Another emotion flashed in his eyes: comprehension. I wondered what he'd figured out, or *thought* he'd figured out. Then it was gone, and he was impassive once more.

Lucy glanced at him. "Something to add, Ronan?"

I wondered if he'd tell her what he'd realized about my plans. Instead, he returned his sword to its sheath on his back in a smooth motion. "I suggest we leave Walliston before you call this situation in to your superiors, or we'll be stuck here dealing with League bureaucracy."

Her eyebrows went up. "Where do you suggest we go?"

He glanced at me. "Alice?"

"We go to the door," I said. "We can't let any more of these things get loose up here." I took the obsidian rock from my pocket. Its dark magic called to me now more than ever, but I couldn't sense whatever trace Daisy was following. Someday soon I hoped to understand how Daisy was tracking the scroll, but that could wait.

I looked around at my cat-dragon, Malcolm, Lucy, and Ronan, then down at my wolf. "The Avengers are assembled, Daisy. It's time to take us to the door."

Daisy showed us her teeth, turned, and ran.

CHAPTER 22

We followed Daisy for nearly twenty miles—Lucy, Malcolm, and I in the jeep and Ronan behind us on his Harley.

My beautiful golden wolf ran like the wind, her paws never quite touching the surface of the road. The jeep's speedometer hovered around forty miles per hour, which was about as fast as we could travel on the narrow, winding road. Daisy kept to the road, as if understanding our vehicles couldn't cut through fenced land and thick woods.

I tensed when we passed vehicles coming the other direction, but either the drivers couldn't see Daisy or they were unperturbed by the sight of a glowing golden wolf flying past them. The former seemed more likely.

As she drove, Lucy radioed in a quick report about what we'd found in Walliston, minus the information about how I'd dispatched the shades. The dispatcher listened to the report, then asked where Lucy was headed.

"I'm trying to find the source of the shades," Lucy said, glancing at the GPS. "Currently heading west."

"Understood," the dispatcher said briskly. "All other Guardians in the area are engaged containing an active ghoul mass rising east of Bakersfield, but we'll request the army set up a containment area and dispatch operatives as soon as we're able. Keep us posted on your location and status."

Lucy signed off and tossed the radio in the console.

"Mass ghoul rising?" Malcolm asked.

"Yeah. That happens sometimes after major magic flares. It's not pretty, but it's not as bad as what we saw in Walliston." She cursed. "I'm going to have a hell of a time explaining all this. They'll find the mausoleum you destroyed, and someone will sense your magic traces." She glanced at me. "Okay, out with it."

"Out with what?"

"When we find that door, what is your plan? And don't say to close it, because I know there's more to it." She slowed on a curve, her eyes on the road. "Ronan's not the only one who can smell a half-truth. Let's hear it."

As far as I could tell, I didn't have much of a choice, because I might need her to cover for me while I was down below.

I drank the last of the water in my Hawthorne's bottle. "I'm going through the door to find a mage named Mariela Diakos and the item she stole from my client. And if we're right and the gravelings and shades came from the Underworld through a door she left open, I am going to bring her back to face justice for the deaths she's caused."

"Did you push Alice to tell you all that?" Malcolm demanded, flitting in anger.

"No, I didn't," Lucy told him. She glanced at me again. "You know I can't let you go through that door."

"Before you decide to get in my way and we have to sort that out, let me tell you the rest of why Malcolm, Daisy, and I are here," I said.

I laid it out as succinctly as I could: Mariela's lost family, the theft of the scroll, why she'd gone to the Underworld, and who she intended to bring back. And then I told her we couldn't get home without the scroll.

Lucy said nothing for a long time.

"This person you were hired to find...she wants to bring back the actual Furies," she said finally.

"Yup."

"Shit."

"Yup."

Suddenly, Daisy veered off the road and disappeared into the trees. Lucy braked hard. "Where the hell did she go?"

"I don't know," I said. Ahead, a narrow dirt road turned to the right. "Try that," I suggested. "She's been staying on the road so far. We'll find her."

As the sun disappeared behind the hills to the west, Lucy turned onto the dirt road. Ronan followed us.

I leaned forward to get a better look at the GPS. "This area is shaded gray. What does that mean?"

"Sacred land." She touched the screen and read the text that appeared. "An ancient burial site belonging to the Chumash people."

I rubbed my prickly arms. "Right on top of a ley line."

"That tracks," Malcolm said. "An ancient burial site on a ley line —there's no better place to try and open a portal to the Underworld."

"But where the hell is Daisy?" I asked.

"Shit!" Lucy slammed on the brakes. The jeep slid to a stop in the middle of the road. I checked my side mirror to make sure Ronan was all right, but the road was empty except for our jeep. Like Daisy, the bike and its rider had disappeared.

Ahead, just before the road ended at the edge of a clearing, a huge man with dark hair and the physique of a Vampire Court enforcer blocked the road. He wore black tactical gear, but no firearms I could see. His eyes were completely black. I'd thought Ronan's poker face was good, but this man had no expression whatsoever. His face was like the side of a cliff.

"Where the hell did this guy come from?" I asked.

Lucy put the jeep in park. Her expression was nearly as cold as his. "Spartoi," she warned. "He can read our lips."

In other words, don't say anything about our companions. I had no doubt Daisy would come to our defense, but Ronan was a question mark. Safest to assume we couldn't count on him.

"What does he want?" I asked.

Lucy's gaze stayed fixed on the Spartoi. "Lots of possibilities. None of them are good." Her hand rested on her door handle. "I suppose it's pointless to tell you to stay in the jeep."

"You are correct, Lieutenant." I opened my door and got out. Lucy followed suit. Malcolm floated out and stood beside me.

Lucy could have nudged me to obey her and stay in the jeep, but she didn't. It didn't make up for her earlier push, but it took a little of my anger away.

I didn't look around for Daisy or Ronan. I hoped one or both were nearby, in case the Spartoi decided to get feisty.

"Lieutenant Lucy Stone," he said, his voice deep and heavily accented, and thoroughly devoid of emotion.

I wondered how he knew Lucy, but I didn't ask, unwilling to either let on that I didn't know the answer or distract her. All my instincts told me he was incredibly dangerous.

"Identify yourself," Lucy commanded.

"Commander Kyrios of the Fifth Division." His dark, unblinking gaze was unnerving. "State your business here."

If Lucy was the least rattled by Kyrios's stare or his presence, I saw no sign of it. "I'm not at liberty to discuss such matters with you, Commander. Why are you blocking our way?"

"This area is off-limits to anyone other than the Brotherhood of Cadmus, by order of the prefect. You will all depart immediately."

"Your prefect has no authority over the League, Commander." The chill in Lucy's voice could have flash-frozen a river of lava. "You're a mercenary. Stand aside. We have business to attend to."

Kyrios didn't move, though he somehow managed to give the impression that he'd just widened his stance. "Final warning,

Guardian and civilian." The change of tone when he said *civilian* implied I was little more than a bug to him. That suited me just fine, because that meant he underestimated me. Being underestimated had worked to my advantage many times.

I took a hesitant half-step back, as if I expected Lucy to back down. Taking my cue, Malcolm flitted. Lucy, however, didn't back down. She also didn't bother to hide her hatred of Kyrios.

We needed to get past him and find the door. Apparently Lucy's thoughts mirrored mine. She reached behind her head and drew her sword out of thin air. She flexed her wrist. The sword gleamed. "I told you to move along, Sprout."

Sprout must have been some kind of insult to a Spartoi—maybe a reference to the legend that they'd been sown from a dragon's teeth. Kyrios's lip curled. He made a sound like the beginning of an avalanche.

And then all hell broke loose.

CHAPTER 23

WELL, NOT *ALL* HELL—JUST SOME OF ITS ANGRIER, MORE DEADLY DENIZENS.

Shades and gravelings erupted out of the trees and from the direction of the clearing. They slithered, bounded, and galloped toward us, howling and screaming.

At first, I thought Kyrios might have called the creatures, but they went after all of us with equal bloodlust. That didn't make us allies, but we were all united in our need to survive.

I hadn't seen him draw his blades, but Kyrios suddenly had a sword in each hand. He waded into the attacking monsters with a roar that made my hair stand on end. He was bloodied almost instantly. As fast as he was—and holy shit, he was *fast*—there were too many gravelings and even more of the much-deadlier shades. We'd all be mincemeat in seconds.

Grabbing a ley line back home was painful and potentially deadly. Latching on to one of the Broken World's crazy ley lines might be damn near suicide, but as far as I could tell, it was that or certain messy death. Kyrios was already down. Lucy staggered, bloody and wounded, and Malcolm was barely able to elude the shades. As for Ronan, he was nowhere to be seen.

I dropped my shields, sucked as much Broken World earth magic into my body as I could withstand to ground myself, and grabbed the ley line.

"Alice, no!" Malcolm shouted.

His voice vanished behind a wave of power that simultaneously brought the most pain and most pleasure I'd ever experienced at once in my life. I might have moaned, or maybe I screamed—it was impossible to tell.

My dark magic roared through the gravelings and shades. With shrieks, wails, and screams, they disintegrated as the wave swept through the trees, across the road, and past Kyrios's bloody, motionless body into the clearing beyond.

This was true power, and nothing had ever, *ever* felt so good.

I caught a flash of something out of the corner of my eye: a glint of silver-blue, but not a blade. My brain struggled to make sense of what I saw, even as my dark magic sought out of the last of the shades and gravelings and turned them to dust.

Someone grabbed my arm so tightly I thought the bones would shatter, but even that pain didn't register through the rush of power.

And just like that, the power vanished like someone had flipped a switch. With it went the pleasure, the pain, and my ability to stand. I dropped in a heap, too confused to do much more than breathe raggedly and cradle my arm. My vision swam and I shivered uncontrollably, though not from cold.

A dark figure crouched beside me. "I warned you if you weren't careful, you wouldn't be satisfied with the magic you were born with."

Ronan.

I wanted to tell him I hadn't had a choice, but the numbness gave way to agony. My entire body felt as though I was being crushed by stones. I set my jaw and tried not to cry out, but the pain was too much. I screamed.

Ronan cursed. His fingers brushed across my forehead and along my hairline. The touch was intimate and unwelcome, but the pain faded.

Finally, I took a shuddering breath and looked up into Ronan's glacier-blue eyes. "Cut it out of me," I said, my voice hoarse. "Please, cut it out of me, while I can still think straight. Before I turn into the monster who gave it to me."

"No blade I know can do that," he said, with real regret. "I would do this for you, if I could."

"Why? Who am I to you?"

He stroked my hair, but not like a lover. His gentle touch reminded me of Sean or Nan comforting a distraught member of the pack. "I don't know," he told me. "But I've come to believe we were meant to take this journey together—the whole strange, misbegotten lot of us."

"Speak for yourself, buddy," Malcolm said, floating into view over Ronan's shoulder. "Strange maybe, but hardly misbegotten."

Malcolm had never said much about his parents other than that they'd died when he was young, but Lucy was the forbidden offspring of a Guardian and a human mother. I was part mage and part shifter, the product of a secret romance between my mother and Daniel. Born of my blood, infection by the werewolf virus, and shifter magic, Daisy was…whatever she was, given physical form by Miraç's black magic. We were certainly a motley, mixed-up group. I thought of the strange glimpse of silver-blue I'd seen while I was destroying the shades and gravelings. Was Ronan giving us a clue about his own origin?

My hand caught his wrist. "What are you?"

"I am just as you see me, nothing more." He glanced up, and his expression darkened. "Unfortunately, the Spartoi hasn't succumbed to his wounds after all."

I pushed myself up and looked toward the clearing. Bloody and breathing hard, Lucy stood just outside the Spartoi's reach, sword in hand. The blade dripped graveling goop. Daisy stood on Kyrios's chest, her paw pinning his sword arm to the ground and her teeth inches from his face.

"Why are you here?" Lucy demanded.

"I have tracked you since yesterday, when you defeated the Underworld creatures near Oakdale." Kyrios spat out blood.

Son of a bitch. Not only had Ronan watched us fight the gravelings from some secret hiding place, but this Spartoi had been crouched in the bushes too. We should have sold tickets.

Lucy was getting madder by the second. "Why the hell did you track us?"

"I wished to know where the creatures came from, and I believed you might lead me to the source of their incursion."

"Easier than doing any work yourself, I suppose," Ronan said, earning a glower from the Spartoi.

"We're here to put a stop to these invasions from the Underworld," Lucy told Kyrios. "So either stop interfering with us or I'll do what I have to do and text your prefect where to pick up your remains."

"I alone will close this cursed door," he ground out, his dark gaze on Daisy. "And I will certainly take this creature. It is magnificent."

"Wrong answer," Lucy said. "And not an option."

Moving almost too fast for the human eye to see, Kyrios palmed some kind of gleaming dark blade in his left hand and drove it hilt-deep into Daisy's side. My wolf let out a sharp sound of pain and staggered away from him. The mercenary soldier flipped to his feet and swung his sword at Daisy's head.

Everyone reacted at once.

I was on my feet before I could form a conscious thought about moving. My cold fire whip blazed out of my hand and lashed across the distance between Kyrios and me. I fully intended to cut him in half and deal with the consequences. Lucy went for him with a battle cry, sword raised. My cat-dragon took to the air with a hiss, her claws extended and ready to rip him to shreds.

Ronan got to Kyrios before any of us, ducking under my whip and avoiding Lucy's swinging blade with impossible speed. He plunged his sword through the Spartoi's chest before his target had a chance to avoid the attack. With a roar, Ronan drove the other man back a half-dozen steps and pinned him to the trunk of a tree with his blade.

I ran to Daisy. My wolf fell on her side, her chest heaving. Bloody foam spilled from her mouth. Black blood soaked her fur and the grass beneath her. My skin tingled with a familiar sensation. Kyrios's blade was silver and spelled.

I knew virtually nothing about my wolf's physiology, abilities, or magic, or about the spells on the blade, but silver was deadly to shifters and I had to assume it could kill Daisy too. I pulled the dagger out. To my horror, its blade was half gone—dissolved into flakes of silver still leaking poison into Daisy's flesh. It was a cruel and deadly weapon meant to kill a shifter. If Kyrios couldn't have Daisy, he intended no one else to have her either.

Fear and fury turned my world silent. I saw and heard nothing but Daisy. She would *not* die. She was me. She was mine. No one, not even the descendant of a dragon's teeth, was going to take her away.

With a snarl Sean would have been proud of, I rested my hand on Daisy's side to comfort her, stuck my fingers into the wound, and used my earth magic to pull the silver out.

She whined and spasmed as liquid silver ran from the wound and dripped to the ground. I pulled harder to get the poison out as quickly as possible.

When the last of the silver trickled out, Daisy shuddered hard and snarled. Before I could react, she flashed out of my hands in a burst of fiery golden magic, crossed the ten feet to Kyrios, and tore the Spartoi free of Ronan's blade.

And then she tripled in size and ate Kyrios in three big bites. His gurgling scream ended abruptly after the first meaty crunch.

Daisy raised her bloody muzzle and howled. The sound rolled through the forest.

"Son of a *bitch*," Lucy said, lowering her sword.

Malcolm made a sympathetic sound. "So much for that rude fella. Hope he doesn't give Daisy heartburn. Is this going to mean paperwork for you, Lucy?"

"The League doesn't even have a *form* for this." She grimaced and touched her bloody shoulder.

He snorted. "You're telling me you don't have a form for seeing someone get eaten? I've only been here three days, but I find that hard to believe."

"It's the Spartoi involvement that complicates things. Has a Spartoi ever been eaten by anything? I don't even know." She glared at Ronan, who withdrew his undamaged sword from the tree with suspicious ease. The blade must be spelled. "You could have kept her from eating him," she accused him.

Daisy licked blood from her muzzle with undisguised relish. Spartoi was apparently quite tasty—or maybe she just enjoyed the taste of revenge.

Ronan took out a cloth to clean his blade. "I'm not entirely sure I could have, Lieutenant, and if I'm being completely honest, I was rather reluctant to get between this wolf and her meal."

"You okay?" Malcolm asked me.

I thought about it. "A little better," I said finally. "I used my dark magic by choice to save us from the shades and gravelings. I could have killed Kyrios the same way, but I used my whip instead, by instinct. That's something, right?"

"That's important," Malcolm assured me. "That means you're still in control, still thinking clearly." Something in his tone made me think he wasn't certain how much longer I'd be able to stay that way.

Ronan watched me as he wiped Kyrios's blood off his sword. His hard mask was back in place, but I figured I knew what was thinking: that I'd used dark magic too much since coming here, that it was only a matter of time until I used it instinctively instead of my own innate power.

"I'm still me," I said. I wasn't sure if I was trying to reassure them, or myself.

When their blades were clean, Ronan and Lucy sheathed their swords. She took a first aid pack from her pants pocket and tore it open. I expected him to offer to help her use it on her torn shoulder, but he didn't; in fact, he ignored her hiss of pain as she cleaned the wound and bandaged it. I scowled, but Lucy didn't seem the least perturbed by his lack of concern.

It was some kind of warrior code, I realized belatedly: pretending not to see a fellow fighter's injury or pain and letting them treat the wound themselves. The dynamics were different between Lucy and Ronan than between she and I. He wasn't uncaring; he was showing her respect.

Meanwhile, he'd helped me rein in the dark magic I'd used to destroy the shades and gravelings before it got away from me and eased the agony I'd suffered afterward. His care for me didn't feel disrespectful, though—rather the opposite. And he'd skewered Kyrios for hurting Daisy and let her get her own revenge for the attack.

Who was leading this group and who was defending and protecting whom seemed very much in flux from one minute to the next. It appeared we'd worked out a de facto dynamic hierarchy, despite the presence of what might be categorized as four alpha personalities and one long-suffering trusty ghost sidekick.

And I'd thought werewolf pack dynamics were complicated.

"Time's a-wasting," Lucy said, cleaning her hands with a wet wipe that she stuffed in her pocket. "I'll figure out what to do about this mess later. Come on."

We followed her to the edge of the clearing, Daisy at my side. A small stone monument identified the ground beyond as a Chumash burial site at least eight hundred years old and asked visitors to be respectful of this sacred area.

"Oh, this pisses me off," Lucy said, surveying the clearing. "If this mage profaned a sacred burial site to cut a door to the Underworld..."

She flexed her hands. "What's justice for her, Alice? All those dead people in Walliston. Isaiah's pack. All the others who've died. And now this. I'm so far beyond caring that your client wants to punish her for stealing."

"Theft is far and away the least of her crimes." I scanned the grassy area in the moonlight. "I don't see any sign of a ritual or any kind of door."

"That's because it's hidden." Malcolm pointed to the far left side of the clearing. "The door's there. Can't you feel it? It's like a wound."

I closed my eyes and reached out with my senses. The power of the ley line and burial ground obscured nearly everything else. I understood why Mariela had chosen this place to make her door, but I hated her for it.

Eventually, I sensed the echoes of a powerful ritual and the door. Malcolm was right: the portal felt like a wound in the earth. No—more than that. Like a horrible, festering wound in the world, made all the worse by where we were.

"Forgive us for this trespass on your homes," Lucy murmured.

Malcolm murmured a short prayer of his own. We made our way silently across the clearing toward the sickening sensation. My magic surged in response to the graves beneath our feet, the lingering traces of rituals conducted here over hundreds of years, and something else I recognized, though I'd never practiced it myself.

"Death magic," I said. "Blood sacrifices to open the door and keep it open."

Lucy inhaled sharply. "Human sacrifice?"

I shook my head. "Small animals. Birds, I think." Magic had echoes, and I recognized these as coming from flapping wings. Poor creatures.

"That's not all." Malcolm looked down at the grass. "There's a ghost here, staked to the ground. No—staked to the door itself. She wanted to make damn sure it stayed open."

We stared at the grass. Even in my Second Sight, I saw no visible signs of the rituals Mariela had performed, or of the ghost she'd trapped. She'd used her earth magic to hide the materials of the rituals under the dirt and grass, and her obfuscation spells were flawless.

Ronan's grim expression mirrored mine. "This is unconscionable," he grated.

"Can we release the spirit?" Lucy asked.

"I don't know," Malcolm said. "That might fracture the spellwork and slam the door."

"Isn't that what we came here to do?" Lucy demanded.

"Shutting the door isn't enough," I pointed out. "Remember, Mariela came here to invoke the Furies. If she succeeds, they're coming up and they're going to slaughter everything Mariela tells them to. I've got to go down there and stop her."

Ronan's glacier-blue eyes turned dark. He'd known I wasn't just here to shut the door, but I hadn't told him about Mariela, or my plans to hop in the elevator and head for the basement.

Malcolm's pain and anger bled over to me and left a sour taste in my mouth. Unsurprisingly, the suffering of other ghosts hurt him deeply.

I entwined our fingers the way Sean did when I was hurting. I'd never been able to really touch Malcolm like that before. I would never have chosen to come to this world—especially knowing we might not make it back home—but when his hand tightened on mine, I wouldn't have traded that moment for anything.

To my surprise, Ronan rested his hand on Daisy's head. "Guardian wolf," he said, his tone strangely formal. I recalled that Torryn had addressed Daisy the same way. "This is why I'm here, isn't it?"

Daisy growled.

"Care to explain?" Lucy snapped.

"The Underworld is vast and dangerous." Ronan rubbed Daisy's head. "You'll need a guide to Edis."

"What's Edis?" I asked.

"The infernal city on the edge of the Darkness. It's the gateway to the deepest parts of the Underworld, and home to a number of very scary things—including the Erinyes."

Lucy crossed her arms. "How do you know this?"

His eyes glinted. "I read books. You should try it. You might learn something."

She took a swing at him. He blocked her punch easily, which made me think she hadn't really been trying to make contact. "I've been there," he said shortly. "End of discussion."

The fact Ronan had been to the Underworld was unexpected, but not altogether a surprise. We still had no idea what he was, but if he'd been down there and made it back, that explained why both Daisy and Torryn had thought we needed him—though *how* they'd known was a complete mystery.

"What's it like down there?" I asked.

"Many realms, like our own world. Some are nightmarish, some quite Earth-like, and some like paradise. Vast wastelands, scattered settlements, some great cities like Edis."

"I thought the name of the city was Dis," Lucy said. She raised an eyebrow at Ronan. "I did read a book once."

"Dante recalled much from his visit and embellished the rest," Ronan said. "And though he didn't get all the details and names quite right, his description of the part of the Underworld he saw was fairly accurate, to a point."

My eyebrows went up. "Dante really visited the Underworld?"

"Many people have visited the Underworld," Lucy reminded me. "They came back with bits and pieces of what they'd seen. Many descriptions exist, some true to a limited extent."

I indicated Ronan with a tilt of my head. "So he's supposed to be our guide?" I asked Daisy.

She stared up at him, her golden eyes glowing.

"Wolf charades again," Malcolm sighed.

"Not just for a guide. I guess we'll find out the rest." I touched my cat-dragon's paw. Her claws prickled on my skin. "Same with her, I suppose."

"A dragon of any size is a great asset." Ronan glanced at Lucy. "Your skill with your blade will be very useful, as will your...other gifts. The Underworld is full of the spirits of the dead, as well as many creatures who may recognize you as one of their own. It's an advantage we'll need to slip through as inconspicuously as possible. We will be as unwanted there as these shades and gravelings are here."

Lucy looked thoughtful. "You may be right," she said finally. "But what about Alice? From what I understand about the Underworld, she'll stick out like a neon sign. The living don't belong there any more than those from Alice and Malcolm's world belong in this one. What do we do about that?"

"That's true." Ronan regarded me. "But Alice has crossed the veil between life and death, am I correct?"

"That is true," I said quietly. "A couple of times."

Lucy flinched. That news clearly bothered her.

"That will make it a little easier to hide her," Ronan said. "The bigger concern is Alice is dying because she carries magic not meant for a human. The Underworld will sense both the dark magic and her imminent death and try to keep her."

I recoiled.

Malcolm flitted and got in Ronan's face. "How the hell do you know all that?" he demanded. "And would it kill you to be a less of a prick? Alice doesn't deserve for you to talk like that. Is your kind born without an ounce of empathy?"

"As a matter of fact, we are." Ronan did something, and a puff of magic pushed Malcolm back a few feet. "Though it *can* be developed, given time. We don't have time for unnecessary coddling or circumspection. If we're going to the Underworld, we need to know each other's skills and abilities—and limitations."

"But apparently you're not including yourself in that, are you?" Malcolm retorted. "You want to know everything about us, but you're going to keep all your secrets. We've seen how good you are with *that* sword. Where's the other one, Ronan?"

Ronan stilled.

"Yeah, we know about that." Malcolm floated back and forth. "So, where's your second sword?"

Expressionless, Ronan turned to me. "You could wander through the Underworld for a century without finding Edis while the Erinyes slaughter thousands here and in your own world." His voice was colder and more remote than on the night we'd met at Hawthorne's. "Either follow me to them now, or I'll leave and you can make your own way."

"Why are you willing to go with us?" I asked. "Because Daisy and Torryn said you should?"

A muscle moved in his jaw. "In a way, yes. I have no more desire to see my—the Erinyes kill those Mariela has identified as her enemies than you do."

"And?" I prompted.

"I have unfinished business in Edis. Apparently, I'm meant to return and settle matters." He jerked his head toward Lucy's jeep. "We need to pack for the journey and hide our vehicles."

"My jeep has a tracking device," Lucy told him as we hurried back to the road. "We'll have to disconnect it. If I don't report in, they'll come looking for me."

"I'll take care of the tracking device," Ronan said.

"If the League, the Brotherhood, or anyone else finds that door before we make it back, they'll shut it behind us," she added. "And I don't know about you all, but I don't know how to open another one from that side."

"I have a thought about that," I said.

WHILE LUCY and Ronan focused on hiding her jeep and his motorcycle, I took my backpack and returned to the clearing with Malcolm, Daisy, and my cat-dragon.

I set the strongest blood wards I could make on the doorway, using the ley line to keep them powered and hopefully impervious to the magic flares. The wards wouldn't stop Mariela from coming through, or any of us, but at least no more shades or gravelings would escape topside.

When the wards were done, I got to my feet. No sense beating around the bush. "Malcolm, I need you to stay behind and guard the door."

"No freaking way." He flitted in place. "How the hell could you even ask me that?"

"Because we have no choice." I touched his arm. "If someone manages to find this place and shuts that door, we'll be trapped on the other side. Someone has to make sure that doesn't happen. And if Mariela gets back to the door before we do, someone will have to be here to know about it and go for help to keep her from getting back to our world. It has to be you who stays. You are the last person I want to leave behind, but you're the only person I trust in *any* world to do those things."

He said nothing, but his fury scoured me.

"I can't make this suck any less," I told him. "I hate the thought of leaving you here—I hate it with every fiber of my being. You won't be any safer than us. I have no idea what might come this way. If you can think of a different solution, tell me. I would love there to be another way, because the thought of going without you makes me want to throw up."

His shoulders slumped. "Damn it, Alice."

Despite everything, I had to smile. "If I had a quarter for every time you or Sean said that, I'd have a mountain of change."

He smiled too. "It does seem to happen a lot." The smile faded. "I will keep that door open, no matter what. If Mariela does come through it before you get back, what do I do?"

"Find the closest League outpost and tell them. We'll find out from Lucy where that is." I hesitated. "It wouldn't be so bad for you to stay here. Your magic isn't as disrupted by the natural magic here as mine, and all the ambient power will keep you from going wraith for a long, long time."

"You mean if you don't come back." His voice was deceptively neutral.

"Yes. We have to think about that possibility too." I took a deep breath. "If you want, you could go back to the portal at Northbourne, in case someone comes through it, and try to hitch a ride back. Or maybe the portal near the bordello back home has another endpoint in this world. You might be able to get back that way if you decide to try to get home rather than stay. It's important to me that you either make it back, or you make a good life for yourself here."

"I will do my best," he said. "But it's important to *me* that you and Daisy make it back so we can all get home together. And the little cat-dragon too," he added, reaching up to rub his fingertip on her paw. She swatted at him playfully. "Have you picked out a name yet?"

"I think Esme." I smiled at my little guardian. "Esme the cat-dragon."

"I like it. It suits her." He glanced back toward the road. "I don't know what the hell Ronan is, but don't put your life in his hands if you can help it."

"I hope I don't have to, but it sounds like we're going to have our hands full down there. I'll keep Daisy at my side and Esme on my shoulder and Lucy at my six, and hope that's enough."

He floated back and forth. "I want to free the ghost who's trapped here."

"I do too. That'll be the first thing I do when I get back. Or you can do it if it doesn't look like we're coming back."

"I could take their place," Malcolm said quietly. "Release them and keep the door open myself."

I opened my mouth to tell him *hell no*, then thought better of it.

"If you do that, will you be able to free yourself and close the door if you have to?" I asked instead.

He considered. "Probably. At least I'd be doing it of my own free will. I doubt this ghost volunteered to be Mariela's doorstop."

"It's your decision." Damn it, it was hard to say that to him. I hated the thought of Malcolm being trapped even more than leaving him behind. "If you do take their place, please make sure you can get free and close the door."

"I will," he promised.

Lucy and Ronan emerged from the trees with bags over their shoulders and identical determined expressions. I imagined my own appearance was similar.

"If you end up going home by yourself, please tell Sean I love him and I'm sorry I didn't make it back," I told Malcolm.

"He knows how much you love him," Malcolm said. "But I'll tell him." He hugged me, then stepped back.

"We good to go?" Lucy asked as she and Ronan joined us.

"I think so." I put my backpack on my shoulders and fastened the chest and waist straps. Given how bumpy the trip through the mirror had been, I could only imagine what we'd face to get from this clearing to the Underworld.

Esme resettled herself, her claws sinking into the padded strap. "Will you be safe there?" I asked her. "This might be a rough ride. I can put you in the bag."

For such a young cat, she had already mastered an expression of total disdain. Then again, I imagined cats nailed that look fairly early in their lives.

"So what do we do now?" I asked.

Ronan startled me by unbuckling his belt. "Whoa there, cowboy," Lucy said, raising her hands. "Not interested in joining the Mile Below Club."

Ronan gave her a bland look as he pulled his belt from its loops. "I have to tie us up. But don't worry—I'll be gentle if you're scared."

"One of these days, someone is going to stab you." Lucy adjusted the straps of her backpack. "What can we expect on the way down, and what will be waiting for us when we get there?"

"What we encounter on the way will depend entirely on the type of door we're going through." Ronan started coiling his belt in long loops, like a lasso. To my astonishment, it stretched into a silver rope that grew in length to more than twenty feet.

"Well, that's handy." Lucy glanced at me. "Let me guess: no enchanted rope back home either?"

"Not that I've ever seen," I admitted. For all its brokenness, this world had more than its share of wondrous things.

"The Underworld is nearly infinite, with many realms." Ronan tied one end of the rope around his waist. "We have no way to know where this door leads. With any luck, we won't fall out into a lake of lava."

Fantastic.

He tied the rope around my waist next, with about eight feet between us, then around Lucy's, and finally around Daisy's front legs and shoulders like a halter. The rope grew longer to accommodate all of us. I tugged at the knot at my waist, but it had no give. I wondered if part of the enchantment was knots that wouldn't give way. I hoped so.

"And the reason for the rope?" Lucy asked.

Ronan tested each of his knots. "So we don't get split up. It's a long way down."

"Sounds like this expedition will require as much luck as skill." Lucy sighed. "Let's hope we've got some coming our way. How do we get through the doorway?"

He shouldered his own pack and gestured at the grass at our feet. "Our blood and earth mage will do the honors." He made a sweeping gesture. "Alice, if you will?"

I crouched and placed my hands on the grass. Unlike the mirror I'd used to travel to this world, the doorway Mariela had cut to the Underworld was like a stab wound with magical sutures keeping it from closing and healing. The boundary strained against the magic holding it open.

My stomach churned. I didn't want to do this. The fact I had no other choice made it all the more unpleasant.

"It's just the Underworld," Ronan said from behind me. "You traveled between worlds to get here. What's one more jump?"

"One more jump," I grumbled. "Sure."

Malcolm pointed to the doorway. "Go get that scroll and kick Mariela's ass so we can go home."

I took a deep breath and exhaled. "Find Mariela. Get the scroll. Keep her from unleashing the Furies. Return to the doorway, get back topside, and go home. That's just six things. I can do six things."

"Atta girl." Malcolm forced a smile. "And don't drag your ass about it."

I dug my fingers into the dirt and pushed magic into the ground. Magic surged and suddenly the maw of the doorway yawned open in front of us, framed with crackling spellwork.

"Shit," Lucy said involuntarily.

A blast of cold air came out, bringing with it a smell that reminded me of a damp cave. "That's promising, maybe," I said. "It feels cool and I don't smell sulfur. Maybe the doorway comes out in one of the nicer neighborhoods."

"We can only hope." Ronan joined me on the edge of the abyss. "On the count of three, we jump."

"Got it," Lucy said. "Ready when you are."

Daisy growled impatiently.

I got to my feet. Esme made a guttural sound I realized was a purr. "Cat, you are so weird," I muttered.

"Oh, hey, Alice?" Malcolm said. "If they've got a Hard Rock Cafe in Edis, bring me back a T-shirt, will you?"

That made me smile. Bless Malcolm. "I'll do my best," I promised.

"One," Ronan said.

I took a deep breath. Malcolm gave me a thumbs up.

"Two."

I rolled my shoulders to loosen up. Daisy crouched. Lucy muttered something I didn't quite catch, but the corners of Ronan's mouth turned up.

"*Three*," he said.

We jumped.

CHAPTER 24

I FELL OUT OF THE SIDE OF A HILL AND LANDED ON SOMETHING SOFT.

"Rrrrr?" Esme asked, her claws digging painfully into my shoulder.

"Ow." Lucy's voice came from underneath me. "Alice, move your damn elbow."

"Sorry." I rolled off Lucy and squinted in the bright light, trying to make out our surroundings.

Something heavy hit the ground on my right. Ronan grunted and cursed. Another thud, accompanied by a chuffing sound. I still couldn't see very well—why the hell was it so *bright?*—but my fingers encountered familiar thick fur. Daisy.

"Everyone okay?" Ronan asked.

"I think so." Blinking rapidly as my eyes adjusted, I sat up and rubbed my aching elbow. I'd banged it on a rock somewhere between the clearing topside and the strange blue-green grassy hillside on which we now sat. Other than that, I seemed unscathed, albeit a little dizzy and out of sorts.

To my surprise, Malcolm's trace still tingled in the corner of my mind. Our journey here hadn't broken our connection the way the trip through the mirror had broken my link to Sean. The familiar sensation was reassuring—not because he'd be able to help if we ran into trouble, but it let me know he was all right.

"Anyone else feel weird?" Lucy asked. "Like a lot of time has passed since we jumped?"

"Yeah." I started to rise, then thought better of it when my vision swam. "Yeah, that's exactly how I feel."

Ronan staggered to his feet and surveyed our surroundings. "I'm sick to my stomach, like I've fallen quite a distance, but I don't recall the fall itself."

"Me either," I said. "I jumped and then I came out of the side of that hill. I don't remember anything in between."

Lucy managed to stand up and offered me her hand. I let her help me up and steadied myself with one hand on Daisy's head. Ronan untied the rope around our waists, coiled it, and stowed it in his bag.

We stood near the edge of a grassy outcropping halfway up a mountainside, overlooking a wide valley that stretched all the way to the horizon. The view was almost disconcertingly like the world we'd left behind, except for the colors. Everything around us—the air, the grass, the trees, even the sky—were alien shades of green and blue. The sky was as bright as noon on a sunny day, though I saw nothing that resembled a sun. The air was cold, the wind full of unfamiliar smells. Below us in the valley, strange dark shapes moved through the trees. Enormous black winged creatures soared overhead.

With a start, I realized the magic here thrummed quietly like the magic of home instead of the intense searing sensation of the world above. The ambient power was far more stable, with none of the surges we'd experienced topside, and almost muted.

Tentatively, I spooled earth magic. To my relief, green magic coiled around my hands and arms. If I could use my magic here, that went a long way toward making me less apprehensive about what we might face.

Gradually my dizziness subsided, but the nausea didn't. My eyes strayed toward the rocky side of the mountain, where the doorway shimmered faintly in my Second Sight. I wanted to retreat through that door and make this sick, almost panicky feeling in my stomach go away.

"That's going to get worse, not better," Ronan said. He gestured at the hand I'd pressed to my abdomen. "Regardless of how many times you've died and been brought back, you're a living being in a world of the dead. You'll feel as though you don't belong here until you go back."

I swallowed hard. The discomfort was annoying but not debilitating—not yet. "Then let's get moving," I said. "Do you have any idea where we are and how to get to Edis from here?"

"Give me a moment." Ronan closed his eyes.

While he was getting his bearings, or whatever the hell he was doing, I checked on Daisy and Esme. Neither had any injuries from the journey that I could see.

My backpack had some light damage that indicated it had scraped along rocks or something similar, but its contents were fine. I checked over everything, drank from my water bottle, and took a moment to study the photo of Sean and me. I tucked it back into the little inside pocket and zipped it closed.

I'd stashed the obsidian rock in the bag for the journey, unwilling to risk it falling out of my pocket. I dug it out and crouched next to Daisy. "You brought us this far," I told her, holding out the rock on my palm. "Any chance you can use this to lead us to Mariela?"

"What's that?" Lucy asked. "Nasty vibes around that thing."

I explained how the rock had been stored with the scroll and soaked up its magic, and how Daisy had apparently been able to sense and follow the remaining trace.

Lucy squatted beside me and scratched Daisy's head. "You are one amazing wolf," she said. "So, how about it? Can you take us to Mariela and the scroll?"

Daisy backed up a few steps, turned to her left, then to her right, and let out a short whine. She chomped the air and looked up at Ronan, who hadn't moved or opened his eyes.

"I think this place is messing with her tracking," Lucy said as we rose. "My internal compass sure as hell is screwed up. Up feels like down, left feels like right...and that valley seems to be moving backward in time."

I stared out at the valley. When I tried to focus on its farthest point, the horizon moved farther away and the valley stretched with vertigo-inducing elasticity. I stumbled. "I see what you mean. Okay, no staring in that direction."

Ronan's voice startled me. "Move back from the edge of the platform."

That didn't make much sense, but Lucy and I took a half-dozen steps away from edge of the rocky outcropping. "What platform?" Lucy asked.

A pitch-black train rounded the side of the mountain from our right, moving with eerie silence. It glided to a stop in front of us, on a track that had not been there a heartbeat ago—a track that faded and disappeared twenty feet in front of the rather sinister-looking locomotive.

The train appeared solid and made of matte-black metal, but the bottom swished and swayed in a way that reminded me, oddly, of the hem of a black robe. I couldn't see any wheels, but there was a track, so maybe the wheels were hidden under the robe?

Or maybe I should stop trying to make things make sense.

"That," Lucy said, nonplussed, "is a train."

"Yes." Ronan put his bag back on his shoulders. If I didn't know better, I'd have thought he was fighting not to smile at Lucy's bafflement. Did he *want* her to stab him? "I enjoy train travel, though I don't get to indulge in it very often. Do you like the train, Alice?"

"I've never been on a train," I admitted. I stashed the stone in my pocket and put on my backpack. Esme switched to my left shoulder and resumed her growly purring. "Are we taking a train to Edis?"

"Did you think we'd have to walk all the way there?" He raised an eyebrow. "This is the Underworld, not *The Lord of the Rings*."

"Ass," I muttered. "Lucy, can I borrow your sword?"

Ronan was saved from certain death when a door on the side of the train that hadn't been visible a second before slid open soundlessly. The car's interior was matte black as well. From where I stood, I couldn't see anything inside but empty space.

I hadn't seen her draw it, but Lucy had her sword raised. Nothing emerged from the train, however.

"All aboard for Edis." Ronan bowed and gestured at the open door. "Ladies first."

Lucy studied our otherworldly transportation, her blade at the ready. "Give me one good reason to step foot on this train."

"I called in a favor, Lieutenant." Ronan's expression turned grim. "One I might need much more urgently in the future, so please don't spit in my face and refuse to get aboard. I give you my word this conveyance will deliver us safely to Edis."

After a hesitation, Lucy lowered her sword, but didn't put it away. "Fine." She got on the train.

Daisy and I followed her inside, with Esme purring on my shoulder and Ronan right behind us. The interior was as black as the exterior. The car was empty except for two rows of seats facing each other near the door. To my surprise, I could see outside the train, as if the walls and curved roof were glass, though from the outside it had all appeared to be solid metal.

Daisy prowled around the car as Ronan, Lucy, and I settled into the seats. He sat on one side and we sat on the other with our bags next to us. The door closed and the train accelerated smoothly. I heard no indication of an engine or the sound of wheels on the track, but we reached full speed in a matter of seconds. Given the surreal landscape and the vast distances between landmarks, I found it impossible to judge how fast we were moving, which was quite disconcerting.

As the train made its way along the mountains, away from the valley and toward a dark horizon, I asked, "Can I ask who's providing our transportation? Purely out of curiosity."

Ronan removed his jacket and sword, stretched out his legs, and relaxed. "He goes by many names. His true name is as old as the universe and isn't pronounceable in any human language. The Greeks called him Charon, though he's much more than just a ferryman. In some ways, he *is* the ferry."

I knew the name Charon from Greek mythology and art. My mind conjured up a painting I'd seen somewhere of a terrifying robed skeleton, ferrying the souls of the dead in a boat on the river Styx.

I recalled the robe-like edges of the train, and Ronan's words, and had a disturbing thought. "We aren't actually, like, *inside* him now, right?"

He thought about it. "Define 'inside,'" he said.

Ick.

I'd eaten several protein bars and the last of the snacks I'd bought at the waystation near Oakdale before going through the doorway, but my stomach growled. That meant either I was burning through calories even faster, or we'd lost some time during our journey to the Underworld. Or both.

My bag contained two boxes of protein bars and two bottles of water—my Hawthorne's bottle, plus another full bottle I bought after we left the motel. I'd left the half-empty bottle of Charles's finest Ronan had brought me in Lucy's jeep. I hoped we'd get to share a toast with its contents when we got back.

Daisy returned from her inspection of the car and settled on the floor at my feet, her back against my shins. Her body heat and warm golden magic eased some of my tension.

My stomach grumbled again. Ronan and Lucy exchanged a glance. "You should eat," Ronan said. "We'll be on the train for a while. Rest. You're well-guarded."

"Don't do that," I said.

"Do what?" Lucy asked with a frown.

"You *know* what. Treating me like I'm fragile. Don't do that."

"We're not treating you like you're fragile," she snapped. "You're hungry and tired. You're *human*. We don't expect you to have the same endurance. Don't make me knock that chip off your shoulder, woman."

Daisy let out a quiet growl. I wasn't sure if she was warning Lucy or echoing her sentiment.

I dug two protein bars out of my bag and tore the wrapper off the first one. "Sorry," I said finally. "I'm touchy about this whole...dying thing."

"Can't blame you." Lucy took a swig from her flask. "It doesn't help that someone threw it in your face earlier." She stared at Ronan. "Seriously, dick move, even for you."

He raised an eyebrow at her but said nothing.

"But thanks for the train," I added between bites of my protein bar. "This is a rather pleasant way to travel."

"If we ignore the fact we may or may not be inside someone," Lucy said.

I narrowed my eyes at her. "Yes, *ignoring* that fact. Why a train, though?" I asked Ronan. "I thought Charon has a ferry—or *is* a ferry."

"Don't think so literally." He took out a cloth and little bottle of liquid and began polishing his sword. "Conveyances in the Underworld can take any number of forms and travel along an equally infinite number of routes. Very few know the ways, and even fewer can travel between realms—or care to. We could just as easily travel by boat, or carriage, or flight, but I prefer the train."

With my own meal finished, I opened a can of cat food for Esme. She climbed down off my shoulder to eat and then sat beside me on the seat to wash her face and head with dainty gray paws. I figured Daisy would be tided over for a while after eating Kyrios. She lay on the floor at my feet, her head on her paws. She seemed at ease, and that made me feel better.

Lucy took out her own sword-polishing kit and set to work. The others appeared lost in their own thoughts, so I turned and sat cross-legged, my elbow on the back of the seat and my chin in my hand. Esme curled up in my lap and closed her eyes for a catnap.

The train wound its way through the mountains, making its own track as it went and leaving no trace of its passage behind. We were not always on the ground; in fact, the farther we traveled, the more the train seemed to take to the air to cross over streams and valleys. I never got entirely comfortable, but after about an hour of smooth sailing I relaxed enough to half-doze as I gazed out the window.

We passed forests and plains, farms and well-tended fields, and even villages and a few small cities. Creatures of various shapes and sizes roamed the grasslands and forests, but none came near enough to the train for me to see them well. The view was surprisingly bucolic.

Ronan's voice startled me out of my reverie. "Many people think of the Underworld in terms of Hell. Hell is something else entirely. We are not in Hell. Some regions of the Underworld are quite hellish, but most are like this one. A few are beautiful beyond imagining—much closer to what you might think of as Heaven than Hell."

"This area is certainly peaceful." I rubbed the silky fur behind Esme's ears. "It's like a continuation of the lives these people lived topside."

"An apt description of this area." Ronan glanced out the window. "We're about to cross into another realm. There might be some bumps."

The bright blue-green light outside darkened abruptly and took on an ominous red-and-purple tone. The train jolted hard and bounced like an airplane in turbulent air. I gripped the edge of my seat, for all the good that would do if we dropped out of the sky.

The train jostled a few more times and swayed sickeningly like a tram in the wind. Finally, the ride smoothed out again. I let out a breath and released my death grip on the seat.

The view outside the window had changed completely. Instead of fields of grain, farms, and cities, the train crossed a flat plain of ash. Behind us, the mountains we'd traversed grew smaller and more distant with each passing moment. The sky was streaked with orange and yellow, as if this realm existed in perpetual twilight. The juxtaposition with the bright mountains and valleys of the realm where we'd arrived was jarring.

When I looked more closely, I noticed trails in the ash, criss-crossing the plain in irregular intervals. Strange dark shapes trudged along the paths. On my side of the train, in the distance, I spotted what might have been a village of a dozen squat buildings. Who or what could exist in such an environment, I had no idea.

Our trip across the ash plain seemed to last for most of a day, though it was probably no longer than the journey through the mountains. Daisy prowled the train car for the entire time, growling at anyone who tried to speak to her. Esme, on the other hand, slept soundly, nestled in my lap.

The nausea that had plagued me since I arrived in the Under-world came and went in waves. When I could, I nibbled on protein bars and sipped water. Once we reached Edis and began our search for the Furies, I might not get much chance to eat.

Ronan finished polishing his sword and moved on to cleaning the knives hidden in his clothing. Lucy cleaned her own knives and checked her gun. Not to be outdone, Daisy yawned and showed all her teeth.

"Do you know much about the Furies?" I asked Ronan. "I read up on the myths—the Greek version, anyway—but how much of that is true?"

"Some of it's true, or close to the truth." He studied a blade, frowned, and went back to cleaning it. "They are very, very old. One myth says they were three daughters of Gaia, born from drops of blood that fell to earth. Another says they emerged from Chaos and Old Night. Both of those stories are beautiful in their own way, and both have elements of truth, but in reality they were archangels once."

"Angels?" Lucy echoed. "Actual angels?"

"*Arch*angels." Ronan didn't look up from his work. "With great wings and swords and celestial power. Like all archangels, they were mighty and terrible warriors. Under the archangel Michael's command, they fought and defeated the darkest forces in existence when the universe was young. As the eons passed, some of their most beloved brothers and sisters died in battle. Angry, hurt, and bitter, they became vengeance incarnate—so much so that they defied orders and unleashed great calamities. They were cast from Heaven and fell bloodied to the earth. They made their home in the Underworld, living either in the Darkness or on its borders, and cut all ties to their sisters and brothers in Heaven, as most of the Fallen do."

"Are there many Fallen?" I asked.

"Not many." Finally satisfied with the gleaming blade, Ronan slipped it into a sheath on his thigh. "A few walk the earth. Others prefer the Underworld. I've heard rumors of one or two who have traveled to other realms entirely, but those are just rumors."

"So the Furies were cast from Heaven and became chthonic deities." I ate the last few bites of a protein bar. "Good to know being an infernal goddess is a step down from being an archangel."

He raised a shoulder in a half shrug. "They aren't goddesses by the strictest definition of the word, though that's how humans categorize beings of great power. They *are* capable of unleashing terrible retribution and death, though I haven't heard of them doing so for a long time. They prefer a quiet life down here. Humans ceased to be more than an irritation for them long ago."

Thunder rumbled. I expected to see storm clouds, but the sky remained red and orange and cloudless.

Ronan glanced out the window. "We're nearing the edge of this realm. And if I'm not mistaken, the next realm is where we will find Edis."

"If Mariela had to get to Edis too, how did she get there?" I asked. "I'm assuming Charon didn't owe her any favors."

"As I mentioned, there are other forms of conveyance here,

though none are as fast or safe as ours." He took a drink from his flask and tucked it back into his inner jacket pocket. "My hope is we've gained some ground on your target—maybe even beaten her to Edis. If we can reach the Erinyes before her, the likelihood of your success increases dramatically."

I wondered if Torryn had told him of her prophecy that I wouldn't succeed in my goals of preventing Mariela from unleashing the Furies, reclaiming the scroll, or bringing Mariela back to face justice. I still intended to do all those things, because prophecies were far from set in stone, and because no way in hell would I accept that Malcolm and I wouldn't get home. No matter what happened down here, I would never accept that fate. I'd fight to get back home to Sean and my life until the end.

Without warning, the train suddenly plunged into total darkness. We jolted, bounced, and shuddered violently again, as with our previous passage between realms. I left one hand on Esme's soft fur and gripped my seat with the other.

A ball of silver-blue light formed across from us. Ronan held up his hand and the light brightened enough for us to see. To my surprise and horror, solid rock zipped by outside the train as if we were passing underground or through a mountain via a very long, very narrow tunnel. In fact, there didn't seem to be any tunnel per se —just the train going through the rock. My mouth suddenly became very dry.

The ball of light brightened, revealing a tall figure in a hooded black robe looming at the front of the car.

I gasped. My earth magic whip spiraled out of my hand. Esme arched her back and hissed. Daisy leaped in front of me and snarled. Lucy jumped up, sword raised.

Ronan, however, stayed in his seat, his legs stretched out. "Hello, old friend," he said with a nod. "Our deepest thanks for the transportation."

"I did not expect to see you again so soon, Ronan." Charon's voice was deep and resonant with old, old magic. The hood of his robe hid his face.

Ronan stood. He was very tall, but Charon was even taller. "We're near Edis, I presume? This darkness seems familiar."

"Quite close. We have only to cross the plains beyond these mountains." Charon glided forward. "You will not be welcome in the city. *She* has placed a bounty on your head."

Ronan sighed. "So I heard. A couple of hunters with lots of blades but no brains even tried to collect it."

Lucy chuckled. "The bounty hunter has a bounty on his *own* head? That's delightful. Who did you piss off, Ronan?"

He ignored her. "Will you take us through the gate?"

"I cannot," Charon said. "I do not believe the guards would grant you passage. Instead, I will deliver you and your companions to a place in the wall where you may find a way in." His head moved slightly, still hidden by the hood. I caught a glint of something under the hood, like the shimmer of magic in dark eyes. I got the impression he was studying the rest of us. "I have heard a rumor of another mortal, seen near Edis in recent days."

Damn it. "Did she get inside the city?" I asked, before I remembered I was addressing a being possibly as old as the universe. "Sir," I amended.

Charon said nothing for a long moment, during which I tried to imagine what he was thinking of me and my impudence. "I do not know," he said finally. "I have sensed great and old powers rising. Many are disturbed by these events. Such darkness has not walked these lands for some time."

Well, crap. That didn't sound good.

"This other mortal may attempt to unleash the Erinyes," Ronan said.

"That would be most inadvisable," Charon replied. "And very difficult to accomplish. They are ministers of justice, and have served in that capacity for a very long time. For them to take up their swords again would require most extraordinary circumstances, or very powerful magic."

His words elicited a rollercoaster of emotions—among them, hope. If the Furies were in semi-retirement, that meant Mariela wouldn't have an easy time invoking them. I doubted she could wield the kind of magic Charon deemed very powerful.

Ronan clearly didn't share my optimism. "If she succeeds, though, can the Furies be prevented from leaving Edis? Or this realm?"

"I do not believe anyone has ever attempted to do so," Charon told us. "I would not say it was impossible, but I know of little that could stop them. The better option would be to prevent this other mortal from reaching them."

"That's what we're trying to do." Ronan gave Charon a small bow. "Again, our thanks."

"I settle my debts." Charon inclined his head slightly. "Speaking of debts, do you continue to ignore messages sent by your brothers and sisters?"

Ronan went preternaturally still. "I've had no messages for a very long time." His tone was icy. "I'm sure I've been forgotten. I'd prefer it that way."

"You were never forgotten," Charon said. His robe fluttered, as if he'd started to raise his hand but reconsidered. "When the next message arrives, pay heed to it."

Before Ronan could respond, the train jolted, throwing us all off balance. Ronan's ball of light went out. When he rekindled the light, Charon was gone.

"People come and go so quickly here," I quipped. No one laughed, or possibly neither got the reference. Malcolm would have laughed. I missed my ghost.

We emerged from the tunnel onto a vast lava field. The air shimmered with the intense heat radiating from the rivers of molten rock. The train traveled well above the lava, and for once I was grateful we weren't on the ground.

Tall pathways made of stone crisscrossed the lava, much like the trails through the ash in the previous realm. Though we couldn't feel the heat, the way the air wavered indicated just how hot it was outside. How Mariela could possibly have crossed this plain on foot, or in anything but Charon's ferry, was a total mystery.

As far as I could tell, we'd traveled in a straight line since leaving the mountains behind. As we reached the middle of the lava field, however, the train banked sharply, and I saw what waited ahead of us.

"Oh, holy wow," I breathed.

Across the lava field, a great walled city stretched almost from horizon to horizon. The lava rivers stopped well short of the wall, forming a kind of steep, rocky beach. Enormous fires burned along the top of the wall, providing light all along its forbidding perimeter.

Beyond the city loomed absolute inky darkness. I recalled Ronan's description of Edis: a city on the edge, the gateway to the deepest parts of the Underworld and home to a number of very scary things. Given it lay in an infernal region of the Underworld, I'd pictured a burning city in ruins, but it wasn't—far from it. The city was magnificent, with soaring towers visible above the walls and enormous gates.

Something moved along the top of the wall near the largest gate: a dragon so huge it made the creature Lucy had wounded look like a house cat. It stretched wings the size of a jumbo jet's and settled on the wall, keeping watch over the lava plain.

Esme climbed onto my shoulder and hissed in the direction of the dragon. "You would not even be a snack for that thing," I told her. "Let's not pick a fight with it, okay?"

She gave me a disdainful look and licked her paw.

"Edis is enormous," Lucy said, standing with her knee on the seat for balance as the train banked again. "How will we find the Erinyes?"

"Charon said the sisters serve as ministers of justice. We'll start at the city's Great Hall, or the bar closest to it." Ronan picked up a stack of clothing from the seat next to him—a stack that hadn't been there a moment ago. He handed us each a pair of pants, a tunic shirt, and a hooded robe. "It will be damn near impossible for us to blend in, but we should try. No need to advertise we don't belong here. They'll figure it out soon enough without us marching in there dressed as we are."

We changed quickly, Lucy and I in the front of the car and Ronan in the back. He faced the rear wall to give us privacy. I didn't see him sneak a peek even once—not that I watched him change, of course.

All right, I *did* watch out of the corner of my eye, because I wanted to know who and what he was. I got no hints about his true nature from seeing him mostly undressed, however. His body was human.

I couldn't say I was entirely disappointed in the lack of clues, given the visual treat of Ronan sans clothes. My heart belonged entirely to Sean, but there was no harm appreciating a work of art— and Ronan was most assuredly a work of art. Had he been on the train with us, Malcolm might have discorporated on the spot.

Like Lucy, who changed with the quickness and efficiency of a trained soldier, Ronan stripped down to his shorts in record time, despite his layers of clothing and gear. His body was all muscle and covered with scars, neither of which was a surprise. Bounty hunting was a dangerous occupation.

I was fairly certain he was aware I was watching. Something about his posture made me think he was smiling to himself and taking his time re-dressing, the gorgeous bastard.

The fact our clothes fit us each perfectly didn't surprise me in the least. As the others arranged their weapons under their robes, which appeared to have strategically placed slits allowing blades to be drawn quickly and easily, I stashed a few items of my own on my person and in the robe. My clothes seemed to have been designed for a mage, who would need to have various blades and objects close at hand.

"Thanks, Charon," I murmured.

The train made a tiny jostle. I liked to think that was Charon saying, *You're welcome.*

By the time the train slowed on approach to the rocky beach and a section of the wall out of sight of the main gate—and the dragon perched nearby, thankfully—we were all redressed.

Ronan took his magic rope from his bag. "There are no wolves in Edis," he said to Daisy. "Certainly none wandering alone. But if you appear to be my property, you will gain less attention."

Daisy curled her lip to show teeth.

I didn't like the idea of Ronan tying that rope around my wolf, especially when I didn't know what it could do, or what he was. "Can't she be *my* property?" I asked. "Why yours?"

"I'm somewhat known in Edis, and my aura is clearly not human," he said. "Most of the inhabitants of the city won't want to start trouble with me. You and Lucy can avoid being noticed with masking and *Look Away* spells, but if you've got a wolf on a leash, you *will* attract attention—especially the kind we don't want. I give you my word Daisy can escape the rope if she chooses to do so."

"How the hell did you know I have masking and *Look Away* spells?" I demanded.

"The same way I knew everything else," he said, which wasn't exactly an answer. "Yes or no on the rope?"

Damn it. "Daisy, it's up to you," I told my wolf. "Do you trust him to do this?"

Her lip still curled so we knew she wasn't happy, Daisy went to Ronan's side and allowed him to tie the rope around her front legs and shoulders again. The rope transformed into a brown leather harness with nasty-looking spikes on the shoulders and a long leash that looped around Ronan's arm.

"Where did you get that rope?" I asked him.

"Bought it from a fae," he said. It could have been true.

"What about Esme?" I picked up my cat-dragon and settled her on my shoulder.

"Dragons of all kinds are not unusual here." Ronan put his bag on his shoulders and sheathed his sword on his back. "A pūķis is less common than her larger cousins, but no one will question that you have one. They will know she's bound to you as your protector."

A thought occurred to me. "Will we get to take the train back to the doorway when it's all said and done?"

Ronan glanced toward the front of the train. "I certainly hope that is the case. I will then owe our ferryman a favor."

The car jostled slightly again. I hoped that was an acknowledgement from Charon.

We were now close to the wall. From a distance, Edis had appeared enormous. Up close, the walls seemed to reach the sky. The city could not look more forbidding if it tried.

The train slowed to a crawl as it snaked along the rocky beach, then stopped. The door slid open. A blast of heat nearly took my breath away. No way in hell we'd be able to cross that lava plain without someone's help. I put those concerns aside for now. One hurdle at a time.

Ronan and Daisy got out first. With my pack on my back and Esme balanced on my shoulder, I let Ronan give me a hand to step out onto the rocky beach. Lucy disembarked last.

We made our way carefully up the steep incline toward the wall. I started sweating immediately. Daisy panted. Lucy coughed. Ronan alone seemed unaffected by the extreme heat.

As soon as we were clear of the train, it accelerated away, banking sharply and heading back across the lava toward the very distant horizon. Thunder rumbled and purple lightning flashed across the sky, which was black and streaked with red. The ground shook, dislodging small rocks that rolled down the hill and caused me to stumble.

Ronan spread his hands. "Welcome to Edis."

"At least it's a dry heat," Lucy said, wiping her forehead with the back of her hand. "You sure this isn't Hell?"

"Very sure." Ronan and Daisy led the way up the hill toward the wall. Lucy stayed on our six, sword in hand as she scanned our surroundings for potential threats. I envied how easily they climbed, while I huffed and puffed and panted and stumbled over the rocks. Neither of them offered to help, which I simultaneously appreciated and resented. Being a prideful human was complicated.

When we reached the wall, Ronan led us along its perimeter for about a hundred feet until we found a large rock against the stone wall. On the other side of the rock, hidden from view until we were right in front of it, a long, deep crack ran up the wall, forming a dark tunnel. Cool air drifted out, along with the unmistakable urban sounds of conversation, strange music, and wheels rattling on stone.

Lucy raised her eyebrow. "A secret passageway? Seems too easy."

"Those who run Edis understand the importance of smuggling to the city's economy." Ronan raised his hand and used his ball of light to illuminate the empty passageway. "These tunnels are for commerce. They're the city's most well-known secret. Getting in is rarely a problem. Getting out...now that's usually a lot more difficult."

"Fantastic," I said. "Well, then let's get in there and find some Furies, shall we?"

CHAPTER 25

EXCEPT FOR THE DRAGON PATROLLING THE WALL, THE UNDERWORLD creatures walking the streets, and the perpetually black-and-orange sky, Edis was like any big city I'd visited: dirty, crowded, noisy, and full of unexpected dangers.

We emerged from the not-so-secret passageway into a dark alcove behind market stalls selling bread, roasted meat, and weapons. Narrow alleyways branched off in several directions, disappearing into the maze of the market and the buildings around us.

Creatures of every size, shape, description, and smell packed the market, talking, laughing, shouting, growling, and arguing in a dozen languages, none of which I knew. I spotted a few humans among them—or beings in human form, in any case. All the competing magics and the fact most of the beings around us weren't alive in the strictest definition of the word made it nearly impossible for me to know for sure what anything was.

As we entered the market, two vendors and several of their customers were embroiled in a fight that had resulted in bloody injuries and damage to nearby stalls. It came to a quick halt when three very large creatures in black moved in and separated the combatants, who shouted at each other as they were dragged away in opposite directions. We used the distraction to slip out of the passageway and blend into the crowd.

The noise and chaos were overwhelming, especially after our very quiet train ride and several days in Lucy's jeep. Ronan didn't give me time to get used to the sights, sounds, and smells of Edis. After taking a moment to look up at the towers and wall and orient himself, he headed off into the crowded market with Daisy at his side. Most shoppers and porters took one look at his imposing robed figure and Daisy's glowing eyes and got out of their way. Lucy and I followed in their wake, moving unnoticed through the crowd.

My skin prickled and my stomach churned from the masking and *Look Away* spells I wore. The former was my own spell, held in a crystal in my left arm cuff, and the latter one of Carly's amulets, which I'd invoked and hidden in one of my pockets. On Ronan's recommendation, I'd given one of each to Lucy as well to hide her. Word would travel fast about anyone arriving in the city, so the longer she and I could stay unnoticed, the better.

He made little effort to hide his own identity, however, and Daisy certainly garnered the attention of everyone we passed. I thought of Charon's revelation that Ronan had a price on his head. Someone else might have chosen to keep a low profile, given the circumstances, but not Ronan. He wasn't about to keep his head down or avoid a fight. I was dying to know who'd put the bounty on his head and why. Maybe we could get the story out of him during our return trip—assuming there was one. In the meantime, I was having fun imagining what the answers might be.

The market was packed, but once we left that area, the streets were less crowded. Carts pulled by beasts or by hand rattled along the wide paved roads, which pedestrians shared in lieu of sidewalks. Narrow roads and alleys seemed designated for pedestrians only. Many pushed small handcarts full of everything from paving stones to food as they hurried past.

I had to walk fast to keep up with Ronan's long strides. He seemed to know exactly where he was going, weaving through slower pedestrians and large carts toward our destination, the Great Hall he'd mentioned. I pictured an oversized courthouse, where the Furies served as ministers of justice. Was that the equivalent of judges in the human world, or something a bit more hands-on, like judge, jury, and executioner?

As we made our way toward what seemed like the center of the city, I had a chance to put together a couple of things: Ronan's explanation of the origin of the Erinyes, what Charon had said about Ronan ignoring messages from his "brothers and sisters," Torryn's description of Ronan as a man with two swords—only one of which we'd seen—and the flash of silver-blue I'd spotted when he intervened to help me rein in my dark magic. That silver-blue magic had nagged at me since the night I first saw it at Hawthorne's. I'd seen it, or something similar, before, but I hadn't been able to remember where...

Until now, when the clues clicked into place like a jigsaw puzzle, and I *knew*.

I stopped so suddenly in the middle of the street that Lucy had to hop to one side to keep from running me over and Esme nearly lost her footing on my shoulder. "Holy shit," I said.

The front edge of a handcart full of bricks rammed into my shin. I bit back a yelp of pain and stumbled. The thing pushing the cart—a tall creature who looked like a cross between a troll and a stack of firewood—blinked at me in confusion. It hadn't seen me because of my masking and *Look Away* spells, and it still couldn't quite see me, though it knew it had run into something. Finally, the cart continued up the street as the creature grumbled.

Perhaps sensing I'd fallen behind, or having heard the impact of the cart against my leg, Ronan backtracked with Daisy. He bent his head so he could murmur in my ear. "What's wrong?"

He smelled like the sea. I should have recognized that, even if the silver-blue magic didn't tip me off, but I'd paid more attention to the smell of leather and tequila. Damn my hormones. Malcolm was going to tease me forever about this.

I decided not to tell Ronan I knew what he was. He'd gone to great pains to hide his true nature; his scars and his wounds from the fight with the werewolf pack were proof of that. He might decide keeping it a secret was worth killing for.

"Sorry to fall behind," I murmured. "I'll do better about keeping up with you."

He held my gaze with his own glacier-blue one. "Are you getting sicker?"

I was, though as a mage I'd worked and fought through pain frequently enough that I'd gotten good at ignoring discomfort. I disliked admitting any kind of weakness, but better he thought I'd stopped because I was queasy than suspect I'd finally put two and two together.

I gave him a wry smile. "It comes and goes. I'm all right."

Clearly unconvinced, he turned and resumed his purposeful stride. Daisy trotted at his side, her lip curled to show her teeth. She appeared to enjoy her role as Ronan's menacing sidekick, complete with her spiked leather halter.

"You good?" Lucy asked in an undertone as we walked quickly.

"Yeah, I'm good." A sharp twinge in my belly almost made me flinch. My arms and legs ached too. Whether it was the dark magic eating at me or my body rebelling against being in the Underworld, or both, I wasn't sure. I snuck a protein bar out of my pocket, tore off the wrapper, and ate it quickly, and that seemed to help. I pushed the discomfort out of my mind and focused on keeping up with Ronan.

The farther we got from the market, the fewer carts and pedestrians we encountered on the streets. I had no idea what time of day it was in Edis, or even if they *had* days and nights. It felt like afternoon to me, for some strange reason, despite the pitch-dark sky. Maybe my body was still on topside time, where it might well have been mid-afternoon.

I pictured Malcolm waiting beside the doorway, worrying about us. I still sensed his reassuring cool blue-green trace in my mind. He could probably sense me too, so he knew I was still alive. It wasn't much, but given where we were and what we might be up against, it was worth a lot.

Ronan led us through a narrow alley into a street lined with what might have been homes. We'd gone only about a hundred feet when our attackers came out of nowhere.

Three of them attacked Ronan with grunts and roars: one of the troll-woodpile creatures and two smaller but stockier creatures with silver fur and very sharp teeth. All carried weapons ranging from a sword to nasty-looking daggers. One of the silver creatures also had a mace that dripped something from the tips of its spikes. I was willing to bet it was poison. Triple shit.

Before I could form blood magic blades or my whip, I heard Ronan's voice in my head: *Do not use your magic. Let us handle this.* It was a command.

With the order came a definite nudge to obey, but one I could resist. Either Ronan didn't have as strong of an ability as Lucy, or he hadn't wanted to actually force me to do something against my will.

What, if anything, Ronan said to Lucy I didn't know, but she shoved me into a doorway alcove, barked "Stay here," and drew her sword.

Ronan and Daisy fought with the troll-woodpile and the silver creature with the mace as the other attacker circled, looking for an opportunity to use his blades. I wanted to run into the fray to fight at Daisy's side, but I had to trust her to take care of herself. If I stepped out now, I'd expose myself and put us in greater danger by attracting more attention than we already had.

With the benefit of the masking and *Look Away* spells, Lucy was almost but not quite invisible. She used that to her advantage. She crossed the distance between my hiding place and the fight and took the head off the second silver creature before it knew it was under attack. In the moments it took for its body to hit the pavement, she was already moving toward the other silver creature with the mace, her sword dripping black blood.

The street was empty except for us. Where were the black-clad giants who'd broken up the fight in the market? Never a cop around when you needed one.

To my horror, the troll sent Daisy flying with a powerful kick and charged straight at Lucy as the mace-wielding creature went after Ronan. The troll must have been able to see or sense Lucy despite the spells. Daisy hit the side of a building and yelped.

I spooled blood magic. Ronan's head whipped around, his angry storm-cloud-gray gaze finding me in my alcove. He must have sensed the rise of magic. *Do not*, he snapped in my mind.

I shoved him out of my head with a furious curse. I was sick and tired of people talking in my head without my permission and trying to force me to do things against my will.

The creature growled something at Ronan and swung the heavy mace with surprising speed. Ronan barely avoided the weapon. One of its spikes tore a hole in his robe. Lucy clashed swords with the troll, who was bigger and slower but many times stronger. The force of his blade striking hers sent her stumbling back. The troll bellowed.

Somewhere out there, Mariela was making her way to Edis to find the Furies. She might already be in the city. We didn't have time for street brawling, and injuries sustained now might affect our ability to fight later if it came to that.

I spun my blood magic into round blades in both hands and spooled dark magic. Glyphs ignited on the blades, and the edges of my vision turned red.

Damn it, Alice! Ronan roared in my head.

I threw my blood magic blades at the troll and the mace-wielding creature. The blades buried themselves deep in the troll's back and the other creature's side. Both snarled and turned to see who or what had attacked. And both died immediately, as Ronan and Lucy swung their swords in nearly identical arcs and separated the creatures' heads from their bodies.

Ronan confronted me as I emerged from my alcove. "What part of *do not use your magic* did you not understand?" he demanded.

"The part where you gave me an order." I knelt as Daisy joined us and checked her side. "You okay, Daisy-dog? Did that mean old troll hurt you?"

"I didn't want you to waste your magic on this." Ronan was still pissed. "The more you use, the faster you burn through your reserves of energy, and the more likely you are to draw attention to yourself. The lieutenant and I would have dealt with this."

Lucy cleaned the blood off her sword and said nothing. I couldn't tell what she was thinking.

Daisy seemed fine, so I got to my feet and offered him the leash. "No need to be condescending. I'm very aware of how magic works."

With a thunderous frown, he took the leash.

"And I didn't give you permission to invade my thoughts and talk to me in my head," I added. "Don't try to make me obey you. I've had enough of both of those things."

"It was for your own good."

My expression went flat. "I was held prisoner and told it was *for my own good.* I was tortured, enslaved, and forced to destroy property and kill people, and more than once they told me it was *for my own good.* Someone manipulated my thoughts and feelings for years because they wanted their own way and tried to tell me it was *for my own good.* So now the only person who gets to decide what's for my own good is me, Ronan."

He slid the loop at the end of Daisy's leash around his arm and flipped up his hood, his eyes dark with anger and something else— an emotion I couldn't quite read. "You were cruelly mistreated, but that doesn't mean everyone who expresses concern for your well-being is doing so to exploit you."

"You didn't express concern for my well-being—you gave me an order and a push to obey you and shouted at me in my brain." My stomach cramped. Blast it, I needed to eat again. "Did these scum-bags come after you for the bounty?"

"Yes."

"So you were recognized by someone. Word *does* travel fast here. More hunters are probably headed this way. We should get moving. Are we far from the Great Hall?"

His forehead creased. Either he didn't like that I'd abruptly changed the subject, or the fact he'd been recognized displeased him. "The sisters are not at the Great Hall at present. We'll find them at their tavern."

"How do you know?" Lucy asked.

"Just a wild guess." He turned on his heel and strode away, leaving the bodies of the bounty hunters on the street where they'd fallen.

Lucy and I flipped up our hoods and followed. She kept her sword in her hand. "That's quite a wild guess," she said, not bothering to lower her voice. He ignored her.

"The Furies run a tavern?" I asked, catching up.

"Doing so suits them," he said over his shoulder, breaking into a jog. "We have to move fast now. Time's running out."

I didn't ask how he knew; it wouldn't have done any good anyway. I just ran.

CHAPTER 26

How far we ran was difficult to tell, since none of the streets of Edis went in a straight line for more than a hundred feet and my sense of time hadn't worked right since we got here. We wove through endless winding streets and alleys, making a beeline for a mysterious tavern and its fallen angel owners.

We saw the Great Hall long before we reached it, towering over all of the buildings nearby. Though it resembled a medieval fortress more than any courthouse I'd ever seen, the building was unmistakably the heart of official power in the city. The towers soared well above the height of the city's walls. Grim and uninviting, its imposing windowless facade loomed over the city. To reach the enormous arched entrance, visitors had to climb steep stairs worn by millennia of use.

"I can't say I blame them for preferring a tavern," Lucy muttered. Like Ronan, she was barely winded, despite our long run. "That place creeps me out."

I was breathing too hard to reply. *Note to self: do more cardio training when I get back,* I thought.

Ronan led us past the Great Hall and through a narrow alley that opened into a busy side street. To avoid attracting attention as we got close to our destination, he slowed to a walk.

We stopped outside the threshold of a dark stone building that looked very much like all the others on this street. Above the arched doorway, several words were carved into the stone in a language I didn't know. The letters pulsed with magic.

"What does that say?" I asked breathlessly.

"The name of the tavern." Ronan read the name aloud. The words rolled off his tongue like music. "It means 'Slay your enemies and pour the wine.'"

"That's a solid name for a tavern." Lucy indicated another set of inscribed words beside the door. "And this?"

"A warning that drawing weapons inside the tavern is forbidden, by order of the management. That includes both blades and magic."

"Any advice on how to approach this?" I asked. "Given what you know about them?"

He considered. "The sisters will do as they will. I see little hope of changing their minds once they've made a decision, but they'll weigh the case fairly. Our only choice will be what to do once that decision is made."

"I won't let them get topside, and I won't let Mariela get away with what she's done," I told him. "This ends here."

He didn't remind me they were fallen angels, or chthonic deities, or infernal goddesses, or that I was more or less just a mouthy human mage currently being eaten alive from the inside by dark magic, or that a clairvoyant witch had prophesied I wouldn't succeed in my mission here. None of that needed to be said. We all knew the score.

"Damn skippy," Lucy said, sheathing her sword. "I know Daisy and Esme are with us. You'll end up having to pick a side one way or the other, Ronan."

He tried to stare her down, but he should have known better. She stared right back. "It's not that simple," he said finally.

"Actually it is, if you think about it." She punched my upper arm. "I got you. Let's do this."

I freed Daisy from her halter, rubbed my fingertip on Esme's velvet paw, and led the way into the bar. I didn't sense any wards on the threshold, but what use were wards to goddesses or archangels?

The interior was lit by firelight and welcoming, though I probably shouldn't have been surprised by that. A bar is a bar is a bar, even in the Underworld.

Even more surprising than the bar's welcoming design was that it was empty except for tables and chairs—no patrons, no bartenders, no servers, no cups or dishes left on the tables. I'd half-expected a crowd like the one we'd seen at Hawthorne's. Instead, the tavern was ominously silent. Even the street noise was muted, though the front doors remained wide open.

Behind the bar, neatly arranged bottles and jugs filled long shelves. I wondered what constituted top-shelf booze down here. I could have used a drink, but whatever they served probably wasn't safe for a human to consume.

"Either this is Edis's least-popular watering hole, or they cleared the place out for our arrival." Lucy's eyes narrowed. "Not sure how I feel about that."

Ronan stepped in front of me. Before I could object, he warned, "We are not alone here."

"You spoil my fun," a woman complained, her voice coming out of thin air from deeper within the tavern.

I had magic spooled, but kept it contained. Lucy's fingers twitched as if she wanted to pull her sword.

Like a curtain had been drawn aside, a large table appeared in an open space in the middle of the tavern. A woman in a long black robe, its hood thrown back, sat with her chin in one hand and a cup in the other. Her white-blonde hair was very long and loose like a cape, her glacier-blue eyes fiery with irritation. Her power crackled painfully on my skin, raising goosebumps.

On the table were two ceramic jugs, a tray of empty cups, bowls of what looked like various jams and honey, and two loaves of bread. They'd known we were coming. I wasn't surprised.

Ronan inclined his head in a respectful greeting. "Tis." His voice was carefully neutral.

The woman at the table studied him and said nothing.

In the back of the tavern, a door banged against the wall. A second woman strode in. Her long dark hair was braided and wrapped with a thin strip of leather. Unlike her sister, she wore the clothes and boots of a fighter—and she was splattered with blood from head to toe. Clearly she'd come straight from work, and she looked supremely annoyed at the interruption.

"Now *that* is looking resplendent in the blood of your enemies," Lucy said under her breath. "I'm a little turned on."

I was too, truth be told. And if Broken World Charles liked dangerous brunettes, he would probably have rolled over at the newcomer's feet, then sat up and begged.

"Aira," Tis said in greeting. "You are late."

"Hardly. The wine has not yet been poured." Aira pulled a chair away from the table and sat. She whistled.

A small demon scuttled out of the shadows near the rear door. Naked except for a scrap of cloth, the red-skinned creature had long, thin arms and legs scarred from the claws of his own kind. Chittering in his own language, he crouched in front of Aira. She propped her feet on his back and crossed her ankles. He looked up at us and hissed. Esme hissed back.

"Behave," Aira said, flicking a finger at the demon. He squealed in pain and crouched lower, chittering apologetically.

She reached for one of the jugs, poured herself a cup of wine, and took a slice of bread. She still hadn't acknowledged us. "Ekto is angry with me."

Tis sighed. "You killed her favorite pet again. She is entitled to her anger."

"*Ro*-nan," Aira drawled, saluting him mockingly with her cup. "You'll be glad to know *she* is not in the city at present. Her many faithful followers would be delighted to present your skinned carcass on her return. I'm tempted to cheat them out of their reward and do it myself."

"You're most welcome to try," Ronan said. "Perhaps after you hear our case, I'll humor you and give you a chance."

Her eyes darkened to storm cloud gray. "Pompous hindquarters of a donkey."

A tiny snicker escaped before I could hold it back. Aira's gaze focused on me for the first time. The temperature seemed to drop about twenty degrees. "You mock me?"

"Not at all." My voice sounded too much like a croak, so I cleared my throat before I added, "It's just that I've called Ronan an ass a dozen times in the three days I've known him."

Her eyebrow arched. The surge of power sizzling on my skin faded. "Indeed. We are of one mind, then."

Ronan made a rumbly sound.

I blinked. Had I just accidentally bonded with a Fury?

A fraction of a second later, I was sprawled on the floor next to Lucy, with Ronan's arms pinning us flat. He'd taken us down faster than I'd ever seen anyone move—vampires included. He'd even managed to grab Esme from my shoulder so she didn't fall, and got severely scratched for his trouble. Daisy dropped to her belly beside us.

Several orbs of silver-blue fire blasted over our heads from the direction of the front door. Aira swatted them away, her hands glowing with the same energy. One fireball vaporized a half-dozen tables and left a smoking hole in the far wall. Another took out more tables and chairs and a chunk of a support column before Tis did something with a flick of her hand and the magical fireball fizzled out in midair.

A third woman stomped past us in a floor-length black gown, bare feet, and obsidian jewelry. Her long flame-red hair swirled around her head either with the force of her power or her anger, or both. She raised her hand to throw another fireball at Aira.

"Enough, Ekto." Tis rose, her palms flat on the table. "We have petitioners. You might have killed them."

Ekto kicked a chair out of her way. It sailed the entire length of the room and exploded against the back wall. "Fine," she spat.

Sensing the immediate danger was over, Lucy and I sat up. Ronan deposited a very pissed-off Esme in my hands and stood, radiating anger.

"You always side with Aira." Ekto dropped into a chair and glared at Tis. "She killed my hound," she added petulantly. "*Again.*"

"It pissed on my front steps." Aira waved her hand dismissively. "You'll get another one, or you'll bring that one back. It's hardly worth fussing about. You're so dramatic, and so careless."

"I am *not* careless," Ekto retorted, pouring herself a cup of wine. "I didn't kill the humans, did I?"

"Had I been a moment slower, you might have," Ronan snapped. "*No weapons or magic to be used on the premises, for the safety of all.* Is that not the one great rule of your Court, Tis?"

She leveled a withering stare at him. "You quote rules to us, oath-breaker?"

Ronan flinched.

Angered by her tone, I scrambled to my feet to stand beside him. Lucy did the same. Despite the edict against the use of weapons, her hand strayed toward her hidden sword. Esme hissed. Daisy showed her teeth, her eyes golden.

"Whatever rules Ronan might have broken, that doesn't change yours," I said. "I didn't come all this way to get my head taken off by a fireball before we even got a chance to argue our case."

Malcolm had told me once there was a better than fifty-fifty chance my last words in this life would be back-talk to someone or something much more powerful than me. I couldn't say he was wrong.

I looked across the table at three sets of glowing storm-cloud-gray eyes and identical glares. That quickly, they'd gone from arguing among themselves to uniting in their anger at me. If they didn't decide to smite me into atoms, that might be a step in the right direction.

I was sick, exhausted, worried about Malcolm, and haunted by the memory of the slaughter in Walliston. And damn it, I missed Sean, I had a score to settle with Valas, and I wanted to go home.

"With all due respect, can we get to the reason we're here?" I asked.

Tis's sharp gaze raked me from head to toe. "I sense little respect, mage who *calls herself* Alice."

"I respect you plenty," I assured her. It would be stupid not to.

"You fear us. That is not the same." Aira shifted position in her chair and re-crossed her ankles, her boot heels leaving marks on the demon's back. "It's smart to fear us. We will hear you."

I took a deep breath and exhaled. "So, did we get here before her?"

"No." Tis gestured at a door to our right, hidden in an alcove. The door swung open.

A woman in clothing much like ours emerged from the shadows, her hood thrown back. She appeared older and leaner than in the photo provided by the Vampire Court. Her hair was short and cut raggedly, as if she'd done it herself. She wore a leather bag on her back. I wondered if the scroll was in the bag. My fingers itched to grab it and find out.

I had no reason to think the Court had given me an outdated photo. Her change in appearance could be the result of many things, but the simplest explanation was that she'd been down here a lot longer than three months. I thought of the strange time-warping we'd seen in the valley when we arrived. Did time pass differently here? No point worrying about that now.

"Hello, Mariela," I said. "We've been looking for you."

CHAPTER 27

"I knew Valas would send one of her pet mages." Mariela's voice was scratchy, either from dehydration or disuse. "I figured someone would try to cut me down outside Edis, but I got here before you could poison them against me."

I opened my mouth to tell her I was no one's pet, but Tis indicated the empty chairs around their table. "Have a seat. You must be tired and thirsty."

"But you—" Mariela began.

Aira flicked her finger. A chair skidded back from the table and hit Mariela in the stomach. "Sit." It was not a request.

We sat.

I took the seat directly across from Tis, my backpack on the floor beside me. Lucy sat on my left and Ronan to my right. Daisy stood between Ronan and I, her sharp golden gaze on Mariela. Esme stayed on my shoulder, watching our hosts.

With bad grace, Mariela pulled out a chair and sat. Daisy curled her lip and growled at her.

Tis gestured at the table. "We offer you water, wine, and bread."

All the lore I knew indicated eating or drinking anything in other realms rarely ended well. When I reached for my water bottle, however, Tis said, "We have offered you hospitality, Alice. Our food and drink is quite safe for you." Her tone had a distinct edge. She pushed one of the jugs in my direction.

I poured a cup of water and took a slice of bread. The water was cool and the bread was warm and slightly sweet. "Thank you," I said.

Lucy followed suit and thanked our hosts. Mariela took a cup of water and downed it.

"We welcome Alice, guardian wolf and dragon, and the warrior Lucy," Tis said formally.

Ronan didn't respond to the obvious snub. He brought out his flask and took a long swallow.

I cleared my throat and folded my hands on the table. "We've come to present another point of view on this case."

"There *are* no other points of view," Mariela countered. "I presented the facts. They know I spoke the truth."

"There are *always* other points of view." Lucy set her cup down. "You may have presented facts and spoken the truth, but we've got some facts too."

"When she opened a doorway to the Underworld to reach you, Mariela left it open topside and a lot of monsters got out," I said. "They killed hundreds of people—men, women, children. An entire town was wiped out. If we're here to talk about justice, let's not forget to talk about that."

"You lie. I put blood wards on the doorway." Mariela's face flushed. "Nothing could have escaped."

"There were no wards when we got there—not even a trace," I said. "Shades and gravelings got out and killed at will. That blood is on *your* hands and no one else's."

None of the sisters seemed surprised by the news, or much affected by it. I tried to remember they were very, very old and had seen countless atrocities in their time, but the memory of the carnage was much too raw. I opened my mouth, then closed it. I wasn't here to confront the Furies, I reminded myself. We were here for Mariela and the scroll. Calling them cold-hearted bitches would not help our cause.

"What do you think appropriate justice is for those deaths, Mariela?" I asked instead. "The shades you let out tore the children of Walliston to shreds and played catch with their heads and bones and organs. You're no better than the people you want them to kill."

She swallowed hard and lifted her chin. "If what you're saying is true, then I'll pay for what I've done. That doesn't change why I'm here."

"I'm not saying the people who murdered your brother and his family don't deserve justice, but slaughter isn't justice," I said.

"Traitors like you are the reason these terrorists get away with murder," she argued. "You're more concerned about protecting killers than your own people. You don't know what it feels to lose your entire family to monsters."

I thought of my parents, burned alive by my grandfather for trying to rescue me. "I do, in fact, know what that feels like."

"Then you can't tell me you don't want revenge," she challenged me. "Hypocrite."

"I want the person who killed my family and those who helped him to face justice. I'm not suggesting wiping out everyone remotely associated with him."

She blinked. "Neither am I," she countered, but a half a beat too late.

I turned to the sisters. "She's not just asking for punishment of the Glen Grove bombers; she wants you to kill everyone who's a member of an anti-supe group. Those people are hateful bigots, but they aren't murderers."

"You're not asking for justice; you're asking for murder," Ronan interjected. "For revenge."

"Why else come to the Furies?" Mariela demanded. "They're the mighty goddesses of vengeance. In my world, a world run by humans who'd rather see us dead than have equal protection under the law, there's no justice for us. Even the severest form of punishment available under human law isn't enough to make this right."

"That's true," I told her. "There isn't any punishment that will make this right. You could burn down the whole world and you'd still be hurting. But you don't get to burn down the world. That's not how this works."

"I'll do what I need to do." Mariela took a dagger and a picture from her robe and set them on the table. Dried blood and something else I couldn't identify stained the dagger's wide blade. The photo was of her brother and his family. The same one was in her Court dossier. Hers was worn and discolored from what must have been a long and arduous journey to Edis.

"I call down the curse of the Erinyes on those who murdered my family, those who protected the murderers, and those who share their hatred." She looked at the sisters in turn and waited expectantly.

Tis picked up the blade and studied it. "Blood of a sheep, a kiss of honey, and purest water from a spring," she mused. "You have read the lore. Had you true knowledge of us, however, you would know we are not goddesses of vengeance now, but of justice."

"Then give me justice for my family and those like me, who've suffered at these people's hands our whole lives just because we're different. Make them suffer the way *we've* suffered."

Ekto moved her fingers. The photo slid across the table and fluttered into her hand. "A lovely child," she mused. "Your niece did not deserve such an end, it's true. It was a monstrous and cowardly crime."

The sisters didn't look at each other, but I sensed they'd made a decision. My stomach knotted.

"Seven people conspired to murder your family," Aira told Mariela. "They may face imprisonment, but only if you return to your world and petition your courts to continue the investigation."

"She has to answer for the murders of the people in Walliston, plus a dozen others," Lucy interjected, her expression hard. "She's not going back to her world. She has to face justice in mine."

Mariela's eyes glowed with blood magic, but she didn't respond to Lucy. Instead, she addressed Tis. "You're supposed to avenge murders of family members. I've traveled across worlds and realms for my dead family, and you refuse to grant me justice?"

Aira's eyes narrowed. "We have told you how you may get justice for your family. If it is justice you want, you must seek it within human law. We sympathize with your losses, but long ago we learned the crimes of man are not ours to adjudicate. We keep the law in this realm. Humans keep it in theirs."

"That's not good enough." Mariela's fists clenched. "I fought my way across a hellscape to reach you."

"And in return, we offer you wisdom and guidance," Tis said. "You would save your own life, and many others, if you were to heed it."

"With all your power, it would be such a small thing for you to do this," Mariela spat. "I don't understand why you refuse."

Aira set her cup on the table. "If you think killing is a *small thing*, Mariela Diakos, you have proven how little you understand what justice means."

Mariela's mouth compressed into a grim line. For someone who'd just seen her hopes for goddess-level retribution go up in smoke, she was much too calm. Lucy and I exchanged a glance. Her uneasiness mirrored mine.

The now-familiar scent of incense and iron drifted past my nose. "It is well, then, that *I* am here." A low-pitched, melodious voice came from the direction of the doorway.

Tis and Ronan were on their feet in a blink. Lucy and I weren't far behind.

The full-figured woman who stood between us and the door wore green robes that appeared sheer from some angles but completely opaque in others. Tiny jewels sparkled in the fabric. Her eyes were yellow, with vertically slit pupils. Visible waves of magic appeared in her dark skin and pulsed in the air around her. Her aura was unlike anything I'd ever seen or sensed. She radiated death magic and pure power that called to my dark magic like the gravelings' had.

As she studied each of us in turn, I caught a glimpse of an enormous mouth, scaly green skin, and rows of teeth. I blinked and the vision faded, but I was certain I'd seen some nightmare Underworld version of a crocodile.

I had a very bad feeling about this.

"Welcome, sister," Tis said.

Sister? Was she another fallen angel? If so, this was turning into quite the family reunion. If we'd been outgunned before, we might have just been outflanked too.

"I hoped you would not come," Tis added. "Do you rise at the beck and call of humans now?"

"I am the Devourer," the newcomer said simply. "I was promised a feast of mortal hearts."

Mariela rose, smiling. "Goddess Ammit, I'm honored to provide you with a great feast."

"Oh, crap," Lucy muttered.

A feast of mortal hearts. I recalled the vision I'd seen at Northbourne of corpses in piles with their chests torn open and the sound of some unseen thing chewing on the missing hearts.

The name finally clicked: Ammit, Underworld deity who devoured the hearts of those who didn't follow the principles of justice and truth. Right-hand crocodile-headed goddess to Anubis, according to myth, which explained the glimpse of green scaly skin and the eyes.

"There won't be any feasting on hearts," I said.

With a reptilian hiss, Ammit turned her yellow-eyed gaze on me. Again, I caught a glimpse of that toothy maw.

"You only devour the hearts of those deemed not pure," I added, hoping like crazy the myth was accurate and I remembered it correctly.

Her smile didn't waver. "I am assured their hearts are far from pure."

"And you don't eat living hearts," I pointed out. "Only those of the dead."

"This is true," Ammit acknowledged. "*He* will serve the dead to me."

Deep beneath out feet, the ground rumbled.

"Mariela, what have you done?" I demanded.

Mariela smiled. "This wasn't my first stop. I didn't come all this way to lose. One way or the other, I'm going back home, and the people who killed my family are going to pay."

The rumbling grew. Aira and Ekto stood. I wondered if they were preparing for battle, or to run.

In a blur, Ronan moved toward Mariela with the same speed he'd used to get Lucy and me out of the path of Ekto's fireballs. Tis intercepted him and blocked his arm from pulling his sword from its sheath. "You will not draw a blade in this Court," she snapped.

Ronan refused to relinquish his grip on the hilt of his sword. "What has she unleashed?"

The rumbling grew in both violence and volume. A crack split the stone floor of the tavern. Something was rising beneath us.

"She has invoked the Son of the Darkness," Tis said.

"Who is the Son of the Darkness?" Lucy demanded.

No one answered her question. "They cannot fight here," Aira told her sisters. "Our city would be destroyed."

"We must send them elsewhere," Ekto urged.

The crack in the floor widened. The entire building—maybe the entire city—shook violently. The bottles and jars on the shelves fell and smashed on the floor.

Ronan's eyes turned silver-blue and sea-scented magic seared my skin. "Tisiphone, you cannot let this go unpunished. You know what she had to do to invoke the Son of the Darkness. She had to sacrifice *a child.*"

Mariela didn't deny the accusation. Her expression hardened.

Any sympathy I'd had for her situation had long since evaporated, but now I could barely look at her. *A child.* Dark magic spiraled up my arms. I couldn't stop it; my fury was too great. Daisy growled.

"Crimes committed in the human world are outside our jurisdiction," Tis told Ronan.

"On whose authority?" he thundered.

Her expression didn't change. "You *know* whose."

"*Michael,*" he snarled. "That sanctimonious prick."

The stone floor burst open. We stumbled back as the head of an enormous black serpent with golden eyes emerged from the hole, its tongue flicking out to taste the air. Quadruple shit.

Daisy lowered her head, fangs bared. Esme hissed. Ronan and Lucy reached for their swords as I spooled blood magic, house rules be damned.

The snake hissed and started to slide out of the hole it had made in the floor.

The sisters reacted as one, their arms extending as their eyes turned from blue to nearly white. Sea-scented silver-blue magic surged.

Behind me, I sensed a burst of power. Light so bright that I had to shade my eyes with my forearm flooded the tavern. I heard a heavy snap that sounded like a ship's huge sails whipped by a sudden gust of wind. Lucy gasped.

I tried to look behind me, but the light seared my vision. I could just make out a silhouette spanning the entire width of the tavern—a silhouette in the shape of a man with enormous wings.

A wave of sea-scented magic swept across the room, picked me up, and carried me away.

Caught in a riptide made of power and magic, I tumbled head over feet through darkness as deep and vast as an ocean. I couldn't breathe, couldn't stop my careening journey away from the tavern, and couldn't see or hear anything or anyone. If the others had been swept up by the wave of magic, I couldn't tell.

Just when I thought my lungs would burst from lack of air, the wave of magic pulled me from the darkness and deposited me face down on a pile of ash.

Gasping and choking, I managed to roll onto my back and suck in a lungful of hot, sulfurous air. My stomach roiled from whatever form of transportation brought me here—wherever *here* was. My surroundings were nothing but a dark blur.

I thought I moaned, but I couldn't hear anything over the ringing in my ears. The ground might be shaking, or maybe it was me. Damn it, I could barely muster a coherent thought, much less get up and figure out where the hell I'd ended up. Magical transportation could go fall in a well.

Something warm, soft, and furry pushed itself under my right hand and licked my forearm. Esme. A cold, wet snout prodded my left cheek. I reached up and found Daisy standing over me. I ran my hands over both of them as best I could and didn't find any injuries —just a lot of dirt and grime. I probably didn't look much better.

"First time in a while I've been thrown out of a bar," I said aloud, or tried to say. It might have come out as a mumble. I still couldn't see or hear very well.

Ekto and Aira had suggested we be sent somewhere else to protect Edis from destruction. Had the sisters dumped us all on this ash heap, or just my wolf, my cat-dragon, and me?

The ground shook hard enough to rattle my teeth. This time I knew it wasn't just me.

I had to assume the sisters had made good on their threat to transport the whole lot of us out of Edis to someplace where we could duke it out without leveling the city. That probably meant the serpentine Son of the Darkness was here, along with Ronan, Lucy, Mariela, and possibly Ammit too. This was no time to be sidelined with magic riptide-induced motion sickness, but I couldn't seem to get my appendages to obey my brain's commands.

Something roared and slammed into the ground. A shockwave rolled through the earth under me. Both Daisy and Esme took off in the direction of the roar, leaving me alone, still half-blind and deaf.

I tried to get up and fell. Son of a bitch. I staggered to my feet and this time I stayed upright. My backpack was nowhere to be seen; it must not have made the journey. Most of the items I'd had stashed in the pockets of my pants and robe had fallen out too, except for one of Carly's amulets and a small dagger in a sheath. Blasted Furies.

My dismay gave way to shock and horror as my vision finally cleared and revealed the scene in front of me.

We'd ended up either in the ash-filled wasteland we'd traveled through on the train, or a realm identical to it. The empty horizon stretched as far as I could see in every direction. The distant black shadows to my left might be the mountainous border that separated this realm from another. The terrain was rockier than it had appeared and utterly lifeless. Purple lightning crackled across the sky and thunder rumbled, though I didn't see or sense a storm coming—not a storm like the ones we had topside, anyway.

About a hundred feet away, a giant with a human-shaped head, a dragon-like mouth, a body made of snakes, and massive leathery wings opened his maw and roared again. In front of him stood a familiar shirtless man in Edis-style trousers, his sword pointed at the monster. Daisy stood on his left, snarling. Esme, in her little dragon form, circled the giant far overhead, out of reach of his hands and wings and the vipers that formed his body.

I froze in my tracks—not because of the nightmarish snake creature or the sight of Ronan's half-clad body glowing with silver-blue power, but because of his enormous silver wings. Magnificent and edged with fiery blue magic, they were almost too beautiful to be real.

Knowing he was one of the Fallen and *seeing* it were two very different things.

I spotted two crumpled forms: Lucy, about ten yards to my right, and Mariela farther away, to my left. Mariela wasn't moving, but Lucy was struggling to get to her feet, coughing and gagging from dust and travel sickness. She'd managed to hang onto her sword during the trip here, but she didn't appear to be able to wield it quite yet. I didn't see Ammit anywhere. Whether that was good or bad, I had no idea, but it was one less thing for us to fight.

The snake giant tried to flatten Ronan with one of its enormous black wings. Ronan slashed it with his sword. The giant bellowed, his torn wing spurting dark blood across the ash.

In a flare of golden magic, Daisy tripled in size. Given the snake-giant's size, I expected her to grow as large as she had when facing the demon lord, Orias, but she didn't. It was definitely possible the different magic of this world affected her abilities.

The damn robe would do nothing but hamper my movement, so I took it off and left it in the dust. I invoked Carly's amulet, stuck it in my pocket, and staggered in Mariela's direction with the small dagger. The snake giant was Ronan and Daisy's to deal with; the murdering blood mage was mine.

You must kill Mariela. Ronan's voice in my head sounded like a hundred voices speaking at once and resonated with what I now knew was silver-blue angelic magic. *We can't kill Typhon, but if you kill the one who summoned him, we can bury him again.*

I knew the name Typhon, but the details of who he was and what he could do according to legend escaped me at the moment. My brain was still foggy and my ears rang like church bells. *I sure as hell hope you know how to bury him,* I told Ronan.

Behind me, Typhon roared and attacked Ronan and Daisy. I half-walked, half-ran toward Mariela, spooling magic and cursing under my breath. Thunder boomed again, louder, and more purple light-ning split the sky. The air felt heavier. Maybe there *was* a storm heading this way. Fantastic.

The ground between Mariela and me rumbled, heaved up, and split open. With a startled sound, I backpedaled. More than a dozen creatures poured out of the gaping hole. They ranged in size from that of a bear to much larger than Daisy's current form, and they were all snarling and gnashing enormous teeth.

I'd thought the gravelings and shades we'd encountered topside were the worst nightmares given form, but these things were so much worse. My brain said this was *so wrong*. I should be home with Sean getting ready to move or working a normal case for a client. My instincts screamed at me to run, though there was nowhere for me to go to escape this horror.

I didn't run away, though. I never had, even when it would have been the smarter, safer choice.

My earth-magic whips spiraled out of my hands, but they were thin and crackly like static electricity—not nearly powerful enough to take on the creatures in front of me. The Underworld had little earth magic for me to draw from, and I didn't have much stored in my own body. My air magic was next to useless in this realm. Blood magic would have little effect on these dead things.

Typhon is the father and tyrant of many monsters, Ronan warned in my head as he traded blows with the snake-giant. *He will summon more until we bury him again.*

Keep him so busy he won't have time to summon more, I thought back at him.

Hissing, Esme flew past me in dragon form, razor-sharp claws outstretched. As she tore into one of the attacking creatures, I spotted Lucy on her feet, hacking at another creature with her sword. Like me, she'd left her robe on the ground so she could move more freely.

Mariela was still down. If I could get to her while she was disoriented, I could try to talk some sense into her. If that failed, I would have to kill her to save countless lives, regardless of whatever sympathy I still felt for the loss of her family. But there were dozens of monsters between us, and I'd have to get through them to reach her.

Lucy's opponent swiped at her and opened a gash across her back with its claws. She bit back a scream and swung her sword, taking off the creature's head. Its body hit the ground and didn't move. Unlike the gravelings topside, decapitation seemed to kill it outright. Small favors.

Dark magic thrummed under my skin. The Underworld was a

full step closer than my world or Lucy's world to the demon realm, the infernal source of the power I'd inherited from Miraç at his death. The faint thread of magic in my mind that was my connection to Malcolm was a reminder that the more dark magic I used, the more deeply it would take hold of me—and very probably the faster it would destroy my body.

Lucy was hacking her way through Typhon's monsters, but more were coming up through the ground and Mariela was trying to get up. I had to figure out a way to plug up that hole, and to do that, I'd have to cut my way through a half-dozen monsters.

When I got back home, I'd never need to use the dark magic again, and I'd do whatever I needed to do to cut it out of myself. For now, to have a prayer of killing these things and getting to Mariela, I figured I didn't have much of a choice but to unleash it.

Something huge hit me from behind. Another hole must have opened behind me. Streaks of fire erupted across my back as the creature raked me with its claws. I screamed and fell to my hands and knees. The monster on my back tore into my flesh with talons, spines, and teeth.

In a rush, my head filled with horrible, bloody memories of blood mages who'd worked for my grandfather stripping skin from my back, and of Miraç in the form of a smoke monster, slashing my back while I was chained in his lair.

Rage and dark magic turned my vision red. My magic erupted with such terrifying force that for a moment I worried my skin would split open. I screamed again, but this time not with pain—with the rush of power coursing through my body.

To my senses, the creatures attacking us felt much like the shades and gravelings we'd encountered topside. I couldn't shred them as fast or as easily as the shades, but I *could* kill them with magic, and much faster than any other way.

I grabbed at the one on my back with my dark magic and ripped as hard as I could. It burst in a spray of flesh, putrid blood, and splintered bones. Its demise filled me with a new source of power: one that hummed with the potent force of death.

I thought I heard Ronan's voice in my head, his tone angry and worried, but the thrumming of the dark magic drowned out whatever he said.

Covered in the creature's blood, I got to my feet. Bits of flesh fell to the ground around me. My aura blazed like a sun—a siren call to every monster on the ash plain.

With ear-splitting screeches and howls, the rest of the creatures abandoned their attacks on Lucy and Esme and came for me.

CHAPTER 28

To my left, yet another hole opened in the ground. A dozen more monsters crawled out, howling for our blood. *Too many...too many,* my brain screamed. I ignored the voice and started ripping the creatures apart.

Behind me, Typhon roared. Whether it was at the sight of his creatures dying or at something Ronan or Daisy did, I wasn't sure, but I couldn't turn to look.

The creatures climbed over the corpses of their fallen brethren trying to get to me. I tore them apart with magic as fast as I could, but for every one I killed, two more emerged from the ground.

Esme, her claws and fangs bloody, ripped into the monsters. They responded by attacking her with their own claws and teeth, opening wounds on her side and one wing. I took pleasure in shredding the ones that hurt my little cat-dragon and letting them suffer a bit before they died.

In the middle of the battlefield, I stilled. I'd killed a number of creatures and even people out of necessity, but I'd never taken pleasure in it. Yet here I was inflicting pain and actually *enjoying* it. What the hell was happening to me?

I glanced down at myself. I was covered in goop and innards, bloody from a dozen wounds, and shrouded in dark magic that licked the air around me like flames. Anyone who saw me in that moment would have thought I was either a sorcerer, a black witch, or something worse. I was immensely grateful neither Sean nor Malcolm could see me right now. That pain—and shame—was worse than any of my wounds.

With an impressive battle cry, Lucy waded into the swarming mass of monsters, slashing at everything within her reach. She moved with the grace of a dancer, killing with her blade almost as fast as I could with magic.

For whatever reason, Mariela seemed to have gotten the worst of it. She'd rolled to her back and tried to rise, but without success. She'd be a threat as soon as she could start throwing magic or spells, but I couldn't get to her with all these creatures between us.

Just as I thought that, I realized I had a much more immediate problem.

A small knot formed in my upper abdomen, just below my ribcage. The knot felt like a snarl or tangle of black magic. Every time I used magic to kill a monster, it tugged at the knot, and the knot grew. *Well,* that *can't be good,* I thought.

Typhon and Ronan had been trading blows virtually nonstop, with Daisy getting in bites whenever she got a chance. They seemed about evenly matched. That would have worried me more if I hadn't been currently up to my eyebrows in monsters.

On the other side of the mass of nightmarish creatures, Mariela finally lurched to her feet. The creatures didn't attack her; Typhon must have communicated to them somehow that she was an ally. She caught my eye and smiled.

Ronan had said we had to kill Mariela to prevent Typhon from following her commands. She'd murdered a child and indirectly caused the deaths of hundreds of people, and I had no problem seeing her die for those crimes. But was that justice, or vengeance? The line seemed blurry now.

Not that I could reach Mariela to dispense either justice *or* vengeance; every time I thought I might be able to get through the horde of creatures, more came out of the ground between us. How the hell many of these things would there be?

Suddenly, a huge creature much larger than Daisy, with a segmented body and a dozen thick tentacles like a cross between an ant and a squid, erupted through the rocky ground, sending ash and rocks flying. It screeched and headed straight for me, giant fangs clacking.

"Alice!" Lucy shouted, but she was too far away and surrounded by a half-dozen monsters of her own.

Dark-magic whips spiraled from my hands. I slashed at the squid creature and lopped off one of its tentacles. It shrieked. With surprising speed, it wrapped two tentacles around my middle and squeezed.

I dug my nails into its hide to get its blood on my skin and used my dark magic to tear it apart. As its flesh split and black viscera splattered me, excruciating pain shot through my middle. The knot within me swelled.

A small monster darted forward and chomped into my arm. The wound bled profusely, and the creature's saliva burned like acid. The pain barely registered over the sensation of dark magic pulsing through me and the discomfort in my abdomen.

I shredded my attacker and a second large monster right behind it. Another wave of pain hit me, this one far more intense. I stumbled, my hand on my stomach. Whatever was going wrong, I needed help. *"Daisy!"*

With a howl the Furies could probably hear back in Edis, my wolf thundered across the rocky ground, leaving Ronan to deal with Typhon. She plowed through the swarm of creatures in front of me like a golden bulldozer, sending pieces of them flying.

Esme and Lucy flanked me, slaughtering every creature that got within their reach, but there were too many of them coming up from the ground.

I stole a glance over my shoulder just in time to see Typhon roar and blast Ronan with black-edged bright orange fire from his mouth like a dragon. When the fireball rolled past, Ronan was on the ground. As far as I could tell, he was unburned, but he didn't get up. Maybe the fireball contained magic. Typhon bellowed.

Ronan? I asked, not sure if he could hear me.

No response came. He didn't move.

A large but surprisingly fast creature slammed into Lucy from the side and knocked her to the ground. With a snarl, Daisy chomped the creature in two, dropped its carcass, and whined.

"Oh, no." I ran to Lucy.

The creature had opened a large wound in her side. She held it closed with bloody hands, her face white with pain. "Damn it, I let that thing get the drop on me. Trev will never let me hear the end—" She broke off and groaned. Blood poured through her fingers.

I thought fast. The wound was bad, possibly fatal. I could heal her with blood magic, at least enough to keep her alive until we got back topside, but it would take time—time we didn't have. Ronan was getting back on his feet, but he looked like hell. Even if he had the ability to heal Lucy, he had his hands full with Typhon.

I pulled a crystal out of the leather cuff on my right forearm and showed it to Lucy. "Tom's blood magic healing spell. It's gonna hurt like a son of a bitch."

"Do it," she said through gritted teeth. "Please."

I slipped the crystal under her fingers, against her side. "Can you sense the magic?" I asked.

She nodded. Her lips were turning white.

"Focus on that magic and when you're ready, say *Stardust*."

"Interesting choice for an invocation word." She took a shuddering breath. "Go check on Ronan and kick Mariela's ass, okay?" In other words, don't watch her use the spell. I understood all too well.

I dragged my heel through the thick layer of ash on the ground and made a circle around Lucy. It wouldn't last, but it would keep her safe for at least as long as it would take for the healing spell to work. I drew runes in the ash, closed the circle with a dab of my blood, and invoked the ward. The circle flared.

I turned away from Lucy to give her privacy. Mariela was making her way toward Ronan and Typhon, spooling blood magic. Daisy and Esme were both bloodied but they fought the creatures tirelessly.

Behind me, healing magic surged and prickled on my skin. I hadn't heard Lucy invoke the healing spell over the snarling and shrieking of the creatures, but I heard her strangled scream when the first powerful wave pulsed out of the crystal and into her body. I flinched. I knew exactly how much a strong healing spell hurt.

Ronan's sword—the spelled one he'd driven through a tree while skewering Kyrios, then pulled free without damage—was broken. He tossed it to the ground. Typhon roared again, the sound strangely like a lion's and full of triumph.

Several of the largest creatures attacked Daisy at the same time. I ripped two of them apart without thinking. The burst of pain in my stomach drove me to my knees.

Halfway between Typhon, Ronan, and us, the ground split again. More creatures clawed their way to the surface. Mariela saw my expression and laughed.

As Esme attacked one of the creatures near Lucy, another leaped and raked its claws across the little dragon's side, nearly slicing her in half and flinging her twenty feet. She hit the ground, rolled until she hit a rock, and lay still. I let out a half-sob, half-scream of rage and grief.

Daisy crushed the creature who'd hurt Esme in her enormous jaws, then ran to the little dragon's side. Esme let out a piercing cry that hurt my ears. It rolled across the plain and echoed even in the emptiness around us.

Daisy raised her head and howled. The sound was the mournful cry of a wolf with a wounded and dying pack mate. She nudged Esme's bloody body with her muzzle, then went berserk on every creature she could get her teeth or claws into.

We were losing this fight.

I didn't want to watch Lucy, Esme, or Daisy torn to bits by these nightmare creatures. I didn't know if Ronan *could* die, but I definitely could. That knot of death magic in my abdomen felt like a lead weight.

My wolf, my cat-dragon, my Guardian partner, and that ass of a fallen angel had to live. I had to live. I had to live and get back to Malcolm and Sean and our pack. And to Valas, who'd fucked me over for absolutely the last time.

Typhon bellowed and raised his serpentine arms to pound Ronan into the ground with brute force. I wouldn't be able to get to him in time, not with more of the creatures clawing their way up out of the hole that had just opened between us.

Typhon started to bring his arms down.

Ronan reached behind his head and drew an enormous flaming sword out of thin air. My breath caught. *Oh, holy cats.*

Typhon's arms crashed down onto the sword. The shockwave and flash of blinding light nearly knocked me flat. When my vision cleared, Typhon and Ronan were locked in battle—the giant's size and powers versus Ronan's honest-to-God flaming angel sword.

Mariela screeched in pure fury. She hurled a blade at Ronan. It sank hilt-deep into his ribs on his right side. If he'd been human, the wound would likely have been fatal.

For a moment, Ronan did little more than flinch. He threw one of the silver-blue balls of magic like Ekto had thrown at Aira in the tavern, but his aim was off and it barely grazed Mariela. She stumbled. Magic shimmered around her: protection spells strong enough to save her from an angel's magic. Damn it.

Ronan took one more swing at Typhon with his sword, staggered, and fell.

Around me, the creatures shrieked with what might have been glee, but didn't swarm me or Ronan. I didn't know what they were waiting for. Typhon bellowed.

Can I wield that fancy flaming sword? I asked Ronan.

His voice was a shadow of itself when he answered. *No.*

I glanced behind me, where Lucy huddled in the circle I'd made. I couldn't tell if she was conscious or not. The healing spell had finished its work, but she'd lost a lot of blood.

Can Lucy? I asked.

No.

Fine. I was a mage, not a swordfighter. I didn't need a damn blade anyway, not even an angelic one.

The lore says Zeus wounded Typhon with thunderbolts and imprisoned him, Ronan said, his voice in my head growing faint. *In truth, it was the Archangel Michael who struck him down, back when the earth was young.*

Thunder rumbled. Purple lightning split the sky.

This is a strange storm, Ronan said in my head. Then...nothing.

He wasn't dead; somehow, I knew that. But he was badly hurt, and now there was nothing between Typhon going topside with Mariela but Daisy and me.

If we were topside, I could use my air and earth magic to conduct the lightning, as I'd done on a rooftop to take out my aunt Catherine when she tried to burn down a condo to get at a rival cabal. Down here, my air magic didn't respond to the power of the lightning, and my earth magic tingled only a little. My dark magic, however, surged along with the lightning.

I caught movement out of the corner of my eye: Esme, trying to get up, despite her terrible wounds. She let out another piercing cry of pain. Daisy shredded any creature that came near them, but more emerged from the ground. Soon we'd be completely overrun.

If I was going down, I was going down swinging.

I dropped my shields and reached for the dark power in the creatures around us. With my magic, I pulled all their death energy into myself, sucking it from their bodies as if I was taking a huge breath of the foulest, dankest, most poisonous air.

These were creatures of the Darkness. That darkness, tinged with the primordial power of Chaos, filled me with the most horrible and sickening magic I'd ever known. The knot in my stomach swelled and hardened.

With shrieks and wails, the creatures fell, their bodies shriveling. Typhon roared and the ground shook.

Lightning burst overhead. In the distance, I spotted a huge, black form silhouetted against the sky, headed our way. When the lightning faded, I lost sight of the creature. Whether it was friend or foe, I had no idea, but I'd have to deal with it later.

Full of dark power and death magic, I reached out with my now almost-black air magic and seized the power of the storm. I expected pain, since every time I'd conducted the power of storms or ley lines it was excruciating. Instead, I felt only enormous power—and grief for Esme, who lay unmoving. *Stay with me, little dragon.*

Ronan was right at Typhon's feet. If I hit the giant with a bolt, I might fry Ronan to a crisp.

"Hey, you big idiot!" I shouted at Typhon. I didn't know if he understood, so I flapped my arms and made chicken sounds, which seemed to be a universal form of communication. "Big ugly idiot, come get me!"

He roared and lumbered in my direction.

"Stop!" Mariela screamed. Whether she was talking to Typhon or me, I wasn't sure. And I didn't care.

I formed the power of the storm into a massive bolt, one larger than any I'd ever attempted to wield before. Tiny threads of lightning sparked across my skin. Daisy crouched protectively over Esme.

With a scream, I brought the bolt down on Typhon's head. The resulting thunderclap was louder and more powerful than two trains colliding.

The shockwave sent me flying. I landed hard on a pile of hot dirt and ash near one of the holes the creatures had made coming up through the ground. Daisy had protected Esme, and Lucy still lay in the circle I'd made for her. She didn't move, but she was breathing. Probably unconscious.

I staggered to my feet. Typhon lay on the ground, black smoke curling up from his body and chunks of his head and left side missing. He wasn't dead, but he was at least down—for now. The snakes that formed his body writhed and hissed and spat in fury.

A powerful blood magic spell hit me from the side and bounced off. The sensation was like being struck with a huge rubber ball. I staggered. Warm magic that smelled like parchment flared: Carly's *Return to Sender* spell, held in the amulet in my pocket.

The spell Mariela had thrown at me rebounded and hit her square in the chest. I expected it to dissolve against her protection spells, but she must have used black magic. It went through her protection spells like they weren't even there.

Mariela screamed.

She screamed as it stripped off her skin, screamed as it ate away at her bones, and was still screaming when she collapsed to the rocky ground in a bloody pile of clothing and liquifying flesh. She finally stopped screaming when her eyes dissolved and ran out of their sockets. In seconds, her body was nothing but blood and bits of blackened flesh.

I put my hands on my knees and took a shuddering breath.

Mariela's death didn't feel like justice, and it sure as hell wasn't a cause for celebration. Without her to demand further investigation into the Glen Grove bombing, would any of the perpetrators face justice now? At the end of the day, it was the bombers who had set this all in motion. Mariela was responsible for a lot of death and suffering, but none of it would have happened if it weren't for their bigotry.

A spell fractured with a puff of foul odor and an echo of death. Mariela's black magic spell that had invoked Typhon had broken. Now that she was dead, we could bury Typhon. How the hell we were supposed to do that, though, I had no idea.

Typhon rumbled and started to rise. The wound in his head was already healing. Blasted immortals.

To my surprise, Esme raised her head again and let out a feeble cry. Overhead, something screeched in reply. Another burst of lightning illuminated the source of the sound: a dragon so huge, it dwarfed Typhon. It was either the one from the walls of Edis or the same species. The dragon swooped toward us, moving so quickly I had no time to get out of its way.

As it turned out, I was not its target.

The dragon grasped Typhon in its claws and settled its massive body on top of him. The giant looked like a mouse in the talons of a hawk. Typhon bellowed and roared as the snakes that made up his body attempted to bite through the dragon's scales, but it didn't seem to notice their attacks.

To my surprise, the dragon didn't take off immediately. Perched on Typhon's body, its weight crushing the giant to the rocky ground, it leaned down toward Esme. Its teeth were larger than Ronan's sword, and there were dozens of them.

I didn't stop to think. I ran in front of Esme and found myself face-to-snout with the dragon. Like Esme's, its eyes were brilliant, glittering emerald green.

The dragon puffed warm, magic-tinged air in my face in what might have been exasperation. It carefully nudged me aside and lowered its nose to Esme's bloody face. My little dragon raised her head and touched her nose to the newcomer's much-larger snout.

The dragon shimmered with violet magic. Warm air and magic blew from its nose and swirled around Esme, wrapping her in a shimmery blanket.

Violet magic was fae magic. I'd seen it only twice before—not counting the traces of fae magic in my aura thanks to a distant fae ancestor—and its beauty and power would never cease to leave me breathless. Daisy paced at my side, clearly uneasy about such an enormous dragon so close to her little pack mate.

The magic faded, revealing Esme curled up in cat form, fast asleep. Her fur was bloody and dirty, but her wounds were gone. I let out a little sob.

Moving very slowly so my gesture wouldn't be interpreted as an attack, I rested my palm on the side of the dragon's head. Its scales were hot and pulsed with magic. "Thank you," I whispered.

Two of the vipers that made up Typhon's body hissed and tried to strike me. The dragon whipped its head around, bit off the snakes, and swallowed them. Yuck.

Under the dragon's claws, Typhon roared. The dragon made a satisfied noise and looked down at Esme.

"I'll take care of her," I promised. "Stuff that asshole back under a mountain, will you?"

The dragon puffed warm air at me and took off with Typhon struggling and bellowing in its grip. Though it was careful not to hit us with its enormous wings, the downdraft knocked me flat. The dragon snuffled in what might have been an apology.

I sat up and watched it rise high into the air and fly off in the opposite direction of the distant mountains, toward a pitch-black horizon and hopefully the deepest pit the Underworld had to offer.

I hurt all over and the knot in my stomach felt like the size of a baseball. I was so hungry that the gnawing sensation was painful, but it was just one more pain I couldn't do anything about at the moment.

Lucy's voice startled me. "Was that a dragon you were talking to, or was I hallucinating?" She sat up, pale and shaky, but alive.

"That was most definitely a dragon. Luckily, it was on our side." Using a rock for support, I got to my feet. I scooped up Esme and headed for Ronan, who hadn't moved since he went down with Mariela's blade in his ribs.

When we got to him, his wings had disappeared, as had his flaming sword. Other than the knife in his side, I saw no other injuries despite the very brutal fight he'd had with Typhon. I wondered how he'd gotten all the other scars. Maybe he could choose when to heal himself.

Lucy staggered up next to me as I knelt beside Ronan. I touched his face, expecting it to be cool because of how pale he was. I hissed and yanked my hand back. "His skin is burning."

Tis's voice came from behind us. "That blade is poison for our kind."

I whirled. Tis stood about ten feet away, with Ammit at her side. "She likely brought it to threaten one of us," she added, studying Ronan. Her face and tone were devoid of emotion. "The bounty hunter had the misfortune of falling victim to its power."

"His name is Ronan." I got to my feet. "Why are you here?"

"We approve of the outcome of this battle." Her tone was beneficent, as if we'd been awaiting their judgment, and I was in no mood for it. Daisy growled.

"Oh, do you now?" I snapped. "How kind of you."

Her eyes narrowed. "Tread carefully, mage."

"You dumped us on this plain to fight for our lives and the lives of thousands more," Lucy said. Her sword trembled. Given how much blood she'd lost, I had no idea how she was even on her feet, much less brandishing a heavy blade. "We barely survived, and Ronan might die."

"All this is true," Tis said.

As maddening as her lack of emotion was, we might have a bigger problem. I turned to Ammit. "Do you still plan to feast on hearts?"

She smiled that eerie crocodilian smile. "Not at this time. Mariela's death and Typhon's return to the Darkness have robbed me of that opportunity."

At least we wouldn't have to fight her too. "Thanks," I said.

She blinked at me with two sets of eyelids. "You seek justice above all else, mage Alice. And you, warrior Lucy, have begun to do the same, after a fashion. See your motives remain true, for the good of your souls." The scent of iron and incense wrapped around us. "I would take great pleasure in devouring your hearts, should they find their way to my plate."

With that threat hanging in the air, she vanished with a surge of magic.

A woman stepped from a shimmery tear in the air about fifteen feet to our right. She was very tall and blonde, with glacier blue eyes. Another fallen angel, I guessed. She wore gray fighting leathers and two swords on her back.

"I have asked our sister Eir to heal your wounds, in recognition of your honor and bravery," Tis said.

"You're a healer?" Lucy asked as Eir approached. "You look like a soldier."

"One does not preclude the other." Her voice was melodious. "Battlefields require medics as well as healers."

"I'm not going into debt to anyone for healing," I stated. "I have healing spells, and there are hospitals and healers topside."

"This gift of healing is freely given," Eir said. I sensed magic when she spoke, as if those words were a bond between us. "At the request of my sisters, and in appreciation for your skill and courage in battle."

Lucy and I exchanged a glance. "You're a mess," she told me with characteristic bluntness. "Blood magic healing spells are good at what they do, but they suck dragon balls. I vote we accept the offer before you fall down."

I sighed and handed Esme over to Lucy. "All right."

Eir's hands glided over my body, her silver-blue magic warm and comforting. My cuts, bruises, and other injuries healed painlessly.

When she found the knot in my stomach, however, she flinched and stepped back. "You can't do anything about that, can you?" I asked.

She looked sad. "I cannot."

I'd expected as much. I couldn't be that lucky.

Since most of Lucy's injuries had already been healed by the healing spell, Eir took only a minute to tend to what was left. Lucy was still pale from blood loss, but when Eir finished, her hands no longer trembled.

I gestured at Ronan. "Now your brother needs your help."

Eir rejoined Tis. "I am forbidden to help him."

"What the hell did he do?" I burst out. "Why doesn't he deserve the least bit of compassion?"

"Whether or not he deserves compassion is immaterial," Tis snapped. "We have orders."

"What, from Michael?" I demanded. "Or from whoever put a bounty on Ronan's head?"

"Both." For the first time, I saw what might have been real sadness in her ancient eyes. "We all answer to someone, Alice, even the Fallen. My sisters and I keep the peace and see justice is done in this realm. Without us, many would suffer and die in the chaos. We cannot risk our own annihilation, not even for our brother."

"Fine." I went to my knees at Ronan's side. "If you won't help, *I* will."

"How?" Lucy asked, crouching beside me. "You take a course in angel first aid?"

"I'll figure something out." I cupped Ronan's face with my hand. His hot skin hurt my palm. His chest barely moved.

I leaned close so I could murmur in his ear. "We are *all* getting back on that train, you ass. Plus I've got a message for you, knight with no court or kingdom."

No response.

I pulled the knife out of Ronan's side and dropped it on the ground. The jagged obsidian blade was full of very black magic. Putrescent flesh surrounded the bloody wound. I gagged.

"You may kill yourself if you attempt to save him," Eir warned.

I snorted and stuck my fingers into the wound in Ronan's side. "If I had a quarter for every time someone told me that." I took a deep breath and closed my eyes so I could focus.

With my blood magic and dark magic, I tried to pull the poison and black magic out of Ronan's body as I'd drawn Kyrios's poison from Daisy, but its tentacles went deep into his flesh and didn't want to come out.

"Damn it." I cut my fingertips on the edge of Ronan's broken sword, sucking in a breath at the pain. I stuck my fingers back into the wound in his side, lowered my shields, and pulled the vile mix of magic and poison into myself instead.

My blood and earth magic burned away most of the poison and black magic as it left Ronan's body. I shuddered. My skin burned hot all over as the remainder entered my bloodstream.

Someone wrapped their slim but strong arms around me and held me tightly so I didn't fall over. Lucy. Daisy chuffed in my ear, maybe to reassure me that she was beside me as well.

I drew poison and black magic from Ronan's body until I couldn't take anymore, and then crawled away from the others to vomit. What came out was black and horrible and tasted like blood and the inside of a dumpster, and cut the inside of my belly, throat, and mouth like razors as I expelled it onto the ground.

Finally, when it was over, I collapsed on my side, my chest heaving with harsh breaths almost like sobs. I was sick and exhausted, but I was alive, and so were Ronan, Lucy, Esme, and Daisy.

The ground rumbled. With my head resting on the hot, ash-covered rock, I heard a distant roar that sounded very much like Typhon bellowing from within the earth. Our dragon ally had found someplace very deep to stash the Son of the Darkness. "Same to you, pal," I rasped.

Someone knelt beside me. I opened my eyes, expecting it to be Lucy. Instead I found myself looking up into Ronan's glacier-blue gaze. He looked haggard, but his hand was only just warm and not scalding when he cupped my cheek.

"I owe you a great boon," he said roughly.

"No debts between friends." My voice sounded no better.

He produced a cloth from a pocket of his pants and wiped my face and mouth. A black scar marked where Mariela's knife had punctured his side. Something told me he'd bear that scar for a very long time.

When his fingers grazed my lips, magic tingled. Whether it was mine or his, I couldn't tell. "I have a question for you," I murmured as he finished cleaning my face.

"Yes?"

"Who put the bounty on your head?"

The corners of his mouth turned up. "Freya. It's a long story."

I blinked. Freya, as in *the* Freya? "I bet."

He offered me his hand. I took it and he lifted me to my feet without showing any strain. And he flexed when he did it. I rolled my eyes.

The ground rumbled one more time, then went still.

We'd won.

Hadn't we?

Torryn's prophecy said I wouldn't succeed in stopping the Furies, bringing Mariela back, or getting the scroll so Malcolm and I could make it home. I hadn't had to stop the Furies, as it turned out, and Mariela was most certainly not returning to our world unless someone scooped her remains into a bucket. That left the scroll.

I made my way through the shriveled corpses of the dead creatures to the puddle of bloody goop that had once been Mariela. With the smell of the poison I'd pulled from Ronan's body still fresh in my nose, I barely noticed the odor of her mostly liquid remains. It was still about a twelve on my personal gross-o-meter.

"Want me to do it?" Ronan asked, making me jump. I hadn't realized he'd followed me.

"I'm going to put a bell on you." I sighed. "I've got it." I braced myself, crouched, and felt around in the slurry of blood, dissolved bones, and flesh. "Eww, eww, eww," I chanted under my breath.

I thought I heard Ronan chuckle, but when I glared up at him he just raised his eyebrows.

I pulled her clothing out first and searched it, then used a rock to nudge several amulets out of the puddle, not wanting to touch them and risk falling victim to whatever magic or spells they held.

When I found her leather bag, I opened it and carefully dumped its contents onto the ground: dirty clothing, a bottle for water, dried meat and fruits in small bags, some toiletries and other odds and ends, and a leather-wrapped bundle so completely devoid of magic that it *had* to be magical and protected by strong wards.

The problem was, I had no way to know what those wards were or what they would do if I tried to open the parcel. They might destroy the contents, kill me, nuke the entire vicinity...the possibilities were endless. I'd bet the wards had deadly landmines that would try to kill me if I tried to unweave them. I didn't want to leave the Underworld until I knew if the scroll was in the parcel, and the apparent accuracy thus far of Torryn's prophecy made me uneasy.

Ronan held out his hand. "May I?"

I hesitated. "There's bound to be some very bad magic in here."

"I know." He continued to hold out his hand. "I'm willing to take the risk. I doubt she thought she'd need to ward it against me."

"She knew she was coming down here to see them," I reminded him, indicating Tis, who watched us without expression. "She had the foresight to bring that angel-killing knife."

"Alice, I know all that," he snapped. "Will you just give me the damn thing and accept help when it's offered?"

Damn it. Of all my many neuroses, that one drove Malcolm and Sean crazy the most.

"I'm not very good at that," I said.

"No shit."

We eyed each other.

"Okay," I said reluctantly. "Be careful, Wings. I've already had to save you once. I don't think I've got another miracle in me today."

His mouth turned down. "Since you did save me, I'll let 'Wings' slide. *This* time. Step back, just in case."

I moved back about ten feet. Lucy and Daisy joined me, with Esme nestled in Lucy's arms. Tis stayed where she was.

With his boot, Ronan made a circle around Mariela's remains and the bundle, then crouched to mark glyphs in the ash along the perimeter of the circle. The circle flared with silver-blue magic. My skin prickled.

Ronan used one of his knives to cut the rope around the bundle. The blade blazed blue as some kind of spell or curse flared, but Ronan seemed fine. The knife must have absorbed the curse. I let out a breath.

With the tip of the knife, Ronan unfolded the top layer of leather wrapped around the contents of the parcel. Another flare of blue magic on the blade, much more faint. The protective spell on the knife had reached its limits. Ronan flinched as the remaining part of the curse hit him, but it didn't seem to do much to him.

Though the knife had no more protection, he used the blade to flip back the other part of the leather wrapping. He stared and jerked in surprise.

Several things happened seemingly at once.

Red and black magic flared so powerfully that I covered my eyes instinctively to protect them. Lucy gasped and turned away from the intense brightness.

Something flew past me with a great flapping of wings, moving so quickly I saw only a blur and smelled the sea. Silver-blue magic seared my skin, but it wasn't Ronan's. I recognized it from the tavern. Tis.

I lowered my hand and squinted.

Radiant with power and magic brighter than anything I'd seen since we arrived in the Underworld, Tis crouched in the center of Ronan's circle, her wings folded to form a shield over the bundle. Ronan lay a few feet away, his body over the line he'd drawn in the ash. He appeared stunned, but he was moving.

A blast of sea-scented cold air washed over us. In it, I caught the distinct odor of something burning and familiar ancient magic.

"Oh, no," I breathed. "No, no, no."

Tis raised her head. Dark streaks spread across her face and wings—traces of the curse she'd contained. She shook herself briskly. Silver-blue magic burst from her skin and wings and pulsed through her body. The streaks began to fade.

My chest tight, I headed for the circle. Tis lifted her wings. Her eyes glowed with power.

The leather wrapping was gone, reduced to fine ash. On top of that ash lay a charred wooden spindle and bits of half-burned papyrus.

"I contained the final curse on the wrappings," Tis said as I stared at all that remained of Valas's treasured portion of the Writings of the House of Darkness—the key to getting us home.

"I also attempted to preserve this bit of foul magic, but it was already destroyed," Tis added. "It is likely your enemy spelled the scroll to self-immolate on the event of her death." She rose smoothly. Her wings folded behind her back and vanished.

Lucy and Daisy joined me at the edge of the circle. Daisy whined.

Ronan got to his feet, his eyes dark gray. "Alice." His tone held sympathy, and I wanted to punch him for it.

I picked up one of the cloth bags Mariela had used for food. I emptied it and gingerly put the charred bits of wood and papyrus into the bag, along with the obsidian stone I'd had in my pocket since the mirror dumped us in the ruins of Northbourne.

I got to my feet. "Tis, I need my backpack from your tavern, please."

She reached to her right, the air rippling and folding around her arm. When her hand reappeared, she held my backpack. She placed it at my feet without a word.

I tied the bag containing what remained of the scroll and put it into my pack. "Thank you for trying to save the scroll, and for protecting Ronan, despite your orders. I'm not sure about your sisters, but you're actually kind of cool."

To my surprise, a hint of a smile turned up the corner of Tis's mouth. "High praise indeed."

"What's the plan now?" Lucy asked.

"Same plan as before." I put my backpack on my shoulders. "Get back topside, get Malcolm, go back to where we landed in your world, and go home. Did you request a pickup for us?" I asked Ronan.

Before he could answer, Tis spoke. "I can send you directly to the doorway back to the human world, if you would prefer a faster mode of transportation."

"I appreciate the offer, but your way is kind of rough on humans," I told her. "Besides, I kinda liked the train."

"Charon should arrive shortly," Ronan said. He bowed to Tis. "My thanks, sister. Please tell Aira she's welcome to try to collect that bounty the next time I'm here."

Tis's eyes sparkled. "If you are lucky, she will have lost interest by then. Safe travels to you all." She vanished.

Ronan touched my arm. "I'm sorry about the scroll."

"I'm still going home," I told him, my eyes tracking a fast-moving black shape heading directly for us across the plain. "And Malcolm, Daisy, and Esme are coming with me. I'll find a way to get through that mirror-door. I don't give up that easily." My stomach cramped hard from hunger. I nearly doubled over.

His fingertips brushed my abdomen where the hard knot had formed. His eyes darkened. "This is death magic."

"I know." I took Esme from Lucy. The little cat-dragon didn't stir. "But there's still time."

He didn't ask me time for what.

We watched the train approach, slow, and stop in front of us. The door slid open. Lucy and I boarded first with Daisy and Esme. Ronan climbed aboard and sat down across from us. The door slid closed.

As the train crossed the plain toward the distant mountains, I ate the last two protein bars in my backpack, drank the remainder of my bottled water, and lay down on the seat with Esme curled up against my stomach, still sound asleep. Daisy sprawled out in front of me and put her chin on the seat. I rested my hand on her head.

Lucy took out her blade and started cleaning it. "You know, I expected your sword to be quite a bit bigger than it was," she told Ronan.

I fell asleep with the sound of his chuckle in my ears.

CHAPTER 29

One by one, the doorway dumped us out topside into the clearing, in the middle of the night—

—And in the middle of a standoff between Malcolm and four Guardians.

Purely by chance, I emerged first, just in time to hear Malcolm shout, "For the *last time*, you are not closing this damn door!"

With Esme in my arms, I landed on the grass and rolled aside just in time to avoid Ronan's arrival. Lucy fell out next, and Daisy last. Dazed and still tied together by Ronan's shiny magical rope, we lay more or less where we'd landed.

The Broken World magic grated on my skin. Given how uncertain I'd been that we'd return from the Underworld, the sensation was weirdly welcome.

"Okay, *now* you jerks can close the door," Malcolm said.

He floated above me, looking worried, relieved, and furious all at once. "Alice?" His eyes went to my middle and widened at the sight of the terrible knot of death magic. "Oh, no," he breathed.

"Lucy?" One of the male Guardians approached us cautiously. "Good Lord, what happened to you?"

"It wasn't a *good* lord who did this," Lucy muttered as Ronan untied us. "Other than some blood loss and one hell of a headache, I'm fine, guys. Had to pop down there with some friends and take care of business so we could shut this door."

"Captain Ellis is going to shit bricks," a tall blonde female Guardian ground out through clenched teeth. "Stone, can't you ever do *anything* according to regulations?"

"Doesn't appear that way." Lucy got to her feet and rolled her neck and shoulders, which popped audibly. She glanced down at the doorway. "Time to shut this for good. Alice, you want to do the honors?"

"I'll do it," Malcolm said quickly, glancing again at the knot in my abdomen. "It's safer for me to do it anyway."

"Did you release the ghost Mariela had staked to the doorway?" I asked.

"First chance I got," Malcolm told me. "I anchored the spellwork myself—and good thing I did, since I had to defend it."

While he picked apart the spellwork that kept the door open, I got to my feet with help from Daisy.

"Who are these people?" the male Guardian who'd addressed Lucy earlier demanded. "And why the hell would you go through a door to the Underworld, leaving it open behind you, without informing your commanding officer or even your partner?"

"It's...complicated," Lucy said. "I'll file a complete report with Ellis."

A familiar man in Guardian officer's uniform stormed into the clearing. "You'll have to do a hell of a lot better than that, Stone," he snapped.

Lucy straightened automatically. "Captain Ellis. You're looking well."

"Stop." He raised his finger in warning as he approached. "You are under arrest."

I took a step forward, but Lucy held me back. "On what charges?" She sounded more curious than angry or afraid.

"A very long list." Ellis put his fists on his hips. "I'll figure out which ones on the way to the nearest Guardian outpost." His flinty gaze raked over the rest of us. "Who the hell are these people?"

Lucy gestured. "This is Alice. She and her guardian wolf assisted me by tracking the location of the door." Daisy sat on her haunches and grinned at Ellis with her tongue lolling like a large dog. Lucy hooked her thumb at our silent companion. "And this is Ronan Smith, bounty hunter, who happened to be down there collecting a bounty and came back with us."

"And what is that?" Ellis demanded, pointing at Esme in my arms, who blinked sleepily at him.

"My cat," I said, as if taking one's cat to the Underworld was a perfectly natural thing to do.

Behind us, the doorway snapped closed with a flare of broken spellwork and blood magic. "It's closed," Malcolm said for the benefit of anyone who couldn't sense the magic. "No more doorway to the Underworld."

"Thanks," I told him. "You're the best."

"I know," he said, but there was no hint of humor in his tone. He stared at my middle, then looked away.

Ellis's face reddened. "You have been missing for *two weeks*, Stone. We thought you were dead. I had to divert valuable resources to search for you."

She blinked. "Two weeks? It's only been a day or two at most."

Malcolm floated back and forth. "It's been two weeks," he told me, his voice quiet. "Thankfully, your wards held and nothing's come up out of the door since you went down. Everything was fine until earlier today, when these guys found Lucy's jeep and the door, and then it all went sideways." He glared at the Guardians. "It's been all I could do to keep them from discorporating me and closing that door on you. You got back just in time. They were about to call in a necromancer to try to *deal with* me."

My stomach contracted, and it had nothing to do with the knot of death magic. The Guardians had tried to discorporate Malcolm and shut the door on us when they knew we were still down there, and apparently we'd been gone a hell of a lot longer than I'd thought. "We've been down there for two *weeks?*" I asked finally.

"Time sometimes slips in the Underworld," Ronan explained. "I thought we would gain time on the way back to the door. We did, but not enough to make up the difference. I'm sorry, Alice."

Two weeks. That meant I'd been gone from Sean and the rest of our pack for nearly three weeks. They probably thought I was dead. The thought made me sicker than the damn death magic. I needed to get to the mirror-door and get home.

"I have to go," I said.

Ellis's expression darkened. "No one's going anywhere until I get a full explanation for this. You're all coming to the outpost." He gestured at the other Guardians. "Arrest them."

Silver-blue magic flared, searing my eyes. When my vision cleared, all five of the Guardians, including Captain Ellis, were sprawled unconscious on the ground.

Lucy glared at Ronan. "What the hell did you do?"

He shrugged. "Put them to sleep and muddled their memories so we can get out of here."

"How did you do that?" Malcolm demanded.

"He's a fallen angel," I said.

"Oh yeah? *How* fallen?" Malcolm asked with interest.

"All the way," Ronan told him.

Malcolm's eyebrows went up. "You don't say."

"*Stoooo-oooop,*" I groaned.

Ronan shouldered his pack. "When they come to, you can tell them the doorway flared when you came through and knocked them out. Tell them you hunted down Mariela yourself and brought her to justice for leaving this door open."

"We can't just leave Lucy here to face the music alone," Malcolm protested.

"Sure you can." Lucy grinned. "You have any idea how many times Captain Ellis has threatened to arrest me? Half the time, he ends up giving me a medal instead. I've got a drawer full of 'em back home."

"Where's home?" I asked.

"Millville, Texas—whenever I can get back there for a visit, which isn't very often these days." Her smile faded. "Go home, Alice. You've got a hot werewolf waiting for you, and I've got to fill out a literal mountain of paperwork on this mess. I'll be writing reports until the trolls come home."

"Until the trolls..." I frowned. "Wait, how do you know Sean's hot?"

"I looked through your backpack when you were in the shower at Hawthorne's and saw his picture." And she didn't look the least bit repentant about it. "I'll miss you, woman. Even though I didn't meet you at your best, you're a damn good deputy. Plus, it was nice having a partner who laughed at my jokes and didn't argue with me about every damn thing for a change."

I rubbed Daisy's head. "I wondered why you and your partner were working separately. If you don't get along, why not ask for a different partner?"

She grinned again. "Oh, we get along just fine, as long as we take a break from each other from time to time. The stick up his ass has a stick up its ass, but he's a hell of a Guardian. Not that I'd ever tell him that. He's insufferable enough as it is."

I sensed she wanted to say goodbye quickly rather than draw this out. That was probably for the best, but my heart hurt. Despite how she'd pushed me to get in her jeep to begin with, I liked Lucy, and I'd miss her. She hadn't done it to hurt me, or to make me hurt someone else, and I supposed that counted for something.

I hugged her. She hugged me back, then released me. "You take care of yourself, Malcolm," she told my ghost.

"You too, Lucy," he said. "You're pretty good with that sword, for a girl."

She flipped him off. They hugged.

When she and Malcolm let go of each other, Lucy eyed Ronan. "You get them safely to where they're going, you hear me?"

"Absolutely, Lieutenant. Keep your blade sharp." He offered his hand.

She shook it. "You too, Wings."

He made a rumbly sound. She laughed and headed in the direction of where she'd left her jeep in the forest.

We went in the opposite direction, where I presumed Ronan had hidden his motorcycle. Esme climbed onto my shoulder and yawned, her eyes half-lidded. Daisy trotted at my side. Malcolm floated along behind us. Having him near me again made the obstacles we still faced seem a little less impossible.

"I don't see how we're going to ride with you," I said as we followed Ronan through the trees and undergrowth. "Malcolm can make the trip in my arm cuff and I might be able to coax Esme into my backpack, but it's not like Daisy's going to fit in one of your saddlebags."

"Daisy can run, remember?" He led us directly to his Harley, which was parked under a tree. Despite being outside for two weeks, it was shiny and clean. "She's a wolf, and wolves love to run."

Daisy showed us all of her teeth.

I worried about her, but I also knew my wolf could take care of herself. "Okay," I said finally. "Let's roll, then. Malcolm, ready to go for a ride?"

My ghost eyed me. "So, we're not going to talk about that?" He pointed at my abdomen.

I covered my stomach, not that my hand hid the death magic from him. "Not right this minute."

He floated back and forth, clearly unhappy. "All right. See you back at our Northbourne, then." He turned to Ronan. "You turned out to be an okay guy after all, Easy Rider." He held out his fist. Ronan bumped it with his own.

"*Contain*," I said. Malcolm vanished. His crystal in my cuff buzzed.

After some initial resistance, I talked Esme into getting in my backpack, leaving it unzipped enough for her to poke her head out if she wanted to. I didn't dare tell her how cute she looked peeking out. Cats had their pride, and I imagined that went double for cat-dragons.

Ronan took a black helmet from one of his saddlebags and handed it to me.

"You ever ride on a motorcycle before?" he asked, swinging his leg over the bike and settling into the seat.

"No."

He put on leather gloves and tightened them. "A virgin. Mmm, my favorite."

I scoffed. "Liar."

He grinned. "It's true—I prefer a woman who knows what she likes. I don't mind showing one who's inexperienced how good it can be, though."

"Ass," I muttered. He chuckled.

I put on the helmet, secured my battered backpack, and climbed onto the Harley behind him, my thighs around his hips. It would have been sexy as hell if it didn't make me miss Sean so much.

He put on his own helmet and started the bike. Its throaty rumble sent a little thrill through me, despite my worry about the knot in my stomach and how long I'd been gone.

Ready? Ronan asked in my head.

I wrapped my arms around his waist. *Ready.*

With a happy growl, Daisy took off through the trees in a golden blur. I smiled.

The motorcycle wove slowly through the forest until we got to the road. As we passed Lucy and her jeep, she waved us to stop and ran over with my half-empty bottle of Charles's finest moonshine. Ronan wrapped it in a T-shirt and stored it in one of his saddlebags. I blew Lucy a kiss. She winked.

As soon as the Harley was on the road, Ronan accelerated with a roar of horsepower and headed north, toward the mirror-door and home.

CHAPTER 30

For nearly sixteen hours, we rode straight through to the ruins of Northbourne. We stopped only for fuel, food, and a short nap under some trees in a park when the pain in my stomach and my exhaustion got to be too much. Ronan gave me a blanket from one of his saddlebags and kept watch while I slept for about an hour, wrapped up like a burrito beside him. When I woke in the middle of a nightmare, his hand was resting on my shoulder, comforting me.

Despite her very vocal disapproval at the idea of riding in my backpack, Esme nestled inside it and slept for almost the entire trip. I tried not to think about how she'd looked when Typhon's monster tore her nearly in half. Instead, I remembered how her much-larger cousin had responded to her call for help and tenderly healed her wounds.

I had no idea what Ronan thought about during our journey. My own thoughts bounced between a dozen topics, from the death magic in my belly to Sean, Valas, and everything we'd seen and done in the Underworld. I had many hours on the back of the Harley to think about all those things and make plans about some of them— most especially Valas.

From time to time I caught glimpses of Daisy keeping pace with us, but generally she ran ahead, presumably in case something big and mean lay in wait in our path. Creatures of various sizes and shapes lurked near the road, but none messed with us.

We said little during the trip. Ronan occasionally took one hand off the grip and rested his forearm on top of my hands on his stomach. Despite his teasing and innuendos, and the way my hormones did a jig in response to his very fine bod, what had developed between us was friendship or a pack bond. I thought it was his way of comforting me now that I had a lead ball of death magic chewing away at my insides. My sickness wasn't just from the way my magic clashed with the ambient power of the Broken World. I could no longer pretend the dark magic I'd gotten from Miraç wasn't damaging my body too.

Ronan was clearly protective of me now. Not so long ago, that would have pissed me off and I've have told him I'd get to Northbourne on my own. Spending time with Sean, our pack, and Malcolm had made me realize when others wanted to protect or defend me, it wasn't because they thought I was weak. I meant enough to Ronan that he'd do whatever was necessary to keep me safe. I felt the same way about Sean, Malcolm, the rest of our pack, and even Ronan when he'd been wounded by Mariela's poison blade, and I didn't think any of them were weak.

With my arms around his waist, I felt the outline of his flask inside his jacket, but he didn't drink from it a single time during our trip. Since it clearly bothered him, I didn't call him "Wings" again, though I did mutter "Ass" under my breath several times. He didn't seem to mind; in fact, I suspected he went out of his way to elicit that response. Our weird camaraderie felt comfortable, like a well-worn pair of jeans.

I hoped Lucy was able to explain her actions to her colleagues and superiors and they'd commended her instead of throwing her in the brig—or whatever Guardians used as a jail. I tried to imagine what she was doing right now. Probably finding out where something terrible and dangerous was happening, like a mass dragon migration, and heading straight there.

One decision I made not long into the trip was that Sean and I needed to own a Harley. The thought of riding a motorcycle with my legs and arms around him made me feel all kinds of things—and stirred up definite heat in some very personal places, which I fervently hoped Ronan did not notice. At one point he shook slightly like he was laughing, but it was hard to tell. It might have just been my imagination.

I dozed off and on during the last few hours, with my head resting against Ronan's back and his arm pinning mine against his stomach to hold me steady. Even through my helmet, I smelled leather and the sea.

As desperate as I was to reach the mirror-door and get us home, I wanted to hold on to this last ride through the Broken World on the back of a fallen angel's Harley, with a cat-dragon in my backpack, a golden wolf running alongside, and a ghost's reassuring magic buzzing in the cuff on my arm.

Someone was carrying me through an endless forest with my head nestled against his broad chest. His arms were strong, and his heart beat in a steady, reassuring rhythm right under my ear. He hummed under his breath.

"Sean?" I murmured.

"Rest," he said. "We're almost there."

Some part of my brain told me that wasn't Sean's voice, but I was too tired to open my eyes. With a contented sound, I went back to sleep.

THE NEXT TIME I WOKE, I was curled up in Ronan's lap in the basement of the ruins of Broken World Northbourne, with Esme in the crook of my arm and Daisy at our side.

He sat against the wall, our backpacks nearby. We were in a dark corner not visible to anyone who might unexpectedly be poking around above. My last memory was of a sunny afternoon, but it was now night.

"Whaaa?" I mumbled.

He chuckled. "For such a little thing, you produce quite a snore. I'm surprised every creature within twenty miles hasn't come to see what terrifying beast is down here making that noise."

"Ass." Bleary-eyed, I wiped my mouth with the back of my hand and raised my head. Pain shot through my neck. "*Owwww.*"

He grunted. "If you think your neck feels cramped, imagine the condition of my spine."

My thoughts were surprisingly clear, so the nap had done me some good. "How long have I been asleep?"

"Not long enough, given what you've been through." His voice had lost all hint of humor. "We've only been here a half hour."

"I'm sorry you had to carry me."

He squeezed me very gently. "I didn't *have* to. I chose to."

"Thank you. I'm surprised I slept through us stopping and you carrying me down to the basement." My eyes narrowed. "Did you put me to sleep? Or *keep* me asleep?"

I heard the smile in his voice when he replied, "Why would I do something so nefarious, when I knew it would piss you off?"

"Oh, shut up," I said, but without rancor. I put my hand on my abdomen. The knot hadn't gone away or shrunk in size, but it hadn't grown. I supposed I'd have to consider that a win.

"Ready to stand up?" Ronan asked. "If not, I'm going to need to reach into my jacket and get a swig of tequila to take the edge off the pain."

Home wasn't going to come to us, so sick or not, I had to get on my feet. "Yeah, I'm ready."

I placed Esme on the floor. She stretched. "Rrrrr?" she inquired.

"I'm fine," I told her. "Just getting up."

"Want help?" Ronan asked.

I clambered off his lap with my usual amount of elegance—which is to say, none at all. "No, I got it."

Despite his complaints about pain and his spine, Ronan rose like someone pulled him up with invisible strings. "You could at least *pretend* that took some effort," I groused.

He didn't say anything while I struggled to stand, though his hand twitched when he thought he might have to catch me. I got to my feet, steadying myself on Daisy, and with only minimal cursing.

When I was upright and walking, I looked for the mirror-door. Our portal home was right where we'd left it. It shimmered in my Second Sight, and its magic, still tinged with my own, tingled on my skin.

Ronan joined me in front of the portal. "I'm sure you have a plan to get back."

"I do have a plan."

"Which would be...?"

"I've got part of the scroll and the stone that contains traces of the same magic. When we're ready to go through the portal, I'm going to damage the scroll. Its spellwork—what's left of it—will flare. I'm hoping that will be enough of the scroll's magic to fool the portal into thinking I've got the whole thing, and it will unlock and send us home."

He studied the portal. "It might work."

"It's going to have to work. I don't have a plan B at the moment. There are precious few ways of traveling between worlds—not that I have to tell *you* that." I glanced up at him. "Speaking of which, how did you get here, if angels can't come to this world?"

He tilted his head. "What makes you think angels can't come here?"

I frowned. "But Tura said—"

A burst of magic sent me stumbling back. Ronan's eyes blazed silver-blue. Power crackled on his skin, and I heard the sound of his wings, though I didn't see them. He seemed to grow several feet taller and towered over me. For the first time, I felt a little stab of fear of him.

"*How do you know Tura?*" he thundered.

As frequently happened, my fear turned into anger. I poked his chest with my finger. "Turn off the fireworks. I am *not* your enemy."

He rumbled. We stared at each other. With visible effort, he dampened his power. I rubbed my arms to ease the prickly feeling.

When he looked human again, I gave him the short version of how I'd met Tura. He listened in stony silence at my account of our conversation on a hill near my grandfather's compound and her claim that I had to deliver the message because angels couldn't go through the mirror-door. After a hesitation, I also told him about her alleged ability to see glimpses of the future, and her warning about my impending death.

"She described you as a knight with no court or kingdom," I said when he was silent. "Your name should have tipped me off, even if it took me way too damn long to recognize that you and Tura have similar magic. Ronan sounds a lot like *ronin*. I imagine that's how you chose that name when you fell to Earth."

"I didn't fall," he said. "I jumped."

I blinked. "You jumped? Why?"

He took his flask from his inside jacket pocket and toasted me before downing a hefty swig.

Now I was even more confused. "You fell—sorry, *jumped*—from Heaven for tequila?"

He took another drink and offered me the flask. "Can you think of a better reason? Whisky, perhaps?"

I accepted the flask. "Very funny." I took a drink, then handed it back. It was good tequila. Not my favorite, but very drinkable. "You're not going to tell me why you jumped, are you?"

"No." He returned the flask to his pocket. "Let's have it, then."

"Have what?"

A flash of exasperation. "The *message,* Alice."

I hesitated.

His brow furrowed. "Charon told me I should pay heed to the next message I received from my former brothers and sisters. In return for our passage back to the doorway, I gave him my word I would at least listen. What's the issue?"

"I have to kiss you," I said helplessly.

He burst out laughing—a real, full belly laugh. I hadn't thought he was capable of it.

I crossed my arms. "I fail to see what's funny about this."

"You should have seen your face when you said you *had* to kiss me," he said when he could speak. "One would think you had to kiss something truly awful."

"I *do,*" I snapped.

Smiling, he stepped close and bent his head. "If it helps, try to remember how you felt riding on the back of my Harley." At my expression, his smile widened. "I thought so."

"I was thinking about riding one with Sean," I protested. "And it's very ungentlemanly of you to bring it up."

"Not a gentleman," he said, very seriously. "Not even close."

I didn't want to kiss him, but I had to. I'd given Tura my word. Oh, what the hell—I'd kissed worse guys, and gals too.

I grabbed the back of his neck, pulled him down to me, and pressed my lips to his.

The scent of the sea swirled around us and magic surged. A wave of sound rose inside me, filling my body and rolling from my mouth into his. It roared like a thundering waterfall, rang like bells, and tasted like honey, and it seemed to go on for hours, though I knew it had been only seconds.

When Tura gave the message to me, I hadn't understood any part of it. The language of angels was far removed from human forms of communication. This time—maybe because I'd pulled that poison from Ronan and with it had come a trace of his own magic—I heard a word repeated several times in the midst of the otherwise unintelligible sounds.

When the message ended, the sudden emptiness left me feeling hollow and nearly boneless. My knees gave out.

Ronan caught me. His eyes were dark, with rings of silver-blue. "And now you're swooning," he said, his voice rough with an emotion I couldn't identify. "That's the effect I have on most women."

I scowled and opened my mouth.

"Ass," he said. "I know." He set me on my feet.

I'd wondered about the contents of the message Tura had given me since she'd asked me to deliver it. Given what I knew about Ronan—or, rather, what I'd cobbled together from clues I'd picked up along the way—I was even more curious now.

His eyes held darkness and pain. Whatever was in the message, it hadn't been a cheerful greeting from an old friend.

"Are you all right?" I asked.

"Isn't that my line?" He smiled, but without humor. "I'm fine. Thank you for bringing me the message."

"You're welcome." I stared into his storm-cloud gray eyes. "Remiel."

He stilled.

"That was the only word I heard out of the whole message," I said. "Something about the way she said it sounded...personal. Were you and Tura close?"

His face lost all expression. "My name is Ronan. Remiel ceased to exist a very long time ago."

Apparently I wasn't the only one who didn't like to talk about their past. Fair enough. I'd delivered the damn message. If Tura wanted to bend Ronan's ear again, she could do it herself.

Before I could try to get us home, I had a couple of things I needed to do. I sat on a rock as Ronan examined the portal. "Daisy, come here," I called.

My wolf approached, but stopped about ten feet away, eyeing me.

"We're going back home," I told her. "That means you need to go back inside me for the trip through the mirror-door."

She sat down and chomped the air between us, curling her lip slightly.

I frowned. "What does that mean? You have to return to my body, or you won't get through the portal. Come on, Daisy-dog. Let's go home."

She wiggled her rump and sat down again, with emphasis this time.

My heart sank. "You can't stay here. I know you enjoyed running around free and being a bad-ass, but you're part of me, and I want to go home to Sean and our pack. We belong with them. I can't stay here anyway. Even if this knot in my stomach doesn't kill me, the ambient magic of this world will."

She didn't move.

I'd worried that talking Daisy into leaping back into my body would be difficult after she'd gotten used to freedom, but I never thought she would flatly refuse to go home.

My stomach cramped hard, either from hunger or the dark magics chewing me up from the inside. I flinched. "Daisy, please," I pleaded. "I can't go without you, and I can't stay."

"It's possible she thinks you won't make it back through this portal, and that's why she's refusing to go." Ronan came over to stand next to me. "Your wolf has had an uncanny ability to guide you since you arrived here. It's worth considering that even if this end of the portal lets you pass, you may not get through the mirror on the other side and end up trapped between worlds."

I thought of the dark, shade-filled nightmare I'd traversed on the way to this world and dropped my head into my hands. "I am not going to die here," I said.

Something clicked. I raised my head. "I'm *not* going to die here. Tura said I would die in my backyard back home. If she's right, that means I get back."

He made that angry rumbly noise. "Tura had no business telling you that."

"Did she lie to me about that the same way she lied about angels not being able to travel here?"

He was silent for a long time. "She didn't lie," he said finally. "You said her exact words were that you would 'soon make a journey through a door we cannot use, to a place we cannot go.'"

"Yes."

"You *did* go through a door angels can't use to a place they can't go. It just wasn't *this* one." He indicated the portal with a nod.

"Son of a *bitch*," I said. "She was talking about the Underworld, not the Broken World."

He nodded. "Only Fallen angels can travel to the Underworld."

"So why the hell didn't she come here and tell you the damn message herself?"

"She's forbidden to speak to me, by order of Michael." A muscle moved in his jaw. "And even if she *had* risked Michael's wrath, I haven't heeded any messages from my brothers and sisters in centuries. She foresaw that our journey would lead us to the Under-world, where I would make a pact with Charon to listen to a message. And she saw that you and I would grow close enough for me to accept delivery of the message."

"I guess being able to see the future comes in handy when you need to use a human as your personal Pony Express," I said, not without bitterness. "It's not the first time someone has lied to me without lying to me. Vampires are damn good at it too." I pressed my hands to my stomach. "If I can't get through the mirror-door, how the hell am I going to get back home so I can die in my backyard?"

A heavy silence.

I looked up. Ronan's expression was grave. Guilt twinged in my heart. "I'm sorry," I said, rising with difficulty. "This has nothing to do with you. You've gone above and beyond to get me here, and you risked your life to accompany us to the Underworld and join in a fight that wasn't really your fight, just because my stubborn wolf said you were supposed to. I'll figure out a way to get us home. It's not your problem." I gestured at Daisy and Esme. "*We* aren't your problem."

My little cat-dragon jumped up on the rock I'd been sitting on and stared up at Ronan with glittering emerald eyes.

"A very long time ago, I was called the Thunder of God," Ronan said, stroking the soft fur behind Esme's ears. Her purr grew as loud as a lion's. "I was a Watcher, an archangel who walked among humans. I commanded a legion of warriors when war demanded it. In times of peace, I was an archangel of hope who guided the souls of the faithful."

I thought of Charon, who guided souls in the Underworld, and wondered if that had made them colleagues of a sort. "So, how do you know Tura?"

"We shared a similar curse, though she never thought of it as such." His gaze seemed to go through me, to a place in the distant past. "Tura served me faithfully. She never lost her belief in me, not even after...all this time."

"You have the gift of prophecy?"

"Not since I jumped. Not if I can help it." His voice and expression hardened. "What use is a curse like foresight if the future can't be changed?"

I wondered if his fall—or jump—and the events that led to him being on Michael's shit list and his *persona non grata* status among even the Fallen were precipitated by an attempt to change the future.

"I can't pretend to know what it's like to be in your shoes, but I do know something about having a gift that's more of a curse." I raised my hand and spooled magic. "My own grandfather held me prisoner and tortured me for twenty years because he needed to control me and my power. Since I escaped, I've spent the last five trying to avoid being recaptured, bought, sold, and owned for it."

"I'm sorry."

"I'm not. My magic heals people now. I can protect the people I care about. And wolves, cat-dragons, Guardians, and fallen archangels too." I mustered a smile. "It's a curse, *and* it's a gift. Life is complicated like that."

He squeezed my hand. "I see what Tura saw: your death. I tried not to, but sometimes things slip through, especially when I feel close to someone. Which is a big reason why I avoid doing that."

I swallowed hard. "Okay."

He blinked. "Okay?" I guess despite his gift of foresight, he didn't see *that* response coming.

"It's okay that you saw it too. That still doesn't mean it's going to happen. And if I can't get back home, it obviously won't."

To my surprise, he spun away and sent a silver-blue fireball sizzling across the lower level of Northbourne. The blast hit the far wall. Broken rocks rained down from the hole the fireball made. The entire building shook.

"Well, it *definitely* won't happen if you bring this place down on our heads," I said dryly when the ruins stopped trembling. "What brought that on?"

He kept his back to me. "I can take you home." His voice was toneless.

"*What?*" I walked around him so I could see his face. His expression was like granite. "You can? Why the hell didn't you tell me that? Why did you let me think the mirror-door was my only way home?"

No response, but the flash of anger and guilt in his eyes told me the answer.

"Because you think if you take me home, I'll die in my backyard, and it will be your fault." I glared at him. "That is *not* your choice to make."

"I know."

I blew out a breath. "Tura told me there's a slim chance I might make a different path than the one she'd seen. Do you see that possibility too?"

He shook his head. "No. I don't know why she would have told you that. Giving someone false hope is cruel. I never knew Tura to be cruel."

"No, giving someone hope isn't cruel—it gives me something to fight for." I poked him in the chest again. "All I need is a chance. My life is proof of that. I'm going to take that slim chance and do something with it. And even if it doesn't work out in my favor, I'll have gone down fighting, having done everything I could."

"You are fierce, like the heart of a star," he said, surprising me by smiling. "If only you weren't human, and taken."

I smiled back. "I thought you weren't a gentleman."

"I'm not." He tucked a stray wisp of hair behind my ear. "But I'm not a bastard."

"You are certainly many things, but you aren't a bastard." I touched his hand. "Will you get us home?"

He took a deep breath. "Home to your world, to your house in the country?"

"Home to my world, and to right where this mirror comes out in that version of Northbourne. I want them to think I'm coming back through the mirror with the scroll."

"You'll need backup." His expression darkened. "They won't be happy when they find out you don't have it."

"I know, but I'll be fine." I hoped. "It would be great if you could just drop me off, so they have no idea I had help getting back."

He smiled—a truly predatory smile, much like the one I used from time to time. His was even better than mine. "I can be unseen if I choose to be," he reminded me.

"These are vampires. They've got more finely tuned senses than humans."

"Alice," he said patiently, "I'm an archangel. If I don't want someone to know I'm there, they won't. I won't interfere...unless things get out of hand."

"All right." I turned to Daisy. "Is this satisfactory, Your Highness?

We're getting an archangel escort home. Doesn't get any safer than that."

She growled agreeably.

"Okay then." I took a deep breath. "Come on home, then, Daisy-dog."

She took a couple of steps and launched herself at me, turning to golden magic in mid-leap.

We'd done this a half-dozen times, but never in the Broken World. Back home, she'd simply returned to my body in a surge of shifter magic and settled into my bones with the pleasant sensation of a puzzle piece finding its home.

This time, the experience was anything but pleasant.

When she hit my chest, the impact was only slightly less powerful than if she'd been completely solid. The only reason I didn't fly backward into the rocks was Ronan was standing behind me and caught me.

And when she passed through my flesh and returned to my body —oh holy hell, did it *hurt*.

My hoarse screams echoed in the ruins. Ronan held me as I doubled over. If I'd thought it hurt when Daisy had jumped out of me when we arrived, that was nothing compared to the agony of her return.

Finally, it was over.

Daisy? I asked tentatively, clutching my aching chest.

Sulking, her tail down and ears back, she retreated into the shadows in my head. Maybe she was upset because her return caused me so much pain, or maybe because she'd enjoyed her freedom and now felt confined. I didn't know the reason for her silence, and she clearly didn't want to talk to me.

Her golden magic gave my skin a light glow as it settled into my bones. The glow slowly faded. I rubbed my chest and straightened with a grimace.

"I'm sorry," Ronan said, releasing me.

"For what?" I wiped my nose on my dirty sleeve.

He helped me sit on the rock next to Esme. "I'm sorry you had to go through so much pain."

"It's not usually that bad, but this place…" I waved my hand. "It's messed with our magic and our bodies. Nothing works right."

"Then I should get you all home." He regarded Esme. "Do you need to ride along in Alice's backpack? Or can you travel with me?"

She put her ears back and made an indignant sound.

"I take that as a yes that she doesn't need to ride with you." He brought me my backpack and helped me put it on, fastening the straps across my chest and stomach. He put on his own pack and pulled me to my feet. "You ready?"

"Will this suck as much as when Tis and her sisters sent us away from Edis?" I asked.

"That was rough travel because of how quickly we had to be moved. Had there been less urgency, it wouldn't have been so hard on you. And just so you know, Tis and the others made it harder on Mariela than on you."

"I wondered why it took her so long to recover. See—I knew Tis was secretly cool."

Ronan snorted. "Lucky for you, she is."

"Lucky for you too, as it turned out." I picked Esme up. She jumped from my hands onto Ronan's shoulder. "I want to get back as soon as I can, but we can take enough time to make this a smooth ride. I have to deal with a vampire I'm pretty pissed at when we get where we're going, and I'd rather not make my entrance looking and feeling like shit."

"Well, I can't do much about how you look."

"Ass."

He wrapped his arms around me. I scowled. "Is this necessary?"

His wings erupted in a blaze of silver-blue magic that blinded me. His mouth brushed my ear. "You said you wanted a smooth ride," he murmured.

Before I could retort, the ground fell away from our feet, and we were gone.

CHAPTER 31

Flying Ronan Airlines was indeed a *very* smooth ride. I made a mental note never to say that sentence aloud when Sean or Malcolm might overhear it.

Instead of an out-of-control tumble through an airless magical riptide, we caught what felt like an ocean current and followed it past dark regions that might have been other worlds, or just my brain playing tricks on me. I wasn't entirely sure if I was actually seeing *anything* while we were inside the current. I certainly couldn't see Ronan, though I felt his arms around me holding tight. I might have even dozed a bit, since the journey was so tranquil.

The landing, on the other hand, was another thing altogether.

In Ronan's defense, I'd made it clear I wanted the vamps to think I'd come out of the mirror, and mirror travelers did not land gracefully or smoothly when they arrived on the other side.

With no warning, and absolutely no control over what my body was doing, I shot out of the peaceful ocean current into familiar-smelling air. I dropped like a rock and landed face-first on what felt like a very expensive rug covering a stone floor. Ow.

With a groan, I rolled to my side. I knew before I opened my eyes that I was home. The ambient magic of my world was unmistakable. Home, home, home. My magic, partially tuned to the Broken World, surged and re-tuned itself. I exhaled in a long sigh and unbuckled my backpack. Sean would sense my return through our bond, I hoped, and know I was alive and home.

The knot of death magic twinged sharply. I wrapped my arms around my stomach, opened my eyes, and stared.

I'd expected to land in the same room I'd departed from in the lower level of Northbourne. Clearly they'd moved the mirror to a room I'd never been in before.

From my vantage point on the floor, I saw stone walls bare except for alcoves where candles burned, a low ceiling, and a tall bed. Over the bed, the ceiling was painted with a mural of two dark-haired women sitting at a table holding cups of wine. An arched doorway to my left led to what looked like a closet filled with dresses and evening gowns. Another led to a bathroom as large as this room, with a small swimming pool in the middle. Or maybe that was the tub.

Other than the elaborate bathroom, the suite was very plain and smelled of a hundred ancient scents I'd recognized instinctively even before my eyes and brain processed the room and its contents. Valas.

They'd moved the mirror to Valas's rooms. That told me a lot—most especially that she wanted to be waiting if and when I returned with the scroll. I didn't see or sense Ronan or Esme anywhere, but I had to assume they were here, hidden by some kind of glamour.

A familiar man wearing enforcer black leaned over me. "Ms. Worth?"

I coughed and struggled to sit up. "Matthias."

He surprised me by offering his hand. I waved him back and staggered to my feet, making no effort to hide how difficult it was for me to rise. I looked like hell, so it should be easy to fool them into thinking I was in bad shape. Okay, *worse* shape. I might need all the advantages I could get.

As it turned out, I was in far, far better shape than the woman on the bed.

"Oh, shit," I breathed.

At first, I saw only Valas's lower torso, legs, and arms, since her shoulders and head were hidden by the woman whose throat she was drinking from. Though she faced away from me, I recognized Niara, another member of the Vampire Court, from her signature brightly colored dress and elaborately styled hair. She was leaning over Valas, almost lying across her upper body, presumably because Valas could not lift her own head from her pillow to drink.

Valas's body was covered by her dress, but her hands and forearms were visible—or what was left of them. Most of her hands and part of her arms had turned to ash, and the flesh that remained was black. The way the dress lay flat on the bed indicated parts of her legs and torso had crumbled to ash as well. She was dying slowly, an inch at a time. Probably the only reason she'd lasted until I came back was by drinking from the other members of the Court. If we'd taken just a day or two more—or our net time in the Underworld had been longer than two weeks—I would have been too late.

Despite everything Valas had done to me, my stomach contracted. Our relationship had always been difficult. From the moment I'd realized she'd allowed Miraç to kidnap and torture me and use me as his puppet, I'd felt little more than hate and fury. And when she trapped me in the Broken World, I'd decided enough was most definitely enough.

That anger didn't go away, but my plan for what to do now had to change.

Matthias stepped between me and the bed. "Give her a moment," he said in an undertone.

I turned away and reached for the familiar buzzing of Malcolm's magic in my arm cuff. "*Release,*" I murmured.

Malcolm appeared next to me. He drifted back and forth and looked down at himself. His face fell at the sight of his translucent body. My heart ached for him.

He touched my arm. *Damn, it's good to be home, but I'm going to miss being a real boy,* he said in my head. *And this is so not what we expected to find waiting for us.*

We figured something wasn't right and she needed the scroll badly, I reminded him. *I just didn't think it was* this *bad.*

So what's your plan now? he asked.

I'm rethinking things a bit, but bottom line, I'm still here to settle a score. In the meantime, I need you to jump to Sean and tell him we're home, where I am, and that I'll get home to him as soon as I'm done here.

Malcolm frowned. *I don't want you to face Valas by yourself.*

I'm not by myself.

He raised his eyebrows and looked around again. *Our feathery friend is here somewhere?*

Yes, he's here. Please go to Sean. I need him to know I'm here and I'm safe and I'm coming home. Tell him I'm sorry I didn't tell him where we went and I'll tell him everything when I get home. Then go see Liam.

Are you sure? He plainly didn't like the idea of leaving me here.

I'm sure. I have a score to settle.

I have a score to settle too, he reminded me.

I know. I'll get justice for us both.

He glanced at my abdomen. *And what about that?*

Later. First things first: Sean and Liam, and Valas. Then I'll deal with this mess.

He didn't look happy. *Okay. Summon me if you need me.*

I will, I promised.

He vanished.

My stomach twinged again—this time, with hunger. I had some protein bars left from the last waystation stop I'd made with Ronan before we got to the portal home. Valas was still drinking from Niara, so I got two bars from my backpack and ate them quickly. Normally seeing a vampire feed would have taken away any appetite I had, but this wasn't just any hunger gnawing at my insides.

I washed the bars down with the last of the water in my

Hawthorne's bottle. The metal bottle had collected a few dents on its travels, but it was quite a souvenir. I stuck it back in the bag.

Niara's dark skin had developed a gray tone. Valas had drunk more from her than was safe—far more.

Niara started to pull away and flinched. I heard a sibilant hiss. Valas wasn't letting her go. Niara would have to tear herself free of Valas's enormous fangs unless Valas would retract them.

"Valas, I'm here," I said, hoping she could hear me. "I'm back with the scroll. Let Niara go. I can heal you."

Valas hissed again. Niara finally moved back and slid to the edge of the bed. Her throat was badly torn. "Thank you," she said hoarsely. In her desperate need for life-sustaining blood, Valas had damaged Niara's vocal cords.

I barely heard Niara. Half of Valas's face and one eye were gone, leaving only grayish-white bone and an empty socket. Most of her lips were gone, and one cheek, revealing her teeth and extended fangs. Blood streaked her skull, jaw, and remaining skin.

No way in hell Valas was moving from that bed, but she still had power and magic. How much she could wield in this condition, I wasn't sure.

Somewhere, Malcolm was talking to Sean and reassuring him we'd returned. I hadn't realized how much strength that knowledge would give me until right now, as I stood in Valas's room, facing the grim reality of her condition and that I had no scroll with which to heal her. I could deal with this as long as Sean knew I was back.

Niara made her way unsteadily to the door. Matthias opened it and ushered her into the hall, where her head of security, Nadya, waited. He closed the door behind her. Wards buzzed on my skin.

"Ver issssss it?" Valas hissed. "I do not sense the sssss...scroll."

"I'm here, and you locked the door so I couldn't get back without it," I pointed out, dodging the question. "Help me understand what's happening to you."

"Do not need...to under...stand." Every word was difficult for her to say. "Bring...scroll."

"We need to talk about a couple of things first." I took a step toward the bed.

Matthias moved to intercept me. At the same time, I caught movement out of the corner of my eye near the doorway to the closet: a flash of a dark figure, part solid and part smoke. A familiar terrible odor hit my nose. Vlad. I might have known he'd be here to protect Valas when she was this vulnerable. He snarled at me.

And then he vanished into thin air. Yay, Ronan.

Matthias's head whipped around when Vlad disappeared. I took advantage of the distraction and touched his hand. *"Sleep,"* I commanded.

Matthias had a little bit of magic, but only a trace—not enough to resist my spell. He hit the floor in a heap, unconscious.

Valas's remaining eye silvered. Dark magic rose, but only a fraction of what I'd felt from her before.

I pushed blood magic edged with death magic from my fingertips to form a blade and held it to her throat. Some of it had turned to ash, and I could see part of her spine.

"Don't call for reinforcements, or you'll die right here and now," I told her. "I'm not here to kill you unless you force my hand."

"Who is with you?" she demanded.

"A friend I met in the Broken World. He's just keeping Vlad on ice until you and I settle our business." At least, I hoped that was what Ronan was doing with Valas's pet and he hadn't already dispatched the creep.

Valas glared up at me with her good eye. "We...made...bargain."

"I know we had a bargain, and I held up my end of it, mostly." I kept the blade at her throat, unwilling to trust her without the threat of immediate permanent death a centimeter from her spine. "I found Mariela and kept her from coming back with the Furies—or the Titan Typhon and the goddess Ammit, Devourer of Hearts."

Her eye widened.

"Yeah, things got a little crazy over there," I said. "It's a really long story. I'll tell you all about it someday, maybe. Unfortunately, I couldn't bring Mariela back. She ended up on the wrong end of a spell she threw at me, and she's goop now on a dusty plain in the Underworld. You'll just have to take my word for that, I guess."

A small vial landed on the bed near me.

I picked it up with my non-bladed hand and wiggled the stopper. A horrendous smell drifted out. I gagged and pushed the stopper back in. "Seriously?" I demanded. "You brought back a vial of Mariela goop?"

No answer.

I set the vial back on the bed. "Fine. Here's proof she's dead. She caused the deaths of hundreds of people—men, women, and children. So the fact she stole from you ended up the least of her sins."

"Sssssssss...*scroll*," Valas hissed.

"Yes, the scroll. Mariela destroyed it. There's nothing left but a few scraps of papyrus and part of the spindle. I'm sorry."

Valas's dark magic hit me square in the chest and sent me flying. I braced for impact against the stone wall, but sea-scented magic caught me and set me on my feet.

She grunted. A dagger protruded from her abdomen, pulsing with familiar silver-blue magic. She strained, but apparently the blade prevented her from throwing more magic at me.

"Thanks," I muttered to Ronan, wherever he was. "Seriously, stop with the Casper the Stabby Ghost stuff, though."

Again, I got no response.

I returned to the bed. "Look, damn it, I said I wasn't here to kill you," I told her. "I mean, I thought about it when you sent me through that mirror-door and then locked it behind me. I can see you needed the scroll badly, but you should have just told me that instead of condemning me to a slow death over there and cutting me off from Sean. That was pretty shitty, even for you. I went over there in good faith to do a job for you, and you fucked me over, *again*."

I leaned on the bed and stared down at her. "This was a result of Miraç's curses, wasn't it?" I said, gesturing at her crumbling body. "He hit you with some really bad magic that night in the garden.

That's why you suddenly needed that scroll back—it had spells that would heal you."

"Yesssssss."

I'd hoped as much, because that meant we could make a new bargain—one that would change everything between us.

"Tell me why I should care right now whether you live or die," I said. "Don't bother threatening me. Tell me why you're worth saving."

Malcolm would be pissed at me for asking her that. Sean too. They'd both say I was too kind, that I let her condition get to me, and maybe they were right. But I wasn't here for vengeance; I was here for justice.

She was quiet for a long time. At first I thought she couldn't talk any longer. "Kill Murphy," she rasped finally.

"It's my job to kill Moses Murphy. Give me a better reason."

She hissed. I waited.

"Release...bond."

Release me from our binding. Now we were getting somewhere. "Keep going."

Dark magic flared and faded. The dagger pulsed.

"No...retaliation," she ground out.

"There better not be," I warned. "Not against me or anyone I'm associated with. Not directly or indirectly."

"Yes."

I made a rolling gesture with my hand.

"Independent...for life," she said.

"You said other members of the Court and employees didn't like that I was an independent contractor," I reminded her.

Her mouth twitched into a nightmarish half-smile. "Will decree."

"Fine. I want all this in writing and duly witnessed."

"Yes." A shudder ran through her. "Please," she whispered. "Afraid."

I couldn't imagine Valas being afraid of anything. My skepticism must have shown on my face. "Something waits..." she rasped. "I fear it."

Her words had the unmistakable ring of true belief. Was it possible the mighty Valas worried about the ultimate destination of her soul?

"I'm sorry I didn't get to bring the scroll back," I told her, and I meant it. "It was a priceless artifact. I'm mad as hell at you, but I have no desire to see you die like this." I leaned over her again so she could see my eyes and know I spoke the truth. "I've never given you reason to think I'd screw you over in this deal. What you did was cruel and I didn't deserve it. Neither did Malcolm, for that matter."

She said nothing.

"I don't expect you to say you're sorry. You wouldn't mean it anyway. I want you to remember I had absolutely no obligation to save you, but I'm going to try anyway."

Her eye moved to look past me. "Come...for my...soul?" she asked.

I glanced over my shoulder and saw the faint outline of a winged figure edged with silver-blue fire.

"Not today, Sala Veli," Ronan said, his voice that of a hundred people speaking at once. "However, if you renege on your agreement with Alice, I *will* return, and no magic or army will stop me."

Dang. I'd wanted to settle things with Valas myself and on my terms, but as threats went, that one wasn't bad.

"Agreed," she whispered. She looked back at me. "Please...heal."

I held my hand over her body. Foul, black sorcerer magic writhed under her skin. Not long ago, I'd found the sensation acutely nauseating. Now, it was a familiar feeling, and uncomfortably close to normal.

I closed my eyes and sank into the layers of spellwork that formed the curses. They were truly diabolical. Miraç had designed them to destroy Valas's body slowly but keep her mind unharmed and clear to the very end, to maximize her suffering. His hatred was woven into every thread of the curse. He'd wanted to make certain that even if he failed to kill her that night in the garden, Valas would die in agony in retaliation for what she'd done to her sister Kassia, his lover from more than a century ago.

I opened my eyes and glanced up at the mural of the sisters—the sight Valas would see each dawn before she slept and each evening when she woke. Charles had a painting of a sunrise above his bed.

"You and Kassia?" I asked, gesturing at the mural.

A tiny nod.

"How long have you had a painting of you two above your bed?"

"Ssssss…centuries," she said.

I closed my eyes, rested my hand on Valas's skeletal chest, and let my dark magic rise. With it, I began to pull apart the spellwork of the curse.

I didn't get far in my unweaving when magic flared and sent a bolt of power through me. I recognized a landmine hidden in the spellwork.

Valas sucked in a sharp breath that rattled in her chest. A small, agonized sound escaped her fleshless lips as her entire left arm turned to ash.

The landmine lashed at me, but I carried Miraç's own magic and it did little more than cause pain.

Screw you, Miraç, I thought savagely. *You're not killing either of us today.*

Forget unweaving the spellwork; there was no time. The landmine had accelerated the progress of the curse and Valas would be nothing but ash in seconds. I spooled blood magic and dark magic and grabbed the curses. Ripping them from her body with brute force might kill her, but the curses and the landmines certainly would.

Valas screamed when I tore the curses out. I was still angry enough at her that I couldn't help but enjoy the sound, just a little.

Spellwork fractured, the landmines detonated, and black magic flared like a star going nova, scouring my skin. That pain was quickly eclipsed by agony in my stomach. The knot of death magic ruptured, spilling its poison into the rest of my body.

I fell onto my back on the bed. My vision tunneled. The roaring in my ears drowned out everything else. Suddenly, I felt as if my body was made of stone. My heartbeat stuttered in my chest. My body was shutting down.

I was supposed to die in my backyard.

I was supposed to get a chance to decide between my life and Sean's.

I wasn't supposed to die at Northbourne, saving Valas's undead life.

Or maybe I was. Since when did I believe in Tura's stupid prophecy, anyway?

A familiar foul odor filled my nose, and a face that wasn't a face appeared above me. Vlad. How the hell did he get away from Ronan? I tried to spool magic to defend myself, but neither my muscles nor my magic would obey my commands.

The smell of the sea cut through Vlad's stench. Cool fingers brushed my forehead. *He has the power to save you,* Ronan said in my head.

I recalled Tom's words when I'd asked if he knew what could cut the dark magic from my body: *It requires dark power to take dark power.* There was no power I knew darker than Vlad's—and no one in the room I trusted less.

Don't let him touch me. My words were little more than a wisp.

"I obey no one but my maker," Vlad snarled.

Ronan's reply was cold. "Your maker only lives because Alice saved her. Therefore, you owe Alice a blood debt. And you *will* obey me, for I know your true name. If you fail or harm her, I will deliver you to the bowels of Hell myself."

Vlad hissed. Fire sliced across my belly. I screamed. Claws raked through my insides, scooping out the poisonous death magic and taking with it Miraç's black magic and power too.

I tried to fight back to keep Vlad from stealing my dark magic. I needed that power. I needed it to kill Moses and protect myself and our pack from anyone who tried to hurt us. Without it, I wasn't strong enough.

You're wrong, Ronan told me. *You are enough. You've always been enough, and you always will be.*

Daisy, I thought desperately. *She was born of this magic. If he takes it, she may die.*

She won't, he promised. *Your wolf is not so fragile as that.*

Vlad's claws ripped through me again and again. I had to be nearly in pieces. No blade or magic could cut this black magic out of me, but his claws could. Saved by a vampire warlock. That was certainly a new one.

I refused to give into the temptation to fade into merciful oblivion, because I feared I would never wake.

Finally, when it was over, I ached as if Vlad had scooped out every organ, bone, and bit of flesh and left just a husk behind. I had no sensation anywhere except for a vague, dull emptiness.

Now get out, Ronan commanded.

Vlad snarled. The stench and disturbing sensation of his presence faded.

I opened my eyes.

As my vision cleared, I found myself staring up at the mural over Valas's bed and noticed a detail I'd missed earlier. Valas and her sister were smiling at each other over their glasses of wine. They appeared to be seated at a table in a garden in front of a villa. Given what I knew about Valas and Kassia's troubled history, was this a memory of a long-ago happy moment, or a fantasy of a sisterly meal? Either way, it must bring Valas some happiness to see it daily. And if Valas still sought happiness, that was worth something.

The sickening sensation of the knot of death magic had faded and taken with it the terrible gnawing hunger. Trembling, I raised my head and looked at my stomach. My shirt was soaked with my blood. When I pulled it up to bare my abdomen, however, my skin was intact. I couldn't sense any death magic or sorcerer power anymore. I missed its potency and power. I should be glad to be rid of it, but I wasn't. Not yet.

Now Vlad had all that power instead. What were the odds that wouldn't bite me in the ass at some point?

I pushed myself up into a sitting position. Vlad was nowhere to be seen or smelled. Neither was Ronan. Matthias was still out cold on the floor.

Valas hissed quietly. She still had only one eye, but her flesh was growing back. Her fangs were out, and her eye was fully black. She was starving and in desperate need of blood to heal. And here I sat, inches away, covered in blood. I had no idea how much strength it took to hold herself back. That level of control was almost scarier than if she'd vamped out.

"Hungry," she rasped. "Send food, and get out."

She didn't have to tell me twice. I woke Matthias and told him his boss needed a couple of square meals. Then I grabbed my back-pack and got the hell out of that room.

Carlos was waiting for me in the corridor. He didn't even blink at my appearance. "Hello again, Ms. Worth. Madame Valas has instructed me to escort you to the garage and provide you with transportation." He held out his hand for my pack.

"Thank you. I've got it." I put the pack on my shoulders and followed him down the hall, through a set of doors, down another corridor, and through a wide steel door that led to one of North-bourne's several enormous garages.

"Take your pick," Carlos said, making a sweeping gesture.

The smell of the sea drifted past my nose.

I scanned the neat rows of luxury vehicles, SUVs, and sports cars, and pointed. "I'll take that one."

Carlos raised his eyebrows. "The keys are in the ignition. Enjoy."

"Oh, I will," I assured him.

Halfway across the garage floor, Ronan fell into step beside me, his bag on his back and Esme perched on his shoulder. Out of the corner of my eye, I saw Carlos twitch, but he didn't demand an explanation or come after us. Valas must have warned him I had company.

Something popped in my head with a sizzle of magic and pain. I stumbled. Ronan caught my arm. "Alice?"

For a moment, I wasn't sure what had happened. Something was missing from my brain, leaving behind a cold emptiness and echoes of gray-and-black magic. The link to Valas that had occupied a corner of my mind since the night Miraç used me as a puppet to attack her in the gardens of Northbourne was gone.

Valas had severed our binding. I hadn't been sure she would, until this moment.

The black magic I'd never wanted, and feared would turn me into a monster before it killed me, was gone too. I'd settled my debt with Valas. I'd never have to darken the doorstep of Northbourne again.

I was free.

"I'm fine." I smiled up at Ronan. "Care to give me a ride home?"

CHAPTER 32

I summoned Malcolm as Ronan and I were leaving Northbourne and found out Sean wasn't at his house, but at our new farmhouse. My ghost was horrified at my appearance, then ecstatic to discover I was rid of both the sorcerer power and the death magic I'd picked up in the Underworld.

He hadn't yet checked in with Liam, so he zipped off to let Sean know I was on my way before heading out to the bordello. I hoped he and Liam could patch things up.

I settled in for the ride home on the back of the Vampire Court's biggest, baddest Harley, with my arms around Ronan's waist and Esme in my backpack. Ronan followed the directions on the GPS on the Harley's dash, letting me ride quietly and adjust. The drive from Northbourne to our new house only took about twenty-five minutes, but I could have sworn it took longer than the train ride to Edis.

My little corner of the world was just as I'd left it, but it felt different somehow. Seeing Northbourne in all its glory and full of people was surprisingly jarring, as was the amount of traffic on the roads at two in the morning. I found myself watching the roadsides for strange creatures and unexpected dangers, and wondered how long I'd do that before it wasn't a habit anymore.

I was so happy to be home, I barely noticed how much my body ached. I was hungry, thirsty, and tired, but only in a normal way— not the gnawing feeling caused by the sorcerer magic.

So this is what you're like when you're happy, Ronan said in my head when we were about ten minutes away from the farmhouse. *I like it.*

Don't get fooled into thinking I'm all sunshine and rainbows, I warned him.

He snorted. *You're* all *sunshine and rainbows tonight, woman,* he told me. When I started to argue, he added, *As well you should be, returning victorious from battle to the man you love. You slayed your enemies—now pour the wine.*

I couldn't argue with that.

We made the final turn onto the road where the farmhouse was. My heart thudded in my ears, and I could barely breathe. I spotted lights up ahead in the darkness. Sean had installed a fence along the road, and a gate. It was open.

The long driveway was lined with small solar-powered lights. Several unfamiliar vehicles were parked off to the side of the driveway next to Sean's Maclin Security SUV. My eyes were on the man standing in the front yard watching us come up the drive.

Ronan slowed as we approached the house. I took off my helmet and handed it to him. Before he was even fully stopped, I jumped from the back of the Harley, left my backpack on the ground, and ran.

In a Pink Floyd T-shirt I'd bought him and jeans, Sean met me halfway across the yard. I would never forget the way he looked at me as long as I lived: worry, relief, happiness, love, and so much heat that I felt it all the way to my soul.

I leaped into his arms, wrapped my legs around his hips, and kissed him hard.

He held me with his hands under my butt and kissed me back, his mouth hungry and demanding. His stubble scoured the skin around my lips. He smelled like forest and wolf and wildness and home.

When we came up for air, his eyes were bright gold. "I love you."

I rested my forehead on his. "Love you too."

He squeezed my butt. "You're a mess, and you stink."

"Oh, God, I know." I let out a half-laugh, half-sob. "I'm sorry. I haven't showered since—"

I was silenced by his mouth on mine.

The next time we broke apart, I noticed the front door had opened and an unfamiliar older man and woman had appeared on the porch. We had an audience. I hadn't thought twice about jumping into Sean's arms in front of Ronan, but Sean had company.

I wiggled to let him know I wanted down. With obvious reluctance, he set me on my feet.

I turned to introduce Ronan, only to find the driveway empty. Esme sat next to my backpack, washing her paw.

Sean growled. Shifter magic prickled on my skin. "Where did he go?"

"Ronan?" I called.

Silence.

"Don't take off until we have a chance to talk, okay?" I added. "Or at least until I can say goodbye."

Still no answer. I sighed. "Well, maybe he'll come back at some point. He does this sort of thing a lot. It's complicated. I'll explain after I've showered and gotten something to eat. And some coffee."

Sean went to get my backpack. Esme hissed at him. He glanced back at me, brow furrowed. "Is this yours? Do we have a cat now?"

"That's Esme. Yes, she's my...uh, cat."

He put my bag on his shoulder, rejoined me, and took my hand. "Let me guess: that's complicated too."

"*Super* complicated," I confirmed.

"Does she need to come inside?"

"Nah, she'll be fine."

"There are coyotes around," he warned.

I smiled. "Trust me—she'll be fine."

Sean kissed the tip of my nose. "Come on, then. There are some people here I'd like you to meet."

I looked down at my bloody, filthy clothes. "Are you serious?" I demanded under my breath. "Can't I clean up first?"

"They've already seen you," he pointed out. "And you wouldn't want to give them the wrong impression by being all clean and dressed up, would you? Not when this is more like how you normally look."

I glared at him. He chuckled and squeezed my hand.

As we climbed the front steps, the older man held out his hand. "Want me to get that bag?"

I expected Sean to say no. Instead, he surprised me by handing it over. "Thanks, Dad."

I froze in mid-step.

Fighting back a grin, Sean slid his hand around my waist and pulled me up to the porch. "Mom, Dad, this is Alice. Alice, my parents, Les and Rita."

I would kill him. I would absolutely one hundred percent *kill him*. And Malcolm hadn't warned me either, that jerk. He was *super* dead.

Les and Rita were both in their late sixties and gray haired. Despite the hour, they were fully dressed, as if they'd stayed up to talk with their son. Like Sean, Les had crinkles at the corners of his eyes when he smiled, and Rita was checking me over for visible injuries. To my surprise, I instinctively liked them—a far cry from the abject terror I'd always felt at the prospect of finally meeting Sean's parents.

"Hello there, Alice," Les said warmly. "Sean told us you're a mage private investigator. This case you're working on must be a doozy." He held out his hand.

My hand was as dirty and bloody as the rest of me. I glanced at my palm dubiously, then at Les's outstretched hand.

"I'm not afraid of a little dirt and blood," Les said, his dark brown eyes twinkling. "I'm a farmer and our son's a werewolf."

I wiped my hand on my pants, but that made it *more* dirty, not less. I shook his calloused hand. "It's great to finally meet you," I managed to say.

Rita elbowed her husband. "Let the poor girl go inside and get cleaned up. She's got to be miserable." She held out her hand. "Hi, Alice. My goodness, you look like a warrior, back from the battlefield."

The scent of sea drifted past my nose. Ronan was lurking around somewhere and probably laughing his fine feathered ass off.

I hid my free hand behind my back and extended my middle finger. The sea scent swirled, then vanished.

Sean frowned. He must have caught Ronan's scent. Before he could say anything, another man appeared in the front doorway. He wore a plaid shirt, jeans, and hiking boots.

I stared. "*Daniel?*"

His bright gold eyes met mine, and he smiled just a little. "Welcome back," my father said.

My mouth opened and closed like a fish.

Sean finally took pity on me. "I think Alice needs a shower, some food, and a stiff drink."

"Not necessarily in that order," Les added with a smile. "Whisky, anyone?"

When we went inside, I found out Sean had sold his house and moved us into the farmhouse while I was gone. My house still needed to be sold, but he'd moved my furniture and combined it with his own to furnish the new place. He'd also painted the rooms the colors we'd picked out before I left and set up the downstairs office with two work areas: one for himself, and one for me.

And he'd done it all without knowing if I would ever come back, because he believed I would.

It was too much to process in front of the others. I scratched Rogue's head, let him sniff me, and then excused myself and took my backpack upstairs to the master suite. My clothes were so disgusting, the only appropriate thing to do was burn them. I stuffed everything into a black trash bag, shoved it into a corner in the bathroom, and got in the shower with the bottle of Charles's finest moonshine.

I shampooed my hair twice. Then I scrubbed and scrubbed and scrubbed my body, washing away layers of blood, ash, dirt, grime, and goop. And in between soaping and rinsing, I took swigs of moonshine.

Already I felt as though the whole experience was some kind of nightmare. For crying out loud, thirty-six hours ago, I was fighting for my life in the Underworld. Two hours ago, I tore curses out of Valas and nearly died from death magic. Now I was home in the farmhouse I was going to share with Sean, and his parents *and my father* were downstairs, drinking whisky and chatting like old friends.

I slid down the wall, sat on the floor of the shower with the bottle, and pulled my knees up to my chest.

That was how Sean found me when he finally came looking for me. He left his clothes in a pile on the floor outside the shower and sat on the tile beside me.

"You smell better," he said, lacing his fingers through mine.

I rested my head on his shoulder.

"My parents went home," he told me. "They were going to stay over, but they figured we needed time to talk. Daniel's gone out to walk around the property. He's been staying here for about a week, in the guest room."

I had so many questions, not the least of which was why Daniel was here and why he'd changed his mind about staying with us, but that would have to wait.

"I'm sorry," I said.

He kissed the top of my head. "For what?"

"Everything." I raised my face to look at him, my tears mixing with the water from the shower spray. "Every fucking thing I've done that wasn't fair to you. Running off to do this job for Valas without telling you where I was going. Letting Charles mess with my head. Forcing you to work so hard to make this relationship work because I make everything so damn difficult. And a million other things I wish I could change about myself."

He cupped my face with his hand. "I know you feel that you owe me an apology, so I accept it, but please believe me when I say I don't need or want you to apologize for any of those things. And I don't want you to change one bit."

"But I *have* changed." I bit my lip. "The sorcerer power is gone. No more powerful dark magic. I'm just Alice again."

He brushed my cheek with his thumb. "You were never *just* Alice. You are wonderful, beautiful, powerful, perfect Alice."

I rolled my eyes. "You're laying it on a bit thick, aren't you?"

He smiled. The corners of his eyes crinkled. "I thought maybe if I played my cards right, I might get lucky later."

"Only if you feed me and make me coffee first."

He kissed me. "And after you tell me what happened when you went through the mirror."

I stilled.

"I read your letter the day you left." His expression hardened. "I had to know."

"You deserved to know. I'm glad you read it." I squeezed his hand. "I hadn't even gone through the mirror before I realized I'd made a huge mistake by not telling you the truth. I worried I wouldn't make it back so I could tell you that." I bumped his shoulder with mine. "Thank you for getting the house ready. I'm sorry you had to do it by yourself."

"I didn't," he said, surprising me. "The whole pack helped. All seventeen members."

"*Seventeen?*"

"Counting the Hayes brothers and the four provisional members you need to meet before we formally bring them into the pack." He kissed my knuckles. "We're going to be stronger than we've ever been."

"What about your sorcerer power?" I asked.

He smiled. "It's gone. Without yours to feed from, every time I shifted, it faded. And I'm glad it's gone. We don't need it."

"We don't," I agreed. I'd feared losing that power meant I would be vulnerable, but that was the black magic's influence talking. We were strong together, Sean and I, and we didn't need Miraç's poisonous legacy.

He rose and pulled me to my feet. His warm hand slid down my side to rest on the curve of my hip. "Let's get dressed, go find Daniel, and have a meal. Then you get to choose: sleep, tell me about your trip, or make love for the first time in our new home. Or any combination of the above."

"Not for the *first* time," I pointed out, shutting off the spray and reaching for a towel. "There was that time on the floor in the living room, that time in the kitchen, that time in the backyard, that time in the *front* yard—"

He kissed me hard. "Point taken. The first time in our bed in our new home, then."

"Of those three choices, I like that option the best."

His smile warmed me all the way down to my toes. "Me too."

SEAN DRESSED QUICKLY and went downstairs to make us something to eat. As I combed and braided my hair, I tried talking to Daisy again,

but she'd retreated into a dark corner of my mind and still didn't respond. I didn't sense anything wrong, so I gave her some space. I put on a T-shirt, yoga pants, and flip-flops and hurried to the main floor.

I found Rogue sprawled on his bed in the living room and Sean in the kitchen, putting a casserole in the oven. "Nan brought some of these," he told me as I slipped my arms around his waist from behind. "Handy for quick meals. Just heat and eat."

"She is an amazing person." I squeezed him. "Any more challengers since I left?"

"Two. They regretted it pretty quickly." He raised my hand to his mouth and kissed my knuckles. "I doubt there will be many more. The word's gotten out."

"And the Council?"

"Still pissed. I'm not worried about it."

"Yes you are."

He chuckled. "Maybe a little. I think they sense that attitudes among shifters are changing and certain members of the Council will always resist change. I don't mind being the pack that blazes new trails and makes pack culture better for more shifters. We have a lot of support among other packs in the area."

I leaned against the counter. "Why is Daniel here?"

He turned serious. "That is a conversation you'll need to have with him. You've got a lot to learn about each other."

"I read Cyro's file on him," I reminded him.

"There's a lot more to a man like Daniel than what's in a file. He's been a lone wolf for thirty years. I'm not sure he'll ever want to join any pack again, even ours, or stay with us long term, but he's here now." He squeezed my hand. "We've got a while before the casserole is ready. Let's go find him. He'll be out back somewhere."

"What's he watching for?"

"Anything and everything. He's restless."

"Even with you here?"

"Lone wolf physiology and psychology are different. An alpha's presence isn't the reassuring and calming influence it is for pack wolves. It's better if we give each other space." He laced our fingers together. "Come on. It's beautiful out there."

We went out the back door. Sean had gotten the deck repaired where Vlad had damaged it, and bought a new grill. The chaise lounges and table from my back porch were already set out. Esme was curled up on one of the lounges. She opened her eyes when we came outside and hissed at Sean, then went into the house in search of food or a more comfortable place to sleep.

"I'll let you choose our outdoor furniture," Sean said as we walked down the steps to the backyard. "I started looking, but there are a lot of options and I figured you had preferences."

"I'm looking forward to picking some out. We'll need a *lot* of outdoor seating for everyone."

Four in the morning in the country had its own scent: the chill of night, dew on the grass, and a hundred more smells not found in the city. The sky was clear and the breeze was warm.

Hand in hand, Sean and I wandered away from the house, across freshly mowed grass. In the distance, I saw the lights of a nearby house through the trees. I made a mental note to warn Esme not to eat the neighbors' pets or livestock. Or fly past their windows in dragon form.

Sean halted us and wrapped his arms around me, his face turned skyward. "I haven't slept well since you left. Sometimes I shifted and went running here or on the pack land. Other nights, I walked around, looking up at the stars and wondering if you saw the same ones where you were."

I looked up at the sky. "I honestly don't know if they were the same or not. I'd like to think they were."

His arms tightened around me. "What was that place like?"

"A lot like this one. Beautiful in many ways. Scary and dangerous too. Good people, bad people. All kinds of supernatural creatures everywhere. Not much air travel because of the dragons, obviously."

"Obviously," he said dryly.

I chuckled. "Also, there's a Charles over there. He owns a roadhouse called Hawthorne's. He wears jeans and T-shirts and smokes."

Sean blinked.

"And he drinks moonshine and domestic beer," I added.

He scoffed. "Now I *know* you're pulling my leg."

"I knew you wouldn't believe me, but it's true. Ronan will confirm it, if he turns up." I glanced around, but I didn't see any sign of him or smell the telltale scent of his magic.

Sean's chest rumbled. "Who is this Ronan?"

"A bounty hunter. He's good with a sword." I kissed his chest. "He was bummed I'm taken. And human."

He slid his hand down to rest on my butt. "And what is he?"

I made a face.

"Let me guess." He smiled. "It's super complicated."

"Not necessarily super complicated, but it's not my secret to tell."

He cupped my face with his hand and looked into my eyes. "I sense your wolf has retreated. Is she all right? Did she try to come out while you were over there?"

I laughed. He frowned.

"She came out, all right," I said when I stopped laughing. "And she stayed out for the entire time I was there. Her name's Daisy now, by the way." My smile faded. "She won't talk to me right now. I'm giving her time. She may just be upset that she's cooped up again. She got used to freedom."

He didn't reply for a long time. I couldn't tell what he was thinking.

"What?" I asked.

He shook his head. "I'm still processing the fact you named your wolf Daisy."

"Don't blame me; Malcolm picked the name. She seems to like it, though." I glanced around. "So, where is Daniel?"

Sean nodded toward the far back corner of our property. "Back there, in human form. He saw us and is headed this way."

His sight was far better than mine. I couldn't see anything but darkness that far from the house lights. We'd stopped about fifty yards from the deck, in an area that had been tall grass before Sean had it mowed.

The back of my neck prickled. I shivered.

"Getting cold?" Sean asked. "We can wait for him inside."

I glanced down at our feet, looked back at the house, and stilled.

We were standing in the exact spot where Tura had told me I would die soon, where she'd said I would have to make a choice between my life or Sean's. But there was never a choice to be made, as far as I was concerned.

A sudden, perfect calm settled over me. I turned toward the trees that lined the back of our property, in the direction I thought someone was watching us.

Sean's eyes turned bright gold. "What's wrong?"

"I love you," I told him.

I struck him in the chest with my palms. Air magic flared bright white and sent him flying back a good twenty feet and hopefully out of danger. He snarled and flipped to his feet.

Something hit me in the upper chest with enough force to send me stumbling. The second shot punched another hole right next to the first. Blood and tissue sprayed across the grass. I took two staggering steps and fell.

Sean howled in rage. Somewhere in the distance, I heard another howl. Daniel.

I sensed frantic movement above me. Something pressed hard against my chest: Sean, compressing his wadded-up shirt to the bullet wounds.

I couldn't see anything, but I felt him nuzzle my face. My nose filled with the scent of blood and forest. "Alice. Look at me, damn it. *Alice.*"

Heavy footsteps pounded up to us. "Give me your shirt!" Sean snapped.

Fabric tore. "Tell me what to do," Daniel snarled.

"Our room. My nightstand, top drawer. Black bag. *Go.*"

Daniel ran in the direction of the house.

Ronan? I asked, hoping he would hear me. *Hey, Wings, are you there?*

No answer. Figures. Never a fallen angel with healing magic around when you needed one.

My torso raised. Sean put Daniel's shirt against the wounds in my back and compressed hard—so hard, I couldn't get a breath. Or maybe one or both bullets had punctured my lungs. Strangely, I felt no pain. Something told me that was bad, but I didn't want to hurt, so why was that bad?

"Alice, if you can hear me, summon Malcolm right now." Sean spoke directly into my left ear, his lips against my skin. "Do not die. Do you hear me? *Do not fucking die.*"

I was having a difficult time thinking, but summoning Malcolm had become an instinctive action. Maybe that was why it worked. If I'd had to think about how to do it, I never could have done it. I found Malcolm's trace in the wolf tattoo on my belly and pulled him to me with the last bit of strength I had.

The voices around me became unintelligible. I recognized Malcolm's frantic tone, and Sean's snarls, and a voice that belonged to Daniel, who must have come back with whatever bag Sean wanted. I couldn't understand a word they said.

A familiar earth magic healing spell flared and rolled through me. Malcolm was trying to heal my wounds. Earth magic wouldn't be nearly strong enough. It would be like trying to use a garden hose to put out a forest fire.

Something cold touched my left shoulder. *Alice, keep fighting,* Malcolm said urgently in my head. *Tura's full of shit, remember? Prophecies are never set in stone. I swear, if you die, I will find you in the afterlife and chew your ass out for eternity.*

Strange magic surged in my chest and pulsed though my body in waves of red and gold: a powerful healing spell, but not one of mine. This one had golden shifter magic in it—magic I recognized as Sean's. Where the hell did Sean get a blood magic healing spell?

I wanted to tell them it was okay if I didn't make it; they'd done all they could. I'd made my choice not to sacrifice Sean to save myself. Tura might be full of shit, but not about this. Eventually, I was bound to run into a wall I couldn't kick down.

I took a breath that gurgled in my chest...which was weird, because just seconds ago, I hadn't been able to breathe at all. That one breath allowed me to speak.

"It's okay," I whispered, and slipped away into darkness.

CHAPTER 33

I woke up in Heaven—which was kind of a surprise, all things considered.

I smelled coffee, and I was in bed next to Sean, with his arms wrapped around me and his nose against the back of my neck. Warm sunshine spilled through the open windows. Birds sang outside, a gentle fall breeze wafted through our room, and Esme was curled up asleep at the foot of the bed. Yep, Heaven for sure.

Sean let out a snore as loud as a jet engine, right next to my ear. I winced.

Either Heaven had a sense of humor, or I wasn't dead. The latter seemed more likely the more aware I became of how sore my upper body was—especially my chest and back.

I didn't want to wake Sean, so I gingerly moved my head and pulled aside the neck of my tank top. Two faint round scars marked where the bullets had punched through my chest. A couple of inches lower, and one or both would have gone through my heart.

Either my movement woke Sean, or maybe he'd sensed I was awake. His snore cut off mid-roar. He raised his head, his hair sticking out in all directions and eyes bright gold. "Alice?"

"Hey." I kissed his jaw. "Do I smell coffee?"

He pulled me against his body and buried his nose in my hair, breathing in my scent. I rubbed my nose against the warm skin over his heart and kissed his chest. We lay like that for a long time, just holding each other, with my lips over his heart and his breath warm on my ear.

I could have gone back to sleep, and Sean probably would have too, but I had questions.

"Who shot me?" I asked finally, my voice muffled by his chest.

He growled. "We don't know. Our priority was keeping you alive, and that took all of us. By the time we found the sniper's nest, he was long gone. Daniel tracked him across the neighbor's property behind us, to where he had a vehicle waiting. No one saw the vehicle, or anyone suspicious. No leads so far, but we'll find out who sent him." He squeezed me. "It wasn't your friend on the Harley—that much we know."

"Of course it wasn't." I tried to sense Ronan's now-familiar silver-blue magic trace, but there was none anywhere nearby. Where the hell had he gone? I hadn't necessarily thought he'd stick around and play bodyguard, but I hadn't expected him to leave without even saying goodbye. I wasn't sure what his abrupt disappearance meant, and it made me uneasy.

"I felt Malcolm using healing magic on me," I said, since I could do little about Ronan's vanishing act. "Where did you get a blood magic healing spell with your own magic in it?"

"I bought some after Caleb attacked you, when you had to rely on Vaughan to save your life." He nuzzled my hair. "I promised myself you would never have to drink vampire blood again for healing if I could help it. I used one of them to heal your injuries when Miraç's witches dropped you off on the side of the road in Landers. I used another one last night—the strongest one I had. It took every bit of it, plus Malcolm's healing spells, to save you."

I frowned. "Why didn't it hurt me? Strong blood magic healing spells are agonizing."

"I had that one made so I would feel the pain, not you." He kissed me before I could yell at him. "Don't tell me I shouldn't have done it. It's my choice to make, and I'd do it again a hundred times."

He would, and there was no use fussing at him about it now. "Where's Daniel?" I asked.

"Out patrolling with Joshua and Jesse Hayes. Ben and Felicia are downstairs. Nan and Karen will be here later."

"Not Karen," I protested. "She's pregnant. Get someone else to take her shift."

He kissed my hair. "She insisted, Alice. Everyone's upset. They all want to do their part. You know that."

That was a fair point. Karen would be pissed if he told her she couldn't help. "So, since we have no leads at the moment, who do we *think* tried to turn me into Swiss cheese?"

His chest rumbled. "Murphy."

I shook my head. "He needs me alive. No way in hell he sent a sniper to take me out. Killing me will be his last resort, and I don't think he's there yet."

"The vamps?"

"I doubt it. Valas and I made a deal when I got back. She removed our binding, agreed to let me stay an independent contractor, and swore no retaliation against me or anyone I'm associated with."

His brow furrowed. "I thought your trip through the mirror to get that scroll was in return for her help in saving my life."

"It was. Turns out, she needed the scroll to save her from curses Miraç put on her before he died. The damn thing was destroyed over there, though, so when I got back, I saved her life in return for some things I wanted."

"If that's what you decided was your best course of action, I support you. I look forward to hearing the whole story." He ran his nose along my hairline to breathe in more of my scent. "What other suspects do we have, then, if it wasn't Moses or the vamps?"

"Someone on the Council?" I ventured. "Or someone from

another pack who's angry at you or me, like one of the Anderson brothers?"

"It better not be." His voice was half growl. "What about someone you've crossed paths with on a case?"

"Maybe. Can't think of anyone off the top of my head who's that pissed at me, though."

He growled. "It was cowardly."

"No argument from me. I prefer a straight-up fight." I stretched gingerly. "Thanks for keeping me alive."

He caught my hand. "You gave up," he accused, his expression suddenly hard. "I can't believe you gave up. Your last words to me were 'It's okay.' The *hell* it was okay." He snarled. "You let Tura's prophecy convince you we couldn't save you."

He was right. If the situation had been reversed, I would have been *beyond* furious at him.

"Before you left for the Broken World, you told me to believe in you," he added. "I *do* believe."

"I know you do," I said quietly.

He held my chin. He was angry, and he was hurt. "Tell me why you didn't believe in *me,* then. Tell me why you'd believe an angel you met once, for five minutes, over me."

My chest ached because I'd caused him pain. "I was lying in the exact spot Tura told me I would die, with two high-caliber bullets through my chest. I couldn't breathe. I couldn't see or hear. I didn't even feel any pain. I've died before. I know what it feels like, and that was how I felt last night."

"Then that was all the more reason to believe in me." His fingers slid through my hair to cup the back of my head. "Don't ever stop believing in me again. I will *never* let you down while there's breath in my body."

My eyes filled with tears. "I know."

He leaned down to kiss me.

Without warning, Daisy emerged from the shadows in my mind. Shifter magic surged. I braced for her to try to force me to shift, but she didn't. Instead, she carefully nudged me aside so she could look out through my eyes.

Sean raised his head and met Daisy's stare. "There you are, beautiful," he said, his own eyes golden and shadowed in a way that told me his wolf was looking at us too. "We'll go for a run later if Alice is healed enough for you to emerge. If not, be patient."

Daisy curled her lip, but not in a threat. *Mate,* she said.

Sean smiled. "It's good to have you both home."

With her tail held high, she returned to the shadows. My shifter magic faded.

"You must have worked things out with her," he said. "She seems content."

"I don't know about working everything out, but she got to be her own wolf for a while, and we got to know each other. That's a couple of big steps in the right direction." I rubbed his bristly cheek with my knuckles. "Seriously, though, is there coffee? And is Malcolm around?"

His expression darkened. "No, he's not."

"What?" I sat up. "What's wrong with Malcolm?"

He ran his hand through his tousled hair. "I'll let him tell you. Summon him, and he'll come."

My stomach in knots, I picked up Malcolm's crystal from my nightstand and tugged twice on his trace in my mind.

More than a minute passed. My anxiety was through the roof, and Sean's ominous silence did nothing to help.

Finally, the crystal buzzed. "*Release,*" I said.

Malcolm appeared beside the bed. I expected him to greet me with relief, or tease us about being in bed, but he didn't. He looked awful—angry, grief-stricken, and lost.

"What's wrong?" I asked.

"The bordello's empty," he said tonelessly.

My brain took a second to comprehend what he was saying. "The ghosts? All the ghosts are gone?"

"All gone. Liam's gone." He floated back and forth. "Someone cleaned the place out. Maybe blood mages, maybe someone else—I don't know. There are no traces left behind, not even of whoever cleaned out the ghosts or how they did it. No traces to follow, even, and I've looked, and looked again."

Shock left me speechless. All those ghosts—dozens, or even hundreds of them—gone.

Malcolm drifted to the windows on the far side of the room. Sunlight streamed through him, making odd patterns on the floor. "When you called to me just now, I was searching for clues or trace. I hoped Liam had escaped and would return to the bordello to see if I came looking for him. But he hasn't been back."

The only person who could have given the order to clear out the bordello was my grandfather. Moses had originally bought the place to turn into a hotel, but the wall-to-wall ghosts had made that venture impossible. No contractors would work on the project, and the building had sat empty for years.

I suddenly had a terrible sinking feeling. "Moses may intend to use the bordello as his West Coast headquarters now that Darius Bell is dead. The location is perfect for that use. Easily fortified and defensible, and accessible by road and air."

I got out of bed and joined Malcolm at the window. "I'm so sorry," I told him, painfully aware of how inadequate my words were. "I don't know what to say."

"I really cared about him," Malcolm said. I'd never heard him sound so broken. "I never told him. And when I left to go with you to the Broken World, he was angry with me because I was risking myself to go. He thought I should stay here where it was safe. All along, it was *Liam* who was in more danger, and I wasn't here when he needed me."

"It's possible he's not gone," I reminded him. "Moses may have had blood mages discorporate the poltergeists and wraiths and put the strongest ghosts into crystals. It wouldn't be like him to waste resources."

The moment the words came out of my mouth, I realized I'd said the wrong thing. "I didn't mean ghosts are resources," I said quickly. "Malcolm—"

He vanished.

"Son of a bitch!" I picked up the closest thing at hand—my jewelry box—and threw it as hard as I could, with some of my air magic in the throw. The box exploded against the wall and left a dent in the drywall. I threw a book and a bottle of hand lotion too, and then I took a swing at the wall.

My fist connected with Sean's palm. "There's a stud right there," he said, gripping my hand when I tried to pull away. "If you want to throw some punches, I've got the heavy bag set up in the workout room, or you can punch my hand as hard as you want for as long as you want. But I am *not* going to let you hurt yourself."

My chest heaved. "Moses." I was so angry, I couldn't finish the sentence.

"I know." He wrapped his arms around me and held me tight.

"I shouldn't have said that about resources. I didn't mean it that way."

"He knows you didn't." He rested his chin on top of my head. "Malcolm needs space and time to grieve. You know what that feels like. Just be there for him when he's ready."

Footsteps approached our door. "You guys all right?" Ben called. "Sounded like World War Three up here. We wondered if Sean needed backup."

"We're fine," Sean told him. "Alice had to blow off some steam. We'll be down in a bit."

"Gotcha. Tell her there's coffee if she wants it and whisky if she needs it." His footsteps retreated down the hall.

I rubbed my face. "I have no idea what time it is. Is it too early for whisky?"

"Never." Sean kissed my forehead. "But you need to eat first, love. I'll make you anything you want, if we have the ingredients. If not, I'll send someone to the store to get what we need."

"Breakfast burrito," I said. My stomach growled loudly. "Better make that two."

He laced our fingers together and walked me to the door of our room. Esme rose, stretched, and followed us.

"Two breakfast burritos coming right up," Sean said.

My heart ached for Malcolm, but I smiled up at him. "I love you too."

EPILOGUE

The first rays of morning sun had just appeared on the eastern horizon when a Guardian vehicle parked alongside Lucy's jeep. The driver cut the vehicle's supe lights and engine, got out, and shut his door.

Bloodied and splattered with graveling goop, Lucy sat with her back against a fallen tree, her sword at her side. She finished taping gauze on a wound on her arm and stuck the used first-aid supplies in her pocket. "Morning," she said.

"Good morning." Arms crossed, her partner studied the field in front of their vehicles. A dozen gravelings lay in pieces, their decomposing bodies filling the air with the stench of rotting flesh and death magic. "How many total have you killed?" he asked.

"Thirty-seven since I got back from the Underworld. We killed a couple dozen before we left too. Nasty things." With a pained grunt, Lucy got to her feet and returned her sword to its sheath on her back.

She leaned against the tree trunk and held her side. The biggest graveling had thrown her against the tree before she hacked it into a dozen chunks. She suspected she'd cracked some ribs. She didn't tell him that. He'd insist she visit the closest healer, and she wasn't in the mood for it.

If he suspected she was more hurt than she appeared, he didn't let on. He was leaner than the last time she'd seen him, and his hair had gotten a little longer than Guardian regulations permitted. Once upon a time she would have mocked him for that, but not anymore.

"How many more of these things do you think are loose topside?" he asked.

"We haven't gotten any more reports of attacks by shades. This might be the last of them. Bummer. I was having a good time hunting them down. I suppose it's back to business as usual—for both of us." She glanced at him. "I hear you had your hands full with the basilisk nest and the ghouls. Shame you had to miss out on the graveling hunt. This was *fun*."

His expression didn't change. "I would have come, if you'd asked—and if I knew where you were."

She said nothing.

"Ellis said you went after a dragon by yourself. *Again*." He was pissed at her—more so than usual. "And you apparently teamed up with a *civilian* to hunt gravelings and shades topside before taking her with you to the Underworld. And then you refused to identify her or the ghost who guarded the doorway. Why you're not in the brig, I have no idea."

"I'm not in the brig because I told Ellis everything that happened."

He scowled. "I find that difficult to believe."

"Believe it, or don't," she said shortly. "I only knew their first names anyway. Without them, a hell of a lot more people would be dead, both here and...other places. They've all gone back where they came from, and they won't return." She straightened with difficulty. Damn it, her ribs ached.

She didn't want to talk about Walliston, or watching Alice shred the shades in the cemetery, or what they'd faced in the Underworld—especially not with her partner. Ellis had let her simply report what had happened and listened in a clinical, dispassionate way. Her partner wouldn't just let it be a report. In the beginning, he would have, but they were long past that. Things had changed between them and there was no going back.

He joined her by the tree. She wanted to touch him, but she didn't. She wanted to apologize too, but she didn't know where to start or what she should apologize for, so she stayed silent.

His scarred face softened. "I did what you asked: I gave you space. While you were going after dragons and killing things in the Underworld, I hunted black dogs, helped clear out a basilisk nest, and spent several weeks dealing with the mass ghoul rising caused by that major magic flare—and then the aftermath."

She flinched.

Some newly risen ghouls found their way home or to the homes of loved ones. Happy to have their deceased family, friends, or lovers back from the dead, people often hid the undead from law enforcement, despite the danger. And they fought like hell to keep them, threatening to shoot the Guardians trying to save them, even when the ghoul was trying to eat them alive. Given what had happened in Lucy's own family, those incidents always hit just a little too close to home.

"Give me gravelings any day, compared to that," she said finally. "I'd even take a basilisk nest again, even though the last time I had to help clear one out, I damn near died."

"I know." He leaned against the tree beside her and watched the dead Underworld creatures turn to black goo. "I should have been with you. You didn't need to face any of this by yourself."

"I wasn't by myself," she said automatically. "I was with Alice, Malcolm, Alice's guardian wolf Daisy, Esme, and..." She stopped. "A bounty hunter. We were a team, at least by the end."

"You, working as part of a team? Hard to believe."

"It wasn't so bad," she admitted. "I think it worked because there weren't any other Guardians in the group—just a mage, a wolf, a ghost, a cat-dragon, and the other guy." Who happened to be a fallen angel, but she kept that to herself.

She would also never admit she hoped Ronan would return and give her a chance to cross swords with him. Her blade had never tasted an angel's blood, and she was sure it would enjoy the chance to rectify that. Its recent diet of mostly graveling goo had only whet its appetite for more...divine fare.

"It certainly took all of us to complete the mission and survive," she added when the silence stretched out too long. "Daisy and the little witch Torryn knew what they were talking about, apparently."

A long pause. "The *wolf* knew what she was talking about?"

Lucy smiled. "She did. Smart wolf. Very big, smart wolf." Her smile faded. "I hope they got home safely."

He rose. "Let's get this radioed in to dispatch. I drove all night to get here, so I'll follow you to the closest outpost to turn in my vehicle, and then we'll head out in your jeep. You can debrief me on the way to Dire Springs."

She frowned and followed him back to their vehicles. "What's in Dire Springs?"

"Reports of Cwn Annwfn sightings."

"*What?*" She stopped with her hand on her door handle. "Does that mean—?"

"Possibly." He opened his own driver's side door. "I'm waiting on confirmation. If it's true, Lord Arawn may be in the area."

The ground beneath them vibrated. Magic blazed up Lucy's arms and sparked from her fingertips, leaving a sizable dent in the jeep's door.

Keeping her own magic hidden during her time with Alice had been difficult but necessary. Others had tried to steal her power. Alice hadn't seemed like the type to stab an ally in the back, but appearances could be deceiving. Dark magic made people unpredictable. And with that death magic eating her alive from the inside, Alice might just have been desperate enough to try her luck. Lucy had liked Alice. It would have sucked to have had to kill her.

Her partner raised his eyebrows at the earthquake and the sound of the metal door bending. "I knew you'd want to know about Lord Arawn."

Lucy took a deep breath and exhaled. Her magic dissipated. The ground stopped shaking. "That cowardly, sneaking son of a bitch." She yanked open her door and got into the jeep. Easy enough to blame the dented door on a graveling. "Let's get to Dire Springs before something else comes up. Arawn's not getting away from me this time."

"Not getting away from *us*," her partner corrected, getting into his vehicle. "That bastard has eluded justice for too long."

Justice, Lucy thought bitterly. *What justice is there for someone like Arawn?*

She caught a familiar scent over the stench of the decaying gravelings and the smell of her own blood: incense and iron. She hadn't expected to encounter that distinctive odor again, but apparently a certain crocodile-headed goddess had taken an interest in her.

"Don't crowd me, Ammit," she said under her breath. "Justice comes in many forms. You should know that better than anyone."

The scent swirled in the air around her, then faded.

"What was that?" her partner called through his open window.

"Nothing." With a smile, Lucy tapped Callie's vampire bobblehead to make it bounce. She turned her key in the ignition and shifted into gear. "We're wasting daylight, partner. Let's roll."

TO BE CONTINUED...

Acknowledgments

First and foremost: thank you, Alice readers, for sharing these adventures. *Heart of Vengeance* wouldn't exist without you!

It's hard to love a Gemini, especially when you're a Libra, so I want to start by thanking my (long-suffering) husband Bill for twenty-one years of love, laughs, and wonderful memories. We love music, travel, road trips, murder shows, the early (funny) years of *Family Guy,* good movies, bad puns, and low-key evenings on the porch with our cats, especially when it rains. Thanks for putting up with me and my craziness. I love you.

As always, a very special thanks to my awesome editor Heather McCorkle.

I owe a huge debt to my alpha reader, Dr. Marie Guthrie, for her very patient reading of early *very* rough drafts, as well as countless Skype calls for brainstorming (or just plain venting). We're coming up on twenty years of friendship, as hard as that is to believe. Here's to the next twenty years of shenanigans!

Thank you from the bottom of my heart to my most excellent squad of beta readers for this book: Luna Joya, Shannon Butler, Dr. Kimberly Dodson, Amy Hopper, Carla Ruehl, and Dr. Robert James. Shannon, Kim, Amy, and Robert have been with me since *Heart of Malice* (and long before!), and words cannot express how much you mean to me. I must have done something really good in a previous life to have such awesome and brilliant friends in this one.

So much love to my very supportive family and close friends, especially my mother. Mountains of love to my sister Susan, brother-in-law Josh, and niece and nephew Alexandria and Madden, as well as my wonderful and brilliant cousins Antoinette and Felicia and sister(-in-law) Amy Hopper. Love and thanks to Mike and Teri Belanger for cheering me on and sending pictures of moose. All my heart to my sistahs from other mistahs: Neda Benitez, Jen Bauer-Krueger, Stacey Kelley, Bridget Talmadge, and Jennifer DeWitt. And a very special thank you to Tiny Editor Joya, for being The Best Pupperino.

I probably forgot someone, so if I left you off the list, I'm sorry and I love you!

ABOUT THE AUTHOR

Lisa Edmonds was born and raised in Kansas. A graduate of Buhler High School, she studied English and forensic criminology at Wichita State University. After acquiring her Bachelor's degree, she considered a career in law enforcement as a behavioral analyst before earning a Master's in English from Wichita State and then a Ph.D. in English from Texas A&M University.

For ten years, she was an associate professor of English at a college in Texas, where she taught a variety of writing and literature courses. Now a full-time author, she shares a cute Victorian-style home called The Storybook House with her husband and their pets, and enjoys writing, reading, traveling, spoiling her niece and nephew, and singing karaoke.

For more information and to join my reader community, please visit LisaEdmonds.com.

9 781963 525151